'Til Death Do Us Part

Austen Butler

'Til Death Do Us Part is a work of fiction. Every name, place and incident are the product of the author's imagination or are real but used fictitiously. Any resemblance to actual persons, living or dead, events or locales, is entirely coincidental, although some of what follows actually happened.

Part 1

Week 1

Austen Butler

1

Sunday afternoon

You know how there are some people you just delight in saying "no" to? Kelli's grandparents are not those people, not even on the list; Kelli would never even consider it. The closest she had ever come, her one and only stab at teenage rebellion, was when she and Sean moved in with "the Gs". The brother and sister were informed they were to call them "Mima" and "Papaw", good old southern honorifics for grandparents. Kelli never voiced her thoughts, just started calling them Granny and Gramps instead and never stopped. Sean, her older brother by almost five years, didn't call them anything, just waited until one or the other was looking at him before he spoke. Easy for him, since he was off at boarding school most of the time, and then college. That was the only time Kelli could remember ever having refused her grandmother. Granny had once asked Kelli to stop calling her that because it reminded her of the old *Beverley Hillbillies* TV show, but Kelli continued. She just felt the names fit them. And she really didn't like Mima and Papaw, sounded like you were calling pigs or something.

It had been almost twenty years since she and Sean had been dumped on the Gs. She had been eight and Sean was thirteen. After the first few months of adjustment, they had gotten along swimmingly. After all they had to adjust to a whole new country. Sure they were American citizens, but they'd never lived here. They'd lived all over the world and gone to religious schools in a multitude of countries; wherever their world-renowned parents were settling for the next big project. Their mother was an archeologist and their father was a paleontologist, famous for their dinosaur finds in Colorado, Switzerland, France, and even Timbuktu. They had met at the College of Charleston and immediately discovered that both their interests in old bones had begun as children finding shark's teeth and megalodon teeth in

3

the marshes and beaches of Charleston, Charleston is famous for them. A whole new dinosaur had even been found in Charleston.

Unfortunately, their healthy marriage-and- bones-partnership did not leave much time for two active children. After carting the kids hither and yon, one summer they finally realized Sean and Kelli needed more stability in their lives. Their next project was rapidly approaching, so Mother quickly called her mother, received permission to store the kids with her "for a little while", made plane reservations, packed trunks, and dropped the two confused children in Charleston with grandparents they had never met. Mother stayed one night and then returned to Father, awaiting her in Cairo.

Stability won out and Sean and Kelli had wonderful schooling, great friends, and a happy life with the Gs in their centuries old house on the Battery of Charleston. Kelli loved the old house with its many rooms and family antiques. Having spent the first eight years of her life rootless, it was nice to have a family and a house with history.

So when Granny called at lunchtime that late-January day and asked Kelli to see about selling the family home, the first words out of Kelli's mouth were "No, Granny, I won't do it. You can't do it." Her words surprised both of them.

"But, darlin', we are so enjoying Arizona. And that house is really too big for us now that we are approaching our dotage." Kelli snorted in a very unladylike way; seventy was hardly 'dotage'. Granny chose to ignore Kelli's unspoken retort. "We really don't think we'll ever move back to Charleston permanently. Papaw is playing golf every day; he's brown as a walnut," she giggled while Kelli tried to get a word in, "Gra…"

"The weather is much drier here in Scottsdale so you don't notice the heat or the cold so much."

"But…"

"And I've joined a very nice bridge group and we're in a dinner group; we've made so many new friends. How soon do you think you can get it listed, Chickie?"

Kelli had to grin. "Granny" had started calling her "Chickie" in retaliation for "Granny." What she didn't know was that Kelli secretly loved having a nickname; she'd never had any form of endearment before.

Granny finally paused for breath. The problem, as Kelli saw it, was that she had always considered it her house too. Except for Christmases, when Bob and Leslie made a point of showing up for the three days of mandatory family time, the children hadn't seen their parents in almost twenty years. But, as far as Kelli and Sean were concerned, that was neither here nor there, no pun intended.

Very soon after their arrival, Sean was packed off to Porter-Gaud; southern boys of good families still went to southern boarding schools. Even though it was in Charleston, Sean boarded and came home on weekends, unless there was something going on at PG; and there was always something going on. Gramps had gone there, so Sean went there. He settled into eighth grade and graduated with a "good foundation for college."

Kelli, on the other hand, got to go to the local public schools. No finishing school for her, even though Ashley Hall was less than a mile away. She always wondered why? Was she too hopeless for them to even try to finish her? Was she not worth the money? Not that she minded; she would have hated it. But she did wonder. It had added to her seemingly insurmountable teenage angst.

Kelli took a deep breath and calmly replied to Granny, "Let me see what I can do, while you think about this. Maybe you should try Arizona for a winter before you make a decision? You've only been out there a month. Maybe they get horrendous blizzards in February. How about renting a house for a year so you get the full experience?" Kelli tried not to sound hopeful. Silence from the Arizona end of the phone. Kelli pictured her grandmother, seated at a desk at the Scottsdale Golf resort, her silver hair carefully coifed, Granny's petite figure ramrod straight. Kelli had Googled the resort and knew what the expansive rooms looked like, well worth their cost. Kelli sighed deeply and said, "Okay. Do you have any idea of how much you are hoping to get for the house?"

"Well, Papaw says we won't take less than four and a half, six and a half if we sell it furnished. If we can't sell it for that we just won't sell it. It's not like we need the money. We just don't want the worry anymore. Someday you'll marry again, maybe even move away, and we'll be stuck with that big old house and no one to help us fill it." Kelli cringed, not sure if it was because of the mention of her former marriage or because the Gs were contemplating selling the furniture too.

Kelli looked around the kitchen and absently scratched Corky's big golden head. Corky could tell by the tone of Kelli's voice that something was wrong and had plopped her head in Kelli's lap, looking up at her with her big soulful eyes, her eyebrows doing their Corky twitch, up and down, one at a time. Kelli tried to smile at her four year old "puppy", but just couldn't.

Everything Granny said was logical and made perfect sense; that's how she knew it was Granny's idea and not Gramps's. Granny was the brains of the outfit, and she was smart enough never to let Gramps know it. Early on she had learned that he liked to feel like he was in charge so she accommodated him by offering "suggestions" and then letting him come to her conclusion. Kelli had watched it thousands of times over the years. She was glad she and Todd had had a more equal relationship, but the Gs seemed happy and that was what counted.

The only part of Granny's logic that Kelli questioned was the part about her marrying again. It had only been six months and nine days. And there was Sean to think about. Marrying again was not on her immediate to-do list, if ever.

Kelli decided to take the high road for her grandmother: get the answers she wanted and just stretch the process as long as she could.

"Do you have an agent in mind, Gran? Know anybody I can call?"

""Call Amanda," Granny replied. Amanda Hawthorne was Granny's best friend and lived directly behind them on Church Street. "Amanda knows everyone, whether it's a society matron or a plumber, she'll know who to call. Be sure and tell her we're just exploring possibilities at this point, or by dinnertime everyone in Charleston will think the moving van is on its way." Granny giggled like a schoolgirl again. Not for the first time Kelli recognized that Granny was a true southern belle, more Scarlett O'Hara than Melanie Wilkes, though. Granny got her way with everyone by playing the "poor little me" role, but she was cunning and a great strategizer. Gramps always told her if she had been a general during the War of Northern Aggression, the South would have won for sure. When he said this Granny blushed and wiggled her fingers at him, saying, "Oh go on, Wilson. You know that isn't true."

"Thank you so much, Chickie dear, this will give you something else to help take your mind off Todd. It's good to keep busy."

"Yes, Granny," Kelli whispered around the lump that was growing in her throat. She walked away from the kitchen desk to the other side of the room, looking out the window for something to cheer her. The camellias were starting to bloom; their pink blossoms always cheered her.

"Call me when you know something, darlin'. We're headed to the club, Papaw has a tee time in a little bit and I'm playing tennis. Love you!" Granny hung up, almost 2,000 miles away. Kelli could see her "doting" grandmother in her short tennis skirt with her long brown legs, her silver hair pulled into a ponytail and through the hole of her visor. Not bad for 70.

Kelli always wished she had gotten her maternal grandmother's looks, but no petite cuteness and dimpled smile for her. She guessed she took her looks more from the Gannon side of the family, even though she didn't look much like her dad either. She could only guess, because his parents were dead and he was an only child. All the family photos had burned in the fire that had taken the Gannon grandparents' lives before Kelli was born.

Kelli glanced at her reflection in the toaster next to her. Definitely no cuteness. She'd given up worrying about her looks a long time ago, about the time she outgrew everyone in her ninth grade class, and a lot of the older boys. At five-nine she had felt like an Amazon among Munchkins.

While she still had the mobile phone in her hand she speed-dialed Amanda and stared out the window that faced Amanda's house. She didn't know what she expected to see; there was an eight foot wall between the houses; all that showed were the second and third floors of the pale yellow, stuccoed structure. Kelli had known Amanda since the day after she and Sean had arrived; Granny had invited Amanda over for tea so she could meet the new arrivals. The children were not at their best, still suffering from jet lag, hadn't unpacked, in a strange house, and missing their friends back in Paris and Cairo. To say they were rude would be an enormous understatement. But Amanda took to them anyway and had been like a second grandmother to Kelli, if not Sean. Back in those days Sean never let anyone get too close. "Somethings never change," Kelli muttered to herself.

"Hi, Kelli, how are you doing all alone over there?" Amanda, a widow too, had been especially supportive since Todd's death. Scratch that, Todd's murder.

"Hanging in there, I guess. You were right, the grief does get easier to bear over time. Not easy, but easier."

"Just give yourself time, honey, and stay busy. You'll never forget Todd, but you will come to live with his absence. You're still young, too. Somebody will come along to fill that gap."

Kelli couldn't even consider the thought of someone else. There would never be anyone like Todd, never could be. They were so perfect together. She took a deep breath and changed the subject.

"You'll never guess why I'm calling! I just got off the phone with Granny and she wants me to talk to a real estate agent; see how much they can get for this house."

"Oh, no! I was afraid of that. I just knew the Arizona life-style would appeal to them. They are both such outdoorsy types, you know what I mean. Not hunting and fishing outdoorsy, but with golf and tennis ten months of the year and skiing six months of the year, they were sure to love it. Damn! I'll hate to see them go." Amanda started to snuffle.

"Whoa, Amanda. So far it's just exploratory. I can't imagine they'll really go through with selling. This house has been in the family for generations, practically back to the age of Blackbeard. For all I know he may have slept here," Kelli said with a chuckle. "Hell's bells, Washington played cards in the parlor with my great-great-great something or other when he visited Charleston in 1791, even though it wasn't this exact parlor since that house had burned down in 1742. I hope this is just a passing fancy. I suggested they rent for a year before they decide and I hope they'll take me up on the idea."

Once more Kelli looked around the updated kitchen, the only room in the house that was modern. All the most up-to-date appliances, Ooba Tooba dark green granite, warming ovens, dual dishwashers and lots of storage. A chef's dream. Not that either she or her grandmother cooked all that much, but Kelli loved to make desserts and breads and she certainly appreciated style and convenience when she saw it.

She looked outside again and saw the white wrought iron furniture on the piazza; she laughed as she remembered having to pronounce it pee-azza, the Charleston way, not pee-atza, the Italian way. They had lived in Florence for two years when she was very young and it had been a hard habit to break. She saw the lush garden beyond. I love this place, she muttered to herself. They can't sell it.

"What, dear? What did you say?"

"Sorry, Amanda, my mind was wandering. Did you say something?"

"I said I'll text you the name and number of the best agent on the Battery, or so I've heard. Keep me posted. Love you." Brisk as ever, or maybe too upset to talk further, Amanda hung up. A minute later Kelli's cell phone dinged with notification of an incoming text.

Kelli just stared at the green icon, not wanting to open it even. She didn't know whether to cry or rage. She slowly walked through the main floor, Corky at her heels, remembering all the good times they'd had here over the past twenty years. The rooms with their eighteen foot ceilings had allowed great tall Christmas trees. Sean had had to get the biggest ladder so he could put the angel on the top; Gramps had passed off the task as soon as they had arrived, claiming "too old to be climbing tall ladders anymore."

Their distant ancestors, the Ellsworths, Granny's family, had built this house on the Battery in 1736. With no air conditioning they'd needed the high ceilings and windows that opened from the top to allow the heat to escape. French windows and doors all around opening to the piazza allowed plenty of cross-ventilation when the breezes from the bay across the street blew. It was worth the occasional flood to have such an idyllic setting. And the new – albeit twenty years old - air conditioning system made it much more livable in the humid summers.

Kelli stood in the oh-so-formal dining room. But it had never seemed formal when the whole family, all six of them, plus any "orphan" friends, those who didn't go home for holidays, had sat around it for lively meals or even more lively games of Yahtzee or Uno. *I really love this Queen Anne furniture,* she thought, *and the green toile upholstery and drapes. Why is it I've never thought about it before? Why do we only appreciate things when we lose them, or are about to? Why did I ever try to get Granny to reupholster in something more modern. Good thing Granny just gave me "the look" that said I'd better not say that again and ignored me.*

The fireplace in the front parlor is probably my favorite part of this floor, even though we had it converted to gas years ago. I always loved the crackle of a wood fire, but neither Granny nor I had the right touch to start one when Gramps and Sean were gone; with the gas we can just flip a switch and have a fire whenever we want. Granny always joked that she didn't need Gramps to "light her fire" anymore. Kelli gazed at the marble surround, envisioning stockings hung with care every Christmas. A formal portrait of Kelli and Sean, painted about a year after their arrival, was hung over the fireplace. Kelli remembered how Sean had hated every second of the sittings.

"The parlor" as the room between the front parlor and the dining room was called, was big enough to hold committee meetings, parties, and small dances. The highly-polished wood floors, original to the house, were perfect for dancing. All they had to do was move back the furniture, open the windows, fold back the oriental rugs, and turn up the music. When the weather permitted they opened the French doors and included the piazza in their dancing. Since the kids from all the surrounding houses attended the parties, none of the parents complained about the noise. *What a great place to grow up!*

I will not get maudlin about this. After all, I'm just going to get information for them. Guess I might as well call the agent and get it over with.

Kelli sat down in one of the gold-and-green brocade-covered wing chairs in the front parlor and looked down at her cell phone. A second text had come in while she was ruminating; she hadn't even heard the ding. She pushed the green icon and the text was displayed. It wasn't from Amanda. "Soon, my darling, soon. We will be together forever."

Kelli just stared at it. *Good grief! Now I'm getting wrong-number love notes. Is technology worth this?* She texted back, "Sorry, wrong number. Hope you get this to your," she hesitated. Was it from a man or a woman or a teenager? She finished the text, "intended." That covered all the bases.

She deleted the text and went to the next one. It was the one from Amanda. She walked back to the kitchen and picked up the wall phone. She dialed the number she saw on her cell screen and went immediately to voice mail. Kelli left her name and phone numbers, the house number and her cell, and asked for a call back. *Great.*

"NO! It's not a wrong number," he screamed at the phone in his hand. He was parked across the street from the Ellsworth house, just two spaces down from the house's black iron front gate. He had a perfect view of the black front door. Would Kelli go out today? She'd already been to church. Sometimes she went to brunch with a friend after she'd come home, sometimes she stayed in all day. He'd watch and see. If she'd go out he could get close to her, a lot closer than he had been in church. Maybe even take her to brunch? No, not yet. Later. But not too much later. He'd waited so long already. He grabbed his latest log book and added an entry for the text and Kelli's response.

Kelli decided to take the intervening few hours and just veg with a good book. As soon as she stepped into her grandfather's library on the second floor, she had a meltdown. *I've already lost so much, I can't lose this house, too.* She sank into one of the two burgundy leather club chairs across from her grandfather's desk, situated in the middle of the room. She pulled her knees up, rested her forehead on them, and sobbed. After a few minutes she quieted, wiped her nose with the tissue from her pocket and looked around the room, her second favorite in the whole house. *This room is where Gramps comes to pay bills, do genealogy research on both sides of the family, and, escape Granny.* Bookshelves on three walls stretched all the way to the ceiling. Books dating back to the first Ellsworths in South Carolina, in the early 18th century. After all these generations and marriages, it was still known as the Ellsworth House, though no one with that name had lived there for ages. The Ellsworth seemed to procreate girls more often than boys; nonetheless the name had stuck.

A dark green tapestry sofa under the window on the fourth wall made a perfect reading spot. The small table next to it was just the right size for a teacup and saucer. *I remember in high school this was my one of my favorite retreats. I would come up here and lose myself in books for hours. I didn't have anything else to do, none of the girls at school liked me, said I was putting on airs with the dregs of my French accent, and the boys were such…boys. Oh, well, if you've learned nothing else in the last few months, you have to move on.* She went knowingly to the shelves on the right of the room and grabbed a well-worn copy of *Pride and Prejudice. Nothing like Jane Austen to cheer me up.*

As she opened the cover of the book, the phone on Gramps' desk rang. At Kelli's answer, an abrupt woman announced, "This is Teri Jackson returning your call."

Equally brisk, Kelli thanked her for returning the call and explained the reason for it.

"Lovely! How about three today? It's so rare to get a place on the Battery, I'm looking forward to seeing it," the woman was very enthusiastic. *That's good in a salesperson,* Kelli thought to herself, *but it can be exhausting for the rest of us.*

Kelli agreed and the woman hung up without so much as a Bye. *I don't think this will work. Not if I have to spend much time with her.*

Kelli returned to her book in an effort to calm down. She glanced at her watch. "Good. A couple hours should give me time to forget my initial impression," she said to the dog resting at her feet, her head weighing down Kelli's right foot.

2

Sunday afternoon

From across the street he watched Kelli's house, really her grandparents' house, just as he had thousands of times before. A car approached slowly, apparently looking for a parking space on the narrow street between the houses and the bay. The car turned right onto South Battery, either giving up or continuing its search around the corner. He chortled as a space opened up directly across the street from him. "Too bad for you, lady," he said to the departed vehicle. He hated people who drove Beamers, always thought they were better than everybody else.

It was a grey, rain-spitting day, normal for late-January in Charleston, and warmer than a lot of places. He pulled his scarf tighter around his neck. Sixty degrees gets cold when you're just sitting, hoping for a sight of the only woman you could ever love. He reached for the newspaper on the backseat of his seven year old Camry.

Just then the light blue BMW came back around the corner. The older woman easily maneuvered the car into the space vacated by the SUV just a few minutes prior. He watched curiously as she got out, big black leather purse in hand, opened the rear driver's side door and removed a matching briefcase.

His curiosity turned to alarm as the pudgy woman marched up the concrete steps to Kelli's front door and rang the bell. As the door opened he strained for a glimpse of Kelli, but the door and the dim interior of the entrance defeated him.

As the door closed behind the two women, he glared in frustration at the woman's car. It was then he saw the small, tasteful sign magnetically affixed to the door: Teri Jackson, Realtor®, Carolina Elite Properties and a couple phone numbers. He started to sweat as he copied the name and numbers into his current Kelli-notebook, in the section he kept for her friends and acquaintances. He hit his fist against the steering wheel and shouted, "A real estate agent! What does Kelli want with her? She can't move. Why would she move? She loves it here, we grew up here." He slammed his fist against the steering wheel again. "Think, damn you, think! You can't let her leave." Gradually he calmed down as he continued to watch and wait for the other woman to leave. He didn't know what he would do then, but he'd figure out something. He had to be prepared. He picked up his Canon SureShot from the passenger seat. He needed a picture of the woman, Teri Jackson. He needed to find out what was going on!

Kelli opened the front door and was immediately taken aback; Teri Jackson was not what she was expecting. In her mind she had envisioned some sleek, tall blonde in four-inch heels. The woman in the wrinkled topaz-colored suit did not match the imagined vision. *Stereotyping?* Kelli asked herself. She hoped her face did not express her dismay.

"Teri Jackson?" she asked hesitantly of the woman standing on the front step.

The fiftyish woman held out her large hand and gave Kelli's a very firm shake. "The one and the same," Ms. Jackson smiled. "As far as I know there's not another in Charleston, at least not in the real estate business." She smiled again as she elbowed her way into the entryway between the two sets of double doors, sort of the 18th century version of a mudroom. Jackson shook out her umbrella and leaned it against the pale green wall. "Well, this is certainly nice." *Is that a note of sarcasm?* Kelli wondered, still slightly speechless. "Do you think you could show me the rest of the house?" *Yep, definitely sarcasm.*

Kelli gave herself a mental shake. "Oh, of course. Forgive me. Would you like a cup of coffee or tea? It's so awfully wet out there." Kelli pushed through to the foyer, the agent following in her wake, rather like a tugboat after a sailboat. Corky was waiting. "I hope you don't mind dogs," Kelli said as Corky walked over to the other woman and gave her a polite sniff.

Teri Jackson patted Corky's head and replied, "Not a bit, have a Golden myself." She straightened and suggested, "How about if you show me the house, then we can have coffee or something, while we talk after?"

Kelli led the way up the sweeping staircase to the second floor, still sizing up the woman she had just met. She decided she liked her, even if she was a bit brusque. Kelli tried to make small-talk as they ascended. "Are you from around here, Ms. Jackson?" Kelli had already surmised from her no-nonsense approach that she was originally from somewhere "up North."

The woman's eyes twinkled; obviously she had heard the question before. "Sure am. Grew up not too far from this very house. Went to Battery Girls' Prep and everything. Went to business school at Harvard, though. Those Yankees may not be worth a damn, but they sure do know business. That's how they won that war 150 years ago."

Kelli's amazement – and liking – grew as they reached the top of the stairs. She turned to the left and stopped at the door to the library. "This is the library and office." Ms. Jackson made a note in the small leather-bound portfolio she had pulled from her voluminous purse.

Kelli moved to the French doors at the end of the hall. "This is my favorite room," she said as she pushed the doors wide. Teri Jackson saw a tiny room with a window overlooking the bay, a chaise lounge with a small table next to it, and a small writing desk with an old French-style rotary phone on it.

"Hardly qualifies as a room, does it?" Ms. Jackson commented with a chuckle and another note on her pad. At first Kelli was insulted, but when she looked at the room objectively she had to agree. She too chuckled. "You're right there. My grandparents refer to it as Kelli's Kloset." The women smiled at each other and they turned and headed back in the other direction. "By the way," the older woman said, "call me Teri. I know it's against Southern tradition, but it makes things go more quickly." They both smiled again. Corky, who had been following the woman ever since she entered the house, seemed to relax a bit at the lighter sound of their voices.

Kelli stopped at the first room on the left, opposite the staircase landing. Teri saw a queen size "rice" bed, tastefully covered in embroidered white linen with a white linen canopy to match. She knew the original "rice" bed got its name from the rice carvings on the bedposts; she had no doubt these were originals. There were nightstands on either side of the bed and a private bath off to the right of the entrance door. Teri oohed and ahhed and made more notes.

At the next door, Kelli said, "These two rooms are rarely used. They're for visiting family mostly." Again Teri saw a tastefully decorated room, about the same size as the one she had just seen, except this one had twin beds and the bathroom on the left.

At one end of the hall was a large bedroom with a king-size bed and antique wooden bedroom furniture. Bow windows on three sides overlooked the expansive gardens and fountains below. Another antique lady's desk was under the window in the right, a large cedar chest on the left. Walk-in closets on either side of the room accommodated extensive wardrobes. "This is my grandparents' room," Kelli explained. "This is their house. They're vacationing in Arizona right now and are considering selling it, but they want to see what they can get for it first." Teri nodded and made more notes.

"The last room on this floor is my room," Kelli said as she stopped at the first room on the right from the staircase. This room was a bit more modern in its décor, maybe turn of the last century rather than late 18th Teri decided. "Nice," she said as she left the updated en-suite bath making more notes.

They headed back downstairs and crossed the foyer to the room overlooking the front steps and the bay beyond. "We call this the front parlor," Kelli offered. "I don't know what you real estate people would call it." Teri saw a small sitting room with a large fireplace. Elegant upholstered Queen Anne furniture. Plaster medallions over the fireplace and plaster rosettes surrounding the chandelier that hung from the high ceiling. "They sure don't make them like this anymore," she commented.

"Is that a good thing or bad?" Kelli asked sincerely. She really wanted to know. Teri just smiled at her and moved into the next room.

"This is the parlor." Teri looked around the larger room, at least twice the size of the front parlor but otherwise a virtual duplicate of it; same style furniture, same fabrics, same pale green paint, same fireplace and marble surround, same light fixtures. She made notes again.

"And finally, the dining room. But I guess you could figure that out," Kelli said ruefully. It was sort of obvious since there was a dining table with sixteen chairs around it.

"I like the way the rooms flow together, rather like an antique version of an open floor plan...except no kitchen. It's got great light, too; those French doors are really a hot item, very popular when the weather turns warmer, as it always does."

"There are pocket doors between each of these rooms so we can close them off if we want, helps keep the air conditioning and heating costs down." Kelli moved them on to the swinging door that opened between the foyer and the kitchen.

As Teri moved through the door she said, "Now this is perfect. Everybody wants a modern kitchen and room to entertain. This will definitely get us bonus points." She strode further in and made lots of notes: separate eating area that looked out onto the piazza and garden, long, deep breakfast and cooking areas, granite on all surfaces, modern appliances. She opened a door at the far end of the kitchen, next to a window. Large walk-in pantry, really large, with floor to ceiling shelving and a library-style ladder leaning ready for the things on the top shelves.

"Only thing missing is a powder room on this floor. Most guests don't want to have to climb to the second floor to pee," she offered with a grin. Kelli was a bit shocked by her language, not because she hadn't heard it before, but because women of a certain age and older were not inclined to say 'pee'.

"Sorry, we missed it. There's a good-sized powder room off the foyer, next to the coat closet. We finally had to put a little tile on each door, one marked coat closet, one marked W.C., because so many people were embarrassed when they opened the wrong door."

"Just be glad nobody peed in the coat closet," Teri said with a loud guffaw that set both women laughing. *It's definite, I like her,*

Kelli thought. Unbeknownst to her, Teri Jackson was having a similar thought.

Just as Kelli was about to offer a beverage again, Teri Jackson jumped right in, "Could I have that cup of coffee now? I run on the stuff and haven't had some in at least an hour." Teri seated herself at the breakfast room table, put on some half-moon glasses, and started reviewing her notes, obviously not expecting any chatter from Kelli.

3

Kelli walked over to the stove and turned on the gas burner under the flowered teapot. She grabbed a coffee mug from the cupboard to the left of the stove. Would Teri notice if she got leftover coffee? It had been fresh that morning. Kelli always made a pot on Sundays, even though she was the only one in the house; for reasons she couldn't understand coffee tasted better to her on the weekends; she never drank it otherwise. And she made a pot in case anybody came over. She just reheated it in the microwave until the pot was gone; nobody had ever complained. She knew Magda would drink lots when she came on Mondays to tidy up. Kelli knew she was not a coffee connoisseur but the reheated coffee never tasted any different to her. She'd learned a long time ago that enough French Vanilla creamer killed the coffee taste. There was just something about a cup of coffee while she read the Sunday paper that appealed to her.

By the time the teapot was steaming Kelli had reheated some coffee in her USC mug, fixed a tray with cream and sugar and a plate of shortbread cookies, and gotten out her favorite porcelain cup and saucer. She trapped some loose Earl Grey tea leaves in the silver tea infuser and placed it into the flowered cup. Gently she poured the hot water over the tea – "never add tea to water" Granny had trained her – and returned the teapot to the stove.

She picked up the tray and carried it across the room to the table centered between two sets of French doors. Teri was just ending a call on her cell phone. As she seated herself Kelli asked, with her most disarming smile, "Teri, are all real estate agents so...vibrant? Or did I just get lucky?"

Teri laughed a big, hearty laugh and crumbs fell and stuck to the front of her navy silk blouse. "Sorry, Kelli, I've been told I'm a bit 'overpowering'. I think that's the polite term for 'loud', or maybe 'bitchy', but it's just me. I stopped trying to be something I'm not when I got divorced twenty years ago and I've been much happier." She paused. "Let me just get another sip of this great coffee and we'll get down to the nitty-gritty." Kelli decided she hadn't offended her with either her question or the coffee.

"Now I feel better." Teri put the maroon "Go Gamecocks" mug onto the table and took a deep breath. "Questions?"

"Are you planning to hold a public open house? I'll need advance notice; there are some pieces I'll need to put up. I'm not sure Granny would be thrilled at the idea anyway; boatloads of complete strangers wandering through the house unattended. Sounds like an open invitation for theft."

"As things stand right now I'm not inclined to hold a public open house. I've found through my years of handling these exclusive houses, and especially the older ones, that the public open houses are not worth the time or effort we put into them. The majority of people who come are just interested in seeing the house itself, not even in the market to buy, or they're out for a Sunday drive , see the sign, and decide to stop in. Especially these old houses on the Battery. It's not often anyone gets to see the inside of them. Would you believe people come to open houses just to get decorating ideas?

"And then there are the footprints; we'd have to get the carpets and the floors cleaned afterward, even if it isn't a rainy day. You would not believe what people track into homes during an open house." She paused, catching her breath. "No, we'll hold off on that idea. Who knows? We could have a contract by the end of the week." Kelli blanched at the thought. *Where will I go once the house is sold? I don't know if I'm up to going back to "our house."* Corky felt Kelli's dismay and lifted her head from where it was resting on Kelli's foot under the table.

"Here's what I'm thinking," Teri continued, seemingly oblivious to the mild panic she had created in the young woman seated opposite her.

"I'll come by tomorrow afternoon and we'll get the papers signed. My assistant, Fran, will come by around one, measure all the rooms, and make a video and stills of all the rooms. As soon as the papers are signed Fran will upload everything to the MLS, my office's website, and my personal site. Once it's on the MLS it will be picked up by Realtor.com, Zillow, and lots of other home-tracking sites.

"Then on Wednesday we'll hold a broker open house. It's much more efficient and productive than a public one. We'll – actually Fran - will email all the brokers in the Charleston area who handle upscale homes and invite them to a buffet lunch here. Offer them food and agents will go anywhere." Teri laughed conspiratorially.

"How does the broker open house solve the problem of people tromping through here unattended?"

"For one thing, there are a lot fewer people, maybe twenty or thirty at the most. Secondly, we know everybody who will be here, they will have been invited. Finally, it's for a limited period of time, two hours max. We'll have a sign-in sheet so we know who was here and what time. Then we can email them afterward and get their opinions of the house, the price, and that sort of thing." She hesitated again. "It's still a good idea to lock up anything that's valuable or that has great family value." She grinned knowingly.

Kelli broke in, "Maybe we need to slow down a bit. When I started this it was just to get information for my grandparents. Since you brought up price, what are you thinking? As I said, my grandparents aren't even sure they want to put the house on the market."

Teri nodded her head and said, "Perfectly normal. I can't say anything about a price until I check the comps, similar houses on the Battery that have sold recently. I'll call you first thing in the morning with a suggested price. We can finalize price tomorrow when I bring the papers for you to sign. That gives you time to talk to them and find out what they want to do. Are they planning to sell the house furnished?"

"I don't think they've decided yet. Would that make a big difference in its saleability? Is that a word?" Kelli smiled, a bit overwhelmed by the pace of everything.

"Furniture makes a big difference when it's antiques of this quality, at least half again the price of the house. The question with selling a house furnished is whether you can find someone with the same taste. If somebody is looking for a really modern house, this furniture probably would turn them off. That's another reason I like the broker open house. The brokers go back to their offices and tell their agents about the house, give their advice about how to show it. This cuts down on those buyers who would never consider this house or who could never afford it."

"Can you give me a ballpark figure on selling price? Something I can tell Granny so they can at least decide if they want to list it or not? I hate for you to go to a lot of work and then have them say 'never mind'"

"Not a problem, happens more times than you'd think." Teri glanced through her notes again and then raised her eyes to Kelli. "I'd guess four million, five and a half to six if it's sold furnished, but that's just a guess until I can do my homework."

Kelli exhaled audibly. "Wow. Well. Okay. I'll call them this evening and call you if they decide against it. Otherwise I'll see you and Fran tomorrow afternoon. Do you have an idea of a time? I'm working from home tomorrow afternoon so I should be here."

Teri pulled up her calendar on her phone, "Can we say one o'clock for Fran, three for me? Does that work?"

"Yes, that's fine. Anything I need to do? Our housekeeper will be here tomorrow so the house will be spotless for the open house. I can have her come in afterward, too, to clean up." Kelli smiled. "Anyway Magda will insist on coming back to clean-up so we might as well let her, this is more her house than it is mine. She's been part of the family since before my brother and I moved in."

"Sounds like we have a plan. The only thing you'll need will be a power of attorney so you can sign in your grandparents stead, or at least until we can FedEx the papers for them to sign and get back to me."

"They left a POA with me, in case anything came up in their absence. I'll have it here tomorrow afternoon. I'm leaving town Wednesday, is that a problem?"

Teri smiled, "Actually it's better if the owner isn't there. What about Corky?"

Kelli patted her dog's head, "She'll be at the kennel; her favorite place after here."

Teri stood and gathered her portfolio and her purse. She extended her hand to Kelli. "I'm sure it will sell fairly quickly, but it could be months. Houses like this either sell right away or it takes a while. This is a very specialized market, very expensive. Buyers who are looking for this age and style house, and who can afford it, are few and far between. Fortunately, we get a goodly number of them moving to Charleston. As I always say, 'It only takes one'." She chortled and heaved herself to the front door, not waiting for Kelli to see her out.

Again Kelli followed in her wake. Teri grabbed her briefcase where she had left it by the front door, and then passed through the first set of twelve-foot double doors. She retrieved her umbrella and opened the left outside door. She glanced outside. "It's stopped raining for the moment. I'll see you tomorrow, Kelli." And she was gone, holding the handrail so she didn't slip on the nine concrete steps, then hop-scotching around puddles on her way to the gate. The gate clanged behind her and she was gone.

Kelli looked down at Corky once the doors were closed. "Phew. I'm exhausted, Cork. How about you?" She patted her dog's head. "Come on, let's go outside while the rain has quit." Corky danced around Kelli as they made their way to the kitchen door and Corky's backyard domain.

4

Finally that woman was leaving. He glanced at his watch. What was she doing in there for two and a half hours? He had just enough time to get home and change. He gave one final look at Kelli's front door but missed seeing Kelli as the door closed behind her. Not long now. Soon she would know how much he worshipped her, had loved her forever.

Ever since eighth grade he had known Kelli was the one for him. It was her first day of middle school in Charleston. He remembered everything about that moment. Old Mrs. Burkholder had introduced Kelli to the homeroom class. Kelli was standing next to her, long brown hair, big brown eyes, and her very classy navy skirt and crisp, white oxford cloth blouse, a bit overdressed for that crowd. Mrs. Burkholder explained that Kelli had been schooled at various places in Europe, and she had now returned to her roots to complete her education. Kelli blushed bright red while this was being related, clearly uncomfortable at being singled out for attention.

Thankfully for Kelli Mrs. B. had kept her comments brief and then motioned Kelli to a desk in the middle of the row, on the far side of the room, away from him.

Everybody knew Kelli anyway, she'd been here for years. Mrs. B. just thought it was cool that she had a student who had studied abroad, even if it had been only convent schools.

That began his worship from afar. They had no classes together, he was actually a year older and had been held back a grade. She was in advanced everything: English, math, French and science. He remembered how excited he was each morning, just seeing her in homeroom lifted his spirits. When she smiled at him, that secret smile they had, he was over the moon.

All the guys in school were falling all over themselves to talk to her, enthralled by her slight French accent, not nearly as pronounced as it had been when she'd first arrived in third grade. Kelli wasn't old enough to date yet. All the boys wanted to ask her out, but very few did, intimidated by her smarts, even though she was even nicer than she was smart. He knew she was saving herself for him, though.

The other girls in school were another matter. He heard them talking about how stuck-up she was, how fake her accent was. That first year of middle school they never invited her to join them for lunch or any of their clubs or anything. Most days she ate lunch by herself or surrounded by boys of all ages, even juniors and seniors. She was always polite to them and smiled sweetly at their jokes and sports bragging, but he knew she saved that secret smile for him.

He had watched all of this from across the cafeteria. That was when he started taking notes and keeping track of names. He had to protect her. She didn't know these kids like he did. Even though he was not one of the popular kids, he still knew them. He watched and listened and recorded...everything. Sometimes he took action; like the time he had slashed the tires of a senior who had spent too much time talking to her. Or the time he covered another boy's windshield with black paint so he couldn't see to drive. Or the girl who was mean to Kelli and then mysteriously disappeared. It was easy to keep track of Kelli back then, he lived close by.

He did nice things, too. He frequently left notes in her hall locker, shoved through the air vents, then waited at the end of the day to see her reaction. He saw their secret smile and the way she carefully tucked the note into a book, pressing it as a keepsake. Their senior year he had flowers delivered to the school for her on Valentine's Day. That one had backfired though because she got into trouble with Mrs. Chittum, "no deliveries to the school office of any kind for students. It's in the student guide." He had been working as an office assistant the hour Kelli came to get them and she was reprimanded. He hadn't thought about the rule, had never read the student guide anyway.

She tried to use logic, "But, Mrs. Chittum, I didn't send them. It's not my fault." Mrs. Chittum just harrumphed and then allowed Kelli to leave them in the office until the end of the day. "After all," she had said, "It's too many roses for you to be caring around all day." He'd saved up for three months to be able to afford them, then he could only get half as many as he wanted because the flower prices were jacked up for the holiday. Crummy crooks. But he'd fixed them, broke their big display window late one night. Just threw a brick through it, with kitchen gloves on, so nobody knew who did it.

He grinned at the memory as he pulled into the parking lot of his North Charleston apartment. He couldn't wait to add his latest photos of Kelli to his collection, but it would have to wait until he got home from work. Once again he worried about what the real estate lady had meant to his plans. Kelli would never leave him, she loved him. She couldn't leave, especially now, after all he had done for her.

5

Monday morning

The next morning Kelli decided to walk the long eight blocks to the Charleston Library Society building on south King Street. It was a beautiful day, especially for a Monday and the end of January. She could enjoy the scent of camellias hanging heavily in the air. The bright sunshine was wonderful after the dreary weather of the weekend. Nonetheless Kelli bundled up in a red car coat, black cloche, and warm gloves; the wind made it feel colder than it was.

As Kelli was going out, she met Magda coming in. The two women hugged on the front step and Kelli walked back inside with the older woman.

"Hey, Magda, I'm glad I caught you, or you caught me I guess," Kelli smiled warmly at the woman she considered another mother, certainly more present than her real one. "You'll never guess!"

Magda, Granny's housekeeper since before Kelli and Sean had arrived, was a woman of few words. She smiled back and quirked an eyebrow at her beloved Kelli.

"Granny is looking into selling the house!" Kelli exclaimed with all the indignation she felt.

"No! Not really?" Magda was crestfallen. Her thoughts had immediately gone to the friend who might be moving away permanently. "For goodness sakes, why?"

"Seems they've decided Arizona is the place for them," Kelli explained with as little sarcasm as she could avoid. "It started as an investigation but when Granny heard how much they could get for it... I suggested they rent a house for a year and make sure it's as glorious as they seem to think. Who knows if they'll do that though? You know how stubborn Granny can be. Anyway, it's being listed this afternoon. The Realtor says it can sell soon or take a long time, there's no telling."

Magda nodded knowingly and with a grin. "Well," she exhaled, "That is a surprise."

"The good news, though, is that we don't have to "stage" the house. Magda looked quizzical. "I didn't know what that was either. Teri, our Realtor, said that's when you take all your personal stuff out so potential buyers can imagine what the house would look like with their stuff in here. Sort of like turning it into a model home. Todd and I looked at lots of models before we bought our house. Frankly, we wouldn't have moved into any of them the way they were decorated. So I'm really glad we don't have to change anything."

Kelli glanced at her watch. "Anyway, I've got to scoot. We can talk more when I get home. I'll be home at lunchtime because the real estate lady and her assistant are coming by to take pictures of all the rooms. I think they look fine right now, but I wanted to give you a heads-up in case you want to do anything."

Magda nodded her understanding and Kelli turned to the front doors again. "Gotta run. See you around noon." And Kelli was off, now hurrying to work. "Don't want to be late on a half day," she called over her shoulder as she went through the gate. Kelli waved and Magda returned it although Kelli was already out of sight.

As she walked to work she remembered Granny's delight when she called her about the visit with the real estate lady; they were forging ahead with the sale. Granny had said, "We'll see what happens. If it sells at our price, great. If not, we'll just pull it off the market and try again next year. Not to worry. I'm just sorry you're the one who has to deal with the paperwork and the showings." Kelli had to grin again at her grandmother's fake regret; her nickname was DOD, delegator of duties, because she was so good at getting people to do things for her, leaving her with the planning and none of the grunt work. Fortunately, everyone who knew her well, knew this was her way and continued to do her bidding.

The few people Kelli passed as she strode down East Bay and across Queen to King Street were smiling, too, apparently enjoying the sunshine as much as she was. She paused a moment before she climbed the marble stairs to her workplace; she looked up at its amazing granite façade and once again thanked her stars that she got to work in such an historic place.

The Charleston Library Society was the first library in Charleston, having been founded by eighteen local gentlemen in 1748. The collection of books and artifacts moved from building to building, sometimes it was even held in the upstairs of houses, until it finally was moved to its current site on King Street in 1914. In 1773, its artifacts became the core collection for the first museum in America, the Charleston Museum. Originally, books were paid for by memberships.

Kelli entered the wood- floored and -paneled lobby and was relieved to see the staff seemed to be perky today as well. The quasi-musty smell of old and new books assailed her nose as she walked past the stacks. She smiled and once again thought to herself *"I am so lucky to work here."* On the way to her office she was greeted and waved at by all seven of the other worker-bees, even Gladys. *Well, it was more of a snarl than a smile, but she did look at me.*

Gladys has been with the Library since "Lee was a corporal" as was said down south. Gladys considered Kelli's job superfluous and inappropriate for an ageless and respected institution. *No matter how often we have all tried to convince her that times have changed and the library needs additional sources of income, she just glares at us and reminds us that we have no respect for tradition.*

Kelli closed her office door behind her and hung her coat on the peg next to it. She sat at her utilitarian metal desk and glanced out the window of her fishbowl office. Except for the wall behind her and the one in front of her, the tiny office was surrounded by glass.

She liked the one that opened onto the garden behind the Library, but the one that faced onto the main floor of the Library she hated; anyone and everyone could see what she was doing. Not that she was doing anything they shouldn't see, it was just the principle. She couldn't adjust her bra or blow her nose without feeling like the whole world was watching.

Now looking out, she saw Gladys once again keeping an eye on her. *She's probably keeping notes of when I arrive and when I leave and how often I go to the bathroom. I know she'd be happy to see the last of me.* Kelli turned away from the window and pushed the power button on her computer. While it booted she considered why Gladys was so set against her.

When I started here four years ago, a newly-diplomaed Master of Information Science, I was definitely out of step. There were three other degreed librarians, all over fifty or nearing it, two long-time desk assistants, one research assistant, and Gladys, the office manager. Everyone was very gracious and welcoming and receptive to new ideas, except Gladys. If I had a nickel for every time she said, "That's not how we do things here." I could pay all Sean's legal bills myself.

With the leadership of our head librarian, Elizabeth Potter, and my recent college courses, we initiated the new bar-code-reader system. Of course that meant more work for everybody as we put a bar code on everything in the building, all three floors of it, from books to library cards to loaner computers to white board erasers. Everything was checked out and we knew who had what. It took almost two years to get everything planned and coded, but now our losses have been reduced and we are saving money on "lost" items.

Once that was successful we decided we needed a Friends of the Library group to help pay for some future purchases that the Library needs, but are not glamorous to taxpayers. But Gladys fought the idea tooth and nail.

She finally came to accept the bar codes and readers, although she still complained they made the Library feel like a grocery store, but marketing, raising funds, "begging" was too demeaning. Her thought was that people would give to the Library out of the goodness of their hearts, they didn't like to be pestered. For reasons I still fail to fathom, Elizabeth put me in charge of the FOL. I tried to get Gladys on board, I really did. Kelli grimaced at the memory of that conversation.

"Gladys, think of it as reminding people we are here, not pestering. Especially those who have moved out of the area. They probably still remember us fondly, but have forgotten about us since they don't use the Library anymore. And there are all the new people who have moved to the area, they probably pass by this building lots of times and have no idea our doors are open to the public."

Her arms crossed on her bony chest, she just growled, "I still don't like it. It's not polite. It's not how things are done in the South." A not so subtle jab at my foreign past.

"But think of all the children's programs we could have if we had just a bit more money." Gladys, a spinster, was in charge of the children's library. Her eyebrows rose in surprise, then immediately settled back to their normal inverted V.

"Like what? Are you saying I'm not doing enough now?"

"No, of course not. I'm just saying you could do more if you had more money. Your story time is a wonderful program and very popular. What if you could bring in some national storytellers once or twice a year? Or puppeteers? Think how many more children might be touched by your programs." Kelli smiled hopefully at her.

Gladys continued to glower, but she was weakening, the children were her Achilles heel.

"We'll see." *She stalked off, refusing to go along with something new. But at least I could see a bit of wiggle room in the fact there was no complete rejection.*

That was two years ago. I spent the first six months getting everything set up. First I had to research donor software to track everything we had to track. Once it was installed, and not without a few glitches, I had to create an extensive data base to track everything we wanted to track: donor names and addresses, how many times they'd been contacted, their responses, and how much and when they had donated. We decided to contact donors only four times a year, and only once to ask for donations; two of the other three times would be a newsletter about Library events and parts of the collection and the last time was a "holiday" card from the whole staff.

The best part of my new position was that I could do a lot of the work at home, so I could be home when Todd was home. As a state trooper his shift changed every month and I liked to see him as much as I could; after all, we'd only been married two years when I started the FOL project.

We sent our first e-letter announcing the Friends; we were amazed at how many donations we received right away: over $26,000, one for $10,000 and lots for $100. It was very gratifying.

After a year of the program we were all feeling comfortable with the FOL, even Gladys. It hadn't proved such a "begging" nightmare as she had predicted. And we had made sure some of the first money went to children's programs.

Kelli's computer pinged, indicating it was ready to go. Kelli just leaned her head back against the chair's high back and let the memories flood over her again.

Then late last May I found out I was pregnant, at least that's what the pregnancy stick told me. But I had to be sure, couldn't just accept it. I knew how excited Todd and my grandparents would be, and how disappointed they would be if it was another false alarm. I decided to wait and be sure. It was so hard, though; I wanted to tell Todd so desperately. But we'd been through three false alarms already and I just didn't want to see the disappointment on his face again. Better he had been disappointed!

It was late June, June 24 to be exact, before I could get an appointment with my doctor. It was right before our fourth anniversary, July 12. I got the good news from Dr. Levine and couldn't wait to tell the whole world, but Todd first. Driving home I planned a wonderful dinner for the both of us, complete with candles and soft music. I stopped at Publix and got the ingredients, then rushed home to prepare. I'd called the Library and said I wouldn't be in the rest of the day. I spent the afternoon cooking and baking. Todd called just as he was leaving work and I asked him to stop and get some raspberries for dinner, I'd forgotten them. While Todd was standing in the check-out line, a man in a hoodie and sunglasses came up behind him and shot him. Killed him. The man ran out of the store and hasn't been found yet, seven months later.

As usual at this point in the memory, Kelli blamed herself. *If I hadn't asked him to stop for raspberries, he'd be alive today and I'd be about to deliver our baby. We would have made a nursery, shopped for clothes, and for stuffed animals. But no. None of that.*

Of course there was a very dignified memorial service, with law enforcement personnel from all over the state. I don't remember much about it; drugs can be wonderful things. Todd's best friend, Dean, and Todd's captain escorted me, but I only know that because Dean told me. He still checks in on me every day and comes over at least once a week to "get me out of the house", as he says.

The investigation began, but there wasn't much to go on. The "perp" had his face turned away from the cameras over the check-out area. He wore gloves. He used a silencer. Nobody else in the line even knew Todd had been shot until he slumped to the floor. By then the shooter had slowly exited the store.

The outside surveillance cameras got the murderer's back as he walked away, but then could not follow him as he took the under-street tunnel to Cane Bay High School across the street. The only thing the video cameras showed was a man a little over six feet tall in sweat pants and a hoodie, wearing combat boots. Strange outfit for late-June in Charleston, where temperatures are usually in the low 90s, but nobody paid any attention to him; you see stranger things everyday on television or the streets of L.A. The hunt continues, but there's not much hope of catching him after this long. The police's best guess is it was a random shooting of a cop. Todd was just in the wrong place at the wrong time...because I sent him there.

A week after Todd's service, I lost the baby. Grief on top of grief just left me numb. For months I could feel nothing, ate very little, slept even less, just laid in bed and wallowed in my grief. The Library gave me a leave of absence. I moved back into my grandparents' house on the Battery the night Todd died; I couldn't stand our little house in Cane Bay anymore.

Granny and Gramps were great. They seemed to know when I needed time to myself, which was most of the time, and when I needed a hug. The first few months Granny brought me tea and toast and fresh fruit, but she never insisted I eat or pressed me to talk. She never even insisted I get out of bed. I changed my pajamas once in a while and that was all the exercise I got. I was too numb even to read. Didn't answer cards or emails.

Kelli's phone rang, thankfully rousing her from her depressing memories. She wiped her eyes, sat up straight, and reached for the phone, aware that everyone on the other side of the glass could see her. "Kelli Cavanaugh, Charleston Library Society, may I help you?"

"Hi, Kelli, it's Teri Jackson. Is this a good time? Do you have a minute?"

Kelli glanced at her watch, 9:30. *Couldn't this wait until this afternoon?* "Sure, what's up?"

"I just wanted to let you know that I did the comps. Naturally in this price range there haven't been a lot of sales, especially recently and on the Battery. But I was able to come up with a figure and I think it's pretty accurate. Do you know if your grandparents want to sell at the price we talked about yesterday or sell it quickly?"

"Granny, she handles all their finances, told me she's not in any rush to sell."

"Great! Then we'll list it at 4.89 million dollars. If they'd wanted to sell quickly we'd list it at 3.5 and probably have it gone in a week. Are they selling it furnished?"

"No, unfurnished. I talked them out of selling it furnished. I used your argument that it lessened the number of potential buyers because we would have to find someone who wanted the same type furniture or was willing to go through the hassle of getting rid of it after they'd bought it. My grandmother is a very rational woman." Kelli grinned again at the image of Granny with her half-moon glasses and her tennis racket.

"Perfect. I'll see you at three then with the papers. It shouldn't take us long to go over them and get your signature.

Don't forget the POA. And Fran's coming at one to take pictures and stuff so she can work her magic."

"No problem. I've got the POA. Magda is there today and I've explained about the house sale but I still need to tell her about the upcoming showings. She may be even more heartbroken than I am."

"Sorry. Got to run. See you at three." The phone line went dead.

Kelli shrugged her shoulders in a "go figure" movement and logged into the computer. She went directly to Outlook and pulled up her emails. She already knew she had no meetings for the day so she didn't need to check the calendar right now. Fourteen emails since Friday, and hopefully all about donations; she recognized a few previous donor names. She quickly started reading through them, oldest to newest. The third one got her attention, a $5,000 credit card donation to the Library. The eighth one got her attention even more: "Soon, my darling, soon."

She rechecked the sender's email address and recognized the name of one of their most loyal patrons. But it was the same wording as the wrong text she'd gotten yesterday. That "my darling" crap. *But this patron is 87 and happily married; I seriously doubt the message is from him. Maybe I should let him know he may have been hacked.* Weird.

Her phone rang again. *Please, no more, Teri, I'm busy,* she thought to herself. She reached for her phone and gave her normal greeting. A male voice responded, "My darling, I see you got my email. Soon, Kelli, very soon. I can't wait to touch you. I know you're looking forward to it, too. Soon. I promise." The phone went dead.

Kelli stared at the phone. *It wasn't a mistake. It wasn't a coincidence. These messages are meant for me. This goes way beyond weird. This is getting scary. But what do I do about it?*

It suddenly occurred to her what the caller had said, "'I see you got my email.'" *Does that mean he's here? Watching me?*

Knows where I work? She looked out through the front window of the fishbowl, scrutinizing each person she saw. She saw no one who looked like the caller, whatever he looked like. *Okay, Kell, what are you looking for? Somebody who looks "suspicious"? Define "suspicious". That guy over there who appears to be sleeping in his chair? Is he really? Sylvan behind the Circ desk? He's obviously trying to hide the fact that he's on a personal call. The guy in the biker shorts on the computer? Maybe he's just looking at porn and isn't your caller. See anybody who looks out of place? Everyday! We get homeless people in here who just want the heat and the bathroom. Mike caught one of them taking a bird bath in the men's room.* Her eyes continued to shift from person to person. *The only one it can't be is someone I know.* Turning back to her computer, she muttered to herself, "That doesn't exactly narrow the field, you work in a public place. It could be anyone." She stared blankly at the screen while she considered her options: call the police, call Dean, do nothing. "It's unlikely the police are going to do anything about a couple phone calls and emails. I don't want to worry Dean over a couple phone calls, either. And what can they do? The voice sounded metallic, like one of those voice synthesizer things. So I didn't recognize it." She heaved a big sigh at her feeling of impotence.

"Okay, I'll do nothing for now. Maybe this fantasy, fascination, delusion, whatever it is, will stop or he'll find another attraction. If the messages continue, I'll talk to Dean, he'll know what I should do. Besides, I'm going to be out of town for ten days, I'm sure his ardor will dissipate in that length of time." She felt much better after talking to herself out loud, somehow her words just made more sense to her when she heard them than when she thought them. "Back to work." She looked at her watch, almost ten. Just two more hours and she'd be gone for the next almost-two weeks. She hoped she could handle the trip without the Ambien her doctor had prescribed; it wasn't going to be an easy vacation.

6

Monday afternoon

Kelli's morning went as usual for the next two hours: she answered emails, sent one to Elizabeth reminding her of her upcoming trip – Kelli couldn't quite see it as a vacation because she knew how hard it was going to be- reviewed the design for a new FOL brochure, and drafted a letter for new donors. She even had time to double-check her plans for the trip. At 11:30 Elizabeth popped in to wish her a good trip, she already knew the reason for the trip and knew how difficult it was going to be for Kelli.

The trip to St. Croix was part vacation, but mostly so Kelli could scatter Todd's ashes in the ocean. They had honeymooned on the island and Todd always referred to it as their "final resting place", the place they would go to retire. It just seemed right to Kelli that she should take him back to the place he had loved so much.

Elizabeth's visit reminded her she had never heard back from TSA about how to transport Todd's ashes; should she pack them in her checked luggage? She didn't feel safe with that idea. Could she get them through security if she carried them on? It was just a small box, about the size of a four-cupcake bakery box. How could such a big man be reduced to such a small container? She felt strange at the thought of stowing Todd in the baggage compartment and risking the chance of some curious baggage handler or security person "spilling him." But she didn't want to get held up at TSA either while she tried to explain the box contents. She could see it now – "What's in the box? My husband." *Nope, don't think that will work.*

Kelli decided to check the TSA web site one more time for an answer. There, under PRESS ROOM she finally found it: Transporting Dead Bodies. *Good grief, how crude, how compassionless; they could have used something less jarring.*

*According to the site, s*he just needed the box sealed with the funeral home's seal, unbroken, and the funeral home's statement of the box's contents affixed to the top. Both of those were already done. She hadn't touched the box since the day she brought it home, two days after his memorial service.

At 12:10 she was still seated at her desk. She just needed to check her to-do list one more time. So much to do and so little time. *At least keeping busy keeps me from thinking about...other things. And now I can add selling the house to my list! Goody, goody. Maybe I'll go for a swim later today. I haven't been swimming since...last summer. The heated pool at the Y would feel really good. I need to get back into a routine, too. Well, maybe I'll start when I get back from St. Croix. No sense starting a new routine just to have it interrupted.*

She printed her enhanced to-do list, grabbed her purse, coat, and hat, and headed out the door. She stopped at the Circulation desk and reminded them she wouldn't be back until Monday, two weeks from now. They all wished her a good trip and made her promise to tell them all about St. Croix when she got back. Kelli smiled as she exited the building. *It is going to be okay; I'll be fine.*

As Kelli walked into the house, Magda was just getting ready to leave. They greeted each other and hugged. "All set for this afternoon," Magda assured Kelli. Kelli smiled at the older woman.

"Not surprising. I don't know what any of us would do without you, Mags."

Magda Rostov harrumphed as she headed to the front door. "If this house sells I guess you'll find out, won't you?"

"Mags, come on. Maybe you'll leave Pavel and come live with me and Corky. I could certainly use the company." Kelli grinned at the older woman, knowing full well she'd never even give it a thought.

Magda shrugged her thick shoulders and grinned back. "Maybe. We'll see." She opened the door. "I'll be here some time tomorrow morning and give the house a good look-over before the open house on Wednesday. Then I'll be back either

Wednesday afternoon or Thursday morning to clean up after those real estate people tear the house apart. I'm telling you, this whole sale thing is a bad idea." She gave Kelli one more glare and headed down the front steps.

"I'm taking the day off tomorrow, so I'll see you some time. I have a million errands to run and I'll probably be on the road before you get here," Kelli called after the departing woman. Magda continued through the gate without even a wave or a nod.

Kelli turned back to Corky. "Boy! She is pissed. No, more likely she's upset that the Gs might be moving. Oh, well, not much I can do about it."

Kelli patted Corky's head and returned to the foyer, thinking of Magda. She had met Magda the morning after their arrival in Charleston. The round little woman had spent more time with Kelli and Sean than either of the Gs; Kelli had always looked to her as another grandmother. Magda had been with her grandmother for ten years before the children had arrived on the scene. Kelli had seen her hair turn from jet black to its current platinum gray, but Magda still wore the same style: a pony tail tied at the nape of her neck.

Many times Magda had voiced her displeasure about Kelli's parents' parenting skills, and the lack thereof. No matter how many times Kelli explained that she really didn't mind being separated from her globe-trotting parents, Magda still disapproved. And that's why Kelli loved her; they could always say anything they wanted to each other.

"We'll just have to find something for her to do once we move back to the other house, Corky. If the Gs really do move, we'll be the only family Magda has left. Pavel is no great shakes in the companionship category, is he? Magda will be really alone." Kelli looked at her dog and smiled. "We'll think of something, won't we?"

7

Monday afternoon

He casually walked down East Bay toward the Battery; he'd found a parking space just a block away on Atlantic. He had slung his camera around his neck so he'd look like a tourist as he strolled on the waterside of the street. He had on a tan Ft. Sumter ball cap pulled low on his forehead. The collar of his Middleton Plantation windbreaker was pulled up against the bay breeze. Every few yards he stopped and took pictures out over the water or of the decorative houses on Kelli's side of the street.

He couldn't believe his luck! He even got a shot of Kelli coming home, a take-out bag from Moe's in her hand. Quickly he snapped photo after photo until she disappeared behind the tall front doors. *Why is she home so early?*

In answer to his unspoken question, a young woman carrying a camera case and portfolio stopped at the gate, pushed it open, went up the steps, and rang the bell. He lifted his camera in hopes of another shot of Kelli. *Got it!* He thought as the door closed behind the younger woman. *She looks like a teenager. Who is she?*

Inside Kelli welcomed Fran Hilton and asked if she wanted a beverage. Fran declined and explained to Kelli, "I'll just go from room to room, taking measurements, and shooting video from each door, as though someone is walking into the room. Teri, Mrs. Jackson, has found this method of shooting very effective. Then, this evening, once all the paperwork is signed, I'll enter all this information into the MLS and Voila! It goes viral." The young woman grinned.

Kelli knew the MLS was the Multiple Listing Service, the Bible for all real estate agents. It gave them visual tours most of the houses currently on the market in their area, asking price, square footage, number of bedrooms and bathrooms, and any special

41

amenities, like a pool, tennis court, or even a fireplace. "What do you mean by 'viral'? Somehow that doesn't sound good."

Fran chuckled. "It's actually very good, for you and for Teri. Other real estate web sites, like Realtor.com and Zillow and a bunch of others snag the listings from the MLS. People outside this area can pull up Charleston listings from anywhere in the world. It helps sell houses. You may not know that the MLS is proprietary and only registered real estate agents and brokers may access it. The exception is authorized online sites. The more people who see the property, the more likely it is to sell. As Teri says, "It won't sell if you don't show it.""

Kelli grimaced at the thought of all the people who would be traipsing through the house. She'd have to talk to Teri about this when she got here later. "Well, have at it, Fran. I'll be in the kitchen if you need anything." She pointed toward the door leading to the kitchen.

Fran nodded and headed for the staircase as she said, "I'll start upstairs." She glanced around as she walked. Her voice became louder as she ascended, "I should be done by the time Teri gets here." She gave Kelli a short wave and disappeared. Kelli shook her head in wonderment of the world of real estate and pushed through the swinging door.

Kelli grabbed her bag lunch and seated herself at the small desk in the kitchen, the one she had come to think of as her desk, because it was, even though it was in her grandparents' house. When Granny had the kitchen renovated she had moved this old maple knee-hole desk from Kelli's room to the kitchen. "It has more drawers than most of those built-in desks. Besides, you're married, you won't need it until you have school-age children. I'll give it back to you then," Granny had promised

Kelli ran her hand across the roughened surface where she used to do her homework, then she reached for the to-do list she had printed before she left work. She grabbed a pen from the flowered pencil cup and amended the list while she talked out loud to herself. "Bank, make a deposit for Granny and get money for the trip." She took a bite of her Caesar chicken wrap and tossed a bite of tortilla to Corky.

At her feet, Corky raised her head every time Kelli said something aloud. The three year old Golden Retriever had been a first anniversary present from Todd, to keep Kelli company when he had to work nights or long days. Corky had been a God-send after Todd's death. Many a night Kelli had cried herself to sleep with her head resting on Corky's shoulder. Those nights Corky didn't move, not once, apparently knowing instinctively that Kelli needed the rest.

Now Kelli reached down and patted her best friend's head. "Don't worry, girl, I'm not going to drop you off until last. I'd wait to take you Wednesday but my flight is really early and I just won't have the time; the kennel doesn't even open until nine." The big head raised and Corky stared into Kelli's eyes while she spoke, "Besides, the real estate lady is scheduling an open house for some time Wednesday and I have to sweep up all your fuzz before I leave; it's better that you are out of here tomorrow." Kelli grabbed two hands-full of the dog's ruff and playfully shook the large head. "I love you, but you do shed! It's like living with a dust-bunny machine," Kelli laughed while shaking Corky. "Enough, back to our list. What else do I have to do tomorrow before I leave?" Kelli turned back to the desk and her list. "Guess I'd better pack, too, don't you think? But not until after I drop you with Jeremy. I know how packing makes you worry."

She continued amending her list until Fran came in a little after two and suggested she vacate the kitchen unless she wanted to be in the video. Kelli escaped to the front parlor with Corky, a pencil, and the list. The doorbell rang a little before three.

Kelli glanced at her watch as she stood. "Good grief, Corky, why didn't you tell me it was so late?" Kelli hustled to the front door and opened it to admit Teri Jackson.

"Right on time," Kelli complimented the older woman. "Can I get you some coffee? I saw Fran go around the corner to the back bedrooms a few minutes ago. She should be about finished, I think."

"Coffee would be great," Teri Jackson said enthusiastically. Today the stout woman was wearing a hot pink pant suit with a striped pink blouse. They walked toward the kitchen. "This shouldn't take too long. I just need your signature on a couple pages, a copy of the POA, and I'll be gone. If it's okay I'll put a small sign on the fence as I leave?"

Kelli hadn't thought about that. Of course there would be a For Sale sign. She was just glad it would be small. And discrete?

Teri seated herself at the kitchen table and started pulling pages from her briefcase. Kelli reheated some coffee and got herself a glass of "sweet tea". She handed the mug to Teri and seated herself across from her. Teri handed Kelli the contract and said, "Read this thoroughly. You would not believe the number of people who sign these contracts without reading them! I guess that means they trust me, but real estate is different from state-to-state. I hate it when they come back at me later and say, 'I didn't know that'. Everything is right here, so I always tell people to read it carefully. Many still don't. I guess you can't fix stupid," she muttered. After this comment Kelli read carefully; it took her twenty minutes to get through all eight legal-size pages of tiny print.

Silence reigned while Kelli worked her way through the eight pages. Silence except for the click of Teri's phone keys as she retrieved and then responded to emails. Kelli had never sold a house before. She and Todd had bought one, and they had both read every word of every page involved in the process – it seemed like thousands of them – and that was before they even got to the closing. She winced at the memory.

Kelli raised an eye at the sales commission and asked, "Six percent?"

"That's the normal rate. It's split between the listing agent, in this case me, and the agent who brings the buyers to the table. Of course, if I sell it, I get the whole commission. I'll drop the commission to five and a half percent if that happens. Since the seller pays both sides of the commission, in reality the listing agent and the selling agent are both working for the seller. Many people don't understand this. Buyers often tell their agent things that should really be kept secret, like how much they are really willing to spend to buy a house."

Kelli interrupted the shorter woman. "That doesn't sound right."

"It may not sound right, but it's the way it is. The only way a buyer can ensure that anything they tell their agent is private is to have a separate contract with that agent."

Kelli looked confused. "I think I remember from when we bought our house that the broker gets a cut, too? That's not spelled out here."

"That's because the broker's commission comes out of the agent's commission, it's between the agent and the broker, not the broker and the seller. I guess in reality my commission comes out of the broker's, because the money is actually paid to the broker, not to the agent. The broker runs the office and manages the sales transactions and the agents. He also has the final fiscal and legal responsibility for anything that goes on in the office. So, for shouldering all this, he – or she, must be politically correct – gets a percentage of all money that comes into the office. He either takes his cut off the top or receives it in monthly fees paid by the agents to him, or her. Geesh! All this PC crap – politically correct, not computers - makes it difficult to talk!"

"Fine," Kelli said after a bit. "Where do I sign?" Teri indicated lots of pink-highlighted places for Kelli's initials and several places for her signature. Kelli signed as indicated.

"I just need a copy of your power of attorney, and we're done."

Kelli went to her small kitchen desk and retrieved a paper from the top right corner. "I copied it off last night so I wouldn't forget," she said as she handed it to Teri.

Teri gathered up all the pages and put them into her briefcase. "Since you're leaving town Wednesday I'll hold your copy of these pages until you get back. If that's okay?" Kelli nodded. "Any questions?"

Kelli remembered she did have one. "Tell me about the showings. Fran was telling me the listing would go 'viral'. Does this mean there will be a lot of showings? I mean, of course, my grandparents want it sold, but I'm not sure I'm ready for showings at the drop of a hat, or multiple showings in one day.

That's just too much disruption. Corky will have a nervous breakdown, too." Kelli smiled at the dog back at her feet. "I can't leave her in the kennel until the house sells, no matter how much she likes it."

Teri chuckled her rough smoker's laugh. "Not to worry. First, in this price range there won't be all that many lookers. Second, I'm putting into the listing that we have to have 24 hours' notice before any showing. And finally, I'm marking it as 'qualified buyers only'. That should cut down on the looky-loos. With the twenty-four hours' notice, that gives me and Fran a chance to see who is scheduling the showing. I know which agents just like to show houses to impress their buyers, and those who are going to bring us qualified buyers. And all the local agents know I know, so you shouldn't be troubled by too many showings." Teri smiled her big infectious smile.

"I'll leave an electronic lock-box on the front door when I leave. We change the code every couple days so anyone who wants to show the house has to call the office to get it; that helps us keep track of who's coming in and out. It's not fool-proof, but it seems to work. Just put up anything you would hate to lose and leave it put away until the house sells, that's the safest way. Does anybody else have a key to the house? We need to give them a heads-up about the open house tomorrow and that there will be occasional showings going forward."

Kelli considered Teri's words. "Sounds like the security bases are covered," she agreed. "As far as the keys go, there are only eight others: me, my grandparents, of course; Amanda Hawthorne, our backdoor neighbor and the woman who gave me your name; Nora, my sister-in-law; Magda, our housekeeper; and my parents, but they were just here at Christmas so they won't be back for a year, at least." Kelli continued to think. "Nine. The spare, it's in the pantry. Ten. My brother Sean's""

Teri was curious at the matter-of-fact tone Kelli used when mentioning her parents, almost like Kelli was talking about the cable repairman. *Bet there's a story there!* Teri thought to herself. "I'll need one of the keys to put into the lockbox. Other than that, I think we're set. Will you let Mrs. Hawthorne know what's going on?"

"I'll be happy to. Will you call Magda if there's going to be a showing while I'm gone? She'll want to come in and tidy up, even though there's nobody here." Teri nodded and Kelli stepped to her desk, "I'll give you her numbers."

"No problem. Anything else you can think of?"

Kelli sighed. "No, I think you've covered everything, set my mind at ease. Who knows, maybe you'll sell it before I get back," she said wistfully to the older woman. "Actually, I'm not sure if that's good or bad."

Teri reached across the table and patted the younger woman's folded hands. "Don't you worry, honey, it will all work out for the best, whatever it is." Teri stood, grabbed her briefcase, and headed through the swinging door. "I'm off." She hollered down the back hall to Fran, "See you back at the office, Fran."

Kelli spoke quietly as they reached the front doors. "I do have one more question." Teri looked at Kelli, her hand on the inside door know. "How old is Fran? She looks like a teenager."

Teri guffawed. "Everybody asks me that. She was a teenager when she started working for me, straight out of high school. But that girl is a whiz with computers and everything related to them. I paid for her to go to college part-time with the understanding that she would work for me for five years after she graduated. That was eleven years ago; she's thirty and I just have one more year with her. I hope she'll stay, but you never know." Teri turned to the door and whooshed her way through the second set of doors and down the steps before Kelli could see the tears forming in the motherly woman's eyes.

Kelli watched her as she stopped just outside the gate and hooked a small sign, almost like a plaque shape, onto the wrought iron fence. Teri secured it with airplane cord and small padlocks on the back side. Teri glanced up at Kelli on the front steps and waved, "Have a good trip if we don't talk before you leave." In a whirl of hot pink she sailed off down the sidewalk toward her car. Kelli grinned after her. But the man passing the gate was not smiling.

8

Late Monday afternoon

He'd been sitting in his car ever since the kid arrived at one and she was still there. He knew because he walked past the house every half hour, this time on Kelli's side of the street. He saw the teenager upstairs through the windows but he couldn't figure out what she was doing. At three the older woman arrived, the real estate busy-body. At 4:30 he saw a small black and gold sign hanging on the fence, just right of the gate. His heart started to race. She's selling the house! Is she moving away? *Don't panic. Remain calm.* He casually took a picture of the sign then breathlessly continued his stroll down to the corner, crossed the street to the bay side and headed back to his car. He continued shooting pictures as he walked.

He walked the dimming streets, muttering to himself and slapping his hands against his thighs, "She can't move! What will I do without her? I tried living without her but it didn't work, the substitute wasn't the same. How will Kelli be without me to protect her? Without me to love her? Nobody can love her like I do. Think. Think."

He calmed himself down as he unlocked the car door and seated himself behind the wheel. He took a deep breath and gripped the steering wheel tightly with both hands. *No problem. Just have to move up the timetable. I was going to give her more time to pretend-grieve, but now I can't. There's probably lots of time. That monstrosity will take a while to sell, probably expensive. Not like when Dad sold and the market was disastrous; the folks were so broke they couldn't even afford college tuition for me, not like they did for the others. Had to move to that shit-hole in Mt. Pleasant. Didn't know anybody, far away from Kelli.* He turned on the heater then sat and thought.

With a grin he thumbed through the recent photos, jotted something into his Kelli journal, picked up his newest burner phone, and dialed. He kept a supply of over-the-counter, prepaid phones in his glove box.

The phone was answered on the very first ring by a perky receptionist. He put on his most cultured voice.

"Hello, I just saw the sign on the house on East Battery. What can you tell me about it?"

"Oh, how wonderful! That's a brand new listing, I didn't even know the sign was up yet. We haven't even had a chance to post it on the MLS yet. You'll be able to see it tonight, though, at the Realtor's web site, TeriJackson.com, one word, Teri with an I." She paused for breath, then continued before he could even ask a question.

"Are you a broker? Teri is having an open house for brokers on Wednesday from twelve to two, lunch is included."

He jumped in. "Can you give me the price? Number of bedrooms, baths, that sort of thing?"

"Everything you need to know will be on the web site." She glanced at the time in the lower right corner of her monitor 4:57. "I'm sure it will be available by 6:30 tonight." He could hear the practiced chirpiness in her voice. "Teri will be back in the office in a little bit. I'll connect you to her voice mail." Without waiting for his agreement she punched in Teri's extension to transfer the call. She grabbed another call and didn't see when the call-light went out on Teri's line. If she had been watching she would have realized the caller didn't leave a voice mail...not that she would have cared, it was almost time to go home.

A few minutes later Teri walked into the small front lobby and started to pass the reception desk. "A man called a few minutes ago asking about the Ellsworth house. Said he saw the sign. I told him about the web site and transferred him back to your voice mail, just like you want me to do. Sounded like he was on a cell phone." She took a chomp of her ever-present gum. "I'll send him right through if he calls back." The almost-graduated high schooler reached for another call.

Teri headed for her office. *A call already. WOW! I could have asked him to help me hang the sign.* She glanced back at the front desk and muttered, "She has got to stop chomping gum in the callers' ears." *Oh well, not my problem, that's what a broker is for. But if he doesn't say something to her soon, I'll say something to him.*

He spent the evening reviewing the online house tour, over and over again. He hadn't been in the house since high school, but it pretty much looked the same. He'd forgotten how big it was. He especially liked the bedroom views. He could tell which room was Kelli's, the one that looked lived in. There was a carafe of water on the nightstand and a book with a marker. The room didn't have the frilly canopy of the one room across the hall, *Kelli isn't the frills type.* Four bedrooms on the second level, two on the first level, behind the kitchen. One appeared to have been Sean's, it had sports stuff all over. *And now he's in jail.* He smirked. All the other rooms looked unused, like Kelli was the only one living there. He thought it over and reviewed his notes in his Kelli book; the grandparents hadn't been seen since January 4th. *They must be out of town. How long? I'd better speed up the timetable before they get back. Just Kelli and the dog in the house. Dog's no problem, just need a bone or a hunk of beef.* His grin was not something anyone would have called 'friendly'.

9

Tuesday morning

Kelli awoke at her usual seven, even though she wasn't going to work. She stretched and mumbled to the dog still sacked out next to her, "I could get used to this part-time gig, Cork. How about you?" Corky raised one eyebrow, opened one eye, and immediately closed it again. Corky knew from past experience that she had a while before Kelli would let her out; Kelli always showered and dressed before going downstairs. Corky was nothing if not a creature of habit, just like Kelli.

True to form, Kelli showered and, today, dressed for errands: jeans and a sweater. "Come on, Corky girl, we've got a busy day ahead of us." Kelli headed down the staircase, leaving room on her left for Corky to descend with her. Corky always took the left side.

The two padded into the kitchen, Kelli still in her black slippers; she never put on shoes until she had to. She dropped a pair of sneakers at the back door and opened it for Corky. "Go on, do your thing." Next she headed for the stove to heat water for her morning cup of tea, Irish Breakfast today, it was going to be a hectic one. She reached into the fridge and grabbed a small tub of vanilla yogurt, no time for a bowl today, she just ate it straight out of the container. While eating she wandered to the back door and let in Corky. Corky got herself a long drink of water, then sat down at Kelli's feet. Kelli grinned as she finished the yogurt and put the empty – or almost empty – cup on the floor for the big dog. "I don't know how you get that big nose into that tiny opening, but you do, and you sure do like it." Kelli shrugged her shoulders and walked to the pantry while the dog got the last few licks out of the plastic cup. Kelli filled Corky's bowl with dry food then fixed a cup of tea in a plastic go-cup she reserved for tea, none of that residual coffee taste for her. She'd tried metal cups, but they just didn't work for tea. Plastic wasn't great either, but she'd broken the only ceramic go-cup she'd found and hadn't gotten around to replacing it yet.

She grabbed her keys from the key rack in the pantry, Corky's leash from the same place, and her to-do list from the desk. Kelli headed to the back door, Corky close on her heels. Corky knew the leash meant she got to go somewhere, she didn't care where, she just liked to go. Kelli chuckled as she attached the leash. "Of course you may ride along." Corky's bouncing made it difficult to attach the leash, but Kelli finally succeeded. Kelli picked up the shoes she had left by the door and the two went out.

A gate in the back fence opened onto two parking spaces, one for Granny's house, the other for Amanda's. Kelli used her remote key to unlock her Subaru Forester and opened the back door for Corky. *Another sign of the times. When I was growing up we never locked doors, neither cars nor houses. It wasn't until Todd, Mr. Security, joined the family and impressed on all of us the need to lock all doors.* "Fat lot of good it did him," she muttered.

The big, fluffy dog jumped into the back seat, grinning from ear to ear, her tongue lolling out. Kelli closed Corky's door, got in, started the engine and turned on her seat-warmer. Corky's panting reminded her to lower the back windows so she could get her nose out, but not her whole head. Charleston's streets were too narrow to have a ninety pound dog hanging out a window, she might be decapitated by an SUV or scare one of the horse-drawn carriage horses. "It's not that warm, Cork, give me a break," she said to the still panting dog. "At least I won't have to worry if I have to leave you in the car for a few minutes, you'd won't get heatstroke today. It's sunny but still in the 60s." Kelli reached down and took off her slippers and threw them into the well of the passenger's side. She turned out the door so she had more room, slipped on her running shoes and quickly tied them so she could get back into the heat of the car.

Kelli slowly edged her way down the narrow alley and turned left onto Meeting Street. "Okay, Cork, first stop the dry cleaners. If there's time this afternoon I'd really like to fit in a swim, but I don't know if there will be time." She continued chatting to the dog. "I'm glad Magda talked me into letting her come first thing in the morning and tidy up before the open house; that means I don't have to worry about that at least."

Kelli drove fifteen minutes to the outskirts of the city to get to her cleaners. She wouldn't have bothered except her favorite teal silk blouse was there and she wanted it for her trip. She pulled up out front and hopped out of the car, saying, "I'll be right back...I hope. You know how Mr. Sanchez likes to talk." She patted the dog and closed the front door.

"Good morning, Mr. Sanchez," she said to the owner who mostly just sat behind the counter these days. He had been her grandparents' dry cleaner when she and Sean had moved to Charleston and she had never seen much reason to switch, even after she was married and moved out to Cane Bay, twenty miles away. Most of her clothes were washable, anyway, so she didn't have that much need of a dry cleaner.

"Ah, Kelli, dropping off or picking up?"

"Just picking up today. I'm going on vacation tomorrow and suddenly remembered the blouse was here."

"No problem, Bert will bring it right out for you." Manuel Sanchez pushed the intercom button. "Bert, please bring Kelli Gannon – sorry Cavanaugh's – clothes up will you?" Bert Grouse had started working there two summers before, when Mr. Sanchez had had his knee replaced and couldn't work for six weeks.

"How's Bert doing, Mr. Sanchez?" Kelli and Bert had gone to high school together. Because of his stutter and a slight case of dyslexia, they hadn't had any classes together, except homeroom a couple years. They had known each other pretty well, though, since they lived near each other and had walked to or from school together many times. Kelli's early nightmarish days in the new school had been made easier by Bert; many days he ate lunch with her so she didn't feel such an outcast. As they got older he held afterschool jobs, lots of different ones; he just couldn't seem to find his niche. Then one day about two years ago she had walked into the cleaners and there he was.

"Wonderful! He's a great worker. Punctual. Never sick."

Just then a lanky, late-twenties type with spiked hair and a big smile came through the glass door that led to the guts of the shop, where the work was done.

"Hey, Kelli, great to see you!" Bert Grouse came around the corner and gave her a big hug. Except when he spoke, and mostly with strangers, no one would ever know he had a speech problem. His dark good looks and infectious smile had attracted lots of girls in high school, until they heard him stutter. *They were all so shallow. Bunch of snobs.*

"Hey, Bert! Got a new girlfriend?" It was a running joke between them. Kelli knew he had had the same girlfriend ever since the year after they graduated, even though she'd never met her.

"Ah, Kelli, you know you're the only one I can ever love." He grinned again. "Want me to put this blouse in the car? Is Corky out there?"

"Yes, please. And yes, she's there, and she'll be thrilled to see you."

Bert grabbed a Milk Bone off the bowl they kept on the counter and headed to the car. Over his shoulder as he headed to the car, Bert replied, "I don't know if it's me or the cookies." Kelli turned back to Mr. Sanchez to pay for the cleaning.

"So where are you going for vacation? Some place fun? Relaxing? You deserve a break. You've been through a lot this year." He handed Kelli her change.

Kelli sighed. Of course everything that had happened around her the last summer had made the papers. Everybody in Charleston knew about the "Cavanaugh Tragedies", as the local, and some not so local, media had called the events of last summer. "Thanks, Mr. Sanchez. I'm going to St. Croix. I'll be gone a week. I hope it will be relaxing, too." She felt no need to elaborate about Todd's ashes. "I'm leaving first thing in the morning and have a million things to do today. Guess I'd better get going." Kelli smiled at the older man, almost Gramps' age, and headed back to her car. She waved as she exited, "Thanks, Mr. Sanchez, see you when I get back."

Sanchez watched as Kelli and Bert hugged again and Bert scratched the dog's head one more time.

Bert pushed through the glass front door and Mr. Sanchez said to him, "I think you're using Kelli, Bert. I think you're using her as an excuse to get to her dog," Sanchez teased the younger man. When Bert had first started working there he hadn't understood the concept of teasing very well, but now he gave as good as he got.

Bert grinned back at his boss, and now close friend. "Maybe so, Manuel, maybe so."

Kelli stopped at CVS and picked up the prescription she needed for her trip. She chatted with the pharmacist, a friend from college, about her trip.

Then she drove to the Wal Mart and purchased travel-size shampoo and conditioner and dog food and treats for Corky. "She's so particular about what she eats and refuses to eat the kennel's dog food," she explained to the sales clerk who insisted on lifting the forty pound bag into the cart. *Not that she'll eat anything the first couple days anyway. Neurotic dog!* Kelli climbed back behind the wheel after loading the dog food into the trunk. She ruffled Corky's head as she grinned at her, "You are a lot of trouble, you know."

"One more stop before lunch, good girl. Let's hit the bank." Kelli headed back toward town and pulled up to the BB&T branch window. She put Granny's check and the deposit slip into the tray the teller had slid open. A male voice spoke to her over the intercom.

"Hey, Kelli, I thought that was you. Actually I saw Corky's big head first. Hey, Corky! How's the good girl?" Corky danced across the back seat, obviously recognizing the voice and happy to hear it. "Corky, calm down. Good grief, do you know everyone in town?"

"Hey, RJ. What are you doing on the teller line?"

Jackson Cobb was a couple years older than Kelli, a friend of Sean's from when they first moved to Charleston. The Cobb family had lived down the street. RJ was also the bank branch manager. He'd known Corky her whole life since Kelli or Todd usually took her along on errands so she could ride in the car. Kelli and Jackson had dated a couple times before he went into the Army; not really dates, just two friends getting together.

Jackson replied, "I work the teller window once a month, keeps me up to date, gives me brownie points with the staff," he grinned at the teller who had moved aside to let him talk, "and I get to keep in touch with the customers. With digital deposits it gets harder and harder to maintain personal relationships, nobody needs to go to the bank anymore. Today is an added bonus; I get to see you and Corky." He smiled and winked.

Kelli could see him smiling at her through the bulletproof glass. Kelli smiled back. She loved the South and everything about it, but why did everything have to include a lengthy conversation? Of course when you grew up in a small town, and Charleston still was a small town in lots of ways, you knew everybody and everybody knew you. She was able to tune out most of Jackson's running chatter until he asked, "Taking a trip?" He responded to Kelli's raised eyebrow, "The check you're cashing. That's a lot of money for just running around town."

"Of course," Kelli replied distractedly, her mind had been on the remainder of her to-do list. "Yep, a little vacation, leaving in the morning."

"Great! Going some place exotic? I mean, not just heading over to Hilton Head are you?" He was referring to the resort island just a few hours' drive away.

"Not Hilton Head. St. Croix, be gone a little over a week."

"Super! You've earned it." Of course everyone knew of her "tragedies" but why did they have to refer to it all the time? Jackson pushed the tray back to her with her cash and the receipt for the deposit, and a large Milk Bone.

"Thanks, Jackson. Corky's very happy. Give my love to Susie and the kids." She smiled at the man behind the window and drove out. She liked Jackson but had always found him a bit too friendly. Maybe that came from being in a big family, four boys and three girls.

"Oh, well, that's probably why he's done so well in banking. He's really a people-person," she said to Corky as she headed for home. "Nonetheless, even though he's married and has three kids of his own, he still creeps me out sometimes. That's why I never go *into* the bank anymore; it's nice to have that barrier between us." She glanced in the mirror at Corky. "Next stop Moe's, then home. We'll try for a leisurely lunch while I go over my list. I'm not taking you to the kennel until the end of the day, around four. Is that okay with you?" She smiled at Corky in the mirror. Corky always looked like she understood every word and was listening intently.

Kelli headed south on I-26 and got off at the King Street exit. She continued south to Moe's at the corner of King and Calhoun. She found a fifteen minute parking space, rushed inside, got caught in the last of the lunch hour crowd, ordered a turkey wrap and a Diet Coke, and scooted back to her car. She drove home with the delicious aroma of warm turkey, avocado, peppers, and mango-lime dressing; Corky was in heaven, too, because she knew she'd get a taste.

Kelli parked behind the house again. She grabbed her blouse, her purse, her purchases, and her lunch and opened the back door. Corky hopped out and ran to the gate, dragging her leash behind her. Kelli juggled her packages and opened the gate, Corky ran in, peed, and met Kelli at the kitchen door. "Okay, give me a minute. I promise. I'll share my lunch. Just give me a minute to put down everything." She dropped the various bags on the kitchen counter, unpacked the lunch and put it onto a salad plate she retrieved from the cupboard near the stove. As she pulled out the bar stool she noticed the light blinking on the answering machine. She decided she'd better answer it in case it was Granny or maybe Teri. God forbid she wanted a showing today! She said to Corky, "Of course, if Granny would get voice mail on the phone there'd be no light blinking and I could eat my lunch in peace before I checked messages." But, being the conscientious sort, she couldn't let a blinking light go unattended, not even for a few minutes. "I know, I know, it would still be there even if I hadn't gotten home yet, but you know me. I can't stand not knowing."

She picked up the phone and hit the replay button on the machine. "I'll miss you, Kelli, but I do hope you have a good time in St. Croix. Hurry back to me. I have big plans for us." Kelli slammed down the phone; she'd lost her appetite.

10

Tuesday afternoon

Kelli went back and forth, forth and back. She paced the rooms downstairs. She did a load of laundry for her trip. She picked up the phone and put it back down. Should she report the calls and emails? Who would she call? The police really couldn't do anything, no real crime had been committed. They'd just tell her to get an unlisted number and forget about it. What would Todd tell her to do? She'd tell him and he'd handle it. Should she call Dean? She couldn't call Sean obviously. And Nora has enough to worry about. For three hours she thought about what to do and finally decided to do nothing. She was leaving town tomorrow and by the time she got back this would all be over. Time to take Corky to the kennel anyway; she didn't have time for the police right now, *not even Dean, who means well, but he can go on. He feels so responsible for me since Todd died; like a big brother. Under the current circumstances it's nice to have an extra big brother.*

"Okay, Corky, let's go see Jeremy." Kelli's efforts to attach the leash were hampered again by her frisky dog's dancing around the kitchen. Kelli doubted Corky recognized Jeremy's name; she was just responding to the tone of Kelli's voice and the sight of the leash. She knew she was going somewhere. Kelli knew Corky was well cared for at the kennel and she didn't have to worry about her while she was gone. She patted the big dog's head, "I'll miss you, but I doubt you'll miss me." Kelli chortled as she opened the kitchen door and let Corky out, once more dragging her leash behind her. Corky went immediately to the gate and waited for Kelli to catch up. "The leash law says it has to be **on** you, it doesn't say I have to hold it." Kelli grinned at her dog and grabbed the leash.

Even though the kennel was a good thirty minute drive from her grandparents' house in downtown Charleston, it was the only one they'd used ever since Todd had given her the puppy for their first anniversary. The whole staff loved Corky, they even gave her the run of the place when they weren't busy, let her spend the day with them behind the big desk; it was like a second home for her.

Kelli started the engine, "Here we go, Big Girl, next stop: North Charleston Vet Services." Corky stuck her head out the partially open window and smelled the smells of her life: sea breeze, camellias, horses, and traffic exhaust. They were on their way! Corky didn't know where they were going; she didn't care. It was a great adventure; it included a car and Kelli, perfect.

From the street in front of the house he had a perfect view of the back alley and the front door. In spring the view was blocked by all those damn hydrangeas. He watched Kelli and the dog drive off. He looked at his watch. Must be taking the dog to the kennel. They close at six. She'd better hurry or she'll be caught in the afternoon traffic. Can't think of any place else she might be going this late in the afternoon. He started the engine and headed down East Bay to Queen, cutting over to Meeting where he was able to see Kelli's car just ahead of him, heading up Meeting toward the interstate. "Yep, must be getting rid of the mutt. Guess she'll be all alone in the house tonight," he said to his empty car. His smile stretched from ear to ear.

11

Late Tuesday afternoon

Kelli and Todd had selected the veterinary/kennel office when Corky was just a puppy because her breeder had recommended them. Even though it was a good thirty minute drive from their Cane Bay home, it was worth it. Corky was always happy there, even when she went for a check-up, none of that planting her feet and having to be dragged over the threshold as Kelli had seen with other dogs. As long as Corky was happy, Kelli was happy. And as it turned out, it was even closer to her grandparents' house, not really closer, but faster to get to than from the house Kelli hadn't seen in over six months. *Maybe I should sell it too? Move closer to the Gs. Get away from the memories.*

Todd and Kelli had bought the house in The Oaks right before their wedding. It was big enough for a growing family but not too big for a working couple. They both had loved it and loved making it theirs, adding all those little touches that make a house into a home: knick-knacks, mementoes, pictures, and books, lots of books. Todd had built bookcases to house all her books – well, many of the – and his books too, mostly military history and crime thrillers. Within a year it was perfect, even the flowers were blooming; Kelli had decided it must be Todd's planting ability because she was known for her black thumb.

Then, right before their fourth anniversary, Todd was killed. Kelli had walked out of the house that same night and never been back. Her grandmother had gone to the house and retrieved clothing for her and her grandfather had hired a local kid to keep an eye on the house, water the flowers, and cut the grass. Kelli didn't know what it looked like anymore and she didn't care.

As they approached the vet's office, Corky started dancing on the back seat, running from window to window with her nose out, sniffing the air. Kelli always meant to ask the vet if it was scent or sight that Corky used to recognize the area, but by the time she'd finished with the doctor, she'd forgotten to ask.

Today they were going to the spacious kennel next door. No doggie-spa, but it had everything Corky wanted: people who fawned over her and other dogs to play with. Kelli liked it because everyone was so nice to her and her dog and because Dr. Harris or one of the other vets was right next door if there was an emergency. She also liked that they had a vet tech stay overnight every night, just in case.

She clipped the leash to Corky's collar and headed inside, Corky leading the way. Fortunately there were no other animals in the waiting area or Corky would have pulled Kelli's arm out of its socket trying to visit them. "Sometimes you can be too friendly," Kelli murmured to the big cinnamon-colored head.

"Corky! It's been a long time! How's my big girl?" The enthusiastic welcome came from Viv, the sixtyish office manager coming from behind the desk to kneel down and hug the big dog. Skinny as could be and with rosy cheeks, Viv ruled the kennel's office with velvet-gloved efficiency.

The older woman stood and hugged Kelli. "We were all so sorry to hear about Todd. How are you doing, Kelli dear?"

Kelli nodded and willed her eyes not to tear-up. "It's…I'm okay." She smiled courageously at the woman she had known for three years. Kelli smiled. "Corky is all excited to be here, as you can see." She smiled more genuinely at her bouncing dog. Corky was trying so hard to remain at "sit" but her butt just hovered above the floor.

Vivian took Corky's leash. "Come on, hover-butt, let's get you settled in." She looked at one of the girls at the desk, "Give Barbara a call, please, and ask her to come get Corky."

Kelli looked confused. "Is Jeremy here today? He's Corky's favorite."

"He's on the night shift this week. He'll be in at six. He's looking forward to seeing her, too." Vivian reached down and patted Corky's head. "Yes, your buddy will be here tonight, don't you worry."

A voice from the tiled hall spoke up, "Hey, Kelli, good to see you and Corky again. We've missed you both." Barbara, one of the twenty-something vet techs, gave Corky a hug and took the leash from Vivian.

Kelli smiled at Barbara. "Wow! Y'all make me feel right at home; we've missed y'all too. Maybe I should have planned this trip sooner." Kelli caught herself as the words exited her mouth. After all, this wasn't really a pleasure trip. The other women laughed companionably.

"Going someplace fun?" Viv and Barb asked at the same time.

"St. Croix. I'm leaving early tomorrow morning. I'll be back next Friday." She hesitated and grinned, ashamed of herself for being so chatty. "But I guess you knew that from my reservation for Corky."

"Never hurts to remind us," Viv assured her as she patted Kelli's arm. "Sounds like a great trip. Need someone to carry your bags?"

"You're too old, Viv, I'll go," Barbara quipped as she backed away from Vivian's shaking fist. All three women laughed.

"Not this time, Barb, but thanks for the offer."

Viv looked at Kelli speculatively. Her excellent memory, especially where her favorite people were concerned, reminded her of Todd talking about their honeymoon on St. Croix. She guessed that Kelli was making a trip of good-bye. Once again she hugged Kelli and patted her back. "I'll hope you'll be able to relax some and recharge. You've had a really rough year. We'll take good care of Corky." Her knowing look told Kelli she had guessed at least part of the reason for the trip.

Kelli hugged the older woman in return. "Thanks, Viv, I will. At least I don't have to worry about Corky. The only problem will be getting her to come home when I get back." The women laughed again.

Kelli knelt down and hugged her best friend's big furry head. "You be good. I won't be gone long." She stood and watched amusedly as Corky dragged Barbara down the hall to the kennels. Kelli looked at Viv and smiled ruefully, "I hope she doesn't mope too much and miss me." The two women smiled at each other. "Obviously she hates it here."

Kelli turned to Viv, "I should be back in time before closing on Friday, but if not I'll call. Then I'll pick her up Saturday morning."

"Not a problem. Somebody will be here all night so if you are running late and still want to get her Friday night, we can work it out for you. Just don't let the word out. We don't do that for just anyone." Once again Viv patted Kelli's arm as she opened the front door.

"Y'all are too good to us. Thanks so much. See you next week." Kelli waved brightly and returned to her car.

As she turned on the ignition she thought *One more thing off the list. All that's left is to write Sean, pack, and get some sleep. Oh, and reconfirm with Super Shuttle for the ride to the airport.* She reversed out of the parking space and headed home.

He had parked next door at the vet's office, with a clear view of the kennel's parking lot, but blocked from view by another car. He watched Kelli pull out of the lot without Corky. *Must be leaving sometime tomorrow. She loves that damn dog too much to be separated for too long.*

"Wonder if she's going to the pool this evening," he said to the air inside his car. "I like watching her swim. She never even knows I'm there, too concentrated on her laps. Hell, she never even knows anyone is there." Kelli swam at the YMCA aquatic center. It had lap lanes, swim teams, and a dive pool. The whole area was surrounded by bleachers for the spectators when they had meets or for the parents when classes were going on. "I can see her from my seat in the diving tank bleachers. Her legs are so long, her breasts so firm. I can't wait to hold her. I'd even hold her soaking wet if there weren't so many people around. Where is she going now?" He followed her onto I-26 Eastbound. "Look's like she's heading home. How can I get into the house while she's gone? That would be magnificent. To get close to her things. To hold them. I must get in." He wiped his sweaty palms on his jeans. "I must," he said again, more forcefully, almost causing himself to have an accident.

12

Tuesday evening

Dear Sean,
Kelli had written that twenty minutes ago and couldn't continue. She stared into space from her small kitchen desk. This was the first time she had been truly alone since Todd's death. Even with the Gs gone, she had Corky. She didn't know how she felt, other than guilty.

Why should she feel guilty about this trip? There was absolutely nothing she could do for Sean; that was the most frustrating part. Kelli was a do-er, never one to sit back and relax if there was something helpful she could do for someone. And now it was her own brother and there was nothing she could do, except write, which she did every day.

Ever since Sean's arrest the night of Molly's funeral, right after last Labor Day, Kelli had been motivated to get him home. The family had little time to grieve poor little Molly's death because everything had happened so quickly. The coroner's office had delayed releasing her tiny body because they "had to run more tests". It was two weeks before they could even hold the funeral. And then, that very afternoon, that lumpy policeman from Child Protective Services had come and taken Sean away with a warrant that read "Felony child abuse resulting in death", and first degree murder.

Sean! That was the most ridiculous thing in the world. Sean loved children, he volunteered at Abbey and Christopher's schools, he coached Abbey's soccer team, he was a Cubmaster. He spent every possible moment with all three of his children.

Granted there hadn't been a lot of time. He'd served two tours overseas with the Marines in what he euphemistically called "hot spots." After his commitment to the Corps was up – what do they say "Once a Marine, always a Marine"?- he had applied to the FBI and been accepted. That meant four months of on-site training at Quantico. Luckily he had been assigned to the Columbia SC office and he was closer to family. Nora had endured his overseas trips, the second one when she was pregnant with the twins, and she was relieved now to have family nearby. An orphan, Nora had immediately adopted Sean's family as her own. Sean still had some travel, but not as much as before and most of it was stateside.

Except for one trip. It wasn't two years after his FBI assignment that he was sent back to one of the hot spots, because he spoke Arabic and knew the area around Fallujah. While riding in an unmarked car through the outskirts of town, they hit an IED and then were fired on by snipers. Sean was shot in the shoulder and had a concussion; his interpreter and the driver were killed, and the armed guard with them lost a leg.

A year later the headaches and nightmares started. Then numbness in his arms and legs. He started self-medicating with alcohol and his temper became short. His V.A. doctor did a thorough work-up and decided Sean had a traumatic brain injury – TBI – and PTSD. He suggested Sean take a leave of absence or a disability retirement. He said Sean was in the wrong line of work for someone with his injuries, that he'd never get over PTSD working with the FBI; too much stress. And one more hit to the head could kill him.

Not Sean, though. He took the drugs the doctor gave him and went back to work. The headaches got worse. The drugs affected his sleep. His drinking continued.

As it turned out, one of the drugs, Benzodiazapine, had a potential side-effect of spontaneous rage. And the nurse practitioner kept Sean on it for months, even though the V.A.'s own safety report said it was contraindicated for PTSD patients. Of course Sean didn't know this until after he was arrested.

Finally Nora gave him an ultimatum: get help or get out. That was all it took; Sean loved his family. He knew he was hurting them but didn't know how to stop. He went to counseling and physical therapy. Things slowly got better. Molly was born two and a half years later.

Then Todd died. Sean and Todd had been close; the big law enforcement funeral and the gun salute had brought back too many memories. Sean stopped counseling for a little while. He had just started back at counseling when Molly died. Then he was arrested, arraigned, and put into the county jail. That was six, almost seven, months ago and he was still there, in virtual solitary confinement.

Protective Custody, where they'd put Sean because of his TBI and his law enforcement background, meant he was in a separate area of the jail, separated from the general population and anyone else in PC. He couldn't be anywhere – hallway, bathroom, yard, visitor area – where there was another person unless the other person was a guard. He was in his cell 23 hours a day; out for one hour in which he could bathe, make phone calls, go to the library or barber, and go outside. Sean hadn't had a hug since his arrest, and he's always been a hugger. He has had no physical contact with his family in six months.

Of course Nora and the kids visit him as often as they can, even though it is through a plexi-glass barrier. Sean is allowed two visits a week. No more than four people at a time. No more than 45 minutes each visit, although the time might get fudged a bit if no one else was waiting for an inmate in protective custody. The PC visitor area was separated from the phone booths for the general population; just three booths compared to the twenty for the others. If someone was visiting another PC inmate, Sean's family had to wait until that visit was completed and the other inmate returned to his cell before Sean could be brought to the visitor area.

Kelli hated everything about the jail. The guards always looked suspiciously at all the visitors. The visitor area was filthy. She couldn't understand how some of the mothers who were visiting could let their kids play on the floor. The walls were institutional beige. The chairs were cheap plastic, looking like hand-me-downs from some 1950s conference room. Fortunately "professional" visits didn't count into Sean's visitor quota. He could see his lawyer and chaplain as often as they wanted to come. Marine Corps chaplains visited frequently.

Nora and the twins visited Sean twice a week, so that left only one slot at each of those visits. Although Kelli went up to see Nora and the kids every weekend and every holiday, she didn't always get to see Sean. Most of Sean's friends have been loyal and supportive, visiting and writing when they can.

So Kelli wrote him every day. Sometimes it was a letter, sometimes a funny card, sometimes a postcard. There were so many restrictions on his mail that it was hard to keep track: no glue, no glitter, no newspaper clippings, no sexual content; the list went on and on. Kelli and Nora kept all the cards that were returned to them because they had glue or glitter on them; they'd give them to Sean after he got out. Kelli tried everything she could think of to keep up his morale. He said mail and meals were the only bright spots in his days, and the food was horrible.

Almost seven months and they were no closer to a trial date. There had been hearings and motions filed, but no forward progress. Kelli organized postcard campaigns, asking all his friends and relatives to send him postcards, especially when they traveled. At the holidays – Halloween, Thanksgiving and Christmas – Kelli asked everyone to send him cards. Despite all the restrictions, Sean received 170 cards at Christmas. She was happy about that and the jail guards were astounded. Kelli couldn't help but think of the movie *Miracle on 34th Street* where the postal carriers dump all the bags of letters on the judge's bench.

And she talked to his lawyer. Granny and Gramps had hired the best criminal lawyer in Charleston – Hank Small - even though it was a ninety minute drive to Columbia for him each time he had a face-to-face meeting with Sean, and the family was charged by the hour. He was giving them the friends and family rate of $450 an hour, half what he was normally paid. Sean had given Hank permission to share anything with Nora and Kelli. So Kelli knew what was going on, but still there was no way to help.

As Hank had told her, "Everything hinges on the medical examiner's report." And it was still "pending". The ME's office had missed their deadline, several times already. Seems they had to get expert consultations and the consultants hadn't returned their findings yet. The judge said that was reasonable and saw no need to hurry them along.

Judge Mathis did agree to bond of $500,000, but Sean would not be allowed to live at home and would only be able to have supervised visits with the family once a week for half an hour each. The ten percent of the bond that Sean, or the family, would have to pay, was nonrefundable. Even though the Gs agreed to pay it, Sean and Nora decided he'd stay where he was; he'd get to see the family more, even though it was through plexi-glass and over a static-filled phone. He lived for their visits.

And now Kelli was deserting him, going off to the sun-filled tropics. She knew Sean would understand how hard this week was going to be for her, but still…

Kelli picked up her pen and continued the letter to her big brother, trying to be as upbeat as she could. Once finished she took a flag stamp from the desk drawer, put it in place, and added a pre-printed label for Sean's address. His address was so long she'd printed labels for him. Apparently these were okay with the mailroom at the jail. She took the letter to the table in the foyer, Magda would put it out in the morning.

Kelli returned to the kitchen and grabbed a raspberry yogurt for her dinner. After downing it, and regretting that Corky wasn't there to lick the empty container, she headed upstairs to pack. She actually enjoyed packing shorts and capris instead of sweaters and jeans. Maybe this trip won't be so bad after all. Kelli carefully packed "Todd" into her carry-on. She showered, set her alarm for six and was in bed by midnight. For once she fell asleep quickly.

He had to do it. He couldn't help himself. He had to let her know one last time he would be waiting for her upon her return.

It was 2 A.M. His hands were sweating. Carefully he punched her home number from memory. Ring. Ring. Ring. Ri

"Hello?" A very foggy, sexy sounding Kelli answered.

He hadn't had her all to himself in years. Not since he had kissed her cheek when she was twelve. Always other people or that damn dog around. He had called her before, at home and at work, but never with such an important message; he had always hung up before he dared speak.

"Hello? Hello?" Kelli was starting to wake up.

He hesitated. Then, "Hi, Kelli, have a safe trip," he whispered.

Kelli was sitting up now; getting angry. Scared?

"Who is this? Tell me or I'm hanging up."

"I'll be waiting for you. Don't worry about anything." Barely a whisper. He pushed the END button.

Kelli replaced the phone in its charger on her nightstand and slipped back between the sheets. She felt a chill. *Is a window open?* Just a few hours until she had to get up for the shuttle to the airport. *Who was that? What did he say? He was so hard to hear. I think he said my name.*

She dozed back off but slept only fitfully and awoke several times, asking herself, "Did I dream it or did some freak really call?"

Finally, half an hour before the alarm went off she gave up, turned off the alarm and took an extra-long shower, trying to wake up.

Even after her shower and feeling semi-awake she still wasn't sure if she'd dreamed the phone call or not. *Oh, well, I'm leaving town. If it was real then whoever it was will have moved on to somebody else by the time I get back. It was probably just some kids being kids, drunk-dialing or that sort of thing.* She paused in her thinking. *But on a Tuesday night? And he called me by name…I think.* She mentally shrugged her shoulders. *Nothing to do about it now. If it happens again I'll call Dean, he'll know what to do.* She zipped her wheelie and carried it downstairs, wheels are no good on a staircase.

Her watch told her she had a few minutes yet before the shuttle was due. She headed for the kitchen and a piece of toast.

She'd barely swallowed a bite when the doorbell rang. She glanced at the clock on the microwave. *How could the shuttle be here already?* She had moved mechanically through her dressing, tossing her make-up bag in last, closing the suitcase. *Did I pack my meds?* The doctor had given her something to combat the sluggishness that comes with depression. She also had something to help her sleep. *Why am I so worn out? Maybe it's the trip bringing it out.*

Kelli opened the door and saw the blue-shirted Super Shuttle driver. "I'll be right with you." She pointed to her bag just inside the foyer. She hurried back to the kitchen and poured her tea into a Styrofoam cup for the trip to the airport. She put the rest of her toast into a paper napkin, slung her tote bag over her shoulder, and headed back to the front door for her trip to St. Croix. She could feel some of the tenseness sliding away. *Maybe getting away will be good for me.* She locked the front door and then closed the heavy gate behind herself. She felt she was coming to the close of a chapter in her life. *Will it be a new beginning? More of the same? What about Sean? God! I need this trip.*

Austen Butler

Part 2

Week 2

Austen Butler

13

Wednesday morning

He was outside Kelli's house very early the next morning, long before her usual time to get up. He wished he knew where she was going and what time she would be leaving. He'd just have to wait and see. He settled into the Camry's fabric-covered seat and sipped his 7-11 coffee. At least at this hour he had had no problem getting a close parking space, directly across from Kelli's gate.

At 7:25 a blue and yellow Super Shuttle van pulled up. He sat up straighter and pulled his ball cap lower. The driver double-parked and tooted his horn. Then he jumped out of the van and loped to the front door. Both men were gratified when Kelli quickly opened the door. The driver ducked into the house and came back with Kelli's wheelie. He easily maneuvered it down the front steps, through the gate and into the back of the van. Just as he closed the van door, the watcher was thrilled to see Kelli locking the front door and coming down the front steps.

As always, he admired her tall, trim figure, decked out in black jeans, black sneakers, and a purple and pink argyle sweater. A jeans jacket was looped through the straps of the large black leather bag she had over her shoulder. He couldn't tell from her wardrobe where she was going. He saw her smile at the driver and the two other passengers as she ducked her head and entered the van. He could feel heat in his cheeks; that smile should have been for him! She seated herself behind the driver and directly across the street from his car window. He desperately wanted to take a photo but was afraid she'd see him.

Okay, now he knew she was out of the house, and he sort of knew when she was coming back. And he knew the housekeeper's schedule. But what about the real estate lady? Would she be showing the house? Wouldn't be great if she walked in on him. No, she is the biggest question mark at this point.

He drove slowly back to his apartment at the northern most end of Meeting Street. He spent the drive plotting ways to get into Kelli's house, ways that wouldn't get him caught. He parked his seven year old car at a few minutes past eight, glad he lived so close to Kelli. He strolled across the parking lot, trying to ignore the empty beer bottles, plastic grocery bags, and fast food bags that littered the yards surrounding his apartment building. "My home away from home," he muttered disgustedly to himself. "How the mighty have fallen." He knew Kelli could never be happy here, he'd have to get a better-paying job, no more of this menial shit. With a better job, Kelli would be okay here as long as she knew something better was coming.

He unlocked his metal front door and slammed it behind him. He dropped the keys on the kitchen counter to the right of the front door, then grabbed a beer from the nearly empty fridge. He took eight steps – he knew, he'd counted them many times - from the fridge to the only chair in the living room. The little bit of furniture he had was "early attic and late basement", from his parents' last home in Mt. Pleasant. The only newish piece he had was his TV and that had cost a month's pay. All his money went to his Kelli project. *I don't need anything else; just her.*

He drank his beer in big gulps and smiled secretively. He'd figured out how to get into Kelli's house. The beer, on top of no food, made him sleepy, so he slept for a couple hours. When the alarm woke him he showered and dressed very carefully. When he looked into the mirror he knew he'd do. He still had the look, even if he didn't have the money to go with it.

At 12:30 he parked a block away from Kelli's and walked to her gate and up to the front door. It was unlocked. He let himself in. He heard voices upstairs but no one appeared. *This is going to be easier than I thought.*

He casually strolled through the two front parlors. He didn't stop to admire the fireplaces' marble surrounds nor the marvelous brocade-covered Duncan Phyfe chairs and settees. He did pause at the portrait of Kelli over the fireplace and smiled secretively. He hurried on; he was on a mission. His pace increased as he hastened through the dining room. He did notice that Kelli's grandmother had had the sixteen dining room chairs recovered since the last time he'd been here, Kelli's high school graduation party. He headed to his goal, the kitchen, figuring everyone kept extra house keys in a junk drawer or on a key rack.

Just as he pushed through the kitchen door a female voice behind him asked, "Excuse me? May I help you?" He turned and saw a bowling ball of a woman, the real estate lady. Her hard, piercing eyes had him pinned to the swinging door.

"Oh, hi. I was just looking for someone. Are you Ms. Jackson?" He smiled his most disarming smile and saw her soften a bit. He held out his hand. She still looked wary but took his hand anyway.

"Yes?" she replied, a question still in her voice. She had no idea who this attractive young man was, but she knew he was not a local broker, she knew all of them. Maybe a friend of Kelli's?

"I'm Jake Naylor. I'm only in town through today. My wife and I are moving to Charleston from Richmond and she sent me to reconnoiter the area for a new house. I saw your sign out front and called your office. I explained my situation to a very nice young woman – Megan?– and she suggested I come over and talk to you." He smiled his most winning smile.

Teri inwardly fumed at Megan. *I really must have a talk with her. She knows, or at least should know by now, not to schedule a showing during an open house. I can't possibly keep an eye on everyone and answer questions upstairs and down.* All this ran through her mind while she surveyed the charming young man in front of her. *Nice suit. Silk tie. Well-mannered. Definitive southern accent. Apparently well-educated. Clean shaven. Looks studious. Maybe a professor?*

"What is it you want, Mr. Naylor?"

"All I really want is to check out the kitchen – my wife loves to cook - and get a feel for the house, not more than ten minutes. Megan said you were having an open house and I know how busy you must be so I don't want to take up much of your time.

Anyway, I just have a bit of time before I have to get to the airport."

He watched Teri Jackson consider the possibilities. She could send him away and hope he'd come back another time. She could give him ten minutes to see the house. She didn't know him, he might be a burglar casing the place. He made a big show of glancing at his fake Rolex.

"I'd be happy to show you around, Mr. Naylor, but only for a few minutes."

"That would be lovely, Ms. Jackson." Damn! The last thing he wanted was an escort.

"How about if you just tell me the basics of the house and show me the kitchen and I'll get out of your way?" He again showed lots of his perfect white teeth and shook his head so a lock of his blonde hair fell over his forehead, giving him that boyish look all older women loved, except of course his mother.

Teri gave him a searching look. He certainly looked as though he could afford the house. And maybe there is some corporate backing there, too. And those innocent blue eyes. She quickly made up her mind just as a voice called from upstairs, "Teri, can you come up? We've got a few questions about the master bedroom and bath."

Teri glanced up the winding staircase and called back, "On my way." She turned back to the young man standing so patiently. She smiled apologetically as she headed for the staircase. "Sorry, Mr. Naylor. If you'll just sign our guestbook over there," she indicated the hall table, "and include your contact information, I'll be right back." As she climbed the stairs she pointed toward the swinging door. "The kitchen is through that door if you want to check it out while I handle this. I'll be back in a jiffy." She turned and hustled her round body up the stairs, amazingly agile for someone with her low center of gravity.

He smiled winningly. "Perfect, Ms. Jackson. I'll wait for you here or in the kitchen." He headed for the guest book as she hit the landing upstairs. "My wife is coming into town this weekend and we'll be back in touch if she's wants to see it in person. Is it all right if I take pictures?"

"Yes, of course. Grab one of my cards near the guest book. I'll be right back." The Realtor rounded the wall and was gone from sight and hearing.

"Jake" hustled through the kitchen door. The first thing he saw was the small desk on the far wall, a breakfast area to its left. He headed for the desk. *Success!* Hanging above the desk was a National Parks calendar with pink highlighter from today through next Friday; in the pink was written St. Croix. *Who would have thought? Guess she's over Todd if she can take a glamour trip like that.* Kelli's flight arrival and departure times were written in black ink. He jotted them on a piece of scrap paper from the desktop.

He quickly rummaged through the desk drawers. No keys of any kind. He stood and looked around the kitchen. Over thirty drawers and cabinets, no time to check each of those before the busybody comes back downstairs.

The kitchen was large and L-shaped. The cooking area, with its own island and sink, stretched before him, around the corner from the desk. At the far end were the refrigerator and two doors. Maybe a pantry or a closet? Good place to hang keys.

He opened the closest door. Linens. Tablecloths hanging from a wardrobe rod. Placemats and napkins neatly folded on wire shelves. Plus a whole lot of items he didn't recognize. No keys.

He pulled open the second door, the one closest to the window. He found a large walk-in pantry. Boxes of pasta, bags of sugar and flour, lots of canned goods, serving bowls, casserole dishes, a waffle iron, and other stuff he didn't have time to consider. *Shit! Keys could be hidden behind any of these.* But they weren't. There was a key rack shaped like a turtle just to the left of the door. There were six keys; four of them looked like padlock or locker keys; the other two were shaped like house keys, but not like each other. He pocketed both of them and silently closed the pantry door.

His shiny loafers were soundless as he sped back across the kitchen and into the foyer. He shouted up the staircase, "Thank you, Ms. Jackson, I'll talk to you this weekend." He turned and hurried out the front door before he could be trapped in another conversation with the saleswoman.

As long as no one notices the keys missing, I can return them tonight. Tonight I'll be in Kelli's bedroom.

Casually he strolled to his car and headed for Ace Hardware to have duplicate keys made. All he could think about was *Tonight.* He started whistling the song from *West Side Story.*

14

Wednesday evening

He had to wait until dark, really dark. Finally all the house lights in the surrounding neighborhood were out except a few front porch lights; car headlights were few and far between. He looked at the luminous hands on his fake Rolex: 1:20. He took a deep breath and quietly, slowly opened his car door; he'd already disabled the overhead light. At 6 p.m. it had been easy to find a parking space on East Bay within sight of Kelli's house. He'd walked over to Meeting Street and lingered over dinner at Toast, linguini with local shrimp in a white sauce, and a vodka tonic, followed by two cups of strong coffee.

At 9:30 he strolled back toward the Battery and stood a long time staring out at the harbor. Eventually he crossed the street and sat on a wrought iron bench in Battery Park until he saw a police car turning the corner and heading his way. *The cold doesn't bother me but I sure don't want to be questioned about loitering; they might remember me.* He casually walked back to his car. The cop waved as he rode past. *All's right with the world.* He grinned.

Finally. He walked to the front door with both of his new keys already in his hand. He fumbled at the front door in the dark. After three tries the bolt turned and he was in. He put the second key in his left jacket pocket so he could keep the correct key separate. Later he'd try the second key from the inside and see if it opened a different door.

Using his mini-mag lite with its pencil thin beam, and keeping it down by his leg, he headed first to the kitchen and returned the two borrowed keys to the rack in the pantry. He exhaled loudly as he closed the door. Surveying the expansive kitchen he puffed up his thin chest and grinned a wolfish smile. *All mine now. And I can get to it whenever I want.* He caressed the key in his right pants pocket.

His fingers trickled across the cold granite countertops as he made his way to the staircase. Palming the mahogany bannister he made his way slowly, possessively, up the stairs, extending the anticipation as long as he could, humming *Anticipation* as he climbed.

At the top he could see three open doors. He turned right and looked into the first room on the left. Nice but unlived in. Guest room. On to the next, another guest room; duplicate of the first except for the beds. He began to feel like Goldilocks. Looking into the room directly across the hall, he said to himself with a sigh, "Just right." It was Kelli's room.

From the street light filtering through the wooden blinds he could tell the walls were a soft, buttery yellow. A white on white quilt covered the queen size bed, no canopy. Soft green and brick red accent pillows stood out against the stark white.

He could tell which side of the bed was Kelli's: the right. There was a book with a marker sticking out, a lamp, a clock, and a mobile phone on the night table. The other night table had only a lamp and a picture of Todd, the loser. He sniggered, "In more ways than one."

He crossed from the bedside to the doors on the opposite wall. The left door led to a good-sized bathroom. No windows so he turned on the light. Again soft yellow. Green towels. Embroidered hand towels. He saw bottles of perfume on a vanity tray near the sink. He opened each and sniffed. He sniffed the scented soaps on the sink and tub soap dishes. Everything smelled of French Vanilla.

Once he'd had his fill, still humming, he was careful to return everything to its original position. The next door opened to a large walk-in closet. He stood on the carpeted floor running his hands over jacket and blouse sleeves, up and down dresses and skirts, holding slacks up to admire their length. He pulled random items out and hugged them to his chest. He even hugged and danced with one dress, recognizing it as one of his favorites. At last he pulled shoes off their shelves and sniffed them, her feet had been here. Overwhelmed he dragged himself back into the bedroom and sat in the tufted tub chair left of the bed. *I can come anytime. Kelli is finally mine.* He leisurely surveyed the room. *Ah. I've saved the best for last.* His pulse above and below his waist began to race.

He stood and walked around the bed to Kelli's dresser. He turned face down the large picture of Todd sitting on the corner of the double dresser. He set his Maglite on the dresser so he'd have both hands free. Breathlessly he opened the top left drawer: *undies. Oh my God! Every color of the rainbow. Mostly bikinis. No grannypants, thank God.* His hands sifted through the fine silks and laces, letting them trickle back into the drawer like a waterfall of color. He grabbed a handful again and pushed his face into them, enjoying the vanilla scent of the fabric softener. He felt himself getting hard.

He opened another drawer: scarves. No interest.

The next drawer: bras. His fingers traced the lacy curves. He admired the rainbow of colors again. He envisioned Kelli modeling them for him. Low cut. Push-ups. Strapless. Sport. His breathing quickened.

The next drawer: cotton nightgowns and nightshirts. No interest.

Another drawer with t-shirts and bathing suits. No interest.

The final drawer held the jackpot: slinky, sexy lingerie. "Must be left over from old Todd," he sniggered aloud. *Maybe she'll model them for me, too. I'm sure I can convince her.* His sweaty palms removed each piece and held it up, his hand running inside each to check its transparency, or running over it to feel its clinginess.

He'd held off as long as he could. He pushed the lingerie back into the drawer and slammed it shut. It was like the elephant in the room; he'd ignored it as long as he could. Kelli's bed beckoned him. The pain in his groin was unbearable. He moved to Kelli's side of the bed. He envisioned her sleeping peacefully, her curly blonde hair covering the pillow like a pool of camellia petals, her thick dark lashes resting against her pale cheeks.

No more! Hurriedly he stripped off all his clothes and pulled back the quilt and top sheet. Clean cool cotton sheets, carefully folded at the top. He slipped under the sheet and pulled it over him. He wriggled all over the bed, trying to push his back deep into the mattress, wanting to feel the touch of Kelli's sheets all over this body. He tossed and jerked like a fish on a line, panting and moaning at the sheer excitement of being so close to Kelli. He came all too quickly, spraying as much of himself as he could between the sheets. Finally relaxed he enjoyed the crispness of the sheets, the softness of the cutwork on the pillowcase. He felt himself nodding off as he imagined he smelled Kelli on her pillow.

After a few hours he woke and resumed his pleasurable thoughts and acts in Kelli's bed. He glanced at the clock: 5:52. *Enough for tonight. I have lots of time. And then Kelli will be home and things will get even better. I'll be back every night.*

He quickly dressed, remade the bed exactly as he had found it except for his deposits, hurried down the stairs and out the front door. He remembered to lock it behind him. He hummed as he unlocked his car and drove to work; he had never felt better.

For the next week he returned every night. Some nights he brought food and ate a late dinner at the dining room table. The first few nights he worked hard to install tiny video cameras and phone monitors throughout the house. One night he brought a bottle of wine, fixed himself a bubble bath in Kelli's tub, relaxed and imagined Kelli in the tub with him. Regardless of how his evenings started, they always ended in Kelli's bed, living out his sexual Kelli fantasies until his needs were temporarily and insufficiently satisfied. *I want Kelli, not a dream of her. I've had the dream too long.*

On Tuesday the house phone rang during his "dinner with Kelli." His fork paused halfway to his mouth. *Who would be calling her at two o'clock in the morning? Must be a wrong number.* He knew the machine would get the call. He heard the female voice over the clicks and whistles of the machine, "It's Amanda. Kelli? Are you home? I thought I saw a light in the kitchen. I'd gotten up for some water. Guess not. Sorry. See you soon then." He shrugged his shoulders, finished his dinner, cleaned up after himself, and paused to look around the kitchen. *My last night here alone. Next time Kelli will be home. At long last.*

He stretched his arms above his head. He could feel his power growing, but first he had to complete his mission: leaving notes for Kelli to find. He had carefully composed each one, careful to use standard computer paper, a cheap pen, and with gloves on the whole time. Now he carefully donned another pair of gloves and removed the five notes from the outside pocket of his leather jacket that was hanging on the back of Kelli's kitchen desk chair.

He opened the desk drawer and put one of the notes inside. He went upstairs and put one inside the moss green afghan Kelli snuggled under when she was in her little reading room; he remembered how much she had used the room when they were kids. She used to watch for him from the window. The third note went next to the little table in her grandfather's library; he was sure this was Kelli's favorite chair. The fourth note went deep into her lingerie drawer. The final note he placed under her pillow. It didn't matter what order she found the notes; he felt certain she'd find the pillow one first. Regardless, she'd know of his desire for her and know that their time together was fast approaching.

He removed the pillow note and placed it on the nightstand. He stripped and climbed into Kelli's bed. *I'll put the note back after I'm done. This will be my last night alone in this bed.* He smiled a big satisfied smile.

15

Friday night

Riding the Super Shuttle back from the airport Kelli leaned her head against the glass of the window next to her, in no mood for polite conversation with any of the other passengers. She was exhausted. *Why are vacations so tiring?* She had hoped the trip would be relaxing; and parts of it were. It wasn't like she was playing tennis or putt-putt or swimming and all those other outdoor things honeymooners do in a tropical paradise. *Sure as hell didn't do any of the indoor things either.* When she had left on her trip she felt as though she had been holding her breath ever since Todd's and their baby's deaths; then Molly's death and Sean's arrest. The lack of progress in either Todd's or Sean's case, and her inability to do anything, kept her stressed. She didn't feel a whole lot better now, nine days since she'd left home.

Dean, Todd's best friend and fellow trooper, called her at least once a week to check in and to update her on the search for Todd's killer. Sometimes he came over for a beer on the weekends or after his shift. He worked so hard to keep up her spirits, but the "nothing new" she kept hearing from him produced the opposite response. For his sake, though, she put on a good front. *I put on a good front for everybody. No sense bringing other people down, too, by having to be around my suffering. I may not be as cheery as they hope to see me, but at least I try not to be gloomy and mopey.*

Almost weekly she talked with Hank, Sean's attorney, but those calls depressed her too. "Still waiting on the Medical Examiner's report." She did not understand how it could take six months! On the other hand, apparently the cause of death was not immediately apparent or they wouldn't have needed outside consultants. *So maybe this is a good thing.*

Right before Christmas she had asked Hank about Sean's right to a speedy trial. Wasn't it a bit long for them to hold him in jail without due process? South Carolina isn't Guantanamo after all. Were they just holding him while they searched for something to corroborate their charges against him? Looking for a way to save face, not to look as inept as they appeared to be? Kelli remembered she'd sort of lost it on that call.

Hank had patiently explained that the right to a speedy trial was a defense call. He and Sean had discussed it and felt it was risky to go to trial without having seen the ME's report, they wouldn't know what the prosecution's alleged evidence was. Together they had decided they had to waive his right to a speedy trial, so he just sat there. Surprises during a trial are not good.

Besides, Hank had told her, child abuse cases trumped everything else. Nobody wants to set loose an accused child abuser and have him hurt or kill another child. So everybody – the judge, the prosecutors, the cops, the social workers - errs on the side of caution when there is even the very slightest possibility of abuse. He reminded her that part of the original charge against Sean was based on a birthmark that the first doctor mistook for a bruise. Sometimes that's all it took for an acquittal.

Her eyes closed, Kelli vaguely heard the voices of the other passengers, apparently a family from Minnesota or Wisconsin, coming to Charleston for the two kids' semester break. She could hear their ooohs and ahhhs as the van approached the historic area. Even at 9:30 at night the architecture and the colors were beautiful. *Just wait until daylight and you can see it in all its glory with the winter camellias blooming. Almost home.*

Kelli had waited until the mid-point of her trip to make her final goodbye to Todd. She had booked herself into the tropical pink Buccaneer, the same hotel where they had spent their idyllic honeymoon. At night she left her sliding glass door open a crack so she could hear the soft tumble of the waves as they hit the deserted white sand beach outside her door. She smiled into the night as she thought of how appalled Todd would have been at the lack of safety. Often she had teased him about his security phobias, locking the cars when they were already in the locked garage, rechecking the doors every night before they went to bed. He had explained to her, "It's not a phobia, not paranoia, it's just important. I don't like to take chances."

Mid-morning she had taken the small dark blue box from her tote and carefully packed it into the sturdy, insulated, six-pack size cooler she had bought at the local hardware store. Not that "Todd" needed to be hot or cold but she wanted to keep his ashes dry. Although, as she thought that, she wondered why it mattered; she was dumping the ashes into the ocean anyway. She had put on her bathing suit, beach wrap, and flip-flops, grabbed a tote already packed with a towel, sunglasses, sunscreen, and a ball cap. She scooped up her room key and headed out. She walked slowly to the beach and the kayak rental shack.

The cooler seemed a lot heavier with each step. She knew this would be her final goodbye. The last thing she would ever do for or with Todd. A couple times she stopped and almost turned back to the room. *I really don't have to do this today, I have four more days on the island.* But she steeled herself and made it to the palm frond roofed "tiki hut" concessionaire.

She found her voice on her second try, "A single kayak, please." The tanned, topless young man explained the hourly rates and that she could stay out as long as she wanted and she'd be charged by the length of time. Except for the hourly amount, the rules hadn't changed in four years.

Kelli smiled weakly. "Fine. Just charge it to my room please. 106." She showed her room key.

The kid smiled back and passed her a stack of paper, in triplicate. It repeated everything he had just told her, basically releasing the concessionaire and the hotel from any responsibility or liability if anything happened to Kelli while using one of their kayaks, whether it was man-made, like the kayak disintegrating, or natural, like getting eaten by a shark. Kelli smiled to herself and signed at the bottom. *If only…. I just want to die and be with Todd. But it has to be accidental. I don't want my family feeling guilty for the rest of their lives, wondering what they could have done to stop my suicide. I wouldn't mind dying. I have nothing to live for now that Todd and our baby are gone. I'm just not going to commit suicide.*

She watched as the kayak wrangler dragged a yellow one down to the water's edge and dropped a paddle next to it. He asked if she had ever kayaked before. Kelli smiled and assured him she knew what she was doing. He warned her about getting too close to the rocks at the point.

Kelli dropped her tote on one of the hotel's cypress lounge chairs near the hut and slowly approached the kayak. Todd had taught her to ocean kayak when they had been here before. She hadn't done it since, but it was easy enough to do. The beach boy took the cooler from her hand and stowed it in the not-so-deep well in the bow, securing it with bungee-type straps.

"You've got a beautiful day for it. I'll give you a push over this first part of surf if you want."

Kelli sat down, stretched her longs legs out in front, picked up the paddle and smiled her thanks to the young man; he looked really young, maybe sixteen? Kelli felt really old. Just three feet from shore the kayak was floating, no longer scraping the shell bottom. Kelli started to stroke as "beach boy" as she thought of him, gave her a final shove, a wave, and "have a good time." He turned back toward his hut and more sunbathing, Kelli was certain. *He didn't even get his bathing suit wet.*

Kelli steadied herself in the kayak and headed to the point where she and Todd had picnicked. Earlier in this trip she had decided a kayak was the best way to get where she wanted to go. If she had walked to the point, just a little over a mile from the hotel, there was no good way to put Todd's ashes into the water. The point stood on a high cliff overlooking a rocky cove. Even if the wind was from the shore, Todd would have ended up on the rocks, *Okay for bourbon, but not for ashes.* If the wind was coming onshore there was no guarantee the ashes wouldn't just blow back into her face. *That would have been too surreal.*

Her strong arms paddled to the point too soon. She was out of sight of any sunbathers or other water enthusiasts. No other kayaks or sailboats. No noodles or inflatable rafts in sight. The large rocks discouraged most water lovers.

Luckily the water out here was dead calm, no pun intended. Carefully balancing the kayak she removed the small red cooler from its restraints. She rested the cooler between her feet and sat staring at it. She worked hard to get her breathing under control. *Would not be good to hyperventilate out here.* She lifted the flat lid of the cooler and lifted the box from inside. She put it on her lap, talking to Todd the whole time. She was still not sure she could do this.

"I love you, Todd. I miss you terribly. Dean is working really hard to find out who did this to us, but it's turning into a cold case, no leads. He won't give up, though, and neither will I." Her eyes filled with tears.

"Sean is still in jail." She rubbed her hand across the top of the dark blue box and broke the wax seal the funeral home had affixed. The seal had been her proof to TSA security at the airport that she had not tampered with the box. Gold letters stood out across the top of the box: Human Remains.

"I wish you were here to help me understand everything that's happening to Sean. You are – were – always so smart about the legal things. I think politics are involved here, too, and you loved to talk politics." She opened the lid and saw, for the first time, a plastic bag full of varying shades of grey ash. "Remember our picnic here at the point? You built that great fire in the fire ring and we roasted hot dogs and made s'mores? That was a beautiful day. Our whole honeymoon was perfect. While our brief marriage was not "perfect", is there such a thing?, it was a good one. I think it would have been even better with our baby." Silent tears streamed down her cheeks. She lifted the quart size bag from where it was firmly packed in the blue velvet lining. It had a plastic zippered top. Somehow the plastic bag with the zipper seemed so...kitchen leftovers to her.

She held the bag and stared at it with watery eyes.

"Logically, or maybe not so logically, I know this is not really you. It's just a bag of ash. I know you, your essence, is in heaven with our baby. I know, I believe, I'll see you again someday. I just wish it was today. I wish this wasn't necessary. I wish we got a do-over." She gently squeezed the sides of the bag. "But this is the only tangible reminder I have of *you*; of your broad shoulders, the big smile, your warm hands, of everything that made you so precious to me." She paused. "Want to hear something weird? I don't even remember what it was I asked you to get at the grocery." She smiled at her little joke. Todd had always told her he loved the way she could make him smile, no matter how down he felt, no matter how rotten his day. And as a state trooper he had some pretty bad days.

Kelli pulled the zipper open and scanned her surroundings. Still no one in sight. She hadn't even asked if this was legal. She wouldn't tell Todd that. "It's just us, Sweetie. Just the way you liked it. I'll always love you. See you and baby soon." Slowly she emptied most of the bag's contents into the calm waters and watched the soft waves carry the ashes down into deeper water. By the time these lazy waves reached the shore, Todd's ashes would be part of the ocean. Kelli left about a tablespoon of the ashes in the bottom of the bag, zipped it closed, and returned the bag to its nest in the box. She closed the lid and returned the box to the cooler. She put the cooler back in its well, but didn't bother with the bungee cords, it didn't matter now. Nothing mattered now.

"Hey, lady, we're here. Wake up. You're home." The mother next to Kelli was nudging her ribs. Kelli smiled a wan smile as she awoke from her reverie.

Kelli smiled. "Oh, sorry, I must have dozed off. Thank you." She crouched her way past the woman's knees and took the driver's offered hand to step down from the van.

"It's a beautiful house," the woman gushed as Kelli stood on the pavement. Kelli stretched her back and looked up at her grandparents' house, the house she'd grown up in. She wondered if she'd ever have a home of her own again. Kelli smiled kindly at the tourist and said, "Yes, it is, isn't it? Thank you."

She tipped the driver a twenty, too tired to do arithmetic, rolled her suitcase through the gate, and hefted it up the stairs to the front door. She unlocked, wheeled the suitcase into the foyer, and heaved a sigh of exhaustion. *Good thing Magda left a light on.* She parked her wheelie just inside the front door, dropped her tote on the foyer table, and looked around the dim hall. It was so quiet. To the air around her she said, "Sorry, Corky. I'm pooped. We had flight delays in San Juan and Miami. It's been a long day. I'll get you first thing in the morning." She looked at her luggage. "And I'll deal with you tomorrow, too. Right now all I want is a hot shower and a good night's sleep."

She sluggishly headed upstairs, not knowing that sleep was a long way off.

Part 3

Week 3

Austen Butler

16

Late Friday night

Sitting on the side of her bed, Kelli was almost too tired to undress, but she knew she'd sleep better in her pajamas. She also knew it was both a tired of the spirit as of the body; *I'm so alone.* Then she perked up a bit. *It's just for tonight, Corky will be back tomorrow.* Wearily she removed one running shoe, toe to heel she pushed, then the other, toe of the left foot to heel of the right. Not for the first time she wondered if all right-handed people put on and took off their left shoe first, and why. *You ask the strangest questions,* she smiled to herself. She slipped off her navy socks. She'd read somewhere that your sock color should always match your slacks color, it would make you look taller. *Not that I need to look any taller. So do tall people wear opposing colors?* She removed her belt and tossed it onto the nineteenth century platform rocker that sat in the corner by her side of the bed; the rocker had been her great-grandmother's.

She knew she had to stand up to get her slacks off, but she wasn't sure she was up to it. *Why do we always need a vacation after a vacation? I didn't even do that much, just sand, water, books, and sunshine. Maybe it's because I've never been very good at doing nothing, probably too much stress on my psyche.* The grandfather clock in the foyer chimed eleven. *You night-owl you! Twenty-eight years old and in bed by eleven on a Friday night.* Grudgingly she stood and slid her navy chinos over her narrow hips.

Across town a pair of lips were licked at the sight of her yellow-flowered bikini pants.

The slacks found the belt on the rocking chair.

Kelli resumed her seat on the edge of the quilt and began to unbutton her cream silk blouse. Her jacket was on the banister downstairs. She was of the old school where one dressed for travel, no capris, t-shirt, and flip-flops for her. Of course, planes were so cold she needed the sleeves on her arms and pant legs for warmth. She tossed the blouse aside, too; it could go to the cleaners later in the week. She stretched her shoulders, working out the post-flight stiffness and kinks.

Again the lips licked, the eyes intensified as they moved closer to the screen where he was watching Kelli's strip show just for him. "The bra, take off the bra," he murmured as he rubbed himself vigorously.

Kelli rose and went into the bathroom. A small shred of decency had kept him from putting a camera in there. *You'll have to fix that* he chastised himself.

A few minutes later Kelli emerged wearing yellow and pink striped flannel pants with a flowered top, daisies and tulips. Kelli walked over to the bed and pulled back the quilt and top sheet.

Now! Now! He screamed silently at the screen. *Get into our bed! Get in!*

Kelli picked up the pillow to turn it cold-side up and she saw the envelope. A confused look passed briefly over her face. She turned the envelope over, apparently looking for something that would tell her its source. *Did Magda leave me a note? Not this way; she'd leave it on the kitchen counter or on my desk. Surely the real estate lady wouldn't have left a note this way? Gag! Oh for heaven's sake, just open it. Stop guessing, it's not a birthday present, just rip it open.*

Slowly she removed the happy-face sticker from the glued flap. She put her finger under the flap and lifted it.

He moaned again, the expectation was too exquisite. Soon she would know of his love for certain. No more guessing on her part.

She opened the note and read it. Her hands began to shake. A look of horror crossed her features: eyes wide, eyebrows arched, mouth forming a round oh. She dropped the note and ran from the room.

"No! No! That's not right. You love me! Don't look like that. No!" Angrily he snapped off the image on his phone. "We'll have to talk, face-to-face. You don't understand. You will, though, I know you will." He hesitated. "Maybe I didn't handle it right. Maybe she doesn't realize it's from me. Maybe she's just surprised. And tired, of course she's tired. I'll make it up to her." He opened the phone icon on his smartphone.

Kelli stood in the hall, her back pressed to the wall. As soon as she caught her breath she went back into her room, sat on the bed, and hesitantly retrieved the note and envelope from the floor. When she had first seen the envelope she had decided it was "weird", but then decided it must be something important. Maybe Granny or Gramps was sick. But when she saw the happy-face she decided that couldn't be it. Besides, someone would have called if it was an emergency; she'd had her phone with her and had had it set for international calls.

Her confusion grew as she turned the envelope over in her hands. Nothing on the outside except the sticker. It was just a plain, cheap legal-size envelope, definitely not Hallmark quality. She remembered feeling a chill climbing up her spine.

At first Kelli couldn't comprehend what she was reading. Now, on a second reading, it made even less sense. Her hands began to shake again as the realization hit her that someone, a stranger, had been in her room. Some whacko had left her this disgusting note, typed on plain computer paper:

> My love. Soon we will be together. I will rub my hands all over your glorious body, bringing both of us to new heights of passion and love. Soon, my darling, soon.

She looked around, almost expecting to see a face leering at her from the closet. Uncertain her legs could support her, she reached for the phone to call 9-1-1. The phone rang just as she touched it. Her hand jerked back. *Who would be calling at this hour? Probably the Gs, they can't keep the time difference straight.* She took a swallow to calm her nerves and answered the phone.

"Why didn't you like my note? I love you, Kelli. We'll be together soon and I'll show you how much I love you. I promise. Then we'll be together forever."

Before Kelli could catch her breath and respond, the line went dead. She stared at the buzzing phone in her hand, her body shaking from neck to toe. Woodenly she pushed the END button and then the TAALK button and dialed 9-1-1. She opened the nightstand drawer and pulled out her gun. She carried the phone and the gun into the guest room across the hall. She couldn't bear to be in her room any longer. She sat on the side of the twin bed and faced the door, the gun held firmly in her right hand.

"9-1-1 what is your emergency?"

Thank God it was a woman on the phone. "Someone has been in my house. He may still be here. He's watching me, I think."

The 9-1-1 operator asked Kelli to confirm her name and address and told her to stay on the phone. "Officers are on the way, I'll stay with you until they get there." And she did, talking reassuringly to Kelli. A few minutes later there was a heavy knock at the door and a shouted voice, "Charleston Police!"

"I'm upstairs. I'll have to go downstairs to let them in," Kelli quaked to the woman on the other end of the phone. The angel on the phone responded, "That's okay. I'll let them know you're coming. Is this a mobile phone?"

"Yes," Kelli whispered as she stood from the bed.

"Then just take me with you. As long as you keep talking I'll know you're okay. If you stop and don't respond to me I'll have those officers to you likety split."

Kelli held the phone in her left hand, grasping it as though it was a lifeline and she was drowning. Her right hand still firmly gripped the gun. "Okay. Right. Good idea." Kelli forced herself to head to the front door. She reached around the doorframe and turned on the overhead light in the hall. The staircase lights came on too.

"Kelli, are you still there? What are you doing? Put me on speaker so you don't have to keep me up to your ear." Kelli did as she was told. Her bare feet noiselessly guided her down the hall. She kept her back to the wall and kept glancing behind her. When nothing happened she felt her strength returning a bit. She spoke up.

"What's your name?" Her polite training returned.

"Yolanda. I've been a 9-1-1 operator for thirteen years and haven't lost anybody yet." The operator chuckled. Kelli guessed she was in her fifties, matronly, and probably black/colored/African American/Negro. *What is the correct nomenclature these days?*

"Sounds like I'm in good hands, or I guess ears," Kelli said more solidly.

Yolanda was encouraged by the girl's little joke, it showed she was getting over her initial panic. Yolanda chuckled again.

"You've got it, girl, best ears in the department. Some say biggest mouth, too." She paused just a heartbeat. "Where are you now, Kelli?"

"About halfway down the staircase. The whole downstairs is dark, but there's a light switch at the bottom of the stairs." Keeping her back to the wall and holding the gun in a death grip, Kelli descended the last few steps and flipped the switch. It seemed an eternity since she had left her bedroom. She put the flashlight on the table at the foot of the stairs. She opened the inside front door with her left hand, the gun held firmly in her right hand down by her thigh. The phone wavered as she turned the knob.

"Yolanda, I can see a shadow on the front steps." She held the phone and the gun more tightly.

"That's fine, Kelli. Should be two uniform officers. Officers Davenport and Seeger. Seeger is the female. Do you have a peephole on the front door?"

"No, my grandparents don't want one. Said it's not correct for the house's era. This is their house, I'm just house-sitting while they're in Arizona."

"Okay. Then just shout through the door and ask who they are."

Kelli shouted the question. A muffled reply came back. "A man said they're Davenport and Seeger."

"Ask them their badge numbers."

Again Kelli did as she was told and replied to Yolanda, "4718 and 2659."

"That's them. You can let them in and they'll take it from here."

Kelli hesitated, reluctant to let go of the woman she had come to trust. "I will, Yolanda, thank you so much. You are **very** good at your job."

"Why thank you! You were very brave, Kelli, you'll be fine. Just tell the officers everything. Good night, sweetie."

Kelli pushed END on the phone, unlocked the outside door, and pulled the heavy door inward. Two uniformed Charleston City police officers stood on the tiny front porch. She immediately noted that one was tall, the other less tall; one was white, one black; one male, one female. Both in the black-on-black winter uniforms she recognized. She swung the door wide and gestured with the silent phone in her hand, "Please come in."

17

Friday night, just after midnight

The two officers removed their hats as they crossed into the foyer. Kelli closed and bolted the door behind them. The woman, the taller of the two, held out her hand, "Kim Seeger, m'am. And this is Don Davenport," she said as she indicated the younger Black man at her side.

Kelli lifted her hand to shake the woman's hand. As she did so they all realized the gun was still in her hand. Both officers' hands went to their holsters and Kelli lowered the weapon. Sheepishly she smiled a tiny smile, "Sorry. I forgot I still had it."

"No problem, ma'am. How about if I just take that for safekeeping?" the woman said as she reached for Kelli's hand. Davenport kept his hand at the ready, his holster unsnapped. Kelli handed the gun to the other woman saying, "As long as I get it back. It was a gift from my husband." Kelli spoke firmly as she added, "I have a permit for it."

Davenport murmured to Seeger, "Husband's either very brave or very stupid." Seeger grinned back. Kelli spoke up. "I know what you're thinking. My husband must have been very brave or very stupid. We've heard it before. I assure you he wasn't stupid. And as it has turned out, I needed it. Todd taught me how and when to use it. He said if I ever heard a noise in the house to lock the door, call 9-1-1, and fire a shot through the floor. He said it was doubtful anyone would break into the room if they knew I was sitting there with a loaded gun."

"And did you?" Seeger asked. Kelli looked confused. "Fire a shot through the floor?"

Kelli smiled a relaxed smile. "Oh, wow! No! My grandmother would have killed me. This is her house, not mine."

"But you did call 9-1-1. Want to tell me about that?" Seeger motioned Davenport to go upstairs. "Is it okay if Officer Davenport takes a look around while we talk?"

"Of course. Please. Would you like some coffee or something?" Davenport raised an eyebrow at the senior officer; they exchanged a glance. They were both confused by the calm of the woman who had just reported an intruder. The offer of coffee they understood; they were both Southerners and fully understood the importance of manners in the South, especially in folks who lived in houses like this.

"No, thank you, m'am." Although only a few years older than Kelli, her mother's training, as well as that of the CPD, required her to be southern respectful, so it was always "m'am" and "sir" regardless of age, unless dealing with children.

You reported an intruder, Ms....?"

"Oh, sorry. I thought I'd given my name to the, to Yolanda, the nice woman on the 9-1-1 line. I'm Kelli Cavanaugh. As I said, this is my grandparents' home, the Gannons. They're in Arizona on vacation. Although they may be moving there permanently. I hope not, though." Kelli hesitated, realizing she was babbling. A frequent flaw when she was nervous. Kelli glanced down and realized her feet were bare on the cold wood floors. "May I just run upstairs and get a robe and some slippers? I was just going to bed when everything happened and then Yolanda told me to come down and let you in and I came straight downstairs." *Babbling again, you sound like a nut case.*

As a woman and a police officer, Seeger knew full well how vulnerable women felt around strangers when they were not dressed appropriately. "That will be fine. You can show Don around the upstairs at the same time."

Seeger gave a knowing nod to Davenport and he headed to the staircase. "I'll go first, m'am, just in case."

Kelli stood and glanced from one officer to the other. "You don't think he's still here, do you?" Surely he knows you're here; he must have heard us talking."

"Better to be safe, don't you think?" Davenport asked from halfway up the staircase. At the top he stopped and drew his gun. "Which room is yours, m'am?"

"Second door on the right," Kelli whispered back.

Davenport raised his Glock 9 mm with his left hand and supported it with his right as he quickly peeked down the hall in each direction. Nothing. He walked toward the first door, tested the knob; locked. "What's in here?" he asked Kelli from eight steps away from the landing.

"It's a storage closet. Luggage mostly. We keep it locked so my nieces – niece – and nephew can't get in."

"Do you have a key?"

"It's on the key rack in the pantry. Shall I get it?"

"Not yet." He waggled his pistol at the room across the hall. "What's over there?"

Kelli felt like she was in an episode of some TV cop show. "Both are guest bedrooms with their own baths and closets. The first one has a queen size bed, the other has twin beds."

"Stay here." Davenport ordered. He did a quick sweep of the rooms, behind the drapes, in the closets, and under the beds. All clear. He noticed an envelope and a folded piece of paper in the twin bedroom.

"What's at the end of the hall?" he asked, returning to the hallway.

"My grandparents' room, bath, closets."

"Any other entry to the room?"

"No, just this hallway." Kelli's nervousness was returning at his questions. Maybe someone could still be here! *Lots of hiding places, that's for sure.*

"And the other end of the hallway?"

"A library on the left and a small reading room at the end." Kelli looked toward the rooms, all the doors were closed. *Magda always leaves them open.*

"Let me check your room, then you can get your robe and slippers. Don't touch anything else, understand?" Kelli nodded mutely.

Davenport entered Kelli's room, his gun still pointed at any unknown surprises. Without being conscious of it, he admired the cozy feel of the room, especially the quilt; his wife had a similar one that her grandmother had made. Once again he checked everywhere and found nothing. He left the closet door slightly ajar so Ms. Cavanaugh wouldn't have to touch the door handle to get to her things. He walked back to Kelli who had moved into the doorway, watching his every move.

"Why don't you get your things and then you can go downstairs while I finish up here. It looks like nobody's here."

"I'm not sure anybody ever was, really. At least not tonight."

Davenport was confused. She'd reported an intruder. *Above my pay grade. I'll let Seeger straighten this one out.* Seeger had six years on him, that's like 200 years in civilian years. "Okay, Ms. Cavanaugh. Get what you want." He motioned Kelli into her room. "Please don't touch anything."

Kelli walked over to the closet and pushed the door wider with her shoulder. She stooped and grabbed a pair of black satin ballet-style slippers from the carpeted floor. Balancing on one foot, she put on one slipper then the other, managing to keep her balance despite her exhaustion and growing consternation.

She came out and headed to the bathroom, no longer embarrassed to be seen in her flannel pajamas. Davenport pointedly asked, "Where are you going?"

Kelli pointed to the bathroom. "My robe's hanging on the back of the door." Davenport nodded his assent, still keeping an eye on the hall.

Kelli emerged wearing a purple flannel bathrobe, snuggly tied at her waist. She'd also grabbed a hairclip from the counter and pulled her hair up into a quicky chignon.

Davenport smiled at her transformation. She looked much more relaxed. "Feel better?"

Kelli gave him a winning smile. "Much, thank you."

"Are you okay to get back downstairs on your own? Can't have you falling over from shock."

Kelli smiled again at his consideration. "Yes, Officer Davenport, I'm fine. The shock is starting to wear off. Now I'm just confused and…" she hesitated. "I really don't know what I am." She looked at him with stark helplessness on her face.

Davenport patted her shoulder like her grandfather sometimes did. "You'll be fine. Don't worry. We'll sort it out for you. You go on then, I'll be down in a few minutes." The younger man gave her a gentle push toward the staircase and watched as she made her way down. Seeger had seen Kelli coming and met her at the foot of the stairs.

While Kelli and Officer Davenport were upstairs, Seeger had done her own sweep of the downstairs. Not many places to hide on this level: half bath, open parlors and dining room, big kitchen with two doors plus one leading to the outside. Door to the half-bath led from the foyer. Seeger had checked and found nothing, no one.

"Feel better? Warmer?" she asked Kelli.

"Yes, thanks, much. Do you mind if I fix myself a cup of tea? I promise I won't contaminate anything."

Seeger looked hard at Kelli. Was she being sarcastic? Ridiculing police work? She appeared very nice, had an appealing, innocent looking face. But she did live in this big house. Often people of this station felt police were more like the hired help, worthy only of their contempt. Kelli so far didn't seem that type. But as Seeger well knew, looks could be deceiving. Just look at Ted Bundy, he'd deceived lots of women with his good looks and then up and killed them. Seeger nodded to Kelli.

"I'd be happy to fix you a cup," Kelli continued as she turned toward the kitchen.

"No, that's fine. We can talk while you fix your tea." Kim Seeger paused and then, "Actually, I will have a cup; thanks."

The two women walked through the swinging door to the kitchen. Kelli filled the tea kettle and put it on the gas burner. She grabbed a paper napkin off the countertop and used it to open the cupboard for cups and saucers, sugar bowl, and creamer. She also grabbed a small bowl for lemon slices in case the policewoman wanted any. Kelli surveyed the room, looking for any changes. The clock on the microwave said 12:40. *Is that all?!* The police had been here less than half an hour. So much had happened it seemed much longer.

Seeger had seated herself at the kitchen bar across from the stovetop. "While the water's heating, why don't you start at the beginning and tell me what's going on?" she asked politely as she pulled a small ringed notepad and pen from her right breast pocket.

Kelli looked at the other woman. She decided she liked the deep blue eyes and warm smile. She felt as though she was in a London fog, though, as she placed the bone china cups and saucers and everything else in front of Seeger. She grabbed a wooden box of assorted Twining teas and put that next to Seeger, too. Kelli took a deep breath and tried to get her thoughts in order.

"Help yourself to whatever tea you'd like," Kelli said as she opened the box lid. She leaned her stomach against the bar and crossed her arms. She rubbed her hands up and down her arms, trying to shake the chill she got every time she thought about someone having been in the house.

The flowered tea kettle gently wobbled on the stove and Kelli grabbed its wooden handle, pleased to see Officer Seeger's tea bag was already in her cup. Seeger noticed the pleasure in Kelli's eyes and guessed its cause. This wasn't her first encounter with Charleston's privileged class.

Seeger grinned at Kelli. "I took the tour at the Tea Plantation. The only thing I remember is that you add the water to the tea, not the other way around," she said as Kelli poured the hot water into the delicate cup. Darjeeling for Seeger, Earl Grey for Kelli.

Kelli surprised Seeger by saying, "That's the only thing I remember too!" Seeger removed the lid from the sugar bowl and was pleased to find sweeteners rather than sugar. Kelli noticed, too. "Oh, sorry. Granny has diabetes so we try to keep sugar out of sight. I have it if you prefer."

"No, this is perfect. I have to cut down somewhere. All those donuts, you know." The two women grinned at each other. Seeger decided Kelli had calmed down enough to talk.

"Ready?" she asked the younger woman.

Kelli looked at the policewoman across from her, nodded, and began. "I just got back from a week's vacation tonight..."

18

Early morning Saturday

He had fallen into a fitful sleep right after his call to Kelli. He didn't understand her reaction. Didn't she know how much he loved her? Had always loved her? Ever since eighth grade?

Voices woke him. Slowly his eyes opened and he looked around. Nothing. No one. Had they been part of his dream? He stood, scratched his naked, hairless chest and walked to his bedroom door. He listened intently. He still heard them but saw no one in his long living room cum computer room. It hit him. The monitors.

He rushed to the bank of monitors he had created, knocking a greasy leftover carry-in enchilada plate onto the beige carpet. He didn't notice.

He stood intently in front of the lit screens, scanning from one to the other. Six showed views from the house at the Battery, two were dark. He rapidly zeroed in on the source of the conversation: the kitchen at the Battery. A uniformed woman sitting at the kitchen bar, Kelli pouring water from the tea kettle into delicate tea cups. Police!

He looked at the time in the lower right corner of one of the monitors, just after midnight. How long had the police been there? Couldn't be long, he'd talked to Kelli a little after eleven. How long had the women been talking? Didn't matter, it was all recorded, he could go back and check it later. But he had to know now. His hands flew to the keyboard and increased the volume on monitor #5. Only two rooms at the Battery house had listening devices, fortunately the kitchen was one of them. He had placed bugs on all the phones but only two had the capacity to pick up voices from the surrounding area, whether anyone was actually using the phone or not. Between the video cameras and the phone bugs, he could keep track of Kelli day and night. He didn't care what she did at work, work is work. The GPS tracking device on her car let him know when she was away from home, too. On top of all that, he could track her on any of his devices, especially his ultra-smart phone. *Don't leave home without it*, he grinned to himself. He knew more about Kelli's private life over the last four years than Todd probably had. *Good ol' Todd.*

"Focus! Focus!" He shouted at his face reflected in the monitors. "What are they saying?" He glared at monitor #5 and strained to hear the words.

19

Kelli hadn't felt it necessary to explain about Todd's ashes. It didn't seem relevant. Nor did the last six months of her life.

"Then just as I was reaching for the phone to call 9-1-1, it rang. A male voice said something about how much he loved me and the note I'd found and then he said we'd get together soon. It was all very creepy. I felt like he was watching me. How else could he have known I'd even found the note?"

Officer Davenport had entered the kitchen about halfway through Kelli's story, giving Seeger a subtle thumbs-up, and then seating himself next to Seeger on one of the forest green leather bar stools. Kelli had interrupted her recitation to ask him if he wanted something to drink, but he again declined. He couldn't imagine one of his big, former-football-player paws holding one of the delicate cups. He did help himself to one of the chocolate cookies Kelli had provided.

Seeger asked, "Have you received any other calls? Any middle of the night hang-ups? That sort of thing?"

Kelli put her tea cup to her lips and took a sip of the warming liquid. It wasn't having its usual effect. She took another sip and searched her memory.

"There were some hang-ups, quite a few actually over the last couple years. I just thought they were wrong numbers." She took another sip. "Right after Todd, my husband, died there was a call offering condolences. It wasn't a voice I recognized and I had been getting calls from total strangers. Of course, I'm not sure I would have recognized my own voice at that point. The only difference about this call was that it was late at night. That's why I answered it instead of letting it go to voice mail." She took another sip, the water was cooling too quickly.

"Any others?" Seeger was making notes in her small vertical-flip notepad. She glanced at Davenport and slightly raised an eyebrow. He excused himself and left the room.

"The night before I left town a man called." She hesitated. "It might have been the same voice. He wished me a good trip. He said he'd see me when I got back. Do you think it's the same person? Maybe a stalker? Good grief, why me?"

Seeger looked up from her notepad and ignored Kelli's question.

"You're a widow? Shit, that's too bad. You're what, 27, 28? How did your husband die?"

Kelli stiffened. She wasn't sure she could tell the story again, she'd told it so many times over the past months and not one of those times had helped find the shooter.

"Is it relevant, do you think?" Kelli stalled, staring fixedly at the policewoman.

Seeger detected Kelli's hesitancy. *What's that about?* "There's no telling what's going to prove relevant and what won't. Don went to call a detective. To us it sounds like something is going on, what with all the calls and now this note. But the investigation is way out of our league. The detective should be here soon. We're just trying to save some time, so maybe you won't have to go over everything again." In reality, Kelli was going to have to go over it many more times, as Seeger well knew, but right now she just wanted to keep Kelli talking. Seeger saw how tired Kelli was, still leaning on the other side of the bar, but now it appeared more for support than when she had started her narrative.

"Is the water still hot? I could use a warm-up on my tea and you probably can, too." Kelli nodded and turned around to the simmering tea kettle. She poured the hot water into each of their cups. Seeger patted the stool Davenport had vacated.

"Come sit down. You must be about out on your feet. It's been a long day for you."

Kelli pushed her tea cup across the bar and came around the end. She seated herself next to the other woman and gave her a weak, watery smile. "Don't be nice to me, Officer Seeger; I can't handle 'nice' right now. I'll fall apart."

"So. You were going to tell me how your husband- Todd? – died."

Kelli looked at her appraisingly. Todd had told her all about interrogation techniques. She smiled at Seeger. "Actually I was trying to avoid telling you how Todd died. But I'll do it anyway." Kelli took a deep breath. "Not much to tell really. Todd stopped at Publix to pick up something I'd asked him to get on his way home. Somebody came up behind him and shot him. One bullet, went right to his heart. I was told the shooter was probably some cop-hater, spur of the moment thing. It didn't appear to have been planned. Todd's stop at Publix was a last minute thing. Still haven't found the shooter. Don't expect to unless he kills again or up and confesses. Wouldn't that be nice? At least the part about him confessing. Otherwise the only way to get justice for Todd is to hope someone else dies, probably another cop? No thanks."

Seeger's head had jerked up halfway through Kelli's story. "Todd Cavanaugh. I'm sorry. It didn't hit me until now. I was at his funeral. That was really tough. You lost your baby, too, didn't you?"

Kelli nodded as she wiped silent tears from her cheeks. *Hope I don't run out of paper napkins.*

"Sorry," she whispered. "I thought I could talk about it by now. It's been a rough week. I went to St. Croix to scatter Todd's ashes; it's where we spent our honeymoon. He didn't even know about the baby. I had just found out for sure that morning. I was fixing us a fancy dinner and decided I wanted some raspberries – that's what it was! – for the dessert. I asked him to stop and get some on his way home from work." She sniffled and wiped more tears away. "If I hadn't, he'd still be here and we'd have our baby." She began hiccupping.

"My God, you have been through the ringer haven't you? You should be a screaming basket case by now. How do you stay so calm? I need to learn your secret." Seeger pushed Kelli's cup closer to her, just as the doorbell rang. Kelli lifted the cup and tried to steady it against her wavering lower lip. Seeger stood and put a hand on Kelli's shoulder.

"That'll be the detective. I'll go fill him in. You sip your tea and catch your breath." Seeger headed for the kitchen door, then came back and gave Kelli a motherly hug, pulling the quaking younger woman close to her chest. "It's not your fault,

Kelli. It's the fault of whoever pulled the trigger," she said against Kelli's forehead. She squeezed Kelli's shoulders and said, "Drink up. I'll be right back."

Kelli shuddered, then straightened her shoulders. "Get yourself together, Kelli, one thing at a time. You have to answer questions for the detective." She swiped the napkin across her face again, took a big gulp of her tea, re-clipped her hair, and pinched her cheeks to bring some color back, a la Scarlett O'Hara. *One of my favorite heroines. I will not be a mealy-mouthed Melanie.* She tried a grin, but it came out more of a grimace. "Better try that one again," she muttered to herself. "Maybe I should be making notes, too, so I don't forget anything."

With a less than firm step she walked over to her desk. She pulled open the pencil drawer and saw the envelope lying there on top of the tray of pens, pencils, and highlighters. Kelli stiffened and bit her lip. She would not panic. She left the drawer open and walked across the kitchen. She pushed the swinging door open and held it. Three people were in a deep, quiet conversation; she saw Seeger and Davenport and another man. They looked up as the door opened.

"I found another note," she said calmly. "I think you probably want to see it." *I think I'm having a nervous breakdown* was what she really wanted to say. Granny's upbringing precluded any public display of emotion, at least not until any crisis was over. *Does this count as a crisis?*

20

What the hell is going on? He frantically searched the six monitors. He had put cameras in the kitchen, the upstairs hall, Kelli's bedroom, the foyer, her reading room, and the front parlor. But there were no phone bugs in three of those rooms, so no audio.

He saw the policewoman open the front door to a tall, good-looking man, not in a uniform. *More police? A lawyer? He looks like a lawyer, all buttoned-down.* He wasn't anyone he recognized; through the years he had come to know most everyone Kelli knew. He knew where she went and who went with her. He had notes of everyone and everything. But not this guy. The new guy entered and shook hands all around. *Polite, too.*

His eyes strayed to camera #5, the kitchen. He saw the desk drawer sitting open. She must have opened it while he was watching the front door. He'd have to watch the recording and see her excitement at finding another note.

He watched Kelli head for the kitchen door. Must be going to the front door. He glanced back to monitor #3; the three at the front door were deep in conversation. *Shit!* He needed to hear what they were saying.

Kelli had stopped halfway through the swinging door, holding it open with her hip and left arm. He could see her lips moving, the other three looked up and moved toward her. All four had deep frowns on their faces.

As they approached the desk, their voices gradually became louder and he could understand what they were saying, thanks to the multi-directional bug he had planted in the desk phone.

"I went over to the desk to get pen and paper," Kelli explained with only a slight wobble in her voice. "I opened the pencil drawer, and there it was. Just lying on top of the pens. It's the same kind of envelope as the note upstairs. I didn't touch it. I just came and got you." Her words were directed at Officer Seeger; she felt she knew her best and she felt comfortable with her. Seeger's innate empathy had gotten through to Kelli. Then she looked quizzically at the new person.

Seeger made the introductions, "Kelli, this is Detective Scott Rae. He'll be taking the lead on this from now on. He's with our Investigations department...and the best."" Seeger deferred to the taller man on her right. "Scott, Kelli Cavanaugh." Kelli was glad Seeger didn't go into any more details about herself, but she may have already told the detective she was Todd's widow.

Kelli looked up at the detective. Taller than either woman, meant he was over six feet tall, but just a bit. Dark brown hair, slightly curly on the edges, either because he needed a haircut or the humidity. Intelligent, warm brown eyes, Kelli could tell they wouldn't miss much. He had on a green plaid button-down shirt and jeans, a navy wool sport coat on top. He held out his hand to Kelli.

"Mrs. Cavanaugh, let's see what we can do to settle things so you can get some sleep, you look all done in." He had a nice smile, but it didn't quite reach his eyes. *What was he not saying?*

Kelli turned to Seeger – Kim. In the face of the two men, she felt a strong alliance with the other woman – she knew how these things went. "So you're leaving now?" Kelli didn't mean to sound desperate, but she felt she did.

Rae sensed a bond had developed between the two women. "Actually, Officer Seeger, I could use your help on this one. Why don't you stick around for a while?"

Sometimes promising beat cops – those who might make good detectives – were given the opportunity to shadow detectives, working real cases. The department had instituted this plan because it gave the officers a chance to see the job for what it was: a lot of hard work, a lot of hours, and a lot of false leads, followed by an occasional glimmer of a clue. And, if the detective was lucky as well as diligent, sometimes an arrest that may or may not lead to a conviction. Nowhere near the excitement and glamour portrayed on television.

The shadow/mentor program also gave the department a chance to watch the officer and see if he or she had what it takes to be a strong detective. Maybe channel a beat cop's interests elsewhere, maybe the Crime Scene Unit, maybe motor pool, maybe PR. Often the cop decided he or she liked being a beat cop and elected to remain there and look for a promotion within the ranks. Those made outstanding community outreach officers. For the department, there were few things more fiscally draining than training and grooming a new homicide detective and have him or her decide detectiving was not a right fit.

But Kim Seeger wasn't about to change her mind. She had wanted that gold badge since she was a kid. She'd gotten her degree in Criminal Justice from USC in Columbia, then researched police departments to determine which was the most receptive to female detectives. She'd settled on Charleston City Police. She graduated first in her class at the academy, even though she was pregnant with her first child. Antonio had been born a month after she started her first beat. Thank goodness they hadn't put her on bicycle patrol; she might have fallen.

Her husband, a history professor at College of Charleston, was very supportive of Kim's ambition and enjoyed the fact that he had the opportunity to spend more time with their two children: Tony, now six, and Brandon, four.

Seeger had had two shadows already, one with Detective Rae. She knew she was up for detective sometime this year. Scott was an excellent instructor and very patient. And he didn't treat her like just a go-fer, as the other detective had. She was looking forward to working with him again.

Turning to Davenport, Rae said, "You, too, Davenport, at least for a while. First thing you can do is call for the forensics team." He looked at his watch: 2:13. "Although at this hour it will take them half the night to get here. Nine-to-fivers," he muttered to himself, or so he thought; the other three heard him and two of them smiled. Davenport walked back toward the front door to make his call.

Rae turned back to the women. "Now, Mrs. Cavanaugh, how 'bout you show me this new note?"

As Kelli moved to the desk, she said to the other two, "Why don't you call me Kelli? Mrs. Cavanaugh is a mouthful." She gave a small smile and paused at the ladder-back desk chair.

All three looked down at the plain white envelope lying across the middle of the drawer, "Kelli" handwritten plainly on the front.

Rae looked at the others, "This is the same type envelope as the other one?"

Kelli nodded, Seeger spoke up, "I haven't seen the first note yet. Kelli had just told me about it when we called you; we left it for you and CSU to handle."

Seeger's left forearm was resting casually on her holster, a normal relaxed pose for police. Kelli's arms were crossed, her hands rubbing her forearms again, obviously trying to warm them.

Rae took a pair of latex gloves from his coat pocket and snapped them on. The noise was like a crack of an ice cube in the otherwise quiet kitchen, even the refrigerator wasn't humming. Rae picked up the envelope and held it up to the overhead light.

"Looks like a piece of paper in there. We'll wait for CSU to give it a once-over." He replaced the note in its original position in the drawer. Kelli stared at her own name staring back at her. "In the meantime, let's go back to the front parlor and you two can catch me up." He led the way back through the swinging door. They saw Davenport near the front doors, still on the phone. Rae led them through the dining room and the formal parlor, to the front parlor, turning on lights as he went, carefully using his gloved hands.

Make yourself right at home, why don't you? Kelli thought snidely.

21

Early Saturday morning

"No, don't go to the parlor! I can't hear you in there," he screamed frantically at his bank of monitors.

Nonetheless the three of them found seats in front of the fireplace with its green marble surround. All he could do now was watch helplessly and hope to gain something from their actions and body language; not for nothing had he taken that psych course. He sat in his wobbly desk chair; he'd found it near somebody's trash can. Chin resting on his hands, he stared forlornly at the top row of monitors, #2 was second from the left, the front parlor. He watched the tall man's lips move.

"Seeger and Davenport have told me a bit about what's going on, Mrs. C..., Kelli. Maybe you can fill in some of the blanks?" His eyes were still, expressionless, non-committal. Kelli had the strangest feeling he didn't trust her. *Good grief!*

Kelli knew a lot about law enforcement from Todd and then from Todd's murder investigation and Sean's arrest. She knew the police would ask the same questions over and over. She knew they could lie to anyone if it would help them get to a resolution. While most of the time she was okay with this, she was not okay with it for Sean; the family had been lied to time and again, by everyone "on the other side" as she thought of the police, prosecutors, and the ME's office. Sometimes investigations arrived at a solution, but not necessarily the right solution, as in the case of Sean. As much as she had loved Todd, and his friend Dean, she would never trust the police again. And that included this man in front of her.

At least he knew it was a parlor and not a living room/family room/den. Kelli knew watchfulness and patience – not her strong suit – were her best course of action. She had to be careful about what she said or they'd end up saying she was a nut case and had hidden the notes herself.

"Whatever I can do, Detective Rae. Would you like some tea or coffee? The water's hot for tea or I can make you a cup of coffee, any flavor."

Rae looked at her steadily. *All the social niceties.* "No, thank you. Not right now." Even though he was desperate for a cup. He'd been up for thirty-six straight hours and had gotten to bed at midnight, barely an hour's sleep before his phone rang again.

"As I understand it, Kelli, you've been receiving strange phone calls for about six months?"

"Yes, although I think the frequency has increased in the last few months. I've had several hang-ups here and at work, more since my grandparents left for Arizona earlier this month. I really don't know. I didn't even think about the calls until Kim asked me about them." She smiled at the officer seated next to her on the settee.

"And tonight you found a note. Where was it?"

Kelli took a deep breath and looked the detective in the eyes. He was seated to her right, in one of the wing chairs, she and Kim were facing the fireplace. "It was under my pillow. I lifted the pillow to turn it over and there it was."

"Is that normal for you? To turn your pillow over at night?" A raised eyebrow indicated the detective did not quite believe this action.

Kelli smiled sheepishly, "Yes. I've done it since I was a child. I like to get the cold side up. It's very comforting, especially in Charleston summers. I do it every night."

Davenport spoke from the parlor entrance and seated himself in the other wing chair across from Rae, "I do it, too, Detective. Lots of people do." He grinned at Kelli. She gave him a thankful look.

Rae looked from one to the other. "Never heard of it." He looked back at Kelli. "How many people know about this," he hesitated calling it a ritual, "habit?"

Kelli was confused. The question was strange and certainly didn't seem relevant. "I don't know. My grandparents. My brother, he does it, too. Maybe my parents. I taught Todd to do it, too." She paused. "Why does this matter? Certainly I would have found the note eventually whether I turned over the pillow or not." *But I would have been in bed then, with my head on the pillow.* She shuddered at the thought. She looked at the detective. Her back was up; he was obviously skeptical about her whole story. Kim reached over and clasped Kelli's hands where they were tightly clenched in her lap.

"Just trying to understand the complete sequence of events," the detective replied calmly.

Right.

"It's just that whoever left that note may have expected you to find it tonight if he or she knew your habits. Gives us a starting point. Or there may be a camera hidden in your room so he or she could have learned your habit. Or he – I'm going to drop the 'she', I'm getting tongue-tied, and it's probably a 'he' anyway – could have figured you'd find the note if and when you put your hands under the pillow. Lots of possibilities. But since he called right after you opened it, my guess is that he's put a camera in there at some time. Or he has some way to see into your room from the outside. Maybe it's just a neighbor boy playing a prank. As I said, lots of possibilities." The doorbell rang and he paused. "Excuse me, that'll be the forensics team. I just need to have a word with them and get them started."

He stood and walked to the door, Davenport at his heels. *At least he's mannerly,* Kelli thought as she watched his broad back.

Kelli and Kim heard the outside front door opening and the clank of heavy boxes banging against thighs. Three people, all in Tyvek white coveralls followed Scott into the foyer. Kelli heard the door close and the murmur of voices, but she couldn't make out the words. She turned to the woman next to her.

"Camera! You don't think there's a camera in my bedroom, do you? Who would do that? How would somebody do that? I would have to have let them in wouldn't I? Me or Magda?" Her hands worked furiously up and down the arms of her purple robe.

"Forensics will find it if there is one. As Scott said, it's just one of the options we have to look at at this point. It looks like you may have a stalker, and we have to figure out how sophisticated he is. Whether he's someone you know or a total stranger who has become fixated on you. There are lots of questions and very few answers right now." Kim patted Kelli's shoulder. "Some of the questions may seem strange, but I promise they're necessary. I've worked with Scott before and he's the best. A bit overbearing sometimes, but really good at his job." Seeger smiled at Kelli as Scott Rae returned to his chair in the parlor. Apparently Davenport had stayed with the others. Kelli heard the heavy steps of several people going up the stairs, equipment banging and clanging.

Rae spoke first, "The team is going to start upstairs. I told them to be sure to check for cameras and phone bugs, but to do it surreptitiously. We may want to leave them in place so we can track them back to their source. We can continue down here while they work up there."

Kelli was looking aghast. "Leave the cameras in place? How am I supposed to go to sleep knowing some pervert is watching me? I don't think I can sleep in there even if you get the cameras out!" Kim once again patted Kelli's shoulder. Her soothing attention helped Kelli calm down. "Well, Kelli, we'll wait and see on that," Rae replied. "I promise we won't do anything without your permission."

Kelli continued to stare at the detective suspiciously. *Promise. Right. I know what that's worth. Like they promised Sean if he gave himself up he'd be home by lunchtime and he hasn't been home since.*

Kelli stole a look at her watch. *After 3. This long night just keeps getting longer.* Unbeknownst to her, the detective was having the same thought.

22

He beat his head against the desktop beneath the monitors. His hands slapped his thighs in rhythm with the beats. Again. Again. A small cut opened over his left eye. He ignored the thin stream of blood dripping into his eyebrow. He shouted at the Kelli on #2, "Why, Kelli, why? Why did you call the police? You know how much I love you. You must by now. I've loved you since the first day we met.

"Remember that Christmas party? The first year you and Sean had moved here your grandparents thought you should get to know the neighborhood kids better, so they invited all the kids in for punch and cookies right on Christmas Eve. It became an annual event. In eighth grade my brother and I were invited since we had moved in down the street. You were just twelve? Thirteen? RJ and Sean were friends, both stuck up because they were older and went to that prep school.

"But you were nice, and very polite. You made a point of greeting everybody and remembering our names. You were already quite the hostess. When you shook my hand you held it a bit longer than anyone else's and you looked deeply into my eyes. That's when I knew you felt it, too.

"That night you gave all of us a tour of the house, if we wanted. Of course everybody wanted, that was why most of them came. I just wanted to see your bedroom. At fourteen I was already interested in girls, very interested. And you especially, because I could tell we were meant for each other.

"And at school, you'd come and sit with me sometimes, in the library or at lunch. Others were sitting alone, but you came to me. I knew it was because you liked me best." He paused, breathing heavily, his right hand down his pants, working furiously.

In a rasping voice he continued, "Remember the time I tied the roses in front of your locker? That was hard! I had to hide at school until after the janitors left. Good thing I had planned ahead and wrapped the rose stems in wet paper towels so they

didn't dry out while I waited. I'm good at planning, very good."
He sighed contentedly as his mind and body joined in pleasure.
"One time the janitor didn't leave until after 2 a.m. I think he was
playing games in the computer lab. I really needed to go to the
bathroom, but I was afraid he'd see me, or hear the flush.

"I loved the look of surprise and delight on your face when you
got to your locker that morning and saw them. You looked all
around, trying to figure out who had left them, but I know you
knew it was me. Each time. I could have killed Brad when he
took credit for them, stupid jock. Like he'd have had the patience
to thread those tiny wires through the air vents of the locker.
And you believed him! Even went out with him! Only took one
date, though, to figure out he had lied. You're so smart, Kelli."
He grinned at her sincere face as she was talking to the police in
her parlor. "If only I could hear!" he moaned.

"And the notes. They were easier. I made them small enough
to slip through the air vents and you found them the next time
you opened the locker. I would have put some in your gym
locker, too, but I was afraid of getting caught. Besides, I had no
easy way of figuring out which gym locker was yours. In the hall I
just had to watch and see where you went. If I'd tried that in the
locker room they would have called me a pervert or something,
probably suspended me, too. Couldn't take the chance of not
seeing you every day.

"All through school I loved you and knew you loved me. You
kissed me! At the Christmas party each year; and then at your
graduation party. Why else would you have even invited me?
My stupid dad had lost all our money and we'd had to move out
to Goose Creek. Goose Creek! What a stupid name for a town.
No class. Certainly not a name like Charleston. I couldn't wait to
get away from there and back to you! As soon as I moved out of
the house I found you and re-started my Kelli journals. I've kept
track of almost every moment of your life for the last eight years.
I know everything.

"But you went up to Columbia and college. I visited you on
campus whenever I could, you never even saw me. But I saw you.
And I kept my notes. Every bit of extra money I made went to

buying things for my Kelli project: binoculars, flowers, more journals. The binoculars came in especially handy. I could watch through windows or from far away and you never even knew."

He frowned. The new man on #2 stood and went to the door with the shorter policeman. He watched intently. They opened the door and three more people came in: dressed alike in white coveralls and carrying big…tackle boxes? As one turned, the watcher saw CSU on the back of the coverall. "Oh, no! This has gone too far, Kelli. They might find my cameras, or the phone bugs. I need to know what you're doing so I can plan. I have to be able to plan.

"Planning is my expertise, I'm good at it. Remember the Christmas party your senior year in college? You brought that jock home with you? Big broad shoulders, sandy brown hair, blue eyes. Looked like some fruitcake model for a magazine, probably Men's Health. His arms looked like he worked out. Tall. Ramrod straight. Been to Afghanistan with the Marines. Big deal.

"And he came to the party the next year, only that time you two were engaged. Todd. Good ol Todd. Stupid name. Took his USC degree in Criminal Justice and joined the state troopers. One of those power-hungry, control freak types. Liked to push people around, I bet.

"But I know you never really loved him, because you had loved me for all those years. I know you only married him to please your parents and grandparents. Well, your grandparents anyway.

"You made it so much easier for me to keep tabs on you and the big guy when you moved from your apartment to Cane Bay. Took me no time to install a couple cameras and phone bugs. Learned how to do it in my technology security class. What a joke! Isn't 'technology security' an oxymoron? Even your super-cool state trooper never suspected a thing. What a loser.

"I know what you talked about. I know when and how you had sex. Where you were going and when. I even knew you were pregnant and Todd never did. Pool ol' Todd.

"I tried to console you at his funeral, but you were right. Too soon to show everyone our love. So I've waited." He glared again at the monitor as the tall guy resumed his seat in the parlor, #2.

"But I'm tired of waiting, Kelli. It's time. Time for us to be together. I just have one more thing to finish up and I'll come for you. Soon, Kelli, very soon. Maybe tonight."

23

"First things, first, Kelli. Officer Davenport has told me they searched the whole house and there's no sign of forced entry. How many people have keys to this house?"

Kelli thought a moment. "I can't be completely sure since it's my grandparents' house. I know Amanda has one; she's the backdoor neighbor. She's 73 years old and my grandmother's closest friend, since forever.

"Of course Magda has one. She's our housekeeper. She's been part of the family since before we moved here when I was eight. She's from Cuba originally. Her father was Russian and her mother was Cuban. Magda is short for Magdalena; made both parents happy; Magdalena is Spanish and Magda is more Russian. Her parents met in Cuba during the embargo, there were lots of Russians in Cuba back in the old days. Pavel's parents stayed in Cuba. Pavel is her husband. Granted he was born in Cuba but he has always considered himself Russian." She thought again.

"Of course my brother and his wife have keys. Although Sean's key came back when he went to jail. I think my parents probably do, but I can't be sure about that. They're rarely here anyway." The other three looked at each other from lowered eyes. *What's with that? She talks about her parents like rare visitors, distant cousins or something.*

Kelli spoke up again. "I gave a key to Teri Jackson right before I left on vacation last week. She's the Realtor handling the sale of the house for my grandparents." She stopped again. "There may be others, but that's all I can think of right now. I can ask Granny the next time we talk." She snapped her fingers. "Of course I have a key and Todd had a key. His came back with his," she hesitated then lifted her chin, "with his personal effects."

"Seeger reminded me of your husband's case. I'm very sorry for your loss." Kelli nodded. *If I had a nickel for every time I've heard those exact words, usually from somebody in law enforcement, I could buy this house myself.*

Detective Rae paused only a heartbeat before he continued, "I noticed the For Sale sign and the lock box on the front gate. How long has the house been on the market?"

"Not long, about ten days. I met with Teri right before I left town and signed all the papers. She put the sign up on that Tuesday, last week, and I left town early Wednesday morning." Kelli gave an embarrassed grin. "Teri had planned an open house – what she called a broker open house – for Wednesday morning, so I was even more glad to be leaving town. I couldn't stand the thought of strangers tromping through my house."

Rae looked at her quizzically, leaving no question unasked; you never know what may prove important. "I thought open houses are usually held on the weekend. Why a Wednesday? Seems an odd day, most people are at work and wouldn't be able to come look." Seeger repositioned her hips on the settee, her gun was starting to dig into her upper thigh.

"That's what I thought, too. Teri said times have changed. Agents only use public open houses as a last resort. Teri said the public open houses have been shown to be counter-productive. That's especially true for houses in this price range and with its age. Lots of people would come to an open house here, just to see the house, maybe to get decorating ideas, but very few potential buyers would actually show up. Then for all that effort, the rugs and floors get dirty and have to be cleaned and there's always the chance of theft.

"These days they hold what are called 'broker open houses' where only the local real estate brokers are invited. And, in this case, only the brokers who are accustomed to presenting houses in this category. The idea is sort of a trickle-down effect. The brokers, who really are in charge of the office and all the transactions, come to the open house then they go back to their offices and tell their agents about the property, hopefully giving it a glowing testimonial." Kelli paused for breath.

"Teri called me Wednesday night and said about a dozen brokers had shown up for the food she offered and the look-around. She said she emphasized to each that we only want qualified buyers looking at the house. That cuts down on the showings right there. Teri seemed pleased at the turnout."

Rae groaned inwardly. At least a dozen more opportunities for fingerprints and thirteen more people to talk to. He'd have to warn the team upstairs; it could take them days to track all the prints. "Do you have a list of those who came?" Rae asked.

"I don't, but I'm sure Teri does; she's very organized. Of course Magda came in and did a thorough cleaning Thursday morning; there may not be many prints to find. Magda is a perfectionist." Kelli smiled sweetly at the detective. She knew he was here to help but he acted like she was unfamiliar with procedures.

This time the groan escaped the detective's lips and he looked helplessly at the other two officers. Davenport rose and went upstairs without being asked. The detective continued.

"How many people knew you were going out of town, Mrs. Cavanaugh?" He caught himself, "Sorry. Kelli."

"Hardly anyone. My grandparents. Amanda, she keeps an eye on the house when no one's home. My office. The bank so they wouldn't worry about foreign transactions. My two credit cards, same reason." She paused, silently ticking each off on her fingers. "Oh, Magda of course." She moved another finger. "Seven," she said proudly.

Scott Rae knew from experience there were probably more, a lot more. "Did you stop a newspaper or have your mail held?"

Kelli looked embarrassed. "Oh, of course. Forgot about them. I stopped the paper and had the mail held. Since I was going to be gone I didn't want the place to look like I was gone. Magda was only going to come in if there were any showings and it was doubtful there would be more than one or two while I was gone."

Rae looked at her with his eyebrows raised, "Stopping both paper and mail was a good idea." He paused, gathering his questions. He looked around the sterile parlor. "What about pets? Do you have a pet-sitter or house-sitter?"

"Oh my gosh! Corky! I have to get her at the kennel tomorrow morning." She looked at her watch. "I guess that's this morning. Will we be through here?"

"Probably not, but we'll see that Corky gets home. What is she? Cat?" He envisioned Kelli reclining with a book and a cat curled up at her side. Maybe a Persian or Siamese. Something fluffy.

Kelli chuckled. "No, not hardly." Kelli had her first full smile since getting home last night. "She's a Golden Retriever, about ninety pounds. She's very friendly and great company. She's also very protective. Although she loves the kennel and has stayed there lots of times, this is the first time since Todd's death. She's probably having a nervous breakdown; she hates change. She misses Todd almost as much as I do. If I don't pick her up she'll be worried. And, friendly as she is, she won't get into the car with a stranger." She paused again. "Well, she might if there was food involved." She smiled conspiratorially. "But I don' think so. It's better if I go get her."

Thinking of Corky and Todd brought back the memories of Todd trying to teach Corky to fetch. He'd throw the tennis ball and she'd bring it back, but only two or three times. Then she'd just lie down and look at him, obviously wanting to say, "You threw it, you get it." If only she could talk! Her facial expressions were almost as good as talking, though.

Scott wondered what had brought the wistful look to her face. She had been so happy just a moment before.

"Were there any showings while you were gone?" he asked, hoping the answer would be "no".

"I don't know. I specifically asked Teri not to call me unless there was a realistic offer made. I just didn't want to think about the house selling while I was gone. I grew up in this house, as did my mother, and her mother; I hate the idea of it leaving the family."

Scott debated about his next question, giving Kelli time to calm down again. It was apparent she loved the house. *Who wouldn't? Must have been a great place to grow up. Right across the street from the harbor. Down the street from the park. That would be the life.*

"Do you park your car in one of those monthly rental garages? Did they know you were going away?"

"No, the car stays in the alley behind the house." Scott raised an eyebrow and Kelli immediately realized what his next question would be.

"I took Super Shuttle to and from the airport; easier than parking and having to schlep my bags to the terminal. I really miss curb-side check-in." She froze in her babbling. "Damn. Super Shuttle had my flight schedule. They knew when I left and when I'd be back. You just don't think about those kinds of things, do you?"

"No, Kelli, most people don't. Even people who know better will make a casual comment to someone and it's usually a lot more 'someones' than they realize. This makes the suspect pool astronomical." He stopped and looked around the room again. He turned back to Kelli. "Now think, Kelli. Who else might have known about your trip? Somebody you might have mentioned it to, even casually. It's easy to do. Somebody says something as innocuous as 'What are you up to this weekend?' and you reply, 'I'm going to St. Croix.' Easy to do. Maybe everybody didn't know your full schedule, but they may have known when you were leaving, or when you were coming back, or maybe just that you were going away." He paused again. "Think hard." He looked at her intently, willing her to remember, even knowing the more names she came up with, the harder his job would be.

Kelli shook her head. She closed her eyes and racked her brain. The other three could almost see the wheels turning.

"Now that you put it that way, I'm sure there were others. I think I told a couple women at the pool. And I got my nails done before I left; I may have mentioned it to Michelle." She closed her eyes again, trying to remember the errands she had run to get ready for the trip. "I ran a bunch of errands the days before my trip: bank, cleaners, CVS, I don't remember where all. I'll grab my calendar so I can give you a complete list." Kelli was up and heading for the kitchen before Scott could react to her comment.

Seeger, who had been quiet throughout the interview, took the opportunity to stand, adjust her heavy belt on her narrow hips, and followed Kelli through the swinging door. Kelli made a bee-line for the National Parks calendar hanging over the desk.

This one showed Hot Springs National Park in Arkansas. Kelli pulled the calendar from its push-pin on the corkboard. The clear pin went flying across the room. Kelli stood staring at the entries for the days preceding her trip.

"Uh oh. I don't think Scott is going to like this." She turned the calendar around so the policewoman could see it.

"You're right. He won't. Oh, well, it is what it is. It's okay. He won't bite you. Most of the time it wouldn't have mattered. Unfortunately, this isn't most times." Kim Seeger gave Kelli an encouraging smile and the two women walked back to the parlor. Once again they seated themselves on the settee, Kim a little closer to Kelli than before. Kelli held the calendar close to her chest, shielding it from Scott's eyes.

"I'm sorry, Scott, it's how I always indicate trips." She handed the calendar to the detective's extended hand.

He accepted the calendar with both hands and looked down at it, mystified by Kelli's comment.

"Oh, shit," he almost exploded, instead he just muttered it. The women heard him nonetheless. And looked at each other. Wordlessly they agreed he didn't like it. On the calendar, under bright pink highlighter, starting the Wednesday before and continuing to last night it said 'St. Croix' in dark blue ink.

Every weekend in the month it had 'Sean' in bright pink for Friday night through Sunday, except this weekend. Scott flipped to February. Same thing. 'Sean' highlighted every weekend. He'd get to that later. He took a deep breath as he turned the calendar back to January. She had long lists in neat tiny handwriting on each of the days preceding her trip; headers on each list read 'phone calls', 'errands' and 'to do'. And she said the real estate lady was organized. *It looks like Kelli is a little hyper, maybe even suffering from Obsessive Compulsive Disorder,* Scott worried to himself.

Scott got his frustration in check, hard to do since he now realized anyone who had been in the kitchen in the last month would have known all Kelli's plans, no secrets there. "What about repairmen? Any kitchen or bathroom or appliance repairs in the last month or so?"

Kelli thought a moment and pulled the calendar back from Scott's big hand. "Yes. The drawer under the oven was stuck. We didn't want to force it. Not a repairman really. Magda had her husband come over and fix it, he's very handy. The drawer had just come off one of its rollers. He was able to fix it in a jiffy. Here, on January 17, it says 'Pavel'; that's when he fixed it." Kelli was very proud she had been able to tell him exactly when Pavel had been in the kitchen. She didn't know why this detective made her feel guilty. *What am I supposed to be guilty about?* She bit her bottom lip to stop her from saying something she might regret.

"Anyone else you can remember telling about your trip?" Kelli was sure she heard sarcasm in the detective's voice. Kelli couldn't tell if he was disgusted, defeated, or just mean.

She again looked at the calendar. All her last minute errands were listed for the previous Tuesday. "I may have mentioned it to Mr. Sanchez and Bert, at the cleaners. But we've been going there forever. Besides, Mr. Sanchez has a bad leg, he has a hard time doing stairs. That's why he hired Bert, to help out while he was laid up, and because Bert can fix anything. Bert has helped Mr. Sanchez in lots of ways." She was babbling again. *Just answer the questions.* She glanced back at Tuesday's entries.

"The week before I had told the pharmacist at CVS. I had to get a prescription refilled earlier than I was supposed to. Pam asked why and I told her I was going on a trip. She said she'd check with the insurance company about a vacation waiver, or I could pay full price. Last Tuesday I went and picked it up. I think I had told Pam I had to have it by the Tuesday because I was leaving town on Wednesday." She stopped talking. *Babbling again.*

"Anybody else," the grim detective prompted her as he looked up from where he had been making notes.

Kelli wanted to slap him. It wasn't as though she had told all these people on purpose, it just came out in the course of normal, everyday conversations. *He probably has no idea about that sort of thing, though.* "Not that I can think of right now. I can let you know if I think of anyone else, though, can't I? Kelli returned his stolid stare. *You are not going to intimidate me* she told him mentally.

"What about Facebook? Twitter? Send any pictures via Instagram from your vacation?"

Kelli laughed a rueful laugh. "No, I'm afraid not. I've never gotten into that whole social media thing. I'm too private a person to share my inmost thoughts, or my lunch, with the whole world. I can't imagine that many people would be interested anyway. I'm rather a solitary person, not so much a love-the-whole-world kind. I have a few close friends, but other than them and my family, I'm not a big talker." Kelli smiled self-consciously, realizing her babbling tonight denied the truth of that statement. "Besides Todd always warned me about the kooks and stalkers who troll those sites. No thanks. Not worth the chance."

Scott said resignedly, "I'll need a list of those 'close friends' and their contact information, please." *At least she did something right. God save me from civilians. They just don't understand how dangerous the world is these days, especially for women and children.*

"So tell me about Sean. He's on your calendar a lot and you haven't even mentioned him. Did he know you were going out of town?"

24

It was five and he couldn't take it anymore. Besides he had to get ready for work.

A short while ago the four had moved back into the kitchen. *At last, I can hear them. No telling what I've missed so far. That stupid forensics team has found nothing! Not even the cameras or phone bugs. But probably they aren't even looking for them. They're more the fingerprint and DNA type. Have to call in the big guns for real technology.* He smiled smugly as he turned up the volume on #5.

Everybody was giving their drink orders to Kelli as she turned up the heat under the tea kettle. Coffee for the men, tea for the women. Just as Kelli started to speak, one of the Tyvek-suited CSU people came into the kitchen.

She motioned the detective over to her spot by the swinging door. She talked softly, but the tiny, powerful directional mic that was in the desk phone picked up her words. "Detective, we've found two more notes upstairs." She held two zippered plastic bags, just like the ones on TV, or the ones used to pack sandwiches in. Each bag had an unfolded piece of paper and an envelope in it. A label was affixed to the front of each.

Rae took the envelopes and read each note. "Thanks," he said to the tech as he nodded and turned back to the three now seated at the bar. Silently he walked over and handed the bags to Kelli. She reached for them and he turned back to the tech. Through the plastic, Kelli started reading. The note was brief. She finished it and passed it to the two uniformed officers seated to her left while she read the second one. She looked up to ask the detective a question but saw he was talking to the tech. This time he didn't bother to keep his voice down.

"Where'd you find them, Suzi?"

Kelli looked closely at the tech: petite blonde, fortyish, gorgeous almond-shaped eyes, hair in a ponytail. Suzi cleared her throat. "The first one," she indicated the one Kelli was holding out to Seeger, "Was in a lingerie drawer in Mrs. Cavanaugh's dresser."

Kelli gave a strangled moan and dropped the clear bag onto the countertop. "He touched my clothes? My underwear?" She gagged and Seeger pushed her tea cup closer. Kelli's hand was shaking as she lifted the cup to her lips; tea sloshed into the saucer.

Suzi looked to Scott for guidance. He checked Kelli and gave the tech an almost imperceptible nod. Suzi continued.

"The other one was in plain sight on a small table in that library room upstairs." Kelli gasped again. She took another sip of her tea and tried to steady herself.

Scott was still talking with Suzi. "Did you bag the first note, the one Kelli found upstairs?"

"Yes, sir." The tech reached into her voluminous pocket and pulled out a third plastic bag, like a magician pulling a rabbit out of a hat. She handed the bag to the detective. Scott glanced at it and passed it over. Kelli read every word, even though she knew them by heart from earlier. She placed the three notes side by side on the counter top.

Davenport, Seeger, and Kelli scanned the notes. They all looked alike. Even the words were practically identical. The theme was certainly the same: "I'll see you soon, Kelli."

Scott said to Suzi, "While you're here, bag and tag that envelope in the desk drawer. Get a couple photos of it in the drawer first, though. Then let me have it."

The tech turned back to the door. "Camera's upstairs, be right back." She hustled through the swinging door. Except for the slow whoosh of the door closing there was silence in the kitchen.

"Say something!" he screamed at the monitors. "What about the notes? What do you think about them? You only found four, though, there's still one out there. And it's the best. You experts will never find it, only Kelli can find it." He started giggling. He had outwitted all of them. "Morons!" He turned and headed for his bedroom; had to get dressed for work. He turned the volume up to max so he could hear the conversations while he was getting dressed in the other room.

"How much longer do you think we'll be, Scott?" Kelli asked in an exhausted voice.

Scott looked at her sympathetically, which surprised Kelli no end. "I know you're worn out, Kelli, but it really is better if we cover as much of this as we can now. Then we'll see about getting you someplace where you can get some sleep."

Move her! They can't move her. How will I know where she is? I have to get over there so I can see where they take her.

"I'm sorry. I can't leave here. And what about Corky? I need to get her. And I need to do my laundry; it's either that or throw away all my lingerie." Kelli was tearing up, the thought of being separated from her dog even longer making her feel even more lost. Seeger patted her shoulder.

Seeger looked at Scott as she said to Kelli, "Let's just see where we are when we finish here. How's that?" Scott and Kelli nodded at the same time and Seeger smiled her motherly smile.

Scott said, "And you can't do laundry until CSU is finished."

At that moment Suzi came in carrying a large 35mm camera with a huge, fancy lens on it. All four stopped talking and watched her work. She took pictures from every possible angle, even kneeling on one of the chairs from the table so she could get the best overhead shot. After about eight shots, she turned the envelope over with her gloved hand and repeated the whole process, this time showing the back of the envelope. When she finished she grabbed a letter opener from the pencil cup on the desktop and opened the envelope. She noticed the pencil cup seemed to have everything in it except pencils.

Suzi spread the note out on the open desk drawer and photographed it, both sides. Then she slipped the note and envelope into another bag, wrote the date and time and location-found on the bag in the appropriate line of the chain-of-custody label, sealed the bag, and initialed it. Kelli and the others had silently watched the expert work. When she started filling in the form, Kelli looked at the other three bags arrayed in front of her, each had its own form: #1, Found under pillow in Mrs. Cavanaugh's bedroom. Under "Found by:" Kelli saw her own name. The other two had identical forms, except where it had "Found by:" Kelli saw Suzi Wu.

Suzi capped her Sharpie with a loud click and handed the bag to Scott. "Anything else, Detective?"

"No, not right now, Suzi. Thanks for the help." Scott placed the desk note on the counter next to the other three.

Suzi wasn't quite done, though. "Detective? May I talk to you a minute?" She walked through the swinging door, sure Detective Rae would follow her.

"Now what? Don't leave the kitchen, I can't hear you out there. Damn you! Come back in here!" The watcher was tucking a polo shirt into his jeans while he shouted at the monitor.

As if the detective had heard his shouts, he reentered the kitchen, a worried frown on his face.

"You know, Kelli, I think you're right. You've had enough drama for one night." He gathered up the four clear bags. "You haven't slept in twenty-four hours, or more, and Suzi said they're about ready to do their sweep down here." He hoped he sounded convincing. Kelli and Seeger were both looking at him with puzzled expressions. *Why had he suddenly changed his mind? Was it really that they needed to get out of CSU's way?*

"How about we get you to a nice cozy room? Seeger will stay with you and you can get some sleep. We'll start again in a few hours, after you've gotten some rest and something besides tea to eat." He smiled his most sincere smile at both women. Seeger guessed he was hiding something and hoped he'd tell her what it was. For now she decided just to follow his lead.

Kelli opened her mouth to speak but Scott put up his hand to stop her. "Don't worry, we'll call the kennel as soon as they open and let them know you've been delayed. Corky will be fine."

"Fine," Kelli said, her question answered before she had even asked it. *Does he read minds, too?*

"May I change clothes, too?" Kelli asked with just a trace of the asperity she was feeling. *Why does he feel he can just order me around like this? I haven't done anything.*

"Why do I have to go somewhere? There are plenty of rooms right here. Granted I can't stay in my room, and I don't want to anyway, but I can stay in one of the other rooms, or even my grandparents' room."

"Because, Mrs. Cavanaugh, the whole house is now considered a crime scene, a B&E, somebody entered, even if he didn't break his way in." Scott was losing patience. Kelli's rational questions and calm demeanor were getting to him. *Why can't she just do it my way and not argue about everything?*

"Fine. I'll just go upstairs and get some clothes."

"Lovely. Just give me a minute with Seeger and Davenport and then Kim can go upstairs with you." The four stood from the bar as Kelli replied, "I'm a big girl, Detective Rae. I can pack for myself. I'm sure you three have something more important to do than watch me pack." Kelli smiled her most ingratiating smile, but her eyes were challenging him to deny her.

"Do you think I'm a suspect so I have to be watched every minute? Do you think I wrote those love notes?" Kelli's voice was dead calm and very cold.

This whole incident was getting out of hand. "Sit down, Mrs. Cavanaugh. Finish your tea. You can't go upstairs unescorted because we have to know what part of the scene you may disturb, somebody has to witness it. That somebody is Seeger. Unless you'd prefer Davenport or I help you pack your undies?"

His logic only angered Kelli more. *Insufferable. Give some men a little power and it went to their heads, and usually other parts of their anatomy.* But, as the widow of a law enforcement officer, Kelli couldn't argue with his reasoning. If she wasn't so tired she would have known it anyway. *But he doesn't have to treat me like a suspect! I'm the victim here. Sure this isn't as exciting as a murder, but it's plenty scary for me. Some stranger was in my house! Handled my clothes! I may be sick…No, I won't give Detective Rae the satisfaction.*

Kelli plopped back down onto her bar stool, took one sip of her tea, *as ordered, Sir*, crossed her arms over her robed chest, and stared at the microwave in front of her. *Six a.m.! No wonder I'm so tired. Practically out on my feet.*

Wait! Stall them. I'll be there as fast as I can. Kelli, I have to know where you are going. He grabbed his keys from the table where he had dropped them and rushed down the two flights of stairs, and out to his car, leaving the monitors on and his front door unlocked. *I have to find you, Kelli, don't leave me!*

Kelli could hear the three talking on the other side of the kitchen door, but couldn't make out the words. A short time later she heard the front door open and close. Seeger returned to the kitchen.

"Scott had to go make arrangements for your stay. Davenport has gone outside to wait for the patrolmen who are coming to help maintain the scene from the outside." Seeger promptly explained the door's opening and closing. "We saw a suitcase in the front hall. Yours?"

"Yes, I was too tired to drag it up the stairs last night. I was planning on unpacking it tomorrow, I guess that's today." Now that all the questioning was over, the adrenaline charge Kelli had gotten was quickly leaving her system. Everything, including her trip from St. Croix, was catching up to her. Kelli tried to stifle a yawn; Granny would be so upset, so unladylike. *Maybe Mr. Macho is right, sleep will help. As much as I want to sleep, I'd hate for him to be right.*

Seeger spoke up. "Think you have enough clothes in there to get you through a couple days?"

Kelli nodded wearily, even though most of the clothes were ready for the laundry or the cleaners. At least the "intruder" hadn't touched them.

"Great! Then we don't have to go upstairs at all. We'll just take your bag and be on our way." Seeger moved to Kelli's side to help her to her feet.

Kelli waved away the helping hand and gave Kim a rueful smile. "I'm not that tired yet. I can still walk by myself." Kelli pulled her robe tighter around her waist and followed Kim out to the foyer. She wasn't sure when she'd started thinking of Officer Seeger as "Kim", but she felt very comfortable with her.

"I'll just grab a couple things out of the bag and I can change here in the powder room." Kelli indicated the second door just outside the kitchen.

Kim nodded and opened the door in the foyer. She took a quick peek around. *Yep, powder room. Pedestal sink, toilet, nicely decorated with pale green grass cloth wallpaper, a small vase of silk spring flowers, and embroidered hand towels. Elegant without being over the top. No place for anyone to hide, nor for Kelli to hide anything. Not that she would.*

"I'll just be a minute," Kelli said as she walked past Kim and closed the powder room door. Seeger noticed Kelli had left the suitcase lying open on the foyer floor. Obviously giving Kim the chance to explore it while Kelli was changing. Kim didn't bother. After all, she could do it at the hotel, once Kelli went to sleep. Better to get Kelli's confidence now.

She could hear Kelli moving about behind the closed door. Inside, Kelli placed her clothes on the toilet seat and looked into the round mirror hanging from a green grosgrain ribbon over the sink. "Good grief! I should have gotten my make-up bag too." Her reflection showed deep dark circles under her eyes, either from exhaustion or smeared mascara. "Probably both," she muttered. "No lipstick. Hair a frazzle. Kelli girl, you've never looked better." Kelli proceeded to wash her face with the hard-milled soap in the floral soap dish. "I love flowers," she said wistfully, almost comatose from exhaustion.

Kelli quickly changed into jeans, a blouse, and a sweater. *Good thing I always pack at least one sweater. As Gramps always says, "You have to be ready for the what—ifs of life." In this case, what if a whacko has invaded your house and you have to spend the night elsewhere?* The fact was that she was always cold; no matter where she was, she needed a sweater or jacket. Warm climates meant air conditioning which was even worse than winter.

It took Kelli more than a minute, but not much more. She exited the powder room, hung her pajamas and robe on the banister and reached down and zipped her suitcase shut. She stood up, the suitcase now upright and on its wheels, and looked at her new friend.

"Where now, oh fearless leader? I'm sure you can use some sleep, too."

Kim smiled as she opened the first set of double doors, then the second one. *At least she hasn't lost her sense of humor.*

Kelli rolled her suitcase to the top of the concrete stairs, parked it, fumbled in her purse for her keys, and then locked the dead bolt on the front door. It occurred to her as she pocketed her keys that she hadn't needed to do that; the CSU technicians were still in there. The two women hefted the wheelie down the steps and then Kelli was able to roll it out to the waiting squad car. Kim nodded to Davenport, waiting in his car across the street.

"No! You can't leave yet. I'm still ten minutes away. I have to know where you're going. Are you coming back here? When?" The intruder shouted at the tiny screen on his phone that he was watching while he drove like a madman, careful, though, to remain within the speed limit; well, no more than five miles an hour over.

Frustrated, he slammed his fist against the middle console of his Camry. He hit so hard his fingers went momentarily numb.

"Don't worry, Kelli, I'll find you. And we'll never be parted again." He raised his hand and shook it, trying to return feeling to it. At the next red light he took a quick scroll through all the monitors at Kelli's house; just the CSU geeks left, and that one cop, the young Black guy. "Never again, Kelli, never again."

Giving up, he turned left at the next corner and retraced his route back toward North Charleston. He'd stop at Hardee's for breakfast and then head on to work. On the way to work he'd start planning. *Have to plan. Everything has to be perfect.*

25

Saturday morning

Detective Scott Rae pulled into the Loading/Unloading Only space directly in front of the historic Mills House, at the corner of Meeting and Cumberland, just a few blocks from Kelli's house. The two women were waiting for him in the lobby, Seeger standing watch, Kelli half asleep in an overstuffed chair. The Mills House was first opened as The St. Mary Hotel around 1801 when the owner used it as her private home to entertain distinguished guests. Prior to the Civil War Otis Mills, the new owner, leased the space to others, including the U.S. Government which used the building as a court house. In 1852 Mills decided to return the building to its former glory as the finest hotel in Charleston. He spared no expense, hiring the best architects and designers, buying hundreds of thousands of dollars' worth of antiques. His hotel was the first structure in all of Charleston to have running water and steam heat on such a grand scale. When complete, The Mills House once more became the queen of Charleston hotels. Its 119 rooms maintain Otis Mills' desire for southern grandeur and hospitality to this day, even though it's part of the Wyndham chain now.

"Okay, ladies, your room for the day awaits. Don't get too excited, though, the department's budget won't go to more than one day." He grinned at Seeger as she moved to meet him, her eyebrows raised in one big question mark. He noted Kelli was slow to rise; his arrival seemed to have awakened here from a quick doze in the lobby chair. As she stood he noticed tears glistening on her cheeks. He patted her shoulders and encircled them in a big, one-armed curl. She looked like a tall waif and reminded him of his youngest sister...sort of. For a moment all Kelli wanted to do was stand there, cuddled against this broad, warm chest. Then she remembered whose it was. She stiffened and pulled back. Scott's arm slipped down to her elbow.

"Come on, Kelli, it's going to be okay. You just need some sleep." His firm hand under her elbow and Seeger on the other side of her, Scott guided the women through the marble halls to the elevator. Just in case, Scott pushed all seven buttons so if anyone was watching they couldn't be sure on which floor they exited. He hadn't seen anyone in the lobby watching them, but he'd been an Eagle Scout; be prepared.

On the ride upstairs he told the women, "CSU has found two cameras so far, one in Kelli's bedroom and one in the upstairs hall. They also found a bug in the phone next to Kelli's bed; the kind that can pick up voices even if they're not on the phone."

Kelli stared at him in horror. "I don't get this. Why me? I haven't done anything to anyone, not anything that warrants this kind of treatment. My bedroom! My God! How long has it been there? I feel so... violated."

The three got off on the third floor and Scott sent the elevator on to the fourth, knowing it would continue to each of the upper floors. The hall was empty and dim, except for a light shining through an open door at the other end of the long hallway. "Probably the housekeepers' closet," Scott said softy. He directed them in the opposite direction and about halfway down the hall. Scott inserted the card key and pushed the door open. Then he pushed the two women inside and quickly closed the door. Two queen-size beds greeted them. Despite the hotel's stately lobby and elegant furnishings, their room was Wyndham modern: turquoise and beige in the linens; Scott decided it must be considered "elegant beach décor."

Scott deposited Kelli's wheelie on the luggage rack. "Good grief! How long were you gone? It feels like a closet's worth of clothes in here." Kelli just glared at him. He handed Seeger an emergency toothbrush he had gotten from the front desk when he registered.

Seeger laughed. "Men. It's so easy for you. Throw in slacks, a couple shirts, maybe a sport coat and you're good to go. We women have it much harder. If you were married you'd know that or you could have learned it from your four sisters. Women have grades of dressing: beach, casual, golf casual, business casual, cocktail, formal cocktail, dinner, dressy dinner, semiformal, and formal. And those are just the ones I can think of in my stuporous state." She grinned tiredly.

Kelli turned to Scott. "Are stalkers ever violent?" Scott debated how to answer. He was worried she was too exhausted to be able to handle the truth.

Kelli watched the indecision flit across Scott's face. That answered her question, but Scott tried anyway, "Sometimes. But don't worry. You're safe here. Nobody knows who you are, the room's registered in my name. Seeger and her trusty sidearm are here." He tried a smile and saw Kelli return it in Seeger's direction. "All you ladies have to do is lock the door behind me and get some sleep." He tipped Kelli's chin up and looked directly into her big brown eyes; he'd swear they'd gotten bigger in just the few hours he'd known her. "Right?"

Kelli sighed an exhausted sigh, "Right." Scott headed for the door.

Seeger spoke up, "Why don't you go ahead and wash up, Kelli, you're dead on your feet." Kelli grabbed her sleepwear and toiletries kit from her wheelie and headed into the bathroom.

Scott turned to Seeger. "Did you call Woody? Is he okay with you helping out with this? Not coming home tonight, or I guess it's today?"

"Yes, yes, and yes. He knows these shadowing opps look good on my record. I explained that you need a woman on the case and I was on the scene, so I got lucky." She grinned at Scott again.

"Not just lucky. Good. You're very good. I would have asked for you if you weren't on the scene already." Seeger blushed at the praise and started to issue a humble denial when they both heard the bathroom door opening. Kelli came out, her face freshly scrubbed, her hair down, and the SCHP t-shirt of Todd's she'd taken with her to St. Croix as a nightshirt covering her like a soft blanket. She stopped in her tracks. "Oh. I thought you'd gone."

"On my way out." As if to confirm his words, Scott opened the door. "You two get some sleep. Get some food from room service. I'll see you around eleven. Okay?"

The two tired women nodded numbly. Scott finger-crooked Seeger out into the hall with him.

"When you wake up explain to Kelli why we left the cameras and phone bugs in place; I don't think she's up to an explanation right now. We'll talk more when I get back. Get some sleep. No way he knows where she is. I'll square everything with your supervisor when I get back to headquarters. I need to get started on that list of names, get background checks, the whole bit. I'm going to need you rested; you may be with us for a while yet."

Scott pushed Seeger back into the room and waited until he heard the dead bolt clunk into its housing. He headed down the hall and into the elevator, then outside to the dawning day and his car. He still had a lot to do before he could even think about catching a nap.

"And miles to go before I sleep," he recited aloud. His favorite poem and too prophetic this time.

Upstairs Kelli rummaged through one of the outside pockets and found a teal-colored St. Croix souvenir t-shirt. She pulled off the price tag and tossed it to Seeger. "You can't very well sleep in that uniform. I bought it for myself, but you're welcome to it." Kelli smiled sleepily at the other woman.

Kim Seeger held it up in front of her, admiring the ocean scene with a sailboat. "Even my favorite color. And probably as close as I'll ever get to St. Croix. Thanks." She grinned and stripped down to her underwear while Kelli climbed into the bed by the window. Seeger headed to the bathroom, gun in hand.

Kelli chortled. "You do know how silly you look, don't you? Black lace underpants, t-shirt and a 9mm in your hand? It's okay, you can leave it on the nightstand. I promise I won't touch it unless Big Foot comes charging through the door. In that case, I do know how to use it."

Kim looked at the younger woman doubtfully. "You sure you know how to use one of these?"

"Just point and shoot, right? Sort of like a camera, only heavier?" Kelli's eyes lit up; Kim could tell she was teasing her.

Kelli grinned and continued, "Yes, I've been shooting since I was ten; Gramps taught me and my brother soon after we got here. He still takes me to the range once or twice a year and I go hunting with him. Todd took me to the range, too, just to be sure I could handle a handgun as well as rifles and shotguns."

Seeger was pleasantly surprised; Kelli looked so fragile. "Okay, then. I'll put it on the nightstand between us. You only touch the gun for Big Foot or one of his cousins. Right?"

Kelli nodded and mock saluted. "Does 'cousin' include Detective Rae?" Kelli asked sweetly with another teasing look in her eyes. Seeger wasn't one hundred percent sure she was teasing; there had been some tension between them, that was sure. Nonetheless Seeger placed the gun down. She turned and headed back to the bathroom. "I'll be right back." The bathroom door closed behind her. Kelli pulled the blanket and spread over herself and was asleep before Kim came out of the bathroom. Kim followed Kelli to sleep shortly thereafter.

26

While the women slept, at least he hoped they were, Scott pulled up in front of the Charleston City Police Department on Lockwood Street. Tucked away behind the Municipal Building, from the front you wouldn't even know it was there. He trudged up the stairs from the parking lot. It had been a long night and another day was just getting started. His watch showed 7:22, less than four hours before he had to be back at the hotel. *No nap for you, Scott, my boy.*

He sat at his government-issued metal desk and reached for a pen. He liked to make notes while everything was still fresh, but not in front of the civilians. He had found that note-taking made them feel more uncomfortable; more like a suspect than a victim.

Twenty minutes later he stood, stretched and headed for the ten year old coffee machine and stale coffee probably sitting there since last night. He made a fresh pot just in case. His mind kept churning while his hands mechanically installed a new filter, added enough coffee for a full pot of strong coffee, added water, and pushed the ON button.

Where to start? Too many potential suspects. Damn! Kelli might as well have taken out an ad in the Post and Courier and announced her travel plans. Start with the most obvious: her work, her neighbors, and that real estate agent. Get Kelli's phone logs, see if there's any kind of pattern to the calls; maybe the stalker isn't as smart as he thinks he is, or as he seems. Maybe he didn't use a prepaid phone. Unlikely. I'm not that lucky.

Run a background check on the housekeeper and her husband. And on Kelli. Get the cyber geeks to work on the cameras and bugs, if they can do it without alerting the stalker. Can they? Doubt it. This guy could be watching from anywhere, even his phone. The curse of technology. Maybe they can track them back to where they were sold. Is there any way to determine when they were installed? Kelli said she's gotten several hang-ups, did that mean she was being watched? It seems the messages she's gotten since she's been home, though, have been more specifically timed; he knew when she found the note. Maybe that means they were installed while she was gone; or was he watching the bedroom windows from somewhere nearby and made a lucky guess? The list of things to do and questions to get answered went round and round; he'd covered four pages of a legal pad with notes, and that didn't include the timeline he'd developed from Kelli's tale of the events or the list of potential suspects.

"Rae, need to talk to you."

Scott looked up and saw his lieutenant entering the squad room, removing his topcoat, still damp from the morning drizzle, as he headed for his office. Scott stood, grabbed his quickly-cooling mug of coffee, and followed the LT. Lieutenant Grouse looked like his namesake and was very sensitive about it, *probably because of having been teased as a child.*

"So what's been keeping you up at night?" Scott looked at his boss quizzically. How did he know about Kelli's case already? Scott hadn't had a chance to tell him.

The lieutenant grinned. "I've still got it you know. You're in casual clothes. You never get in this early unless you haven't been to bed. I haven't lost all my detecting skills just because I'm stuck behind this desk thirty-six hours a day." Chuck Grouse smiled at the younger man. He liked and respected Scott; Scott was a good cop and an even better detective. "So, what gives?"

As succinctly as possible Scott brought Grouse up to date on the past almost-eight hours, ending with his massive to-do list and even more extensive list of potential suspects. And he hadn't talked to the real estate agent yet.

"Okay, get some uniforms to canvas the neighborhood and Mrs. Cavanaugh's office. You take the real estate lady. Have Sissy get the phone logs and review them; she's good at finding patterns. Sissy Brewster – the only female on the team – had been nicknamed "Sissy" by Grouse's not-lamented, chauvinistic predecessor. Unfortunately the Southern nickname for "sister" stuck; by now it was a term of respect for their only female detective. Susanna had been on the force ten years longer than anyone else on the squad and they all respected her dedication and talents. Grouse rubbed his hands across his bald head; he feared this was going to be a long one. "I sure hope Sissy never retires; it was bad enough when she was on maternity leave."

Scott smiled, "You got that right, and I didn't even know her well then. I can't imagine what y'all went through." He'd come to feel like Sissy was truly an older sister in the eight years he'd been with CPD.

"Right. Where were we?" Grouse brought them back to the case.

Scott mentally reviewed his to-do list. "I'm going to get the cyber guys working on the technology, see what they can find. Sissy on the phones. Blues on the neighbors and co-workers. I've got the real estate lady. That leaves financials and background on Kelli and her grandparents. Any cameras in the area that might have picked up the perp or a car circling the block. If we still have nothing at the end of the day, we'll have to start on everyone who knew she was going out of town, which is practically everyone she knew, everyone in the whole damn city," Scott finished dispiritedly. The two men eyed each other, knowing what a time-consuming, and probably futile, task it could be to have to do backgrounds on everyone Kelli knew. "See what you can do to shorten that list," Grouse advised.

Scott tapped his index finger against his South Carolina Aquarium mug. "I think we're going to have to look at motive. Too many people knew she was going out of town and when; plenty of opportunity. Other than stalking and semi-threatening calls and notes, the only crime that has been committed is the E part of B&E. Not that stalking isn't serious, Kelli is scared out of her mind and I don't blame her. I'd just as soon we catch this guy before he becomes violent."

"I'm with you, Scott. It's not often we get to stop a murder or a rape before it happens. That would be quite a coup, locally and maybe even nationally."

Scott could see Grouse's wheels turning. He liked his boss because he was not one to play politics and many times had fought "the brass", as the top-most police officials were called collectively, when others would have taken the politically safe route. Grouse was also realistic enough to know good press never hurt. "Charleston has a low crime rate, compared to similar-sized cities in the South, and I'd like to keep it that way. Looks like you've got your work cut out for you. Just remember, this is a low priority case…unless something happens to Mrs. Cavañaugh. Get to it." Grouse reached for his phone as a way of enforcing the dismissal.

Scott was not offended by his boss's brusqueness; after eight years he was used to it. And he was right. He did have a lot to do.

Back at his desk Scott made the requisite phone calls to get the canvasses started. He left a voice mail for the real estate agent to call him ASAP – as soon as possible; he even left his cell number which he tried never to give out.

He called Stu in the cybercrimes unit and filled him in on the cameras and bugs and what he hoped they'd find. Scott apologized that he wanted Stu to do all this without letting on that he knew where the bugs were.

"We'll take a look," Stu said. Everyone joked that the sixty-year old had invented computers, not just personal ones, but when it came to ferreting out clues, there was no one better. And Scott was one of his favorites. Once Scott filled him in on the fact that it was the widow of a fellow officer, Stu's motivation jumped. "I'll get someone over there right away. Good chance to show the newbies how it's done," Stu chuckled and hung up on Scott, anxious to once again show his expertise and astound the department. Scott stared at the silent hand piece.

Scott looked at his watch as the desk phone rang: 9:08. A breathless female voice on the other end said, "Detective Rae? I'm sorry I didn't get back to you sooner. I had an early morning showing. Saturdays are my busiest day." As she took a breath to continue, probably with a sales pitch of some sort, Scott jumped in.

"Ms. Jackson. No problem. Thanks for returning my call, I'm sure you're very busy." Flattery was always a good ice breaker he'd found. Before the saleswoman could start again, Scott continued, "I need to talk to you about the open house you held at Kelli Cavanaugh's house about ten days ago."

"Why? Is something missing? I'm sure none of the brokers would have taken anything. Besides, Kelli assured me she had locked up anything of value or family significance. It's not her house anyway."

Scott wasn't sure what this last had to do with anything, but he let it pass. "No, nothing like that. Something else has come up and I just need your help. Do you have a list of everyone who attended the open house?"

Scott could hear papers rustling as if the woman was searching through piles on her desk. "Oh, somewhere here. I know my assistant has the list and she gave me a copy, but she's not here today. Her mother fell yesterday and broke her leg and the poor girl has gone over there to help out. Now really! On a Saturday? Fran knows that's our busiest day. It's not like she doesn't have siblings, and her father there to help out."

Scott halted this rambling monologue. "Do you think you could fax me a copy of the list?"

"What? Today? Didn't you just hear me say it's my busiest day and my assistant's not here?"

Scott waited her out, silence usually worked with these self-important types. "Well, I can call Fran and ask where her copy is. I'm much too busy to spend time searching for it. I have another showing in ten minutes."

Scott grinned and hoped it didn't show in his voice. "Thank you, Ms. Jackson. You have no idea how important your help is to our case." Scott laid it on as thick as he thought he could without gagging.

Slightly mollified, the woman responded, "Of course, Detective. I'll call her right now. Kelli's not in any trouble is she? She's such a sweet girl." Scott could hear the quest for gossip in her voice. "No, not a bit. I'd be happy to tell you about the case if you could spare me some time this afternoon. I'd like to go over the list with you, too, get your input on the names on it. Your expertise would be especially helpful." He thought he might barf, but anything for the case, and he was really good at charming the ladies, of all ages.

Teri Jackson purred into the phone, "Of course, Detective, anything I can do to help the police. And of course Kelli. Last year I helped raise over ten thousand dollars for the police widows and orphans fund. I know how difficult, and thankless, your job is." *Now who's pouring it on?* Scott grinned to himself.

Just then one of the CSU techs who had been at the house handed him a sheaf of pages. Scott mouthed "thanks" and started to glance through them as he listened to the woman go on and on about how she loved and respected the police, fire, and military. He had the phone wedged between his shoulder and chin and occasionally issued an "How nice" or "um hmm" in response to a brief silence on the other end. Each page was watermarked "Preliminary".

On the next to the last page a line was highlighted in yellow. Shocked, Scott slid his desk chair back and reached for his stack of file folders.

The voice on the other end of the phone inquired, "Detective Rae, are you there?"

"Yes, of course, Ms. Jackson, I was just making notes of your conversation."

"I said I can't meet you until at least six today, I have showings all afternoon and the last one is at four."

Distracted, Scott replied, "Perfect. I'll see you at your office at six. And you'll fax that list over right away? Thanks so much, Ms. Jackson." He put the phone down, grabbed his coat, and hurried out the door. He'd have to wake them a bit early, but he had to talk to Kelli now.

27

Where is she? He once more checked the video display on his smartphone, scrolling through the six active monitors. Since he worked in the back, usually there was no one to look over his shoulder to see what he was watching. *She left with those cops hours ago. The CSU people finished a while ago, didn't even find the last note. Still didn't find the cameras and bugs either. How useless can you get?* He grinned at his own intelligence. *She should be home by now. It's not fair that I have to work when I have to find her.* His dirty index finger hustled through the monitors again, showing nothing going on at the house on the Battery. *Nothing. She has to come home today or she'll mess up all my plans. We have to be together.*

At the same time Scott was banging on the door of room 316 at Mills House. Kim Seeger carefully opened the door, her gun held down by her left thigh. "No need to hammer, Scott. You said eleven and it's only 10:30," Seeger snarled.

Both women were dressed, Kim in her freshly pressed uniform and Kelli in slacks and a sweater; It was obvious they were just finishing breakfast. Kelli was seated on the far bed, balancing a plate of toast and a tea cup. Seeger's breakfast was on the small desk. Scott could see the remnants of a bowl of oatmeal, orange juice and coffee.

"And you got up on the wrong side of the bed. Let's talk." Scott motioned Seeger back to the desk chair while he moved over in front of Kelli. She smiled sweetly at him as she asked, "Coffee? I think there may be a cup left, Kim's only had one so far."

"Not now, thanks." He looked down at Kelli propped up against the headboard with what looked like every pillow in the room. "Your husband died about eight months ago, is that correct, Kelli?"

Confusion crossed her face. *Why is he asking that? Todd's death can't have anything to do with this stalker.* She gritted her teeth, confused and mad at the question. "Yes, June 24th of last year. It's easy enough for you to check. Why are you asking me that?"

"And since that time have you had sexual relations with anyone? Specifically, anyone in your own bed?"

Kelli turned bright red and almost dumped her plate and cup as she started to stand. She caught the dishes and set them onto the already-crowded nightstand between the beds. Then she stood and faced the detective, fury in her eyes. "I fail to see how that is any of anyone's business except my own, Detective Rae, and certainly not the business of the CPD." Her teeth were tightly clenched, her lips drawn and white, her arms crossed beneath her breasts. Kim, watching the exchange, thought Kelli looked as she had always imagined a banshee would look.

"It is my business, Mrs. Cavanaugh, because CSU found a great deal of semen stains in your bed. I assume the sheets have been changed at least once since June 24th," he snapped sarcastically as he stood and glowered down at her. "So we need to know if you can tell us who else might have been sexually active in your bedroom. Otherwise we will assume the stains were made by the intruder."

Kelli's face had turned from bright red to graveyard grey as she plopped onto the edge of her bed. "He was in my bed?" Her hand flew to her mouth as she rose and ran to the bathroom door, slamming it behind her. Kim and Scott could hear the distinct sounds of vomiting coming from beyond the bathroom door.

Kim Seeger just stared at Scott, "Well, you handled that well. You certainly won't get any awards for diplomacy." Now it was Scott's turn to be confused. "What? I don't think diplomacy is in my job description. She still hasn't answered my question."

Kim looked up at the tall man still standing in between the beds. "Yes, I think she has." She canted her head toward the bathroom. "She has not had sex with anyone since her husband died. And now she'll never sleep in that bed again, either. This guy has a lot of gall and a bad fixation on Kelli, if you ask me."

Kim walked over to the bathroom door and knocked. The toilet had flushed and water had been run in the sink. "Kelli? Sweetie? You okay?" Receiving no answer, Seeger tried the knob; unlocked. She opened the door, went in and closed it behind her.

Kelli was seated on the narrow side of the claw foot tub, a damp turquoise hand towel covering her face, muffling her sobs.

Kim sat down next to Kelli and put an arm around her shoulders. "It'll be okay, Kelli." She felt like she was comforting one of her kids, although there was less than six years between the two women. "We're going to find him and then he won't be able to bother you any more. But we need your help. Sometimes it's as much about eliminating suspects as it is focusing on one or two. You are the best help we have; we can't find him without you. Well, actually, we can; but it will take a hell of a lot longer."

Kelli could hear the smile in Kim's voice and lowered the towel, giving Kim a watery grin. "Okay, Kim, I understand. And I'll help, but make sure he," she indicated the man on the other side of the bathroom door, "shows some respect."

Kim continued to grin. "Will do. Wash your face and come on out. I know Scott has a million more questions. The sooner we start, the sooner we catch this pervert." Kim squeezed Kelli's shoulder one more time and exited the bathroom. The tub was big enough for two, but not the floor space.

Scott gave Kim a questioning look. Kim saw he had helped himself to some coffee after all. She gave him a thumbs up. "She'll be out in a minute. You know, you might remember that tact is not one of your many virtues. And remember she's the victim here. You could have phrased your question a bit more...delicately."

"Delicate! I'm trying to catch this guy before he..." Kelli walked out of the bathroom. Her eyes were red-rimmed but still fierce. She had brushed her hair and pulled it back into a ponytail. She was ready for battle. But battle with whom?

"Before he what, Detective Rae?"

Scott hesitated. "Nothing, Kelli; I'm sorry I upset you." What he didn't understand was why the tech report had upset *him* so much. "Can we start again?"

Kelli nodded and resumed her seat against the pillows. This time she pulled the blanket up to her chin, too. Scott sat on the edge of the other bed, facing her; Seeger adjusted her heavy belt and resumed her seat at the desk. She gave Kelli an encouraging smile.

Kelli turned her dark eyes back to Scott and regarded him coldly. "No, Scott, I have had no sexual relations since Todd – and my baby – died last summer. Not in that bed nor anywhere else."

Scott winced. He didn't remember if he ever knew she had lost a baby, too. Poor kid.

"Okay, isn't Sean your brother? Why is he on your calendar every weekend?"

28

Kelli pulled her knees up under her chin and rested her chin on them. Her arms and the hotel blanket were wrapped around her legs and shoulders; it seemed to Scott she might never get warm again, or maybe she's just one of those women who can't tolerate cold; he'd met a few. Kelli let out a deep sigh. *How many times do I have to go over this?*

She stared solemnly at the man seated on the side of the other bed. He looked nice enough, but most of them do. She knew better than to say anything that might get back to the prosecutors of Sean's case. Scott is still law enforcement and on the side of the angels; at least I used to think the prosecution was the side of the angels until all this came up. Used to think they worked to find the guilty and put them away so they couldn't hurt anyone else. But these two in Columbia seem to be looking for another notch in their belts rather than getting at the truth. There's a long, twisty road between legal and justice, and I think they took the fork to legal. Gathering her strength for one more recitation, Kelli began.

"Sean is my older brother. He and his family live in Columbia. On Labor Day last year he was arrested for long-term child abuse and first degree murder in the death of his two year old daughter – my niece and goddaughter – Molly. I'm sure you can look up the case.

"I try to go up there every weekend to give my sister-in-law Nora a break with the twins – they're eight – and to see Sean. I stay with Abbey and Christopher so Nora can get out of the house and have some time to herself, have a bit of a break from all the stress and worry. She hasn't had a chance to grieve since Molly died; no one has; Sean was arrested two weeks later, the day after Molly's funeral. We couldn't have the funeral sooner because the ME wouldn't release her body. Even though her organs had already been donated and removed."

Kelli gasped as she tried to control the rapidly rising sobs. Kim had come over and sat next to her on the bed, holding one of

Kelli's frozen hands in her own warm one. It was obvious to Scott Kelli had told this story many times and had managed to reduce it to its bare bones facts. He knew there was more to it. *Could someone related to Sean's case be involved with Kelli's? It seems far-fetched, but not impossible. Add that to the to-do-list.*

"My God, Kelli, I had no idea you'd been through so much." Kim put her arm around Kelli's shoulder but Kelli shrugged it off. She turned and gave Kim a watery smile. "Please don't be nice to me right now, I can handle everything okay unless someone is nice to me. I'm not much used to nice and I don't know what to do with it. It's not you, Kim, I know you mean well. It's just I'm teetering on the brink of an emotional breakdown and I have to be strong; I'm the only one who can be.

"Nora's a wreck, not unexpectedly. Sean can't do anything because he's in jail. So it's up to me to put a good face on everything and keep all the pieces and the family together. Sean had always been the strong one, my big brother, he took care of me after we were left here by our parents. Granny and Gramps have been great, but we never really knew them before we got here. It was just us against the Southern life-style, totally foreign to our BC – Before Charleston - lives." Kelli smiled a quick smile and croaked, "I'm trying." She cleared her throat, wiped her eyes with a tissue she pulled from her slacks pocket, straightened her back and turned back to the detective.

"Anything else you need to know about Sean, Detective?" For once there was now belligerence in her voice. Scott decided he liked the fighting Kelli better than the defeated one. Scott had been watching the rapport of the two women, close in age, but each different. Seeger so motherly, Kelli much stronger than she looked.

"Actually, yes. You need to start at Sean's arrest and tell me the details. I can get the facts from the prosecutor but it will be helpful to get your perspective. Could someone related to Sean's case be stalking you? Trying to put pressure on him by getting to you? Has he made any enemies while he's been in jail?"

Kelli laughed ruefully, "I don't see how I can be hurt any more. But I guess you mean physically. Do you really think I'm in danger?"

Scott looked at Kim and gave her a quick nod.

Kim turned to face Kelli more directly and forced Kelli to face her more head-on. "Kelli, we don't usually do anything about stalkers until they get physical. CPD just doesn't have the manpower to help every potential victim. Usually the best we can do is suggest you move, get an unlisted number, or get a dog." Kim smiled. "You're way ahead of us on the dog."

Kelli smiled back. "You haven't met Corky yet, she's a lover not a fighter. Though I'm sure she'd be very protective of me if I was in any outright danger; most dogs are I think, even the little ones." Kelli paused. "But why do I think you're treating this case differently? I've been with you all night, Kim, and not once did you mention me moving or getting a new phone number. Is it because of Todd? Because I'm part of the blue family?"

Scott took over. "Todd's death is part of it, law enforcement does try to take care of our own. But there's another side to it. It's the sophistication of the stalker and the notes. The notes constituted actual threats. His "we'll be together soon" lines make it sound like he has definite plans for you. The cameras and bugs require a level of know-how not common in your everyday "fascination stalker". A "fascination stalker" usually has a type: tall/short, dark hair/blonde, athletic/or not; you get the idea. But if thwarted, normally he'd just transfer his affections elsewhere, to someone else who fits his type. That isn't a permanent or useful solution for the cops, but it buys us some time. In this case, though, he seems fixated on *you*, not a type.

"I explained all this to my lieutenant and he agrees with me. The guy sounds like he's in love with you and ready to take it to the next level." Scott paused again, trying to gauge the impact his words were having on Kelli. Her back was stiff, her lips tight in a grim line, her chocolate brown eyes were focused on his face.

"As Kim explained to you this morning, we left the cameras and bugs in place so maybe we can trap him." Kelli shook her head.

"But won't he know you found them and left them there for just that purpose? Doesn't sound like he's stupid. If he was watching he saw those CSU people find them."

"First, I told the CSU techs ahead of time to do their best at ignoring the cameras, don't look right at them; usually they're not so good at ignoring evidence, but since they had a heads-up they think they were successful. They found six cameras: your bedroom, the upper hall, the front parlor, the foyer, the kitchen, and one in the dining room that could give a view all the way to the front windows. Phone bugs were in your bedroom phone and the kitchen phone." He paused again, not sure Kelli was ready for this next part.

"On the other hand, even if he guesses that we know about the cameras, we believe his desire for you will force him to keep watching." Kelli shivered and pulled the blanket tighter around her shoulders. "So I'm bait? Guinea pig?" The other two kept silent, allowing Kelli time to digest all she had heard.

Kelli exhaled and sat taller. "Okay, what do you want me to do?" Kim looked at Scott with a told-you-so kind of grin and he looked relieved. He could only work this case until something bigger came up so they needed to get ahead of the guy...assuming it is a guy. He leaned forward, elbows resting on his knees, hands clasped. He looked directly into Kelli's dark eyes.

"Let's start off with you telling me more about Sean's case. We've got detectives checking backgrounds on all the people and businesses you contacted before your trip, but that will take a while. Can you think of anyone who might gain from putting pressure on Sean?"

Kelli put her fingers to her temples and pushed. She shook her head. "After Molly died and Sean was arrested, some people set up a blog, calling Sean horrible names, ranting about him being a baby-killer, or a pedophile, or a child abuser. All those holier-than-thou types who have no idea what's going on or how much they're hurting the family. They even picket the courthouse every time Sean has a hearing. Sean is none of those things. He loves children; he would no more hurt a child than that," she looked around the room, "than that pillow would," she said pointing to the lone pillow remaining on Kim's bed.

"Unfortunately, Nora found out about the blog and checks it daily. I've tried to get her to stop, she's already a nervous wreck, but it's like an addiction; she can't stop. Hank, Sean's lawyer, told Nora not to respond to any of their postings. Her frustration at not being able to rebut any of the comments has just added to her stress. None of us can say anything to anybody because we never know who might be taking notes and reporting back to the prosecution.

"Then add the fact that Child Protective Services keeps hinting they might have to take the twins away from her; CPS sent a social worker to the house once a week for the first three months after Sean's arrest to talk to the twins and check the "home environment"; of course they found nothing, but still CPS hints that the twins might have to be put elsewhere, just in case." Kelli's voice started to rise, "Just in case of what? Sean's locked up and he's their scapegoat. Why would they have to remove the twins if Sean's supposed to be the one guilty of abuse?"

Scott gave her a minute to calm down. *Sounds like a royal screw up, maybe. Of course the family always claims innocence or frame-up.* "Do you know the blog address, Kelli?"

"Not off the top of my head. I read it the first month, then couldn't take it anymore. Those people are sick and malicious. Forget about innocent until proven guilty, let's just string him up now. Sean is a war hero and an FBI agent; he's given his life for his country; you'd think he would get a benefit of the doubt at least, but 'no' just give him a fair trial and then hang him. He's been in jail six months now without a trial, he's lost his job, his reputation is ruined, some of their neighbors won't let their kids play with the twins anymore; the twins are bullied at school. It just goes on and on. It makes no sense."

Kelli took a deep breath to try to calm her disgust at the judicial system and her rising blood pressure; she always got like this when she had to recount Sean's story. No matter how many times she told the story, nothing helped Sean. And that was the worst of it, her inability to do anything. She wrote him every day, knowing every letter and card would be read by someone at the jail, so she had to censor what she could say. The stress of her last eight months was unusual, to say the least; unbearable and intolerable, too. *I can come up with lots more adjectives if I have to.*

Scott looked at Kelli calmly and made a mental note to check the blog; it would probably come up if he Googled Sean's name. He'd see if he could read through the case files, too.

29

Scott leaned back, crossed his arms on his broad chest. *Right. Yet another 'innocent' victim persecuted by the system. Poor little rich boy can't take it in jail?*

"Okay. Your brother's a good guy who flipped out. I still don't see the point."

"Where do I begin? I just told you about CPS threatening to take the twins away. Isn't that enough? When the cops came to arrest Sean the morning of Molly's funeral, Gramps convinced the arresting officer – Mike Taylor, a walking caricature of a redneck cop if there ever was one: big belly, ketchup stains on his tie, poor fitting jacket, all he needed was buckteeth to make the picture complete – anyway, Gramps convinced him that Sean would surrender the next day. Clark agreed, pretty readily I might add considering Sean was supposed to be a child abuser, and said Sean would go before a magistrate and be home before dinner. Sean's been in jail ever since." Kelli clenched her hands around the blanket. She felt her blood pressure rising more.

"We're so confused and mad and frustrated, which I assume is normal under the circumstances. Unless, of course, you're used to all this. Every time I go visit Sean there are families there acting like they're on a picnic, laughing and joking. I've heard them talking about 'other times' they were there, like it's routine. But for those of us who find this all new and degrading, it's infuriating. Kelli took another breath. "Sorry. You asked. It's been a long six months of petty crap. The whole family is on edge, depressed, and scared. Nora hadn't even had a chance to grieve poor little Molly before all this was dumped on her."

Neither have you, Kim thought from next to Kelli.

"It all mounts up," she said softly. She looked defiantly at Scott. "Aren't CPS and the ME's Office arms of the prosecutor? It's not even the individual events I'm talking about. It's the cumulative effect on the whole family. She hesitated and then smiled. "But they don't know the Gannon family, and that includes Nora. We'll wait them out as long as necessary to prove Sean's innocence.

"It breaks my heart. Tell me, Scott, how would you feel if you were innocent and this happened to you?" Tears formed in her big brown eyes once again. "How would you feel, Scott?" she whispered.

Again he hesitated, giving the question time to fade from the room's atmosphere. He looked at Kim, who gave a tiny shrug, and then back at Kelli. His voice had an edge to it now. "Do you really believe the blog people or people associated with law enforcement are out to get you so they can get at Sean?"

Kelli continued to stare at him. Then her shoulders slumped and she gave up. "No, not really. As much as I hate everything they've done to us and I would love to believe they're behind all this, I just can't. That tiny shred of faith in the judicial system that remains won't let me think even they would go this far. Despite all the unintended consequences we have had to handle – and the intended ones- I don't really believe they're behind this. The family is just collateral damage." She smiled a wavering smile at Scott and Kim. "Damn! I wanted to go after them."

She looked up at Scott. "So now what? Back to square one?"

"Not quite. I'm going to drop you and Kim at your house, Kelli. You can unpack and try to get your life back to some semblance of normal. While you do that, I'm going to the office and see what we've found from all our morning's research and legwork. I'll be back at your house about seven this evening and bring you and Kim up to date."

All three stood. Kelli and Kim grabbed their keycards from the nightstand. "We can shred these at the house," Kelli told Kim. Kim nodded and glanced triumphantly at Scott, as if to say, "She's no dummy. She was married to a LEO after all; give her some credit."

They left the hotel and headed for Scott's car parked in the loading zone on the Queen Street side of the hotel. Suddenly Kelli stopped in her tracks. "What?" Kim asked worriedly, her hand sliding to her holster. She noticed Scott's hand had slid under his jacket as well. "Did you see something?"

"Corky! The kennel is only open until two on Saturdays. I have to go get her."

The other two visibly relaxed and smiled sheepishly at each other.

"Is it okay if I go get her? I really hate for her to have to stay another night." Kelli tried not to look too pleading.

Scott relented. He'd never had a dog but knew how attached some people could become to theirs. "Sure go get her, as long as Seeger goes with you."

30

Late Saturday morning

"Perfect! Corky will love you, Kim."

The three got into Scott's unmarked Crown Vic and he drove the three blocks to Kelli's house. Scott silent, the women, mostly Kelli, talking about the dog they would soon see. Scott pulled up next to the line of parked cars and the women got out and retrieved Kelli's luggage. He waved briefly as he drove off. Once more the women hefted Kelli's wheelie up the steps.

As they went through the tall front doors, Kelli gaped at the interior of her grandparents' home. There was forensic dust everywhere, drawers not completely closed, furniture left just a bit off from the carpet indentations. She sighed. "I see Magda and I have our work cut out for us. She'll have a heart attack, she's such a perfectionist."

Each woman grabbed an end of the wheelie and hefted it up the ornate central staircase. "Glad you are here, Kim, and not just because you're helping with my suitcase." Kelli smiled down at the other woman as her feet hit the second floor landing. Kelli up-righted the suitcase and rolled it to her bedroom. She had to keep a firm hold on herself not to take a look at the camera she now knew was over the bathroom door, nestled into an arrangement of silk magnolias. Scott had told her it had a wide angle lens so the whole room was visible. She hated it!

As they hefted the suitcase onto the bed Kim asked, "So what's the latest on Sean?"

"Whew! Thanks, Kim. I have to say I've learned a lot about the judicial system, I guess I should limit it to the court system, since dealing with all Sean has been going through." While she started unpacking her suitcase, Kelli said, "There's so much logistics involved, you'd think it was the Normandy invasion. Every time there's a hearing, everybody has to be there: the trial judge, the prosecutor, the defense attorney, and Sean. They have to bring him from the jail he's in to the processing facility and then to the courthouse. So they have to find a date that works for everybody but Sean; as he says, 'he's nothing but available.'" Both women grinned at each other.

"Sounds like he's keeping his sense of humor anyway," Kim observed.

"That's about it. Hank, our attorney, filed a show-cause motion before I left asking why the ME's office shouldn't be held in contempt for not complying with the judge's previous order telling them to provide the report by Jan. 15. They didn't and now it's February and still no report. I've been away and haven't talked to Hank since before I left. He'll probably call tomorrow or Monday."

"Even as a cop I'm dumbfounded by the slowness of all this. Of course I've only been involved in what I would consider "big" cases in my eight years on the force, so I don't have a lot of cases to go by," Kim responded.

"Bless his heart, Sean is so bored! Nothing to do and twenty-three hours a day to do it in. We finally figured out he could receive subscriptions so Gramps and I sent him newspaper and magazine ones; they have to come directly from the publisher. Nora was able to reroute subscriptions he was getting at home. I tried sending him books directly from Amazon, but they were a no-no. The jail returned them, unopened. Of course, many times the COs read the magazines and newspapers before they get around to giving them to Sean. And they're not even *Playboy* or *Cosmo*."

She straightened her back. "There. All unpacked and put away. Let's go get Corky. I'll feel much better once she's home."

Kelli grabbed a stack of clothes still sitting on the bed. "I'll drop these at the cleaners after we get her. Then we can get to-go from Hall's and bring it home. Corky loves their fries." Kelli grinned again, obviously regaining her balance after the previous night's sleeplessness.

Kim grinned back, "Sounds good to me. I don't get there any too often, as in never, on my pay grade." Kim adjusted her thick black leather belt and followed Kelli back down the staircase.

31

"She's back! She's on her way. I'll see her soon." He'd overheard the conversation in Kelli's bedroom. His smile lit up the room full of equipment but there was no one else to see. He smiled at his smartphone, watching Kelli and the cop exit the kitchen door. "Won't be long," he murmured.

"Did you say something," the older man asked as he walked in.

"No, no, just muttering to myself about an email I got."

"Well, turn off the phone and get back to work. We've got customers waiting."

Screw you. Soon I'll be out of here and not answering to you anymore. Kelli and I will be together. He paused in his twisted thoughts. *But I have to get rid of that lady cop first.*

"Kelli, hey! Corky's been missing you." Vivian once again greeted Kelli with a broad smile that dimmed a bit as she lifted an eyebrow toward the police officer entering behind her.

Kelli laughed. "I know that's not true. I think Corky is happier here than at home. Here she had people around her all day." She looked over at Kim, "Kim, this is Vivian. She runs the place."

Kim reached across the raised reception desk and shook hands with the woman who had risen at their entrance. "Hey. I'm a friend of Kelli's. Just came off shift and haven't had a chance to change." The two women smiled, obviously liking what they saw in each other.

Vivian's smile widened. "I was afraid you'd followed her in here to give her a speeding ticket. That road leading up here is a favorite for speed traps." Vivian reached for the phone. "I'll have Corky brought up front right away." She spoke into the phone, "Bill, would you or Jeremy bring Corky up. There's somebody here who wants to see her." She turned back to Kelli, "It'll just be a minute. So how was your vacation?" Vivian leaned her hip against the desk, taking some of the weight off her sore right knee, "an old football injury," she told people who noticed her favoring her right side.

Watching the hallway for her dog, Kelli replied distractedly, "Nice. Very nice. But it's nice to get home, too."

A mad scrabble of nails against tiles indicated Corky had heard her voice from around the corner and was dragging the person on the other end of the leash as hard as she could. Kim heard heavy breathing too, as Corky labored to get to Kelli. A laughing deep voice said, "Hold on, Cork, wait for me."

A large cinnamon colored Golden Retriever lunged around the corner, her red leash hitting the floor as she galloped for Kelli. An obviously frustrated attendant hurried in her wake.

"Knew it had to be you, Kelli, you're the only one she gets this excited about," the attendant said with a shy smile.

Kelli was kneeling on the hard tiles, nose to nose with her dog, Corky's huge front paws bouncing off the floor. Kim was standing aside, a bit overwhelmed by the size of the dog. "She must weigh, what? A hundred pounds?"

"Not quite," Vivian replied, still smiling. "Ninety-six. She's a really big female."

Kelli stood and turned to the dog handler, "Jeremy, you've been giving her too many treats. She's gained weight since I left her here." At her mock serious tone, Jeremy hung his head, lanky brown hair falling over his face. Then he looked up and smiled a winning smile. "I can't help it, Kell. I've known her since she was a puppy. I even went with Todd when he went to pick her up. Remember? So I guess I've known her even longer than you."

A shadow crossed Kelli's face briefly at the mention of Todd, but she shook it off. "Where are my manners? Kim, this is Jeremy Deets, dog handler extraordinaire. Jeremy this is my friend Kim Seeger. She's going to be staying with me for the weekend." Kelli reached over and gave Jeremy a one-armed hug while she continued her attention on her dog.

Kim said nothing, just smiled at the nice-looking young man and nodded her head, the big dog in the way precluding the opportunity for another handshake. Kim stood back and continued to listen. Kelli seemed awfully familiar with "the help", but maybe that's just her way.

A sarcastic voice came over the intercom, "Need Jeremy back here if he can spare the time."

Jeremy shrugged his shoulders and handed the leash to Kelli. "Duty calls." He patted Corky one last time, hugged Kelli, and headed back down the hallway.

Vivian broke the silence, "He's great with all the animals, but there's no doubt Corky is his favorite."

"And Corky loves him," Kelli replied as Corky tried to pull her out the front door. "If he could only teach her to walk calmly on a leash. Bye, Viv," Kim laughed as Corky got out the door and Kelli struggled to point her in the direction of the car. Kim followed bemusedly, *maybe getting a dog for the kids needs some more thought.* Kim was relieved to see Corky get into the back seat, she had been afraid she would want to ride up front, in her lap.

Apparently reading Kim's thoughts, Kelli said, "Corky loves to ride in the front. But she got so big Todd trained her to ride in the backseat without complaint. The 'without complaint' was the hard part, Corky can whine like you would not believe." Kelli smiled at Kim and fastened her seat belt.

"We'll just run real fast to the cleaners and then lunch. You okay with that?"

"Whatever works for you, Kelli. We had that late breakfast so I'm fine. Besides, I'm just along for the ride." Kelli backed out of the parking space and headed back to town.

Kim decided she might be able to do some subtle sleuthing on her own. "Jeremy and Vivian seem very nice."

Kelli's grin widened. "Aren't they? The whole staff is like that. Even though the kennel is a bit of a drive from the house in town, Todd picked it because he'd heard good things about them from my grandparents. We just love everybody there," she ruffled the big head resting on the center console. "Don't we, girl." Corky's eyebrows twitched. "Even Bill. The disembodied voice on the intercom? He's big and gruff, but so gentle with the animals. I always think of Santa without the beard when I see him."

"So you've known everybody there for what? Four years?"

"Just about. Except Jeremy and Bill; I've known them since high school. Corky will be four in May. Todd got her for me for our first anniversary, the end of June. She swallowed and spoke softly. "This year would have been our fifth. Our baby would be almost a year old." She swallowed again, shook her head and gave Kim a small smile.

"Sorry. I really am trying to do better. Not inflict my pain on everybody else. Sometimes something just catches me by surprise." Kelli shook her head again.

Kim reached over and patted Kelli's hand on the steering wheel; Corky's head raised watchfully. "Don't worry, Kelli. I'm a pretty good listener. I mean, shit! After all you've been through you're entitled to feel sorry for yourself now and then."

"Thanks, Kim. I have been seeing a grief counselor and she's helped a lot. I think there's a lot to be said for this 'talk therapy.' It's nice to have someone objective to talk everything over with, somebody who's not involved in Todd, the baby, Sean, and now this whoever he is who's after me. Dena is a nonjudgmental ear. She just listens and then offers suggestions. This way I get to vent without burdening my family." Kelli smiled. "I've tried yelling into a mirror, but I get the strangest reactions back, and absolutely no words of wisdom." Both women laughed, easing the somber mood.

"I think that's what I miss most about Todd. Having someone I could talk to about anything and everything. And he understood. He was a really caring person."

"While we're talking about Todd, what's the latest on his case? I don't remember hearing anything recently." Kim knew Scott was reviewing the case file to look for any possible leads to Kelli's stalker, but never miss the chance to collect more information, especially from someone so closely involved.

Kelli sighed. "It's gone cold, as best I can tell. No videos of the area around Publix that show anything helpful. Whoever he was, he wore a hoodie, the current coward's choice of apparel. No witnesses who were worth a flip, even though it was eighty-five degrees and here stands a man in a hoodie and sunglasses. No forensics. Todd's best friend, Dean, is keeping an eye on the case and bugging the Summerville detectives as much as he can. Of course they're thrilled to have a state trooper looking over their shoulders, as you can imagine. Dean checks in on me once a week, keeps my chin up, gets me out of the house, that sort of thing.

"Bless his heart, he has as isolated a life as I do these days." She sighed again. "But I know from talking to Todd and Dean and watching every cop show on TV that it's going to take a lucky break to solve his murder. Random shootings with no witnesses are probably harder to solve than terrorist attacks." She sighed again. "It doesn't matter, really. Nothing is going to bring Todd back, whether the case is solved or not." Kelli turned into the cleaners' parking lot.

As Kelli started to get out, Kim put a hand on her arm and said," You know, you're right, a large part of solving crimes is luck. Or intuition. Or gut feelings. Call it what you want. But a lot of it is dogged determination, too. And a cop-killing won't go unsolved. Not around here anyway. There are too few of us to let a good one go unavenged. Todd's shooting may have been random, maybe not. Somebody will figure it out. It might not be this year, or next, but eventually it will be solved. I promise."

The two women stared at each other a moment. A small spark started deep in Kelli's eyes. She'd lost Todd and found a friend. Not a perfect trade-off, but better than nothing.

Kelli squeezed Kim's hand where it rested on her forearm and smiled, "Thanks, Kim, that helps. You help." She reached into the back seat, pushed Corky off the stack of clothes, and opened her door.

"I'll just be a minute." She exited the car into the bright sunlight of early February in Charleston, almost spring. Corky sat up in the back seat and watched carefully as Kelli entered the small storefront shop. She put one paw up onto the center console and leaned forward to get a better view.

Kim put her hand up and patted the big fluffy head. "She's okay, Corky. She's getting better. And we'll keep her safe, won't we?"

Corky turned and looked solemnly at the policewoman, her golden eyes staring deeply into Kim's. Kim laughed and ruffled Corky's mane. "You almost have me convinced to get a dog for the kids. But only if I could be sure to get one like you."

32

Saturday afternoon

Kelli hustled inside the glass door of the dry cleaners. Bert was seated behind the cash register. He stood as she entered and gave her his biggest smile.

"Kelli, great to see you! How was your trip?" He craned his neck to see through the reflection on the windshield. "Corky with you?"

"Of yes, just got her back from the kennel. She'll be happy to see you. As much as she loved the kennel, she loves being home more."

Bert smiled his genuine, but slightly vague, smile and reached for a dog cookie from the bowl on the counter. Kelli was accustomed to his vagueness. She also knew his face belied an exceptionally technical mind. He could build machines or take them apart or fix anything. Mr. Sanchez said Bert had saved him a lot of money in repair costs; something broke, Bert fixed it, from conveyor belts to computers.

"Where's Mr. Sanchez? Taking the day off?" Kelli asked with a grin. She and Bert both knew the store was Mr. Sanchez's life, he never took a day off.

"No, he's taking a late lunch. Said he had some errands to run. He'll be sorry he missed you."

"He must be feeling really secure if he left you alone," Kelli said encouragingly.

Bert stood a bit straighter. "Yep. He's been doing it lots lately. I think his knee pain is slowing him down a bit. Plus, he doesn't sleep well. Some days he looks like he's been up all night." Bert paused and looked toward the back. "You picking something up?"

"No, just dropping these off." Kelli pushed the stack of blouses and slacks across the counter so Bert could reach them better.

"Tuesday okay?" Bert asked.   Kelli nodded. "You can just leave them, I'll do the ticket after I give Corky her cookie."

The two headed out to the car as Kelli said, "By all means, let's not keep Corky waiting." Bert opened Kelli's door and then the rear door as Kelli climbed into the front. He reached in to give Corky a pat and the cookie. "Wow! A police officer! Cool! What'd you do, Kelli?" Bert laughed in his high-pitched way at his own joke. He scratched Corky's ears as she inhaled the Milk Bone.

"Bert, this is my friend Kim. She just got off her shift; we're on our way to my house for a girls' night."

"Have fun," Bert said as he slammed the back door and turned back toward the shop.

Kelli put the car in gear and looked at Kim, her silence deafening. "What?"

"Do you always do that? Tell everyone you meet your plans?"

Kelli caught her breath. "Oh for heaven's sake." Then she caught herself. "I guess maybe I do. Up until now I've never really thought about it. Guess I'll have to watch it in the future."

Kim tried to calm the air. "He seems nice. He scared me half to death when he just opened the door and reached in. I didn't know how Corky would react."

Kelli laughed. "No problem. Corky knows Bert gives her cookies, so he's an immediate friend. She's a firm believer in not biting the hand that feeds her." Both women grinned as Kelli continued, "Bert's a doll. My grandmother has been coming to this dry cleaner since before Sean and I moved here. Bert's a little slow, mentally, but really good with tools and stuff. A couple years ago Mr. Sanchez hired him and it's been a great match, especially since Mr. Sanchez's knee surgery. Even after Todd and I got married and lived in Cane Bay, I still came here. Since I visited Granny once a week anyway, it wasn't like it was out of my way; just drop stuff one week, pick it up the next. Bert and Mr. Sanchez are both so sweet."

Kim made a mental note to have them both checked out.

"Now, how about some lunch? It's after two and I'm getting hungry." Without another word Kelli headed to Hall's on King

Street, just a few blocks from the Battery. The ten minute ride was spent debating menu options. They finally both settled on Hall's steak sandwiches with fries for Corky and Kim phoned it in. Kelli miraculously found a parking spot around the corner from the restaurant. She hustled in and got their order then drove the three of them home for a well-earned lunch. After lunch Kelli started a load of delicates, hoping to get something dry before she ran out of underwear. Fortunately she always packed extra on her trips.

33

While Kim and Kelli were running errands and then enjoying their sandwiches, Scott was catching up with all the field reports. Nothing unusual from the neighborhood canvas, except one report of a light in the upstairs while Kelli was out of town. Nothing on the house phone logs other than what he had expected: several calls from prepaid, throwaway phones, lots of heavy breathing but nothing else and no way to trace the phones. Kelli's credit reports were as expected, too: clean. *She's a librarian. What do you expect?* Scott continued wading through pages of reports, skipping lunch and fueling up on bitter coffee.

He looked at the employee lists from the places Kelli had visited the previous week: at least the ones they'd been able to get over the weekend. He immediately cut the lists in half by crossing out the female-sounding names. The caller's voice had been male so he'd start there. Stalkers usually worked alone so Scott doubted there was a female involved. He'd show the lists to Kelli this evening and see if she had any vibes about any of the names. Or maybe she could eliminate some of the names. *Legwork. The most tedious part of police work, but always the most productive. Except for luck, of course.* Scott smiled to himself remembering his conversation with Kelli about luck.

Then he paused and thought about Kelli some more. *She's tough. A lot tougher than I'd have expected from a librarian. Am I stereotyping? And smart. And brave. I think I want to learn more about Kelli Cavanaugh.*

All he needed now was the list from the real estate lady, since she hadn't faxed it yet. He looked at the round atomic clock on the wall over the coffee station: 5:40. "Shit! I'm supposed to meet her at 6:00." He jumped up, grabbed his topcoat off the coat rack. Opting for the stairs over the aging elevator he hurried down the three concrete flights and out into the darkening evening. He hustled to his car, the cold wind billowing his coat behind him and snatching his breath away. *Damn! I thought today was supposed to be warmer.* He jumped into the car, slammed his key into the ignition and headed out.

Fortunately, the drive was just a few blocks. But with Charleston's narrow one-way streets you just never knew. He pulled in behind the Carolina Elite Properties building and parked in one of their two "reserved for clients" spaces. 5:57 by his watch. *Perfect.* He opened his door and hurriedly walked around the lavender-stuccoed cinder block building, buttoning his coat and pulling on gloves as he went. He was almost done insulating himself when he entered the overheated lobby and had to start undoing what he had struggled to complete. *Oh, well, the joys of the South in winter.*

Scott walked over to the receptionist's desk. Looking at the name plate on her desk he said, "Hi, Rachel. I'm here to see Teri Jackson." He gave his most winning smile. Few women could resist a six footer with a broad chest, dark hair, dark eyes, and that smile. The teenager at the desk was not about to be the first.

"Mr. Rae? Ms. Jackson just called. She's running a bit late but should be here in about ten minutes. If you'd like to have a seat?" She smiled her most seductive smile and waved her hand like Vanna White toward the empty fiberglass chairs across the utilitarian lobby.

Scott looked at them with decided lack of interest. "I'll stand, thanks. Been sitting a lot today." He smiled again.

"Can I get you some coffee or water or something?"

Scott held her gaze a moment and then, "Coffee would be great, thanks. Black."

Rachel stood and pulled her mid-thigh length sweater tighter across her thin chest and wiggled her way down the hall behind her desk. There was no noise in the office except the low voices coming from *The Weather Channel* on a TV in the corner of the lobby. *Everybody must be out on 'showings' or at home watching the Pro Bowl. Lucky them. I don't even remember who won the Super Bowl last week. What a week it's been!*

The teenager returned with Scott's coffee in a Styrofoam cup with a java sleeve that said *List with Carolina Elite Properties; you won't regret it* in dark red script. Rachel tried moon-eyes at the older man, but figured out she was getting nowhere. She returned to her desk and busied herself with her cellphone.

Scott strolled around the lobby, picking up and putting down the variety of real estate magazines displayed on the end tables. He searched and found Teri Jackson's photo on the office's wall of fame. Just as he found her 8x10 glossy he heard the glass door open behind him. He recognized her immediately, even all bundled up. He put his cup with the dregs of his coffee on top of one of the magazines and went to meet her before the door had closed completely.

"Ms. Jackson," he said as he helped her out of her coat.

"Mr. Rae." She emphasized the 'Mr.', obviously not wanting her office, namely Rachel, to know he was a cop, bad for business he was sure. "Sorry I'm late," she wheezed, not sounding sorry at all. Scott had draped the stout woman's unflattering purple boiled wool coat over his arm. She gave him a tentative smile as she removed her lime green cloche and matching mittens. "Let's talk in my office."

Teri marched down the hall behind Rachel's desk and entered the last office on the right. "Have a seat," she directed Scott as she closed the door behind him, retrieved her coat from his arm, tossed it onto a chair next to her desk, and plumped herself into the high-backed desk chair.

Her soft brown, bird-like eyes looked soberly into Scott's dark ones. "I really don't know what else I can tell you, Detective. I have the list of everyone who attended the open house last week." She pulled it from a pile on her desk and handed it to him. Scott gave it a cursory glance.

Scott smiled "the smile" that had worked for him through the years and said, "Please call me Scott. I appreciate your time, Ms. Jackson. Sometimes, though, when people talk out loud, it sparks memories they didn't know they had." He handed the list back to the Realtor. "Would you mind looking over the list again. It's only fifteen names."

She took it from him. "Sure, but I really don't..." She stopped as she got to the last name. "Oh, right, I had forgotten about him." She had the good grace to blush. "I didn't actually review the list before. I just had my assistant pull it together for me." She looked uncomfortable.

She tapped the copy paper page in front of her. "This one, the last name? He wasn't actually a broker." Her cheeks turned a darker red. Scott's left eyebrow crooked up.

"I *never* do this, you understand, but he seemed so nice. He walked in just a little after I'd started the open house, about 12:30, I think. Said he had seen the For Sale sign and the open door and wondered if he could take a quick look around." She hesitated, trying to recall as much as she could to appease the detective for not remembering sooner.

"He had on a Brooks Brothers suit and Italian leather loafers, I remember. Glasses. Nice looking in a prep school kind of way, if you know what I mean; not rugged like you." She blushed again. Did he think she was flirting? She hurried on. "He said he and his wife were moving here, to Charleston, and he was here on business and just happened to see the sign." She snapped her fingers. "I remember, he said his wife was coming to town the next week, guess that would have been last week, and he was trying to narrow down her search. He knew she would love the Battery and just wanted to take a quick look around." She looked directly at Scott. "Now that I think about it, he never called back to make an appointment." She looked royally miffed, as only a salesperson who has lost a possibly lucrative sale can look.

"Anyway, he was very nice, well-spoken, well-mannered." As much as to say "He couldn't have done anything wrong." Scott bit his tongue and maintained his silence. Teri Jackson scowled, either from straining her memory or at Scott's silence, he wasn't sure which. He could feel the subtle prickle of success on the back of his neck that told him something important was coming.

"Of course I told him it was just not done, but he was so nice and so sincere, I let him look around, but just the downstairs. He said his main interest was the kitchen anyway."

Scott smiled encouragingly. "Was he alone or were you with him?"

Ms. Jackson sat up straighter in her chair. Her eyes searched the ceiling for an answer that would put her into a good light. Scott thought she looked like a plump pigeon with its feathers ruffled. Ms. Jackson took a deep breath, "Oh, the hell with it." She'd given up trying to get out of telling him something. Scott held his breath.

"I seem to recall that just as we got to the kitchen door I was called upstairs to answer some questions about one of the bathrooms. That's why I told him to stay downstairs until I got back." She squirmed in her leather chair. "That seemed the prudent thing to do. If he was a thief there wasn't much he could steal from the kitchen. And I did hurry."

Scott maintained his silence but fuming at the woman's stupidity. She'd probably be in breach of contract, too, but that was not his problem. "Anything else you can remember?" His tone was less than warm.

"Yes!" She said in a remorseful voice. "He left very quickly, before I even got back downstairs. He hollered up to me that he'd just remembered a meeting or something. Next thing I knew, he was gone." She tried to smile at the disbelief on Scott's face. "I did get him to sign in, though. That should help you, won't it?"

Scott looked at the name: HArold HAnnigan. HA HA. He decided he still needed the lady's help so he wouldn't tell her exactly how little help the name would be, if this was their guy, and he thought it was.

"Do you think you could help a police artist come up with a sketch of the man?"

Eager to make amends, Teri Jackson replied, "I certainly can try, but I'm not very good at remembering faces. I'm much better at names." She smiled weakly again. "But I'm certainly willing to try."

Scott rose without smiling. "You know where CPD headquarters is? On Lockwood Street? Could you be there in an hour? I'll have a police artist ready to work with you."

"Of course, an hour, I'll be there." She paused and smiled up at the man. "Does Kelli have to know about this? I'd hate to lose this listing."

Scott stared at her in disbelief and no small amount of disgust, turned on his heel and left the small office. *Save me from salespeople!*

34

Saturday evening

A little after seven Scott parked a block away from Kelli's on the bay side of the street. He turned off the engine and stared at the tall house down the street, upstairs and downstairs lights twinkling through the light rain. Slowly he reviewed his day, listening to the light plink of raindrops on the roof and windshield.

He couldn't figure out why this was happening to Kelli. *Not because of her money; besides, according to her financials, most of the insurance money she received when her husband died has been used on her brother's attorney. She seems like a nice person. A librarian for God's sake.* This made him smile. Maybe if he could figure out the *why* then he could figure out the *who*. The list of possible suspects was too cumbersome to prove helpful anytime soon, but maybe Kelli could help reduce the list. Maybe a name on the list would spark a thought or a memory. He was worried that, from the tone of the notes, the stalker was ready to strike, and soon.

Scott pulled up the collar of his topcoat and wished he was the type to wear a hat or carry an umbrella. Instead he slammed the car door, beeped the lock closed, and walked hurriedly across the street and into the shelter of the dripping oak trees in Battery Park. In the dark the stolid Civil War cannons looked like fat cigars pointed at Ft. Sumter. His heel caught on the uneven pavement but he caught himself before he landed in a big puddle at the intersection of South Bay and East Bay. A few more feet and he ran up the front steps of the Ellsworth home. He rang the bell and wondered why the front porch did not have some kind of portico to keep visitors dry on nights like this.

Kim opened the door and let him into the true entrance hall. He stopped between the two sets of double doors and removed his topcoat. He figured it was better to shake it off here, over the inlaid tiles, than inside over the polished wood floors. "Hey" they greeted each other as Kim relocked all the doors.

"Kelli's in the kitchen cooking. Bring your coat in there before it drips all over," Kim ordered, sounding much like Scott's older sister, even though he knew she was six years younger than he. He smiled and obediently followed her to the kitchen, holding his coat as close to his body as he could to avoid dripping and any further scolding.

"Hey! You're soaked! There are towels in that drawer to the right of the sink," Kelli indicated with her hip as she continued stirring something that smelled Italian.

Scott hung his coat on the back of a bar stool and grabbed a towel. Rubbing his face and hair, he commented, "Smells good. I haven't eaten much since..." he paused in thought. "I guess dinner last night. I didn't even realize I was hungry until I started smelling this." He lowered the towel and sniffed the air again appreciatively, smiling at both women.

"Nothing exotic. Help yourself to a beer or wine; wine's in the wine frig behind me, beer's in the big frig. Or something stronger if you prefer; liquor is in the sideboard in the dining room." Kelli continued stirring, adding pinches of Kosher salt and fresh ground pepper as the ingredients cooked.

"Beer's perfect, thanks." Scott pulled a Sam's Winter Ale from the refrigerator and unscrewed the top. He saw "the girls", as he referred to them in tandem, were having white wine, probably Chardonnay from the deep amber color.

Scott turned to Kim. "You look comfortable. I don't think I've ever seen you out of your uniform." He blushed at his choice of words. It was so difficult talking to women these days. Kim and Kelli broke into peals of laughter.

"And you never will, Scott Rae. I'm very happily married, remember?" Scott wasn't sure if the other two were laughing with him or at his discomfort.

Kim settled the question. "Oh, come on, Scott, lighten up. Kelli loaned me these." She indicated the stretchy pants and sweatshirt she was wearing, "So I wouldn't be quite so conspicuous. We played with Corky in the yard and decided blonde hairs all over my uniform were not a good idea."

That reminded Scott that he hadn't seen the dog yet. There'd been no sign of her since he came in. "So where is she? Locked outside?"

Kim tilted her glass toward Kelli. Scott stood and looked over the bar and saw a large goldish-brown dog resting on the floor next to Kelli. The dog's big head rested on her forepaws and her eyebrows twitched at his perusal. Otherwise, she didn't move. Scott could tell she was watching him very closely, however.

"Whoa! Some watchdog. I guess as long as people trip over her they're in big trouble?" Scott asked with a slightly snide tinge to his voice.

Kelli gave him a long appraising look. *Must not know much about dogs.*

"Oh, she's protective. But we've been apart for almost two weeks and it's hard for her to leave me. She's used to Kim now and since Kim let you in Corky decided you must be okay." She glanced at the dog and back at Scott with a twinkle in her eye, "But I'd say the jury's still out on you. Probably better if you don't get too close to either me or Kim."

Scott laughed. "What would that big powder puff do? Sit on me?" He moved around the counter and closer to Kelli. Corky's head came up. Scott took another step. Corky's hackles rose and a soft growl started deep in her throat. "Hush, Corky, it's okay. He's just playing." Kelli turned and gave Scott a schoolmarm look. "Really, Scott, go sit down. You do not want to upset her. I promise you." Scott took another step. Corky jumped to her feet and moved solidly between Kelli and Scott with a look that said, "You have to go through me, big boy." Scott threw up his hands with a dry chuckle and returned to his seat next to Kim at the other side of the bar. "Okay, point taken. You're in good hands – paws – with Corky here. Does she sleep inside or out?"

"With me."

"In your room?"

"On my bed."

Scott stared at her, dumbfounded. "Isn't she kinda large?"

"I prefer 'snuggly'." Again the women looked at Scott's face and laughed. Corky's tail thumped.

"I take it you've never had a dog either?" Kim chortled. "Corky has me almost convinced to get a dog for the kids. I'm just not sure I'd get one as beautiful or as smart as Corky. She has spoiled me already." Again Corky's tail thumped.

Kelli piped up, "Not to change the subject, but let's eat."

The three moved to the breakfast room table which Kim had set earlier under Kelli's direction to the location of plates, glasses and utensils. Kim poured more wine while Kelli spooned her concoction onto the plates. Then she returned the skillet to the stove and returned with a loaf of freshly baked whole grain bread.

"Smells good and looks gorgeous," Scott said enthusiastically, helping Kelli with her chair. "What's in it?"

Kim gaped at him. "You sound just like my son, but he's six. Don't tell me you're a picky eater?" The women were aghast.

"Not hardly," Scott scoffed. "But I like to cook and this looks like something I could try." He looked from one woman to the other, then down at his plate. "Chicken, spinach, pasta. Peppers, onions, baby Bellas. I saw you adding salt and pepper. Anything else?" Kelli shook her head as she took her first bite.

"Nope. I just grilled the chicken first, then cooked the veggies in olive oil. I added the cooked pasta and chicken cubes at the end, just to get everything heated through. If you want it a bit spicy you can add red pepper flakes. Sometimes I put in sundried tomatoes, too. And voila! Now eat."

The room was companionably quiet while the three indulged their hunger. Corky had placed herself on the floor between Kelli and Scott, all the while looking hopefully for someone to drop a tidbit.

The meal continued in friendly conversation until Scott said, "Kelli, we need to go over something after we finish."

Both women sat back, placing their forks on their plates, hands in their laps, appetites suddenly gone. The similar motions made Scott think again of his sisters.

"I guess we're finished then," Kelli said as she glanced at Kim. "I'll bring coffee to the parlor where we can talk more comfortably."

"No! Stay in the kitchen! I can't hear you in there." He had been following their conversations since the two women had gotten home that afternoon. As least as much as he could when they were in either the kitchen or Kelli's bedroom. He knew they had napped on the twin beds across the hall from Kelli's bedroom for most of the afternoon. The hall camera had let him see them go in there, but he had no camera or bugs in the guest rooms.

He had moved his Camry a couple times so he wouldn't catch the attention of the roaming police cars. The last move, just before 4:30 had left him directly across the street from Kelli's house. He'd used his phone to keep an eye on all the cameras he had at the Battery house.

He'd watched, but there had been no movement until after five when the women and Corky exited the bedroom and went downstairs. They took Corky out into the yard and played catch; the cop seemed to enjoy it as much as the dumb dog.

Then they all went in and Kelli started food prep; he thought it looked like they were in for the night. Kelli paused at one point and fed the dog. The cop poured wine and Kelli went back to slicing and chopping. After a bit he found himself salivating. He realized he'd skipped lunch. He grabbed his survival kit from under the front seat and pealed open a protein bar. The rain began about 6:30, obscuring his view of the house exterior, but not the interior.

Just after seven he caught a glimpse of a tall man hustling up the street from further down the Battery. He laughed when the guy almost fell in a puddle. He stopped snickering when he recognized the cop from the morning. He saw the lady cop open the door for the man, then close it behind him. "Go to the kitchen," he snarled. "I can't hear you otherwise."

He switched to the monitor of the front hall and saw the two police types in a brief conversation, then the watcher saw them following his direction and heading for the kitchen. He switched back to the kitchen monitor and turned up the volume.

For the next hour and a half, he listened intently and learned nothing new, except the lady cop has two kids and the man is not comfortable around dogs. "Jerk! If you're not comfortable around Corky, you're a moron. She's the most placid dog in the world."

And now, just when they are about to start talking about the case and I can learn something meaningful, they're going where I can't hear them. He slammed his fist against the steering wheel repeatedly. "Shit! Shit! Shit!"

35

Once they were all comfortable in the parlor, the women on the settee once again, Scott in the green brocade-covered wing chair, Scott began. He had retrieved a sheaf of papers from his top coat pocket.

"I've got a couple things here I need you to look at, Kelli." He handed her four typed pages, a list of names. Kelli looked up at him quizzically when it dawned on her all the female names had been crossed out with a black marker. Seeing her look, Scott explained, "We're focusing on males for the stalker at this point. You said it was a man's voice on the calls you received."

Kim was leaning closer to Kelli, reading the list with her.

"There are names on here I recognize, but most of them I don't." Kelli started to hand the list back, but Scott shook his head.

"Think hard, Kelli. Maybe names from your past? School? Friends of Todd? What about USC? Even if it is just a name that rings a bell, even if you never met the person..."

Kelli slowly reread the list, handing each page to Kim as she finished it.

"I don't think so, Scott. There are only a few names I recognize at all; Jeremy and Bill from the kennel, Bert and Mr. Sanchez from the cleaners; RJ from the bank, and Watts from CVS. Most of them I know only in passing, because of their job. I might recognize others if I see their faces, but don't know their names. I've known Bert and Mr. Sanchez, RJ and Jeremy as long as I've lived here, and Bill since high school." Scott took the sheets and used a yellow highlighter to mark their names.

"But now that you bring it up, you've got me thinking. There were some weird things that happened in high school. I didn't think about them at the time, just figured they were jokes. I haven't even given them a thought since then, probably ten years ago. Do you think they could be related?"

Scott replied without answering her question. "What kinds of things?" Scott was all interest, leaning forward, his shirt sleeves now rolled up to his elbows, elbows resting on his knees; his undivided attention focused keenly on Kelli. Kim watched the two of them. She liked the way he focused in like a laser; she realized she still had a lot to learn about being a detective.

"Oh, stupid things: notes stuffed into my locker, Valentine cards at strange times of the year. A couple times there were roses tied to the outside of my locker. It all stopped though when I went up to Columbia for college. I hadn't thought about it since then."

"So which of these highlighted names have you known since high school?" He handed the sheets back to her.

"All of them. Except Watts, he just moved here about a year ago."

"Mr. Sanchez, Bill Loudon, and RJ seem a bit old for you to have gone to high school together."

Kelli laughed her deep throaty laugh.

"Good catch! That must be what makes you a super detective." The two women shared a look of sarcastic humor that Scott did not miss.

"I've known Mr. Sanchez as long as I've lived here, since I was eight. Granny has been going to his dry cleaners forever; it used to be owned by his father and now it's his. I think you can cross him off your list. Besides his age, he's got a bad knee, just had it replaced recently. I can't see him climbing the staircase, let alone a ladder to have placed the cameras." She motioned toward the foyer and the long spiral staircase. "His knee is why he hired Bert originally. So Bert could do the fetching and carrying while Mr. Sanchez can sit up front and deal with the customers. It's worked out perfectly for both of them."

"How so? Bert's what 28? 29? Is he satisfied with such a menial job? Maybe he's looking to move up in the world? Get Sanchez blamed for this and take over the business? Force you to marry him? Stranger things have happened."

Kelli hesitated, she didn't want to disparage her friend. "Bert has always been a bit slow. He talks slowly. He thinks slowly. But he's wonderful with his hands. He can fix anything, build anything. He's had a bit of a problem holding a job since high school because his people skills are not quite what they should be. When Granny told me about Mr. Sanchez's knee pain a couple years ago, I went and talked to him, convinced him to give Bert a chance. It's worked out." Kelli gave a shrug and a smile.

Scott looked up at her from beneath his dark brows. "You two went to school together? You're still in touch? Are you still in touch with your other classmates?"

"Well I wouldn't say we're still in touch, but his mother's aunt plays bridge with Granny and she sort of keeps her up to date on Bert and then Granny tells me." Keeping tabs on people this way seemed perfectly straight forward to Kelli, a bit too invasive for Scott.

"And Bill Loudon?"

"Oh, he was the janitor at our school, first middle school then he transferred to our high school. Always very nice, except when he was grouchy. Although I never saw that side of him, but there were stories, some said he had a drinking problem. I was really happy when he turned up at the kennel one day." Scott raised an eyebrow in question.

"I guess about three years ago, soon after we got Corky."

Scott put a tick next to Bill's name. "What else can you tell me about him?"

"Nothing. I just saw him around school and now at the kennel. It's not like we were friends or anything. I just knew who he was. I smiled and said "hi" when I passed him in the hall. That's it."

"And Jackson Cobb? How well do you know him?"

"RJ? He was really more my brother's friend than mine. Sean and RJ are five years older, really not part of my group of friends. Sean and RJ went to the same prep school. RJ lived down the street so he and Sean became good friends, visited back and forth on holidays and summer breaks, that sort of thing. He and Sean have kept in touch, see each other when Sean's in town. I know RJ married and has three kids, works at the bank, manager at the branch in N. Charleston. That's all I can tell you."

Scott put a question mark next to R. Jackson Cobb. Possible, but better suspects than a man with a family, too hard to camouflage his activities from his wife, or so he'd been led to believe. Stalkers liked to work alone. Looking at the lists again a thought occurred to him.

"Would Mr. Cobb and your real estate agent, Teri Jackson, be related?"

Kelli looked at him blankly. "Not that I know of, but I guess it's possible. What makes you think that?"

"I don't know. Seems awfully coincidental that they both have Jackson in their names."

Both women responded with a peal of light-hearted laughter. When they had regained their composure, Kim explained, "Scott, this is the real South, and we southerners have long memories. Ever hear of Stonewall Jackson? Hero of the Northern War of Aggression? Brilliant general? Died too young from an infection after losing an arm to a bullet fired by one of his own men. You'll probably find a number of Lees on that list, too. It's a southern thing." The women were grinning from ear to ear. He could just read their "Dumb Yankee" thoughts. He did not consider himself a Yankee; he grew up in Maryland and went to school in Virginia after all.

"Okay, got it. I was born in Missouri, we tend to downplay our Civil War participation." He tried to bring the conversation back on track.

"That leaves Jeremy. What about him?"

"Jeremy, Bert and I were in school together. Jeremy was a year older but he'd been held back at some point. I don't remember how we met. He was just there. I never knew him well even though he lived just down the street. I seem to recall something about his dad losing all their money, a Ponzi scheme or something. I don't remember the details. I don't think I've seen him since we graduated, at least not until he showed up at the kennel a couple years ago. He's great with animals and Corky adores him. Sometimes I think she loves him more than she does me." Kelli rubbed her slippered foot across the big dog's back; Corky had been asleep on the floor next to Kelli's feet since they had settled into the parlor.

Scott put another tick on the list. *Could Bill and Jeremy be working as a team? Possible.*

"Anything else?"

"Not that I can think of. I never knew him well. I just knew who he was, saw him in the halls a few times, sometimes we'd eat lunch together, just like Bert and I did. No big deal. I'd say we were acquaintances more than friends." Scott stared at Kelli. *What is it about her that somebody finds so compelling? She's pretty, but certainly not gorgeous, except those big brown eyes. Maybe cute is a better word. Nice figure. Warm smile.* He realized the two women were waiting for him to continue.

"Any of the names on the last page look familiar? Those are the brokers who came to that open house and the agents who showed the house while you were gone. We're still waiting to get the names of the clients who saw the house while you were gone."

Kelli bit her lip to compose herself again. "No, no names I recognize."

"There was a man who got into the open house under suspicious circumstances. Teri Jackson is working with a police artist on a sketch; I'll show it to you as soon as I get it. She said he was blonde, a little over six feet, nice suit, glasses, well-mannered. Ring any bells?"

Kelli shook her head, "Could be lots of people."

Scott stood. "Study that list another minute, I want to check something in the kitchen." He left and returned in under a minute.

"Who has access to that key rack in the pantry? I noticed it last night when I made a quick sweep of the house, but I guess it didn't register."

"Access? What do you mean? The pantry doesn't lock, so I guess anybody who comes into the kitchen." She paused. "Oh my God! Do you think he has a key to my house?"

"How many house keys were on the rack?"

"I don't know, one or two? And duplicate car keys. And keys to Gramps' gun case." All color had drained from her face.

"It looks like all the keys you mention are still there, but he could have duplicated a key and then returned it to the rack." Now it was Scott's turn to blanch. He looked at his watch; after ten. "Got time for a little more?"

Kelli looked at him expectantly. *What else could there be?* "Sure. I had a nap today. But what about you?" She looked at the dark circles under his deep brown eyes. "You look exhausted. I know you haven't slept since last night, and maybe not before then." Her concern touched him.

He hesitated. "I'm fine. I started to ask you the other day, but we got sidetracked." He paused again. "Tell me what you remember about the day Todd died."

36

Saturday night

The watcher could spend the rest of the day – maybe night? – with Kelli. Before starting his car he checked his phone one more time; the three were still in the parlor, still in deep conversation. "What are you saying?" he yelled at the silent phone. Then he glanced furtively around the Battery, making sure no one had heard him. At this time of night it would be too weird if anyone else was around. "Too dark to see anyway."

He started the car and backed out of the parking space, following East Bay north until he cut over to Meeting Street. Then I-26 and the short drive to his North Charleston apartment, on the south side of North Charleston, closer to Charleston...and Kelli.

He unlocked the door to his second floor apartment. His eyes immediately went to the wall of eight monitors he had set up directly across from the front door. He saw the threesome hadn't moved; it was like watching an old black and white movie without the subtitles but in color.

He threw his fleece jacket onto the back of the rolling desk chair in front of the monitors and headed for the kitchen. A beer would be great about now. He unscrewed the top on a bottle of Holy City ale and returned to the living room cum computer room. Five of the monitors showed still photos of empty rooms and hallways, two monitors were completely black, turned off. The final monitor showed a long view from the front parlor to the French doors in the dining room.

He noticed the three were sitting more relaxed now, the women drinking tea from flowered porcelain cups, the cop using a mug. He knew those cups, they were from the kitchen cupboard to the left of the stove. Each cup had a different colored rose on it. He had fixed himself a cup of tea on one of his evening visits the prior week. "You're using the same one I did,

Kelli, the yellow rose. Can you feel my lips on the rim? It's like a kiss, isn't it?" He walked closer to the monitor and outlined Kelli's face and figure with his fingers. "Tonight, Kelli, tonight," he whispered.

In answer to Scott's question about Todd Kelli asked him, "Why can't you just read the police report, Scott? I'd really rather not have to go through this again."

"I have read the report, Kelli, but I want to hear your memories, because you're here and he's not," Scott replied, more patiently than Kim might have expected.

"Duh! He's not here because he's dead! And nobody tells me anything about the search for his killer." Kelli was growing angry all over again.

Kim and Scott glanced at each other and maintained their silence, giving Kelli a chance to calm down.

Kelli took a deep breath and lowered her hands, clasping them tightly in her lap. "I'm sorry. I'm tired and everything is getting to me. Okay. Once more. It was our anniversary and I had just found out that morning that I was pregnant. I was fixing a splendid dinner for the two of us...and Corky, of course. At the last minute I called Todd and asked him to stop at Publix for some raspberries because I had forgotten to get them and I needed them to garnish the chocolate mousse I had fixed for dessert. It kept getting later and later and the next thing I knew a Sheriff's department car pulled into the driveway. Two men came to the door: Todd's captain and another trooper. They told me he had been killed at the Publix, standing in line to pay for the raspberries." She turned and looked solemnly at Scott, "Is that enough for you?"

Scott was the one to break the silence. "I don't know any more than you, Kelli, so I can't speak to the outcome. I do know the LEOs in this state will work their hardest on a case involving the death of a fellow officer. But when it comes to a trial, any trial, there is a fine line between 'just' and 'legal'. We all, and I mean the public as well as those of us in law enforcement, we all seek justice. Fortunately, most of the time 'just' and 'legal' work out as the same thing; good guys get off, bad guys get convicted. Sometimes there's an aberration. Things are not as obvious, not as clean, as we'd like them to be. At those times some may err on the side of legal, doing what they can legally to support the greater good. He paused and looked deeply into Kelli's watery brown eyes. She still had some fight left in her, he could see it smoldering beneath the tears.

Scott looked frustrated. "I'm sorry, Kelli, I can't explain it any better than I have. I just hope it turns out the way it should." They stared at each other. Scott smiled tentatively. Kelli smiled back. "Okay, Scott, that was very diplomatic of you," Kelli's smile was rueful.

Kim stood up. "Hey, it's really late. What say Kelli goes to bed?" She turned to Kelli. "Is it okay if I sleep on this settee tonight?"

Kelli looked at Kim blankly. Slowly it dawned on her; Kim was planning to stay the night. "No, you don't have to stay. I'll be fine. You will sleep better in your own bed and with your family. Really, I'll be fine." Kelli smiled her most convincing smile. "Corky will protect me." Corky raised her sleepy head at the mention of her name, then put it back down between her paws and closed her eyes.

The two police officers laughed. Scott said, "Oh, she'll be a lot of help."

Kelli turned defensive, but continued to smile at her beloved dog. "She is a big help. She barks whenever someone new comes into the house. You just doubt her because you haven't seen her in action; she knows both of you, now."

Scott looked doubtful and turned to Kim. "Kelli's right, though. You go home. I'll stay here. I've had more sleep than either of you."

Kelli stood up and glared at both of them. "No. You're both going to leave. If either of you stays I won't get any sleep. I'll be worrying that I need to get up and play hostess or something." She smiled pleadingly at both of them. "And I really need some sleep." She snapped her fingers and Corky stood, shook herself, and came to stand at Kelli's side. "We'll be fine. Please. Both of you go get some sleep. And take tomorrow off. I'm just going to swim and church and then curl up with a good book. I appreciate your help and concern, but I'll be fine. I just need some sleep and the chance to get my life back into some semblance of normal."

Sean admired her strength if not her decision. *This nutcase could come back anytime and he has a key.* After wrestling mentally with his decision he agreed, on one condition.

"Okay." He turned to Officer Seeger. "Kim, you go on. I'm just going to check that all the doors and windows are locked and call for some patrols to watch the house tonight."

Kelli started to protest but Scott held up his hand. "It's patrols outside or me inside. Take your pick."

Kelli stared at him a minute trying to decide if he was bluffing or not. Then she grudgingly gave in. "Outside. Better warn them I have a gun, too. Is it okay if I fix them some coffee?" She grinned.

"I'm sure they'd appreciate it," Scott said as he left the parlor and headed upstairs to check that everything was closed and locked. *Not that it will do much good if the guy has a key* he thought as he climbed the stairs. *But maybe it'll help Kelli sleep.*

Kelli walked Kim to the front doors and hugged her. "Thank you so much. I feel a lot better knowing a woman, especially you, is working with me. It won't get shuffled aside, will it?" Kelli paused. "I mean just because he hasn't actually hurt me yet?"

"Not if I can help it." Kim squeezed Kelli's hands and headed down the front steps. "I'll call you tomorrow, but you call me if anything happens, or you just want to talk. I left my home number and personal cell numbers on your desk."

Kelli waved at the other woman as a squad car drove slowly past the house. Kelli gave a small wave to them, too. She and Corky turned back into the house. As they entered, Scott was just returning from checking the kitchen doors and windows.

"All set." He kept walking through the front doors. He turned back to Kelli at the top of the outside steps. "Lock all these doors and leave some lights on." He stared at her seriously; Kelli gave him a mock salute and a grin. "I don't like this, but I respect your decision. I'll call you tomorrow and check in." He continued to stare. "Get some sleep," he said as he awkwardly patted her shoulder. He turned and headed down the steps.

"Good night, Scott, thank you." He gave a wave over his shoulder without turning back.

Kelli watched his broad back disappear into the dark bay mist rolling at the foot of the steps. She heard the clang of the iron gate and then turned once again to the house. She locked the deadbolts and then turned the big brass key to the right of the brass door knob. No one in the family had actually locked the old fashioned lock in years, but it gave her some added sense of security to hear the tongue fall into place. "Good thing Scott didn't know this door was never locked until all this started," she whispered conspiratorially to Corky, "He'd have a sissy fit."

Next she locked the deadbolt on the inside doors and returned to the kitchen. She loaded the dishwasher with their dinner dishes, cups and saucers and wiped off the countertops. Corky cleaned the crumbs from the chairs and the floor under the table. Kelli filled Corky's water and food bowls, turned out the kitchen lights, and headed to bed. "Oops. Better take care of my undies or pretty soon I won't have any to wear." She turned left outside the kitchen door and walked down the long hall; passed Sean's bedroom and a guest room then into the laundry room. She got out a wooden folding rack, stood it up, and then took her lingerie out of the washer. She carefully placed each piece onto the rack then turned to Corky, "Finally," she said as they both climbed the stairs.

Knowing the camera was in her room, Kelli changed into her pajamas in the bathroom. As she exited the bathroom she turned out the light, leaving her bedroom in the dark. Since she had turned off the upper hallway light when she got to her bedroom, the whole floor was dark. This allowed her to quickly move from her bedroom to the bedroom across the hall. She knew there was no way she would ever sleep in her old bedroom again. Corky jumped up onto the queen size bed next to Kelli and they were both asleep within minutes.

"Finally," he echoed. "I thought they'd never leave. She's alone now. Soon she'll be asleep and then she'll be all mine. I'm on my way, my darling. On my way." He grabbed his black fleece jacket, looked once more at the monitors to ensure Kelli was still heading upstairs to bed and headed for his car. He fumbled his keys from his pants pocket, locked his apartment door, and headed for his rendezvous with Kelli, just a short drive away. "Finally."

37

His heart was racing. His big hands kept sliding on the steering wheel; he wiped them on his jeans and left a sweaty palm print. He had a hard time staying under the speed limit even though he knew at this hour cops were as scarce as slaves around here. *Probably getting donuts and coffee* he chortled to his car's messy, dark interior. Even the ornamental street lights seemed darker than usual, giving him a greater sense of impending success. *Of course it is still Saturday night,* he reminded himself, *cops are still out there even if technically it is Sunday morning. Don't get cocky.* He laughed at his unintended pun as he looked at the rock-hard bulge between his legs. *Have to tell that one to Kelli. She has such a wonderful sense of humor.*

Twenty careful minutes later he approached Kelli's house by way of Meeting Street; then left onto South Bay and another left onto East Bay. He was now heading north on East Bay and just a few houses south of Kelli's house. All was still. The earlier mist had thickened to a sure-nuff fog. Slowly he drove past the front of the house; lights were still burning downstairs and a small light was on upstairs. Was Kelli still awake? He turned left onto Atlantic and pulled over in front of the large Victorian house on the corner. He carefully looked around. Nobody. No lights. He reached for his phone on the passenger seat and pulled up the view of the downstairs at Kelli's. Nothing. A light on the dining room sideboard and one on the small console table at the foot of the staircase.

He checked the upstairs cameras. Another small light coming from under the door to Kelli's reading room; that was all. The upstairs was totally dark. Kelli's room was dark, very dark. *Where's Corky? Must be sleeping with Kelli, there's no sign of her any place else. She could be a problem.* He scowled. He didn't want to hurt Corky, but he didn't want her in the way either. He rummaged through his "bag of tricks" that he kept ready on the backseat. He found a can of Mace. *That'll keep Corky occupied.*

He started the car and slowly circled the block once again. This time he was surprised to see a CPD squad car parked directly across from Kelli's gate. *Where did they come from?* His hands were slippery once again. He watched the car in his rear view mirror; he saw a cop get out and go through Kelli's gate. The last glimpse of him was as he circled around the house to the left. The watcher continued north and back to the same quiet parking space around the corner on Atlantic. *What now? Are there more of them? Any waiting on the piazza?* He slammed his fist against the steering wheel in frustration. *Calm. Calm.* He leaned his head back against the head rest and took several deep breaths, like he'd learned in group therapy years ago.

*Damn, stupid parents. Locked me away because they said I had anger issues. Just because they saw me throwing rocks at squirrels in the back yard. At least I wasn't throwing the rocks at them like I wanted. Good thing they never figured out what happened to RJ's guinea pig Nutmeg. If they had, I'd probably still be locked away. But I **am** able to control it. I haven't had an episode in over six months. I fooled them all. Saps.*

He suddenly raised his head. The alley. He knew there was an alley that opened off Meeting Street and went straight through to the backs of the houses on E. Bay. *That's where Kelli parks her car. What if the cops are walking around the yard? They'll see the car lights coming down the alley. Can't drive that alley without lights, too narrow. They'll hear the car scraping the walls or the trash cans and know something is going on.*

He rubbed the bridge of his nose with his thumb and forefinger. Concentrating made his head hurt. He looked out the windshield, his eyes glittering coldly. *First, the cops.*

He made a U-turn on the dark side street and reversed his circle of the block, daring to take a quick peek at the two cops as he passed their car; the driver had his head back and his eyes closed; the other one was reading a magazine by the light of his Maglite that he was holding shoulder high. *They didn't even look up as I passed. Worthless, but good for me.*

He made two right turns and he was back on the south end of Meeting Street. He drove almost to Atlantic and turned right into the narrow alley. With just his parking lights on to keep him centered he drove slowly toward the other end of the alley. The fog helped mask his approach. He drove until he saw Kelli's car parked just off the alley in a private space. He stopped and looked around. He had noticed another empty private space just behind him; if nobody was using it at this hour they probably were out of town. He reversed the car into the space. He turned off the overhead light and quietly opened and closed the door. He listened for any indications that he had been detected. Nothing. Quiet. The fog hid more than lights.

Stealthily he walked back toward Kelli's car and the gate leading to the Ellsworth house's back yard. He hoped the gardener kept the gate well-oiled...and that there were no cops waiting on the piazza. He knew Kelli's grandparents had a service that came every Tuesday to take care of the yard and the plants, *and of course Mr. and Mrs. Gannon take all the credit for their beautiful landscaping.* Since the yard guys use this gate for access, *can't have the help coming through the front gate*, it made sense that they kept it oiled. *Old Mrs. Gannon would not want to hear it squeak every time they opened or closed it.*

He pulled a pair of black leather gloves from his jacket pocket and silently slid them on. Again he checked for any sounds of discovery. Nothing. Slowly he opened the black iron gate. Not a sound. He smiled to himself. *I'm coming, Kelli. I'm right here. Can you feel me coming to you?* He silently closed the gate behind him. He looked up at the neighboring houses. All dark. He couldn't make out the windows even because of the fog; *so they can't see me.* His smugness and exhilaration had returned. *Everything is in my favor, our favor.*

He crossed the damp grass to the kitchen door. He stopped before stepping up the two steps. Nothing. No cops. No nothing.

He pulled the house key from his pants pocket, fondling himself in preparation. The fog and danger of cops being so close were adding to his excitement. "Calm, calm," he whispered to himself.

The dead bolt released with a reassuring *snick*, too quiet to be heard more than two steps away. *Probably keep it oiled too*, he grinned. As long as Corky didn't hear it. But he'd deal with her if he had to.

Even without light he walked assuredly through the kitchen to the swinging door. His forays into the house the week before had given him time to memorize the floor plan. He didn't even need a flashlight beam; he didn't want to take a chance of the neighbors or the cops seeing it.

He pushed through the swinging door. The small light was on in the foyer. He pulled down his balaclava so only his eyes were visible. He turned up his jacket collar. Slowly he hugged the left wall and made his way to the table at the foot of the staircase. His black sneakers made no sound. The foyer couldn't be seen by the cops out front. The only tricky part would be when he passed in front of the light; that momentary blip of darkness might be seen and questioned by the cops; it was a chance he decided was worth it. *Kelli is at the top of the stairs...alone. Waiting for me.*

Gathering his confidence he quickly passed in front of the table lamp and over to the far wall of the staircase. *There's no way of knowing if the cops saw me until they show up.* He waited. His back was tight to the wall; it felt like he might push right through the two hundred year old bricks that formed the foundation and outer walls of most of these old homes. At least the ones that hadn't burned down. Even the ones that had been rebuilt had used old bricks.

Nothing. He slowly mounted the stairs, still hugging the right hand wall, thankful the bannister was on the other side. He knew Kelli's room was the first door on the right. *I should. I spent enough time there while she was gone.* He had to restrain the giggle of success rising in his throat. Once more he checked his phone view of the upstairs. All was dark. He could barely see the light coming from his phone. His breathing quickened. His hands inside the gloves were moist. He licked his lips. *Almost. Almost. At last.*

Slowly, quietly he approached Kelli's door, listening for any sound, especially that blasted dog. He moved the Mace canister from his jacket pocket to his right hand, to use on the dog at the slightest movement from her.

He turned into Kelli's room and approached the bed. Hesitatingly he put out his hand and reached for Kelli's head on her pillow, ready to cover her mouth and stifle any screams. He knew she'd be afraid, being so suddenly awakened.

Nothing. Kelli was not in her bed. The bed in which he had indulged so many fantasies last week was empty. He felt the entire bed. Nothing. "Shit!" he snarled through gritted teeth. *She has to be here. The others left and I saw her come upstairs. I saw her come in here and get ready for bed. Think!* He stood woodenly next to the bed. Frustration leaking from every pore. *The note scared her. She must be in one of the rooms across the hall. Probably not in her grandparents' room, that would be creepy.*

He knew the room directly across the hall had a queen size bed, the other one had twin beds. Since Corky slept with her, he guessed the queen one.

Holding his breath he walked the twelve steps to the partially closed door across the hall. With his gloved right hand he quietly pushed open the door. He had his Mace ready in his left hand. Silence.

Suddenly the bedside lamp came on. "Looking for me?" Kelli asked. He was frozen in place at the sight of Kelli sitting up in bed across the room, a steady .357 revolver pointed at the doorway, the large dog seated next to her growling deep in her throat, a snarl showing her big teeth. Kelli was holding tightly to Corky's collar. Suddenly Corky laid down, her head on her paws, her fluffy tail wagging.

"Just hold still while I call the police," Kelli instructed him in a firm voice. Without thinking she released Corky's collar to free her left hand to reach across the dog's body for the phone, keeping the gun and her eyes steady on the intruder. She took one quick glance over her shoulder to confirm the phone's proximity to her hand.

He took that instant to turn and run down the stairs, through the kitchen, out the back door, through the gate, and into his car.

Corky jumped down and followed him, barking an excited bark, her tail wagging furiously. He had his car started and tearing down the alley before Kelli got herself untangled from the bedcovers and out the front door to yell for the police. Then she turned and raced out the kitchen door and after Corky who had followed the intruder out to the open gate and down the alley. Corky sniffed around and then looked up at Kelli with a very confused look; she couldn't figure out where he had gone.

Kelli grabbed Corky's collar and led her back through the gate, closing it firmly behind them. "It's okay, girl; good girl." The two policemen came running through the kitchen door and met Kelli and her dog in the back yard.

Kelli smiled weakly at them as Corky bounced around gleefully at the two new people. She accepted them immediately because they'd come from inside the house, and Kelli wasn't giving off any bad vibes.

"Are you okay, Mrs. Cavanaugh?" the taller one asked. He reached down. "May I take your gun?"

"Yes, I'm fine. It was an intruder." Kelli was now gasping for breath, the most recent events starting to register. She handed him her gun, butt first, as Todd had taught her. "Corky and I scared him off." She grinned and patted her dog's head. She pointed to her gun. "I'll want that back; it's licensed and so am I."

"My partner called Detective Rae. He should be here soon. He told us to stay with you until he gets here," the shorter one said.

Kelli was starting to feel the damp through her flannel pajamas. "Well, then, I guess there's nothing to do but go inside and make some coffee." Kelli smiled at the two men and led them back to the kitchen door, Corky at their heels.

The shorter one turned and said he was going to look around. Kelli spoke up, "Corky followed him to about halfway down the alley, or at least his scent. I didn't see anyone when I got to her so I guess he was already gone. I did hear a car tearing down the alley as I was running through the back yard."

"Thanks. I'll check it out." He turned and was lost in the fog.

"Just knock when you get back," Kelli yelled after him. "I'm sure we'll be in the kitchen." Kelli ushered the other officer into the kitchen and closed and locked the door behind them. "Fat lot of good you did," she muttered to the heavy dead bolt. She turned on the overhead lights and headed for the coffeemaker. "Guess there won't be much sleep for either of us tonight, so I might as well make some coffee, regular instead of decaf this time." She smiled again at the young officer. "Would you mind going and checking that the front doors are locked?" He smiled wonderingly at her composure. She was kind of amazed by it too.

38

He rushed home, panicked, constantly checking his rearview mirror to see if the police were following. Halfway home he began to calm down and realized he was way over the speed limit. *Slow down!* His mind screamed. *Don't get caught speeding, they'll ask stupid questions.* Again he wiped is palms on his jeans. He checked the mirror as his foot came off the accelerator. Nothing. His heart rate started to slow.

That was close, too close. There wasn't a gun anywhere last week. I would have seen it. I opened every drawer, every closet, every cupboard. She couldn't have taken it with her, unless it was unloaded and packed in her suitcase. But who would do that? It'd probably get stolen by a baggage handler or a 'guard'. They'd see it on the luggage x-rays and just help themselves. Kelli is definitely not stupid.

She must have locked it up somewhere while she was gone, probably her grandfather's gun safe. But that's meant for rifles and shotguns, not pistols. There's nothing to say they couldn't keep other things in there, jewelry, silver, maybe even a pistol or two. You are so stupid! You can't do anything right! Think! Or you'll get yourself killed before you and Kelli get together. Better make it soon, the way you're going. Moron. He hit his forehead with his left fist, twice; it hurt but not as much as Kelli pulling a gun on him.

He glared at himself in the mirror. *After all, she was married to a cop, stands to reason she'd have some type of firearm available. Okay, so now I know, just have to come up with a new plan, and soon. It must be soon.*

He parked and scurried to his apartment.

The front hall monitor he had placed at Kelli's showed the detective entering and Kelli locking the door behind him. He didn't like the way the cop scanned Kelli's face; it seemed to take longer than necessary. His anger grew again. *At least I have tomorrow off; that gives me plenty of time to plan.* He settled into his swivel chair and watched the activities at the house.

39

Early Sunday morning

Just inside the locked front doors, Scott glared. First at the two cops standing a bit down the hall, then at Kelli standing next to them. "Will one of you please tell me what the fuck is going on here?" he snarled through clenched teeth.

Kelli put her hand on his tensed forearm, pleased to see her hand had stopped shaking. "It's okay, Scott, nothing happened. Everybody's okay."

Scott continued to glare. Slowly he let out his breath, surprised to realize he had been holding it. He turned to the patrolmen waiting nervously for his notice again. Scott had a reputation for being a hard-nose, never one to suffer mistakes in silence, especially if it involved peoples' lives, as it usually did with him. Scott saw them shifting from foot to foot, their hands poised defensively at the front of their broad belts. *Better they learn now than later, or worse, not at all.* He turned his gaze back to Kelli, "I'll deal with you in a minute."

He determinedly strode to the young men. They stiffened, expecting a thorough ass-chewing, or worse.

Scott stood silently before them, switching his burning gaze from a set of brown eyes to a set of hazel. He was glad to see remorse, but nothing to indicate they were cowed. *Maybe there is hope for them after all. We'll see.*

He hoped they weren't like too many rookie cops who got off on the power trip. Fortunately that type usually didn't make it very far up the ranks. They either quit, screwed up enough to get dismissed, or eventually their arrogance got them killed. Unfortunately, they did a lot of damage while they were on the force: PR problems, discipline problems, and worst of all, deaths. All this ran through Scott's mind in a flash. The cops still looked nervous.

"Richardson and Harris," he said, reading from their nametags. "How long have you been with CPD?"

Richardson, the taller, replied, "One year, sir."

Harris said, "Four years, sir."

More calmly than he had expected, Scott looked directly at the more experienced officer. "Then, Harris, the blame is on you. I don't want to know what did or did not happen tonight. I don't want to know if you fell asleep, or went for coffee, or decided it was warmer in the car than out in the fog. I don't want to know if you're just plain lazy or royal screw-ups. I don't want to hear anything out of your mouths." Scott paused for breath, daring them to utter even one word in their own defense. The two remained silent.

"I just want to remind you that your failure to do your duty almost got that lovely young woman killed tonight." He motioned over his shoulder to where Kelli still stood, looking especially young with her hair down the back of her flannel pajamas with the penguins on them.

"I'd also like to add that this perp could have killed both of you, too. Has that occurred to either of you?"

Richardson's eyes grew wide. Harris continued to stare guiltily at Scott.

He continued, calmly, coldly. "Now, I like to think everyone is allowed one minor mistake and I have no reason to believe you've already had yours. So here's what I'm going to do. I am going to write up both of you, full and complete details of this evening's events, which, fortunately for you, turned out to be relatively minor."

Both cops grimaced. Richardson looked pleadingly at Scott, he loved being a policeman.

"Then I'm going to file the report," he paused for effect, "in my desk. We'll consider this a learning experience. But if I *ever* hear of either of you screwing up like this again, I'll file the report and you'll both be in big trouble, with two strikes against you. So it's up to you. Do your job the best you can, keep out of trouble, not even a hint of trouble associated with either of you." He looked from one to the other. "Got it?"

They both nodded with relief.

"Good. Not get your flashlights and cordon off the whole yard and the back alley. Harris, call for the crime techs. And try not to mess up any potential clues."

They both murmured "Yes, sir." Richardson turned toward the swinging kitchen door and Harris took a step toward the front door. Scott stopped them both with a stern look and then a grin.

"It's cold and damp out there. I'm sure Mrs. Cavanaugh has already made coffee for you. Mugs are in the cupboard to the left of the sink. Fix yourselves some coffee and get to work...and don't spill anything on my crime scene." The other two smiled back and went into the kitchen, anxious to prove themselves and feeling very lucky. Maybe Scott Rae wasn't as bad as they'd heard.

"And don't break the mugs," Scott hurled at them as the door swung back toward him on its well-oiled hinges.

Scott composed his features and turned back toward Kelli. In two long strides he was beside her once more, having assumed his stern detective demeanor.

Kelli started to speak but quickly closed her mouth at the ferocious look on Scott's face. He took her elbow and steered her into the formal parlor, the one between the dining room and the front parlor. He seated her at one end of the gold-brocade-covered sofa and then walked over to the fireplace. He flipped the switch on the right side of the mantel. The gas logs immediately sprang to life, providing warmth and light to the dark room. He turned on the Tiffany-style lamps, *probably real Tiffany* he mused, on the tables at either end of the sofa.

Kelli sat quietly where he had placed her, watching his every movement, waiting for him to pounce. *He does look rather like a tiger, waiting for its kill to come into view. Tightly coiled, tense. Oh, boy.*

Scott stared at her. He realized she looked more confused than fearful. He stood before her, not knowing what to do with his hands. He knew he wanted to shake some sense into her, but felt that would get him nowhere. Finally he said, "Cup of tea?" He was pleased to see his question had dumbfounded her.

"Yes, please. I'll get it," she said in a soft, dismayed voice, afraid to wake the sleeping tiger.

He motioned her to stay still. "You sit still and get warm. I'll get it."

Scott headed for the kitchen. *So far so good.* Kelli stretched her hands toward the fire, then rubbed them up and down her arms. She took stock of how she felt: physically, fine; emotionally, confused. *Why is Scott mad at me for pity's sake?* Mentally, fine. Todd had trained her well. She knew she might have some after-shocks when she thought about tonight, but that would be normal. *And it's not like I killed anybody. I didn't even think about it. I just wanted to keep him here until Scott got here. I wanted this to be over.*

Scott returned with a porcelain cup for Kelli and a mug of coffee for himself. The kitchen had been empty and he could see the misty halo of flashlights in the backyard.

"Earl Grey," he said as he handed the cup and saucer to Kelli. "One Splenda." He sat down on the other end of the sofa, enjoying the warmth of the fire. He turned so he could face Kelli. She had one pajama-clad leg tucked under her, the other bare foot just reaching the floor; mauve nail polish on the visible toes. She turned and looked over the rim of her teacup. Her eyes were as big as any he had ever seen, watching him patiently, fearlessly. She had slipped through the parlors and around them into the kitchen while the three men had been "discussing"; that's how he had guessed she'd made coffee, not realizing it was the second pot since she'd come back inside. Harris and Richardson had just about finished off the first one. After a few minutes she had slipped back to the front door, where he had told her to wait for him.

"So. Do you want to tell me what happened since I left here," he looked at the watch on his left wrist, "not quite four hours ago?"

Kelli's warm brown eyes turned icy, not liking his implication that somehow she was at fault. She gritted her teeth and said in her softest, most sarcastic voice, "Oh, nothing much. A man broke in. He got away. You're here." She smiled her most insincere, sweet smile at Scott.

Scott felt he had just been put in his place, but he didn't know why. *Coffee. I need coffee.* He took a sip and regained his composure, not sure why he felt so angry at Kelli, she's the victim. He set the mug onto the table next to him and rubbed his hands over his face.

In his most conciliatory voice, he said, "Okay. Let's start over. Please walk me through what happened here since Officer Seeger and I left. Step by step." He took another sip and returned the cup to the tabletop. He removed his notepad and pen from the inside pocket of his tweed jacket.

Kelli held his gaze a moment longer then decided he was just doing his job, and on almost no sleep. Once again she reached down and patted the dog sleeping at her feet. Then she straightened and began.

"I turned out the lights and double-checked all the doors," she smiled, "even though I knew you had checked them all before you left." She took another sip of the perfectly steeped tea.

"I left some lights on, as you had instructed: the back hall light and the one on the console at the foot of the stairs. I had the staircase lights on until I got upstairs, then I turned them off." She closed her eyes, visualizing her progress up the stairs, trying to remember as much detail as possible. "I went into my room. I went into the bathroom to change; I knew the camera was still live in the bedroom. I didn't want to stray too far from my normal routine, but I wasn't giving him another peep show if I could help it." She looked to Scott for…what? Admiration? Congratulations? His eyes continued to watch her without the slightest change of expression on his square-jawed face. *Men! I thought it was a good job of dealing with the camera. After all, it's not every day I'm stalked. Well, actually, maybe it is, but it's not like I knew it.*

"I changed into my pajamas in the bathroom, brushed my teeth, brushed my hair, and returned to the bedroom. I closed the drapes and turned down the quilt. Then I turned off the bedside light and quietly snuck across the hall. There is no way I will ever sleep in that bed again!" Kelli shivered at the memory of what had happened in her bed while she was gone. Scott's jaw tightened but he said nothing. Kelli sensed his displeasure and looked at him sheepishly. "Sorry," she whispered. "I hope I haven't messed up your surveillance."

"Why did you turn off the light?"

"So I could sneak out without the camera seeing me. That room is on the north side of the house and is very dark at this time of the year. I hoped if I turned down the quilt and turned out the light, he'd think I was getting into bed and going to sleep. I planned to get back in there before light and mess up the sheets so it'd look like I had been there all night. I figured he'd think I was in the shower or something if he didn't see me in the bed."

Scott looked at her admiringly. "Good thinking. So where did you sleep?"

"I took the guest room across the hall with the queen bed; the one with twin beds was too narrow for me and Corky to sleep; the queen bed is big enough for both of us. She paused. "I feel kinda like Goldilocks, retelling it this way." She got a tentative grin from Scott.

"Anyway, I got into the other bed about an hour after you left, so I guess it was about one? Corky jumped up and assumed her normal position, head toward the foot of the bed, back legs stretched out and under Todd's – the spare- pillow, pressing her whole body against me. I never need a heater with her there! We both were asleep immediately. I was exhausted." She took another sip, getting to the hard part of the story.

"About three Corky started to growl, very deep in her throat. It took me a bit to wake up and figure out what the noise was; it's rare for Corky to growl." Kelli took a breath. "Once I figured out she was upset about something I grabbed her collar so she wouldn't go running off to investigate, then I grabbed my gun from the top of the nightstand and aimed it at the door." She looked at Scott again for an attaboy.

"Can you give me one good reason why you didn't call 9-1-1?" he growled through gritted teeth. Kelli looked at him in surprise. That was not the reaction she was expecting, that was for sure.

"9-1-1? I didn't even think of it. I was only half awake and I had to hold Corky and I had my gun. I didn't know what or who had gotten Corky riled, but, maybe subconsciously, I knew I should keep quiet. I don't know. I just didn't." *How dare he criticize her? She was fine. Nobody got hurt. She had almost caught the guy, too.*

Scott blew out another breath. He could see her point. "Okay. Move on. What happened next?"

Kelli glared at Scott and gritted her teeth as she continued. "Corky was still growling and her hackles were up. After a bit I thought I heard a noise in the hall. Corky's growls became stronger and I gripped her collar tighter. Suddenly there was a figure in the doorway. I pointed the gun and told him to hold still. He did, but when I reached for the phone to call 9-1-1, see I didn't forget completely, he ran off. Corky broke free from me while I was juggling the phone and ran after him. By the time I got downstairs and unlocked the front doors to call for the patrol, he was gone. I thought I heard a car in the alley and Corky was outside barking down that way."

Scott looked up from his notes. "How did Corky react when the intruder came to the bedroom doorway?"

Kelli was confused again. "What? Corky?" She looked down at her dog who had sat up and put her head onto Kelli's lap when she had heard her name mentioned. She realized what Scott was getting at. Kelli closed her eyes and reviewed the events in the bedroom. Her eyes flew open. "Corky relaxed. She stopped growling. She was doing that whiney thing she does when I hold her back from jumping on people." Kelli hesitated, her eyes as big as a fawn's once again. "Corky knew him."

Scott nodded. "That means you do too. Did you recognize anything about him? I assume he was wearing some sort of mask or you would have already told me who it was."

"Right. He had one of those ski masks pulled on, the whole face ones that pull down from the top of the head? It was dark, black or dark blue. He was shorter than you, maybe five-nine or – ten. He had on a dark fleece jacket; kinda bulky so I don't know about his body type; he could have had a sweater on under the jacket. Jeans, black, I think. I didn't see his feet, but he must have had some quiet-soled shoes on. I saw his hands just for a second. But I couldn't tell if he had gloves on; if he did, they must have been like leather gloves or ski mitts, something black."

Scott looked skeptical. "You said it was dark. So how did you see anything?"

"The room I was sleeping in has more natural light than my room. There's a long clerestory at the ceiling. There was lots of foggy moonlight coming in and the angle was directed right at the doorway. I could see him better than he could see me. Plus my eyes had had a chance to adjust to the light level; I'd waited for him for what seemed forever. He had just turned in from the dark hall into the lighter room."

Scott was impressed by her logical, concise retelling of the events. "Is that all? Did he have a weapon? Did he say anything?"

"Not that I saw. Not that I heard."

"Would you say Corky went after him because he was an intruder or because she knew him?"

Corky's eyebrows had started to twitch, as though she knew they were talking about her. "Definitely because she knew him. She was barking at him while she ran, but it was her playful bark, like she was playing a game, not angry."

Scott closed his notepad and finished the last of his tepid coffee. "Okay, I think you can go back to bed and get some sleep. Take Corky with you," he said nodding at the dog who was now looking at him. Kelli and Scott and the dog stood.

"You don't think he'll come back, do you?"

"No, not tonight. But we'll be here anyway. I'll be down here, Richardson and Harris will make the rounds outside; they're doing penance." Scott grinned and Kelli was struck again at how it made him look...almost human.

Scott continued as he walked Kelli to the staircase, "The crime scene techs should be here soon. I doubt they'll find much of anything, it sounds like he was pretty well covered up, but you never know." He looked at his watch. "If you hurry you can get at least a couple hours before they have to start on the upstairs."

"What about my gun? I'd like it back."

"In the morning. Go get some sleep. We're going to have a busy day. I've got another list of names for you to review, there'll be the artist's rendering from the open house, and we'll go back over everything from the beginning."

Kelli looked at him resignedly as she put her foot on the first step. She shrugged her flannel-covered shoulders. "Okay. Whatever." Corky trotted up the stairs after her. Kelli turned and smiled at Scott. "Thank you, Scott. I hope you get some rest."

Scott watched the two until they rounded the corner, heading for a bedroom. He thought Kelli looked like a forlorn little girl, but he was coming to see that her looks could be deceiving. *Yeah, a forlorn little girl who handles a .357 like a professional.*

40

Sunday morning

While Kelli and Corky slept, Scott maintained a vigil from the front parlor. Mentally, he reviewed all his notes and the various reports he had obtained. Still nothing. His gut feeling at this point was that it was someone Kelli knew – for sure someone Corky knew - but she didn't know who she knew at this point. Didn't know about the stalker's infatuation with her.

Being someone she knew could be good or bad. If indeed she reciprocated his feelings it might keep her safe and maybe they could live happily ever after, if Kelli was able to forgive his stalking. Could anybody? Scott's observations made him believe she had never loved anyone but Todd, her deceased husband, and had not started dating since his death.

If she did not share the stalker's feelings it would probably send the stalker into a rage. If that was the case, there was no telling what he would do, but it wouldn't be good for Kelli. His talk of them "being together soon" worried Scott. He'd have to have a talk with Kelli, warn her, scare her enough that she'd be careful, but not so much that she would lock herself in a room and never come out. They'd never catch the guy if she did that. Besides, the guy has a house key.

At 6 a.m. he left another message for a team of crime scene techs to come to the house ASAP. Techs worked on their own schedules and their own priorities. The team of four arrived at 6:30, loaded down with cases of technical gear to check for fingerprints, fibers, footprints, bodily fluids, and anything else that might point to the stalker.

Scott heard Corky woof as he opened the front door. Immediately the big dog ran down the curving staircase and approached the techs, a growl deep in her throat, tail down, ears flat. She stopped at the bottom of the stairs, blocking anyone from going up. Looking at her Scott wasn't sure she was the same dog who had gone up the stairs with Kelli just a few hours earlier. Now he understood what Kelli meant when she said Corky could take care of her.

"It's okay, Corky. Good dog." Scott patted the top of her head. Immediately Corky's whole demeanor changed; her head came up, her tail wagged and she approached each of the techs with a smile on her shaggy face. She allowed each of the newcomers to pat her and scratch her ears. Then she trotted off to the kitchen in search of water and food.

As Scott started to explain what they needed to do, Kelli came down the stairs. Five pairs of eyes watched her descend. She pulled her robe tighter and ran her fingers through her tousled hair. She felt terribly underdressed or like she had mascara smudges or something. She wished she'd done more than brush her teeth before coming downstairs, but she hadn't wanted to slow the work of the techs. She figured they had better things to do on a Sunday than work at her house.

As Kelli stepped off the bottom step, Scott introduced her to them. "This is Mrs. Kelli Cavanaugh. She lives here and last night someone broke in and entered her bedroom." Scott grinned, "And she scared him away with a very large .357." The four techs looked at her with admiration. One's hand went up to give her a high-five, but he immediately dropped it at Scott's scowl.

Kelli was embarrassed. "It was a gift from my husband on our first anniversary." Kelli grinned as the female tech murmured, "Romantic devil."

"Well, he gave me the gun and Corky for our first anniversary, for my defense he said. As you no doubt picked up on, the gun is more effective than Corky, although she has a really good bark." They all laughed.

"May I get y'all some coffee or tea?" Four heads nodded. "I'll be right back, I'm sure Scott needs to talk to you."

Kelli headed to the kitchen as she heard Scott restart his instructions. She patted Corky and started a fresh pot of coffee. She put the kettle on, too. She filled Corky's food bowl and opened the door for her to go out. Next Kelli pulled out a large wooden tray, put sugar, cream, and a bowl of sweetener packets on it. She added five mugs, five spoons, and a stack of paper napkins. Plus a teacup and saucer for herself.

Corky trotted back in and received her "Greenie". Kelli closed the back door as Corky laid down in the sun puddle coming in through the breakfast room window. "Are you sure you aren't part cat?" Kelli asked her mellow dog. "I guess it's a good thing you can't get up onto the backs of chairs or sofas." Kelli smiled at her dog, poured the coffee into the mugs, poured hot water over her Irish Breakfast Tea bag, hefted the tray, and headed back to the front parlor.

Kelli and the tray arrived just as the little meeting was breaking up. Each tech grabbed a mug, doctored it as needed, and thanked Kelli for her trouble. One man and one woman headed upstairs, another man went to the kitchen, and the fourth went outside to survey the perimeter and alley for any sign of the intruder.

Scott motioned Kelli to join him in the parlor. She fixed her tea, stirred it, then took it to the settee. She looked at Scott questioningly.

"I just want to bring you up to date, Kelli, and have you review the list of names again."

Kelli sipped her tea and watched Scott in silence.

He was almost undone by her silence. He had never met anyone so composed, especially not a woman with an unknown stalker on her trail.

"All the checks into the phone calls you received yielded nothing. It appears the caller used prepaid phones, a different phone for each call. We can track them to their source, but finding a specific sale on a specific date takes a while. Once we know the source, we have to hope they have a security camera and recorded the sale being made. Then we have to hope they still have the recording and haven't deleted it or recorded over it. Like I said, not much. We may be able to get something, but as you can see it will take a while, not much like TV where solutions appear within 60 minutes, minus commercial time." Scott paused. Still Kelli said nothing.

"What it looks like at this point is that we've got a very smart, very determined stalker. And it's probably someone you know." Kelli's right eyebrow quirked, she continued to stare into Scott's eyes as she took another sip of her tea. "Unless...could there be someone Corky knows that you don't?"

Kelli thought seriously about his question. "I almost answered 'no', but I guess there are deliverymen, repairmen, people who come to the house while I'm at work. She'd at least recognize them but I wouldn't. We can ask Magda about them."

"Obviously it's not someone you would consider as a," he hesitated. "As a lover. But it's someone who wants that role." He found her calm stare very disconcerting.

Kelli set her cup and saucer onto the small table at her elbow. She pulled her robe more tightly around herself. A troubled look crossed her face. At last she spoke.

"Someone I know? I can't imagine who it might be. I've never given anyone any romantic encouragement, at least not since I met Todd."

"This is the hard part, Kelli. You didn't have to. You may have just been what you think of as friendly. You may not have said or done anything out of the ordinary. Some of these stalkers get fixated on a particular person, or a particular type; maybe brown eyes, or blonde hair, or tall, or a combination of features. Who knows? Every one of the stalkers I've encountered had a different reason for picking the person he did."

"Have you encountered many?"

"Not many since I moved to Charleston, but a few when I worked in D.C."

"So what are you trying to say without saying it, Scott. You seem to be avoiding something."

Scott drained his coffee mug.

"I'm just saying this guy is going to be hard to catch and it may take a while. You will have to be hyper-vigilant until we do. He could be anywhere, anybody."

Kelli gave a scornful laugh. "'Hyper-vigilant?' That's one of the first symptoms of PTSD, like my brother. Look where it got him."

"I know and I'm sorry. If we don't catch this guy in a couple days, we won't be able to keep patrols around to keep an eye out. It will be up to you to protect yourself. Keep the doors locked, after you get them changed. Keep your phone handy, make 9-1-1 a speed dial. Keep Corky and your gun close by. You'll probably want to get an unlisted number, too."

"That's all well and good, Scott, but he has a key. And you say he's someone I know, so Corky probably knows him, too; she's not going to attack someone she knows."

"True. That's why you need to get the locks changed first thing Monday. All we can do is the best we can do. I'm sure if Corky detects a menace or senses fear from you, she'll be highly protective; it's just the nature of dogs, or so I've heard."

Kelli considered his words. "Okay. I'm sure you'll catch him; I trust you, Scott. What else can I do? Where's that other list you want me to look at."

Scott groaned inwardly. The three worst words a cop – or a man - wants to hear: "I trust you". He knew Kelli did not intend to lay a guilt trip on him, but it amounted to the same. He felt responsible for her now; she trusted him to keep her safe. *Guess that's what I'll have to do.* He removed the two typed pages from his jacket pocket and handed them to Kelli along with a yellow highlighter.

"These are the people from the open house and some state troopers you may have met. Just mark any names you recognize, just like you did before. This time, write down how long you've known them and how you know them. Again, it's just the men. We've also included anyone associated with Todd's death, people you may have come in contact with." She was already reading through the names.

"From what you've told me, it sounds like this may have gotten started when you were in high school and has grown over the years. So read through these carefully, it may be someone from your past who you haven't even seen in years, but he's seen you. He's probably followed you, knows your patterns."

Kelli was frowning at the list of about forty names. "Okay, if you think it will help." She uncapped the marker and read more slowly through the list.

Scott smiled at her serious concentration. He picked up his mug and her cup and saucer. "I'll get refills and check on the techs while you do this." He smiled again and headed for the kitchen. Kelli highlighted a name and began to make a notation beside it.

When Scott came back Kelli handed the highlighted sheets back to him. He glanced at the pages and looked back at her. "Is that all? Just three names you recognize out of forty?"

Kelli nodded. She had the feeling she had failed him somehow. "I'm sorry, but that truly is everybody I can think of. And you can even cross off a couple of those names because they couldn't be the intruder; too tall or short, too fat, or I've known them forever."

"No. Don't apologize. This is great. As I'm sure you know from Todd, an investigation is a winnowing process. We start with a large pool of suspects and then work our way down and down until we get to just a few. In your case we started with all the people who possibly could have known you were leaving town, from your housekeeper to the kennel, the drug store to your friends at the pool. Then we eliminated all the women, and men over sixty. You just reviewed the list of real estate people and highway patrol cops and only found three. The smaller the list, the less time it will take to find your stalker."

Kelli looked at him soberly. "What if I'm wrong? What if we eliminated someone from the lists and it's really that person?"

Scott hesitated, a small frown on his face. "That's always a possibility," he answered opting for honesty. "We have to play the probabilities. In this case we know it's a he; you saw him. Even though he was masked and bundled up you got a sense of his height, his body type. And stalkers are more often someone the victim knows. So we'll work with your names and do full work ups on them."

"What if it's not someone I know directly?" It was obvious to Scott this was someone she didn't like. *But how could she dislike them so much if she didn't know them?*

"It's obvious you have someone in mind. Who is it?"

Kelli looked into Scott's intelligent eyes, willing him to tell her she was being stupid. She spoke in barely a whisper, "Somebody from that blog, the righteous indignation of strangers." She rushed on at the incredulous look on his face. "Before Labor Day I would have had the same look on my face. But they have been so vicious in their comments, it's like they're on a personal crusade. At this point I wouldn't put anything past them. These are people we don't know, worse, people who don't know Sean or us." She crossed her arms over her chest and leaned back into the corner of the settee.

Scott settled into the wing chair. He steepled his hands in front of his face, pausing to consider his answer. He knew Kelli was smart so she wouldn't be saying this if she didn't think it was possible, if unlikely. "I'll look into it. In the meantime, let's table that idea for the moment, but you do bring another thought to mind. Has anyone in the family received threatening letters about Sean? There are a lot of weirdos out there who might just see it as their responsibility to punish the wicked, maybe through their families."

Kelli looked blankly at him and replied stiffly, "No, I haven't. I'm sure Nora would have said something if she had. But for this thought to work it would have to be somebody – or somebodies – I don't know. I thought we were looking at people I do know."

Scott ran his hands through his hair. "Hell, I'm just throwing out ideas. It could be the postman for all I know right now." He looked pointedly at her, "Is your postman on the list?"

Kelli grinned. "We have a post office box, not home delivery."

Scott stood. "I'm going to check in with the techs and then go to the office and get a start on these names. You'll be okay here? I'll try to be back before the tech team leaves."

Kelli stood, too, and walked him to the door. "I'll be fine. I'll get a shower and head to church. I may go for a swim this afternoon."

"I would prefer it if you'd stick around here until I get back."

"What I'm saying, Scott, is that I'll be fine; you don't need to come back. I'll be surrounded by people at church and my watchers out front can follow me there and back." She smiled her warmest smile. It was obvious to Scott that stubbornness ran in the family; apparently Sean wasn't the only one.

"To appease you I won't go to the pool. I'll take Corky for a walk after church then settle in with a good book. But I will not let this person dictate my life." She opened the front door and gently ushered Scott out. "Thank you, Scott, for everything. I know it's just another case to you, but you make me feel safer. I appreciate it. I really do."

Scott was speechless. He just walked through the brick red outer doors and muttered, "Call me if you need me. Otherwise I'll see you later this afternoon." He started to say more, but finally settled for "Be careful."

If only they had both known they would see each other sooner than "later this afternoon."

41

It was almost nine when Scott finally left. The day promised to be spring-like, warmer than the previous week, and sunny. It wouldn't be long until the redbuds and azaleas would be in bloom. Kelli hurried up the stairs to check the techs herself.

She peeked around the door frame of the room where she had slept earlier this morning, careful not to touch anything. "Is it okay if I shower and change? I can use my grandparents' room if that's better for you."

"Your room is the one across the hall?" the female asked without looking up from the bathroom doorknob she was dusting with a grey powder. At Kelli's "yes" she replied, "Sure. We're done in your room, haven't found any prints except yours and one other. We've already made copies so you're good to go."

"How long do fingerprints last?" Kelli asked, always willing to learn something new. "I mean would our last guest's prints still be there?"

The woman sat back on her heels and looked seriously at the young woman in the purple flannel robe. *Why does she want to know? Curiosity or future planning?* She mentally slapped herself. *This job! It makes you suspicious of everybody.*

"It depends on how long the room goes undisturbed, how much oil or sweat there is in the print, the surface of the object where the print is left. Neat freaks, those who dust and polish every nook and cranny, will ruin any prints in a heartbeat. A room left alone, rarely used, like an attic or those storage rooms down the hall, can keep prints forever. Fortunately we are usually called to a scene pretty soon after a crime so we don't have to worry about either the neat freaks or the length of time. If we find something without any prints after a crime that usually means the perp wore gloves or wiped the place down. That just makes us work harder. No matter what criminals think, it's hard to remember every place you touched. So they're getting smarter and wearing gloves like we do." She held up her purple latex gloved hand. "We wear them so our prints don't get mixed with any evidence; the criminals wear them so they don't leave any prints in the first place. TV has done wonders for the criminal elements!" She chuckled.

Kelli listened intently. "Sounds like your job is pretty interesting. Science and crime. Modern day Sherlock Holmes." She smiled back.

The tech replied, "Yeah, but no violins or cocaine, at least none unless it's left at a scene." Kelli's smile broadened, a literary kindred spirit.

"Well, I'd better get going or I'll be late for church. Will y'all lock up if you leave while I'm gone? I'll get you an extra key and you can just leave it in the first potted plant on the piazza. I'll leave it on the lamp table at the foot of the stairs."

"Sure, no problem. We may be done before you leave."

Kelli smiled, turned, and headed across the hall to her room, mindful of the camera's tiny eye over the bathroom door frame. *Even if there is a slight nip in the air, I feel good today. It's a sunny day and that guy, whoever he is, can't get to me.*

Kelli shuddered as she approached her dresser, knowing "he" had touched everything. She grabbed the only clean underwear left from her trip from the virtually empty second drawer of her dresser; everything else was still hanging on the drying rack in the laundry room. Next she got a silk blouse and slacks from her closet, and headed into the bathroom. *A hot shower will help, too.*

Twenty-seven minutes later Kelli poked her head into the room across the hall. "I'm gone. Thanks for your hard work. There's still coffee if y'all need a refill." She smiled and hustled down the stairs, shouted to Corky to be good, and rushed out the front door. While showering she had decided to walk to church; it's such a gorgeous day.

She crossed East Bay and stopped at the Team car parked directly across from the gate. "I'm walking to St. Philips. Does one of you want to walk with me or do you want to follow in the car?" Everybody knows where St. Philip's is, it's the oldest church in Charleston, founded in 1680. Even though it's not in its original location, having been badly damaged by a hurricane n 1710, it's still considered the oldest. It's been in its current location since 1723 despite fires, Indian attacks, epidemics, and more hurricanes. Not for nothing is Charleston known as "The Holy City", even though it really has nothing to do with the number of churches per capita as most people think. It received the moniker from an editorial in the *Post and Courier* many years ago. The author thought Charleston the most perfect place and referred to it as the Holy City.

Kelli continued her chat with the patrolmen, "The front door is still unlocked, so one of you can go inside and be comfortable. I'm coming straight home after church and I'll fix us all some lunch."

She smiled at the two uniformed officers, turned and headed up East Bay. It was just a few Charleston blocks to the old church, its steeple one of the tallest in the city. Soon she heard a car moving slowly behind her. Kelli glanced over her shoulder to confirm it was the police car and continued her long-legged walk to Queen Street, turned left for one block, then right onto Church Street for another two blocks, then up the steps and into the narthex. As she always did, Kelli admired the stained glass windows behind the altar and the forty foot ceilings graced with Corinthian columns. Glancing at her watch, she hurried into the box pew in the fifth row and grabbed a hymnal. *Not a moment too soon!*

Officer Meyer waited in the narthex where he could observe everyone coming and going and still keep an eye on Mrs. C.

Surreptitiously the watcher slipped into a pew behind her. As soon as he'd seen her getting clothes from her closet he knew she was headed to church, she tried to make it every Sunday. He knew that, he'd followed her for years, he knew her routines. He'd left his apartment right away and gotten to the church ahead of her. He knew she preferred the left, the Epistle, side of the main floor of the church so he'd gone to the balcony and stayed there until right before the first hymn. He found the back of her head just as the choir's processional began. As soon as the singing started he went downstairs. He reached inside the box pew door, undid the latch, and seated himself six rows back of Kelli and to the left, alone in the pew. He held the hymnal high enough, or kept his head bowed enough, so she couldn't see his face if she turned around. He gazed at her through the whole service, admiring her long neck bowed in prayer, her obvious delight in the hymns. *Soon that look will be for me.* He even managed to snap a photo of her as she turned to watch the choir's recessional. He snuck out before the final blessing, making sure she didn't see him.

The sermon was about forgiveness. Kelli was thinking about it as she and Officer Meyer strolled home, not sure if she was the "turn-the-other-cheek" type or the "eye-for-an-eye" type. She'd have to give it more thought; she'd never given it serious consideration before. *I always assumed I was a forgiving person, but I'm not so sure any more. With everything that's been going on, Todd, Sean, Molly, this idiot stalking me, I just don't know. It's certainly a lot easier to be a forgiving person when nothing serious is going on; much harder even to consider forgiveness when your family is involved.* As she and the patrolman entered the house, she was still puzzling over the question. One thing she was fairly certain of, though, it was a lot easier to forgive than to forget.

Seeing her frown, the officer seated in the parlor rose and asked, "Everything okay, Mrs. Cavanaugh, you look worried?"

Kelli jumped at the voice, startled from her thoughts. Then she smiled at the young man. "Oh, no, everything's fine, Officer." She stepped forward and looked at his name tag. "Officer Sullivan. I was just thinking about what to fix for lunch." She mentally switched gears. "I'm going to run upstairs and change, then I'll fix us some soup and grilled cheese. Is that okay? No need for you two to eat fast food and sit out in your car. After all, you're doing me a favor." She smiled again.

"No need, m'am; we're just doing our job." Officer Sullivan tried not to sound like a television cop.

"Well, you don't have to be uncomfortable while you do it. I seriously doubt anybody is going to break in during the day, and if he does, you and Officer Meyer will be here to stop him." She gave her most winning smile at her logic, *but why do I have to sound like a "schoolmarm"?* Officer Sullivan couldn't be more than five or six years younger, but she felt so much older. She headed for the stairs. "I'll meet you both in the kitchen in a few minutes."

At a distance he followed her and the policeman as she walked home. He wanted to make sure she was going home. Once she was inside he returned to the parking garage on Cumberland and retrieved his car. With his smartphone he was able to observe Kelli talking with the two policemen and then Kelli headed upstairs. He quickly switched to the view of her bedroom. He saw her selecting jeans and a sweater and once again heading to the bathroom to change? *Why does she keep changing in there? She didn't before, at least not the night she got home from St. Croix. Does she know about the camera? I thought those crime techs would have found it, but maybe not. I guess they're as dumb as I thought. Maybe it's because of the men downstairs.* Kelli exited the bedroom and headed back downstairs. He followed her with his various camera views from the foyer to the kitchen. *At last! I can hear what they're saying.*

Lunch was very enjoyable. The day had turned warmer so they ate out on the piazza at the large round wrought iron table. Since they knew Kelli had been married to a cop, even if he was a state trooper, the two felt comfortable discussing some of their more interesting collars. Kelli listened and laughed as the men vied for her eyes to sparkle at them. It made them both feel good to know they were helping her forget her troubles for a few minutes. After finishing their bowls of chicken noodle soup and three-cheese grilled cheese, Sullivan and Meyer helped take the dishes to the kitchen.

Kelli refilled their glasses of sweet tea and said, "I'm going upstairs and read for a while. You two just help yourselves to more tea and make yourselves comfortable. There are cookies in the cookie jar, too, so help yourselves." She pointed to the owl-shaped jar on the counter by the sink.

The two young men looked at each other. Sullivan, with only nine months on the force, looked to Meyer for guidance. Already he knew not to get in bad with any of the detectives, especially Detective Rae; he'd heard him called a "bad ass" and not to be messed with.

Meyer spoke up, "Thank you, Mrs. Cavanaugh, we'll try not to be in your way."

Kelli smiled back as she ascended the stairs, Corky close on her heels. "You won't be in my way, I'm just glad you're here. Thank you both." Kelli and Corky made it to the upstairs landing as the two policemen found comfortable seating: Meyer in the parlor, Sullivan headed for the kitchen. "Hey, bring me a couple cookies, will you?" Meyer shouted after him. "I'll just radio in and let them know where we are."

Kelli looked into all the rooms upstairs, fingerprint dust everywhere. "Good thing Magda's coming tomorrow; I'll just clean up the bedroom and the reading room and leave the rest for her. Knowing her she'll clean everything anyway, whether I do anything or not." Corky seemed to smile in agreement.

Kelli grabbed an older hand towel from her bathroom and quickly gave all the surfaces a once-over. "There. That's enough to make the room breathable. Magda will be mad that I used a towel, but it'll wash and I didn't feel like running downstairs for a paper towel or a rag. Come on, Cork, let's go read."

He had smiled to himself when he heard Kelli say she was going to go read. He knew that meant she would be in her reading room at the front of the house. He had placed another small camera in there so he would be able to see her reaction. A hopeful smile spread across his face. This camera fed directly to his phone, not to the monitors in his apartment.

Kelli tossed the dirty towel into the hamper, grabbed *The Dutch House* from her night stand, and walked down the hall. Her reading room was a small lounge on the east side of the house that Kelli had appropriated as hers a month after moving in with her grandparents. Now the whole family referred to it as Kelli's Kloset. It had floor to ceiling bookcases along the north and south walls, full of books Kelli had collected her whole life. She just couldn't get rid of a book, it felt like sacrilege. Years ago she had pulled an old leather wingback from her grandfather's library and it faced the window. There was a small table next to the chair, just big enough for a book and a cup and saucer. A flowered afghan her father's mother had made was draped over the matching ottoman.

The room was especially nice in the mornings when sunlight streamed onto the bay and into the big mullioned window. Not nearly as bright and warm at two o'clock on an early-February afternoon. She turned on the floor lamp just behind the table and grabbed the afghan as she circled the chair to sit down.

Kelli put the book on the table, curled her legs under her, then flapped the afghan open to spread over her lap.

An ivory envelope sailed softly through the quiet air and landed to the right of Kelli's chair. Kelli stared at the words written on the front: "My Darling Kelli." It took her a moment to recover. She reached into her jeans pocket and pulled out a clean tissue. "Thanks, Granny, I knew your lady-like training would come in handy someday." Corky's ears rose at Kelli's voice. Woodenly Kelli straightened her legs, pushed the afghan to the floor and stood. She bent down and picked up the envelope with the tissue between her thumb and forefinger. Slowly she walked downstairs to Officer Meyer. "Look what I found," she said holding the envelope out to him. "Why me?"

42

Sunday afternoon

She found it. The last note I left. And this was the good one, the one that promises our future. Ever since those stupid cops found the others I've waited for her to find this one. The look on her face was beautiful! The joy at finding another note from me. But why didn't she read it? Why share it with those cops? Is something wrong? Has she changed? Doesn't she love me anymore? We have to talk.

He darkened his phone's screen and continued watching the front of her house. It had been torture to sit so close behind her in church and not be able to talk to her, to touch her. He was disciplined, though. *I know it will not be long until we are together forever. Then she will understand how much I love her, have always loved her.*

"What the hell?" Scott shouted at the high ceilings as he stormed through the front doors. "How did tech miss this note?" He hadn't stopped to ask any questions after he had gotten the call from Meyer. He'd just raced to his car and broken all speed limits getting to the house. Meyer, having been left in charge by Harris at the shift change, cowered back from Scott's wrath.

"Get one of the techs on the phone," he shouted at Officer Sullivan. Richardson walked over to the younger officer and told him how to reach the tech office.

Scott looked at Kelli, curled and covered, relaxed on the parlor's settee, watching as the fury slowly drained from the tall man's face and shoulders. "I'm sorry, Kelli. Are you okay?"

"I'm fine, Scott, thanks for asking. I was a little shocked initially, but Officer Sullivan made me some tea and I'm feeling much better." She smiled encouragingly at the young officer in the foyer.

Scott saw a socked toe and a jeans leg peeking from under the soft green blanket she had wrapped around herself. Her dark hair was pulled back in a ponytail. Again the fireplace was burning. Corky was at her feet, her head resting on Kelli's knee. Kelli was her usual composed self, watching him very carefully.

Sullivan held out his phone to Rae, "Tech Moss, Sir." Sullivan backed away. Whether from courtesy or fear was unclear to the others in the room.

"Moss, another note from the stalker was just found in that little lounge room on the second floor, front of the house. It was wrapped inside a blanket folded on the back of the chair. What I want to know is how your people missed it." Scott's anger was growing again. The others could see his jaw tighten as he listened to Moss's explanation. "You do that. Call me back on my cell." Scott handed the phone back to Sullivan as he reported, "Moss said he didn't do that room, but his guess is that the 'new' tech was confused, maybe thought they were just dusting for prints." Scott rubbed his hands over his face. Could this investigation get any stranger?

"There was print dust in the room. I cleaned it up before I went in to read." Kelli looked apologetically at all three policemen. "Maybe he left it last night when he broke in? Maybe it wasn't there when the techs were here yesterday morning?" She hesitated, afraid to incur Scott's wrath. "Besides, does it really matter who found it when? I can't imagine there's any way to determine when it was left, other than that it was after the last time I was in there, or the last time Magda cleaned in there. So there's no sense in trying to lay blame. Why don't we just see what it says?" Kelli pointed to the envelope resting like a dead flounder on the coffee table in front of her.

Scott really wanted to chew out somebody, but knew he couldn't, not now. Not in the face of her logic and the two witnesses standing like silent sentries at the side of the room. He shook his head in defeat.

"Okay. You're right." He pulled a pair of latex gloves from his coat pocket and a pocket knife from his front right pants pocket. He looked at the two officers. "You two can get back outside now. Your relief should be there. Explain the situation and what is expected of them. If they want to trade off sitting in the kitchen until dark, that's fine, but after dark I want them both outside and wide awake, patrolling the grounds." Scott paused as the two men walked toward the front doors. He spoke again, "And thanks. You've done a good job."

The two men gave Scott a thumbs-up and mumbled "No problem" as they went out. Kelli smiled and said "Bye" to their retreating backs.

Kelli patted the seat next to her on the settee. Scott sat down. He reached for the envelope as he said, "Okay. So you went up to read, opened the quilt, and this fell out. Then what?"

Kelli knew it wasn't worth the effort to explain the difference between quilt and afghan, instead she just told Scott what she had done. "I took a clean tissue, picked up the envelope, and brought it down here to Officer Meyer. He told me to put it on the table." She pointed to where it sat, "And there it's been until just now."

"And what time was all this?"

"About half an hour ago, maybe forty-five minutes. We finished lunch and I went up to read. I had to dust first, so I guess it was a little before three when I found the note. The sergeant called you immediately and you came right over. Now you're up to date." She paused, looking for any signs of anger remaining in Scott's face. All she saw was the calm professional she'd been dealing with for the past almost-two days.

"Can we open it now? After all, it is addressed to me. Technically I don't think I even had to wait for you." She smiled sweetly at him, daring him to argue.

Scott just glared at her and slid open the envelope with his knife. He pulled a folded sheet of plain computer paper from inside. He unfolded it and read the message aloud

My darling, within the month we will be together at last. I cannot wait. I have looked forward to this day for so many years. Finally, we will be one, as was destined the day we met. I know you are happy, too.

Scott looked up from the paper, shock registering on his face. "What? Scott, what is it? Is there more? What does it say?"

"I'm not sure you need to hear the rest of this, Kelli."

"What are you talking about? Of course I do. What does it say?"

Scott looked back at the paper, then back at Kelli, seeking reassurance. He continued reading with a more husky voice, like he was having trouble swallowing

Once I killed Todd I knew it would be just a matter of time until our joining. These six months have been unbearable, but I know we had to create the illusion of distance from your sham marriage. But it's been long enough. Soon I will hold you close, kiss your soft breasts, your eyes, rub your arms, your legs. And we will be one. Just a bit more time, my darling. Be patient. Very soon.

Scott looked up into Kelli's horrified face, silent tears coursing down her cheeks. "He killed Todd," she whispered. "Why? How could he?" Scott started to tuck the letter into his pocket, but Kelli reached and took it from him. She reread it. The tears slid in a torrent now.

"Kelli, we can't worry about Todd right now. We have to worry about the future. Did you read what he wrote about you?" Todd's murderer had gotten lost in Scott's visions of what this sociopath might do to Kelli.

Kelli rose, tossed the letter back onto the table, and said through gritted teeth, "I have been waiting over six months to find out who killed my husband and now we have a suspect. I'm not worried about the future, I assume you and Charleston's finest will see that nothing happens to me. But I can never rest until Todd's killer is caught.

She headed to the kitchen, tossing over her shoulder, "I have to call Dean. I'm sure you can play nice with others and solve the murder of one state trooper." He heard the swinging door whoosh open and then close.

He leaned his head against the back of the settee and muttered to himself, "I guess that answers that question. This case can get worse."

43

Sunday, late afternoon

Dean Hamilton arrived forty minutes later. Miracle of miracles, he had found a parking spot close to the house and walked over. He walked in without knocking and was met by Scott's service piece pointed at his nose. Dean immediately raised both hands. "Whoa, whoa. I come in peace. I'm Dean, Kelli's friend." Just then Kelli came through the kitchen door with yet another coffee and tea laden tray. Her eyes on the liquids, she missed the confrontation occurring thirty feet in front of her.

"I thought I heard you, Dean, can't miss your basso profundo," Kelli looked up and grinned at the two men, her eyes widening at the sight of Scott's .9 mil being replaced in his brown suede inside-the-belt holster. She opted to say nothing about it. Men! She made the introductions, "Dean Hamilton, Scott Rae. Scott, Dean Hamilton. Let's go into the parlor and Scott will catch you up, Dean." Dean took the tray from her hands and placed it on the long coffee table before the fireplace. Corky followed patiently at his heels, waiting to be recognized. Kelli could feel the two men sizing each other up. Kelli walked around the table and hugged and cheek-kissed Dean with a whispered, "Thanks for coming."

Scott saw a man of his own height, but surfer-blonde and blue eyes. Dean had the natural erect posture of both military types and the best in law enforcement. It showed he was comfortable with himself and not likely to take anything from anybody. Scott knew several people like that; he liked to think he projected the same image of self-confidence. From that standpoint he liked what he saw. What he didn't like was the easy familiarity the new man had with Kelli...and Corky. Could he be the stalker?

Scott interrupted the long-time-no-see hug and chatter with, "Okay, Dean, let's talk."

The three settled themselves around the coffee table, Dean and Kelli on the settee, Scott back in his familiar wing chair. Corky had deserted him for the new arrival.

Over Kelli's shoulder, Dean had eyed the detective and decided he liked what he saw: calm, strong, no-nonsense. He did wonder about the small frown that had crossed Scott's face when Kelli hugged him.

"In a very small nutshell, Dean, Kelli is being stalked. The stalker has a key to this house and while she was away last week apparently he left some rather explicit notes for her to find. He also installed some sophisticated video and audio gear; at least we think he did this while she was gone because there had been nothing to indicate he was able to see inside the house before then. We've left it all in place in case we want to use it for disinformation." Dean quirked an eyebrow at this. Scott continued, "Unusual, I know, but worth a try." Scott looked at Kelli and continued his summary, "Then, last night, he broke in. Kelli scared him off with her gun."

Dean grinned at Kelli and high-fived her. "Way to go, Kell. At last that anniversary gift came in handy." Two chuckled, one looked confused.

Scott once again diverted their reminiscences, "In the latest note we've found, he says he killed Todd 'for Kelli'. So it appears violence is not out of his bag of tricks. We don't know exactly why he killed Todd, or if he is just saying he did to get Kelli's attention. On the surface it looks like he may have killed him just to make way for his romantic attachment to Kelli. We do know he is likely dangerous when thwarted."

Dean listened in silence then turned to Kelli, fire in his eyes, "Why am I just now hearing about this? What were you thinking?" Kelli opened her mouth to reply but Dean held up his hand. "No. No excuses. Obviously you weren't thinking. Todd's killer is the number one priority of the State Patrol. We have worked our tails off trying to catch this guy and you get a lead and don't tell us?" The muscles in his jaw were rigid; his anger barely contained.

This time it was Scott's turn to say "Whoa!" as he jumped to Kelli's defense. "Hang on, Dean. Kelli did call you. We only found the note about Todd's murder about an hour ago. Kelli called you as soon as I let her, as soon as I had finished debriefing her. She insisted that she had to call you before she did anything else, even make more tea." The two men glared at each other, then both grinned at Scott's reference to tea.

Somewhat mollified, Dean leaned back against the settee. He hung his head a moment, then looked across to Kelli and patted her leg, "Sorry, Kell."

She smiled at him and handed him a coffee mug. "Coffee?" she said and they all burst into laughter. Scott liked that she could laugh at herself and lighten the tense mood.

Dean and Kelli sobered up shortly after Scott did. "Sorry, Scott," the blonde trooper said. "I'm what they call around here a 'blue belly'; of course not to my face; they're all too polite for that. I'm from Philadelphia originally. Even though I've lived in the South since I was three, I'm still a Yankee. If you can't trace your relations back to the rice plantations, or have lots – and I do mean 'lots' – of money, you're not a true Charlestonian. I always tease Kelli that her true southern solution to everything is food or drink. You can always turn the tide of an argument with a cup of something, a plate of cake or cookies, or a glass of sweet tea or bourbon. Unfortunately, that theory sort of fell apart in 1860 during the War of Northern Aggression, but she keeps trying." Dean and Kelli smiled fondly at each other and she leaned over and kissed his cheek.

"Worked this time, didn't it?" she quipped with an impish smile at both men.

"For the moment," Dean warned her. "Why don't you get out of here and let us do men's work?" He was smart enough to grin when he said it. "Maybe get us some more cookies?"

Kelli punched him in the shoulder and smiled back. "While you two work out my future, I'll get something started for dinner. Just don't make any decisions without consulting me." She stood. "Holler if you need more coffee, Mister Hamilton," she quipped in her best Melanie Wilkes interpretation. She sashayed her way to the kitchen with an exaggerated hip swing.

Dean spoke first, "Cooking helps settle her nerves." He hesitated then said, "I can see you like her, and it's not all professional. I have no problem with that. Just an FYI, I'm gay. My interest in Kelli is purely familial. She's the little sister I never had and the widow of my best friend. Todd and I met in college, went through Highway Patrol training academy together. I was best man at their wedding. The three of us used to hang out almost every weekend. If one of us was on duty, the other hung out with Kelli. They both know – knew? – I'm gay and couldn't care less. Although I know she worries about me." Dean was staring right at Scott, daring him to make a negative comment. Scott remained silent.

"All I'm saying is, take it slow with Kelli. She loved Todd with every bit of her soul and it's going to take her some time to get over his death. She went to St. Croix last week to spread his ashes; that's where they had honeymooned. It was a big step for her. Catching his killer will go a long way to help her heal. In some ways, this whole stalker thing is a blessing in disguise." Scott's eyebrows shot up in disbelief.

"No, really. It's taken Kelli's mind off the St. Croix trip, it's giving her a puzzle to solve, and we'll catch Todd's killer at last. Perfect." Dean smiled, evidently very proud of his logical thinking.

Scott reminded Dean, "We have to catch him first. I take it you're offering to help?"

"No problem. I called my captain on the way over, told her Kelli said we might have a lead on Todd's killer. The captain said to stick with it and see where it leads."

"Great!" Scott replied enthusiastically as he leaned forward, hands clasped between his knees. "And by the way, my interest is purely …I don't know what. I can't figure her out. One minute she's screaming at me to do something, the next she's calm as can be. She's a librarian who isn't afraid to face down her stalker, and with a loaded gun in her hand. She definitely is not my picture of a librarian." Scott hesitated and then changed the subject, "Here's what we know, or mostly know, so far about Kelli's stalker." The two men consulted, argued, and theorized until Kelli called them to dinner.

44

Sunday, dinnertime

Sure, look at them, having the time of their lives. Good old Dean, can't find his ass with a road map. At least I can hear them now, figure out what they're up to. They don't know I'm watching and listening. Good for me, not so good for them.

At 6:30 the three sat down to a dinner of pork chops, grilled asparagus, cinnamon applesauce and corn on the cob. "Just what I had on hand," Kelli apologized. "Fortunately I'd gone to the grocery right before I left town and put everything but the asparagus in the freezer. I always have applesauce, comes from Granny, she serves applesauce with every meal." She grinned at the two men.

"And you grill, too?" Scott asked in amazement.

"Actually I do. But tonight I just did these on the stovetop in a grilling pan we gave Gramps for Christmas last year. It's cast iron and gives the lines on the meat and veggies like on a grill, so I didn't have to go out in the dark." Kelli smiled at the two men, one dark, one fair. She grinned to herself, *but I never expected to be serving this dinner to two good looking men.* Kelli motioned the men to the small breakfast room table and they all took seats.

Scott took a bite of his pork chop, swallowed, then looked at Kelli. "I've brought Dean up to speed on what's been going on. He's gotten permission to work full time on Todd's case, in conjunction with your intruder case." Kelli looked at him in alarm; had he forgotten about the phone bug just a few feet away from them?

Dean picked up Kelli's update, "Scott and I have gone over everything that's happened, the time lines, the list of names, and the notes. One thing that stands out is Corky. Corky must be comfortable with the person who broke in here last night. You said she didn't bark." Dean took a second helping of applesauce.

Kelli reviewed the events like a slow motion newsreel in her mind. "She woke me, I remember. She was growling and then she stopped; she just sort of watched the bedroom door." She paused again, trying to bring the scene into sharper focus. "Her tail started to wag." Kelli reached down and patted her dog, on her usual place under the table, watching for any tidbits that might come her way.

Scott asked the other two, "Is Corky likely to be distracted by treats? If the guy gave her a treat as he came into the room would that have kept her from barking?"

Dean and Kelli looked at each other and laughed. Dean recovered first. "No way. She may be big and fluffy but Todd trained her as a watch dog. Even had the K-9 trainers work with her. I'm sure you saw the first time you came here; she doesn't trust anyone new until Kelli says the person is okay. And Corky was trained not to accept treats from anyone but family, unless Kelli or Todd gave her the okay."

"Impressive," Scott replied. "Are you considered family, Dean?" Kelli didn't like the suspicious tone in his voice. She jumped in, "Of course he is. He's my second big brother." She rose, gave Dean a peck on his square jaw and started clearing the table. "Chocolate mousse for dessert. Coffee?" Both men nodded.

"You were busy while we were talking," Dean observed to Kelli.

"Not really. Just quick and easy stuff. I have to keep busy or I may lose it. Besides, I can't have you protecting, serving, and starving. Or worse yet, living on fast food."

Scott spoke up, "Speaking of which, Kim will be spending the night here for a while. She should be here in a bit, as soon as she gets her youngest to bed. We're keeping the patrols, too, but they'll just do periodic drive-bys since Kim will be with you. A patrol officer will get you to work in the morning and stay with you through the day."

Kelli nodded over her tea cup. "Sounds like a plan to me. Guess, we'd better save Kim some mousse, though." The two men looked guiltily at their all-but-licked bowls. "It's okay," Kelli laughed. "I made a double batch."

"After we clear the dishes, let's take another look at the names and narrow it down by the ones Corky knows, too," Scott suggested. "Good idea," Dean agreed. Kelli just nodded. It was hard to imagine the intruder was somebody she knew; she almost preferred it to be a stranger. Almost. They each stood, moved their dishes to the counter by the sink and headed for the parlor, mugs and tea cup in hand.

He had heard every word. Nothing he didn't already know, except that one little piece that might come in handy. He'd have to investigate that a bit more. He stared over the monitors in his apartment. The long wall behind was a collage of Kelli photos. Kelli at the pool. Kelli going to work. Kelli walking Corky. Kelli at church. Kelli and Todd. Kelli. Kelli. Kelli. Pictures going back to high school, then college, then Todd, then no more Todd. He gave the finger to the last photo of Todd, at his big police funeral. *Poor Todd.*

"Shit! They're getting too close. I'll have to move fast. Not too fast, though. Watch her. See if these new police plans affect her routine. You've waited this long, you can wait a bit longer. It has to be perfect."

He grabbed another prepaid phone from the desk drawer, he had them everywhere. Each bought at a different store throughout South Carolina, good thing it's a fairly small state. He chuckled as he dialed Kelli's cell number. He watched her pull her phone from her jeans pocket. She said something to the two men seated with her in the parlor. She punched the phone's buttons twice and held it away from her body.

"Hello?"

"I don't care if you have me on speaker, Kelli, it won't help them. No more than anything helped Todd."

Watching the monitor showing him the front parlor, he saw Kelli stiffen, but she remained silent.

"Soon, my darling. Nothing can keep us from being together. Especially not those stupid cops." He sighed deeply into the phone and hung up.

He watched the looks of consternation on the three faces. If only he could hear their words, their confusion, their frustration. He had them outwitted and it was so easy. *They are no match for me. After all these years Kelli will finally be mine.*

He laid down on the sofa across the room from the monitors. He was asleep so quickly he did not see Kim arrive nor the men leave. It was a quiet night for everyone.

45

Kim arrived about nine Sunday night. As soon as she had been brought up to speed, the men left, headed to CPD headquarters. Kim checked in with the roving patrol to let them know she and Kelli were going to bed. Kelli let Corky out the back door and then had to go find her. Corky was sniffing at a dead squirrel under one of the camellia bushes. "Bad dog! You get into that house right now," Kelli admonished her dog…and still gave her a treat.

By eleven the women were tucked into their separate beds, the twin beds in the other room across from Kelli's. Corky opted to sleep on the floor between the two beds.

Kelli leaned up on one elbow and looked at her new friend across the gap between the beds. The soft moonlight from the ceiling windows assured her Kim was not asleep yet. "Kim?"

"Yep."

"So what's with Detective Rae? Sometimes he seems almost human, but most of the time he's an absolute bear. What gives?"

Kim roused herself up on her elbow and looked back at Kelli. A small smile played across her lips. "Yeah, he's hard to figure out. I've spent a good bit of time with him, though, so I've learned a bit. He's the best detective on the force. I was lucky enough to get to spend a couple mentorships with him and I learned a lot, about police work and about him, maybe more than he wanted me to learn. It's because of him I'm determined to become a detective, too. Take my exam later in the spring."

Kelli sat up straight and smiled her biggest smile. "That's great, Kim! We'll have to go celebrate after you pass."

"Whoa, one thing at a time. I've got a good chance because there's only one other female detective, that gets me extra points on the exam. But I want to get the promotion on merit, not affirmative action. I want the other detectives to respect me and know that I'm one of them. Getting the job just because I'm a female is not the way to do that. Anyway, enough about me. You asked about our intrepid Detective Rae.

"He's been on the force six years, came in as a detective right out of D.C. Believe me that did not sit well at all. But it didn't take long for everybody to see that he deserved the position, he started closing cases right and left. He was made for this work. He comes from a law enforcement family: his dad is a big prosecutor in northern Virginia, two brothers are in federal law enforcement, and he's got four sisters, all lawyers."

"So why isn't he a lawyer? With a pedigree like that I'd think he could be a U.S. Attorney or with some big firm."

"He was. A U.S. Attorney that is. Four years after Georgetown Law School. Rumor has it that he felt he could do a better job at catching the bad guys than prosecuting them. He paid his dues, big time, with D.C. police, rose to the rank of detective in just three years. Then he moved here. Needed a change he said. The other rumor is that his fiancée was killed in a drive-by while she waited in her car outside D.C. headquarters, waiting for him."

"Oh, my God. How terrible for him! I am so sorry. I'll try and be nicer to him."

"No, don't be any different or he'll know I told you about him. He'd hate that. Like I said, just rumors. I tried to Google more information but found nothing except his official police info, no mention of a fiancée. So pretend that you don't know any of this."

Kelli's big eyes glistened at unshed tears for the man who was helping her. "I'll try," she gulped.

"That's about all I can tell you. So let's get some sleep. I have the feeling we're going to need it."

Kelli felt she would never get to sleep, worrying that the intruder would show up again, thinking about Scott's sad history. While hoping for sleep to overcome her hyper-active brain, she made a momentous decision: *I will not let this man, whoever he is, ruin my life. I will get back to my normal routine. I have to feel in charge again, for the first time since Todd and the baby died.* What surprised her was that now she wanted to live, but she could remember wanting to die for the longest time. Even in St. Croix she had wanted to just go into the water with Todd and never come out.

She remembered Scott telling her to vary her routine so the stalker couldn't find her. Instead she decided to keep to her usual routine and make it easier for Scott and Dean to catch the guy. *After all, the house is bugged, he'll know where I am lots of the time anyway.* Having made the decisions, her brain calmed and she quickly fell into a deep sleep.

46

Monday

It was the best night's sleep she'd had in months. For sure the best one without benefit of Ambien. Kelli rose at seven and told Kim she was going for a swim and then off to work. Kim quickly dressed and radioed for the new patrol to come to the house. Kelli grabbed her towel, goggles, and clothes for work and went downstairs. While Corky did her morning rounds outside, Kelli scrambled some eggs and microwaved some bacon.

Over breakfast the two women coordinated their activities for the rest of the day. The doorbell rang as Kelli went for the coffee to refresh Kim's mug.

Kim motioned Kelli to stay put while she went to the door. They were expecting the patrolmen, but Kim knew it never hurt to be cautious. A minute later Kelli heard Kim in conversation so she assumed it was the new shift. She opened the back door to let in Corky and she traipsed right over to the table staring longingly at the remaining strip of bacon on Kelli's plate.

Kelli chuckled at her silly dog, topped off Kim's mug and dropped half the bacon strip into Corky's bowl. "No food from the table is not the same as no table food, right?" she asked her contented dog. "Spoiled rotten dog," she admonished as she ruffled Corky's mane.

Kim offered to do the dishes and Kelli drove to the Y, followed by the squad car. She went to the locker room, changed into her teal tank suit, put on her teal flip flops, and went to the heated indoor pool. It was her routine to try to swim at least fifty laps twice a week, but she hadn't swum since before her trip to St. Croix. She found swimming laps was a lot less boring since Todd had given her the underwater iPod; she had loaded all her favorite songs and listened to them as she swam. At home in Cane Bay she had a pool she could walk to, but not here "in town".

She thought about their house in Cane Bay. Maybe she would just sell it and buy something closer in, the Gs weren't getting any younger. Or maybe she'd move to Arizona with them. Or maybe she'd move back to their house once she got over Todd's death. "Not likely!" she said out loud to herself and got a mouthful of water. Her head came up gagging and spluttering. She reached for the floating lane divider and hung on until the coughs subsided. "Let that be a lesson to you, girl; don't talk underwater," she said forcefully to herself.

After 45 minutes she exited the Y, waved at the officers, got into her Subaru, and drove with her escort to work. Kelli was thrilled and privileged to work at the Library Society. Most days she couldn't wait to arrive, hated to leave at the end of the day. Today she had really wanted to stay home and have a pajama day; she knew what lay ahead at the office.

And she was right. After having been gone for ten days, she spent the morning getting caught up on emails, voicemails, and questions from the other staff members about her trip. "How was St. Croix?" "Was it gorgeous?" "Did you scuba dive?" "Did you get to do any shopping?" "What's with the cop?" Kelli gave as many short replies as she could to each question and to ones about the patrolman she just said, "I'm helping the police research something."

Her only real break came at mid-morning when Hank, Sean's attorney, called to let her know the ME's report was finally back. He was able to tell her in strictest confidence that the report showed no signs of abuse or neglect. But it did find a subdural hematoma that probably killed little Molly. Since Sean hadn't touched her, it might have happened when she fell down the stairs a couple days before her death.

"This is a good thing, isn't it, Hank? Do you think the Solicitor's Office will drop the charges?" Hank heard the hopefulness in Kelli's voice.

"In all reality, Kelli, I doubt the charges will ever be dropped. The Solicitor's Office still sees this as a high profile case; death of an adorable two year old girl, FBI agent, former Marine. If they do drop it, that's an admission of error on their part. It's better for them to see it through to a verdict, then, when he gets acquitted, they can say they did their best; it was the jury's decision to turn him loose."

"But he's been in jail six months now. How much longer can they keep him in there without a trial? What happened to justice? He might as well be at Guantanamo. Shoot, he might be freed sooner if he was."

"Unfortunately the legalities here don't have a lot to do with justice. They can stall for – oh maybe another year, maybe two. And it's all perfectly legal, but most definitely not just."

Kelli's former joy disappeared as quickly as it had come. "That's not right," she murmured into the phone held tightly against her ear.

"Well, let's not lose hope. There is evidence of a hematoma killing a victim days, even weeks, after it occurred. Even with President Carter they found a hematoma that probably occurred when he had fallen a couple weeks prior. Fortunately they found it and he survived. It definitely works in Sean's favor." The attorney paused and then continued, "The next step is another hearing, this time to set the trial date. We want at least ninety days to study the ME's report before we even think of a trial. I need to get our experts to look at it and let me know what they think. So we're looking at early summer, or whenever we can find two weeks when everybody's available. Of course summer means we will have to factor in vacations, too. I wouldn't expect anything before September."

Kelli gasped. "But that will be a whole year then!"

Hank was silent, then decided to continue. "That's if we're lucky. No telling what other stall tactics the other side will find, at least they can't say they need more time," he tried to lighten the mood. "Hang in there, Kelli. I'll set the date as early as I can, but we don't want to jeopardize Sean's defense either. I want time to round up professionals to refute the prosecution's case."

"What 'case' do they think they have?"

"Right now they're still saying first degree murder and child abuse resulting in death. That's because that gives them the most leverage to get him to accept a plea somewhere down the road. I'm guessing they'll try to get him to agree to the child abuse charge because the statute gives them a lot of leeway. The statute ranges from locking a kid in a closet without food or water for days, to failing to give a child medicine in a timely manner." He paused. "Since they have finally complied with the judge's order, the hearing that was scheduled for this week is off. I'll let you know as soon as the next hearing date is set."

"I know you will, Hank. I want to be there for it. It's just so depressing. Will you call my grandparents or shall I?"

"I'll be happy to, give your grandfather a chance to tell me how much golf he's playing." He paused again. "I already talked to Nora, gave her the abridged version of this news." He paused again. "You okay?"

"Sure. Don't have much choice, do I? Thanks for calling, Hank." She hung up the phone and slumped back in her chair, her head resting on the high back, eyes closed. "What else can go wrong?" she said to the ceiling, forgetting the officer who was seated across her office trying to look invisible.

After a few minutes she returned to her list of messages to return. Around ten Kelli called Magda's cell to fill her in on the cameras and phone bugs and to tell her not to touch them. Kelli told her she'd fill her in on everything else when she got home. They chatted about Kelli's trip after Magda's initial attempts to interrogate Kelli about the cameras.

At lunchtime Teri Jackson called to check in and let her know there was a showing scheduled for Tuesday morning at 9. Kelli had the feeling the Realtor really wanted to know what was going on with the stalker, but she refrained from telling her anything; the fewer people who knew the better. After Teri's call Kelli called Magda back and gave her a heads-up about the showing.

By the end of the day Kelli was worn out, but caught up. *All I did was get my mail done, I shouldn't be so tired. It just seems the phone rang constantly.* She was debating grabbing another protein bar from the stash she kept in her drawer for days like this when her phone rang for the umpteenth time. She looked at her watch. "Good grief, I'm done for the day," she said to the room and the officer sitting stoically across the room. Kelli glared at the phone, "Why call at 4:53?" But she answered the call anyway.

The throaty voice said, "Soon, my darling, soon." He hung up. Kelli did, too, furious. "You are not going to win. You are nothing but my own personal terrorist and I will not let you steal my life," she growled at the silent phone. It rang again. Kelli reached for it; she'd tell him.

"You look so tired. Why don't you go home? It will soon be dark, my darling. Soon."

Kelli slammed the phone. "I will not let you scare me." She grabbed her purse, held her keys firmly, turned out the light, and headed out the front door, Officer Bewley close on her heels. The bored policewoman had been sitting patiently with Kelli all day and was glad finally to have some action, even if it was only following Mrs. Cavanaugh home. He didn't know why she was babysitting the woman, but the reason must be something big. CPD didn't have enough money to park like this for just anybody. Kelli stopped at the patrol car just long enough to ask the officer inside to let Scott know that she'd just had two more calls from the stalker and that she was headed home. Then she walked around the building, got into her car, and drove home, followed by the squad car.

At home Kelli found Magda sitting at the kitchen table reading a magazine. "What a mess! What happened? It looked like a fireplace had blown up. You weren't gone long enough for there to be that much dust; it looked more like ash." Magda was properly incensed at the extra work.

Kelli smiled and hugged the grey-haired, round woman who came almost to her shoulder. She'd known Magda ever since her first week in Charleston, twenty years ago.

"I'm sorry about the mess, Magda. It's been a strange weekend. How about a cup of tea and I'll tell you all about it. Let's take it out on the piazza, I think it's warm enough with the sun out there."

Over tea and shortbread cookies, looking over the burgeoning garden, Kelli filled in Magda on everything that had happened since her return from St. Croix Friday night.

"And the police think it's someone you know? That's ridiculous. We only know nice people. Nice people don't do things like this."

Kelli smiled and patted the older woman's shoulder; she almost felt like she was patting Corky. "It'll be fine. Don't worry. Dean is working the case, too, and there are some very nice police from CPD. One of them, Kim, is spending the night with me, at least for a while. She'll be here after a bit."

The plump woman crossed her arms under her ample bosom. "Well, I'm staying here until she gets here. And I'll stay nights, too, if she can't."

Kelli grinned at the mental image of Magda, looking like a ruffled partridge, confronting the stalker; he'd be sorry! She had no idea what actual physical help Magda could be, but there was no doubt she was a force to be reckoned with.

"Okay, I'll fix us a pot pie for dinner, then. You can meet Kim and get home to Paco. I don't want him coming after me, too." Magda's husband's real name was Pavel but Magda had started calling him Paco back when they were dating in Cuba. The Gannon family had adopted his nickname, too.

"Oh, Kelli! A man came today and changed the locks. He said the police had asked him to do it. Was that okay?"

Kelli froze with a box of pie crusts in her hand. *Scott had told me he was sending someone to change the locks and I forgot to tell Magda. What if it wasn't the right man? Could it have been the stalker? If it was, now he has the new keys too.*

"I'm sure it was okay, Magda. Did you get his name? Did he show you any identification?"

"No, I didn't know I needed to ask. I think his name was Dave, or maybe Don. He told me when he came in but I didn't really pay attention. The new keys are on the table in the foyer. I already took one."

Starting to unwrap the pie crusts, Kelli said, "No problem. I'll just check with Scott and make sure it was his man." *No sense giving Magda a guilt trip; she didn't know.* She left the crusts warming on the counter and grabbed her phone. "Pour us some wine, will you? It's well past five o'clock." Kelli moved to the porch to call Scott, while Magda went for the wine, and a sweater; it wasn't as warm out on the piazza as it had been before the sun went down.

She quickly dialed Scott's number, from memory. When he answered she explained about the locksmith and asked him to check. Then she went back to her pot pie. It wasn't five minutes later when Scott called and confirmed the locksmith was the one he had sent.

"Thanks, Scott, that takes a big load off my mind."

47

Monday night

After assuring Scott she was not alone and the patrol was still there, Kelli and Magda awaited the pot pie and Kim's arrival. Kelli brought Magda up to date on Sean's case and the house sale. Magda was obviously enraged, her Cuban temper coming through.

"Two things I cannot believe: my darling Sean in jail and your grandparents selling this house. Has the whole world gone mad?" She threw up her hands in Latin frustration.

Kelli chuckled, Magda's reaction was so similar to her own. "It would seem so." The doorbell rang. "That'll be Kim. Will you get her a glass of white wine, too, while I let her in?" Magda headed for the frig and Kelli went to the front door, Corky close on her heels. Kelli opened the door to Kim's smiling face and casual clothes.

"I could get used to this no-uniform gig," she grinned. "Woody is going to get the boys to bed after the Tony's soccer practice and homework. I'm sure they'll hit Bojangle's for dinner so I decided to come on. Last thing these hips need is another buttery biscuit. Hope you don't mind?"

"No, of course not. The pot pie is almost ready and Magda is getting you a glass of wine. We're in the kitchen," she said as a reminder to Kim of the technology hidden there. Kim nodded.

Kelli, Kim, and Corky rejoined Magda and three full wine glasses at the table. "Are you going to be okay to drive?" Kelli teased the older woman.

Magda huffed. "Hah! I am Latin, remember. I was drinking wine before you were born. But, if I have too much, I will stay here tonight; there's plenty of room."

The three women spent a comfortable couple hours over pot pie, leftover mousse, and wine followed by coffee, and stories of Kelli's childhood.

At 9:30 Magda insisted she was fine to drive and headed home. There were hugs all around and Kelli's reminder to Magda of the showing the next morning and to call when she got home. Kelli and Kim quickly took care of the dishes. Kim made her rounds and advised the patrol they were going to bed while Kelli let Corky out for her final time. It had been a long day and Kelli was exhausted.

She made sure Kim was comfortable, then she crawled into the other twin bed and was half asleep when her cell phone rang. She fumbled for it on the nightstand. "I forgot about you calling, Magda," she said without even a hello. "Glad you're home safely. Night-night." She started to hang up when the voice stopped her, "I'm glad Magda got home safely, too; if she did. You and that cop sleep well." The phone went dead. Kelli slammed the phone down hard enough to bring Kim running from the bathroom.

Kelli's glare was enough to tell Kim it had been the stalker again. Kelli told Kim what he had said. "I'm worried about Magda, what if he hurt her?"

Kim grabbed her radio, "I'll call it in and have somebody drive by and check on her. You go on back to bed. I'm sure it's nothing, just him playing with your mind. Try to sleep. I'll wake you if there's any problem." Kim was very reassuring.

"Wait. Let me call Magda first. If she's home there's no need to send a patrol." Kelli hit the six key – Magda's speed dial number – and waited. And waited. Then the phone was answered by a sleepy man. "Hi, Paco, it's Kelli. Is Magda there?" She waited while Pavel got his brain around the phone call at this hour. "Hi, Kelli. I thought she was with you?"

"She was, but she left about twenty minutes ago and I just wanted to check that she got home safely. We put away a good bit of wine." Kelli said with a forced chuckle. No need to worry Pavel over nothing.

"Well she's not here in bed or in the bathroom. Let me go check the downstairs. Sometimes she makes herself a cup of tea before she comes to bed. I'll take the phone with me." Kelli could hear his footsteps going out of the bedroom and down the stairs. Then Pavel's voice, "Did y'all have fun tonight? Mag so loves her girls' nights with you. She's not downstairs. Let me look in the garage."

Kelli held her breath as Paco walked across the kitchen and opened the door to the garage. Kim looked anxious, too, waiting for Pavel's response. "Nope. Not home yet. But it's just now the time for her to get here; it's about 30 minutes from our house to yours." Kelli heard the inside garage door close and Paco returned to the kitchen. "She may have stopped at the grocery. She does that sometimes. Why are you worried?"

Kelli decided not to tell Pavel what was going on and why she was worried. "It's just that we…"

"Oh, wait a minute, I hear the garage door opening now. I bet she drove slowly so as not to attract a cop's attention. Do you want to talk to her or shall I just tell her you called?"

Kelli smiled at Kim to let her know Magda was home. Kim returned the smile with a bigger one than Kelli had. She would have hated to have to investigate Magda's assault or worse.

"No, that's fine, Paco. She probably needs some sleep. Love you!" Kelli hung up and collapsed onto the bed. "Oh, my God. That was scary. I have to get some sleep or I'll be totally useless."

Kim replied, "That goes for me, too. Maybe you should take an Ambien tonight; I'm here so it's okay if you sleep soundly; I won't. I'm a mom; I sleep with one eye and one ear open all the time."

Kelli smiled weakly and said "Nice pjs" and was asleep almost before her head hit the pillow. Once again Corky took her post between the two beds.

Kim looked down at the print of fancy high heels all over the pajamas; her oldest son had given them to her last Christmas. She wore them not because she necessarily liked them, but because he gave them to her. She grinned and called Scott Rae to tell him about the latest phone call. He told her not to worry as long as Magda was safe and to get some sleep. Kim dropped off to sleep, snuggled in her silly pajamas.

Damn! That cop is there again. I sure got both of them scurrying around. Just a little phone call and Kelli was calling

Magda. Fun! No way I can get close to Kelli tonight. No matter. I need a couple nights of prep anyway, now that that cop seems joined at Kelli's hip. I have to see if it changes Kelli's routine. Everything has to be perfect. As soon as he saw the lights go out upstairs he drove off and headed back to his apartment. Once parked, he grabbed a gym bag from the trunk of his car and carried it into his apartment.

He quickly checked the monitors. All was dark except the light in the upstairs hall. He unzipped the gym bag and started placing the contents on his small kitchen table: flashlight, the K-bar that he'd gotten from Sean's dresser, duct tape, zip-ties, towels, rags, band-aids in case one of them got nicked with the K-bar, rope, syringes, and a bottle of chloroform. The last few things he would get tomorrow, after work. *Don't forget something to take care of that big ball of fur*, he reminded himself. *A couple more nights to observe, make sure the cops haven't messed up her routine, then it's show time. Need to check our happy home, too, make sure it's ready for its new mistress.* He chuckled wickedly at the play on words of "mistress". *She'll be **my** mistress, not the house's.*

48

Tuesday morning

Kelli was glad she only swam a couple days a week; that meant she didn't have to get up so early Tuesday morning. She lounged in bed until 7:30. Then showered and dressed for work. She found Kim fixing breakfast when she got downstairs.

"Wow! Such luxury, not having to fix my own breakfast," Kelli said as she opened the kitchen door and let Corky out.

"I thought I'd give a quiche a try. My kids hate eggs, so it's usually cereal or oatmeal with a pound of bacon. I'm usually just getting in from shift or just leaving for one so the faster the food the better. It works out for all of us: I don't feel too creative at that hour, and they don't want to eat it anyway. But, today, since I was able to get a good night's sleep and I have the day off, sort of, I decided to cook something I want for a change."

Kelli smiled. "Hey! You don't hear me complaining." Kelli opened the door to a damp dog and grabbed a towel before Corky shook all over the room, then fixed herself a cup of tea. "So what are you going to do with all this free time?"

Kim turned beet red and tried to ignore the question. "Do you want toast, too?"

Kelli had never seen Kim other than totally controlled, so this obvious discomfort was intriguing. She studied her new friend.

"What? Do you have a hot date or something?" she teased. Kim turned an even darker red.

"You do!" Kelli chortled.

Kim carefully studied the quiche as she pulled it from the oven and placed it on the countertop. She looked at Kelli totally embarrassed. "Well, it's just that Woody has the day off, too, and we've always wanted a girl, so we thought maybe today we would work on it." She blushed and rushed on, "It's so unusual for us to be home alone and not completely exhausted." She gave a sheepish grin and served big slices of the bacon and asparagus quiche.

Kelli hooted and gave Kim a big hug. "You go, girl! You don't have to make excuses, I'm sorry I pried." Kelli smiled slyly, "And if it doesn't work this time you and Woody will just have to keep practicing." Both women laughed and sat down to eat.

Tuesday was much like Monday with fewer phone calls and emails. It was a drizzly day, too, unlike the sunny day Monday had been. Once again Officer Bewley sat quietly near the door to Kelli's office. Kelli spent the better part of the day beginning a new fundraising campaign. She researched possible guest speakers and dates. Maybe Ken Burns? Then started writing her proposal for the Board. Although Kelli was a firm believer that you have to spend money to make money, not everyone on the Board agreed, preferring to hold onto the money they had rather than spend it on possible future income. It was a constant battle between new age thinking and "that's not the way we've done it in the past."

For lunch Kelli decided to take her minders to Poogan's Porch. The women had salad and Officer Tillmans had a really big burger. For dessert Kelli insisted they all have the crème brulee. As they were leaving Kelli noticed Bill Loudon seated across the room. *Now that's a coincidence.* They were all glad of the walk back to the Library, even in the rain.

At 3:30 Teri called with an update from the showing. The people loved the house and its location. She said they were deciding between this house and another one. They might want to see it again this afternoon.

Kelli thanked Teri and slowly hung up the phone, unsure how she felt, but pretty sure she had hoped it would never sell, even though that was what her grandparents wanted.

She absently reached for the phone to update her grandparents just as it rang, for the tenth time that day. "Soon, Kelli, very soon. I promise we will be so happy together."

Kelli slammed the phone and called Scott. "Might as well put Scott on speed dial," she muttered as she waited for him to pick up the call. Scott told her to get the patrol officer and head home. "Tell the officer she's to stay inside with you until I get there."

"Okay, Scott, but I can't just run out the door, I have a couple things I need to finish up here first. And I have to let my boss know."

"In that case have them both sit with you. You are not to be alone. Understand?"

Kelli's hackles came up, she felt like Corky. "Yes, Scott, but do you understand what a can of worms that will open? Me bringing a policeman into my office is one thing, but two will raise a lot of questions. I haven't said anything to anyone here about what's going on, for just this reason. Librarians are terrible gossips. Might as well take out an ad on the front page of the *Post and Courier*."

Save me from strong-willed women! Through gritted teeth he replied, "I don't care. Either go home or bring in the other officer; your choice." He felt like he was negotiating with a teenager.

Kelli must have felt the same thing because she said sarcastically, "And am I grounded for a month, too?"

Scott took a deep breath to cool his temper. More calmly he repeated, "Your choice."

Silence rippled over the air waves. Finally Kelli agreed. "Okay." She forestalled his next comment by adding, "And I'll have one of them call you when we get ready to leave here." She hung up without even a good-bye.

Kelli is pissed. Except she'd probably say "miffed". He grinned and picked up the phone to call Kim and Dean.

Kelli told Officer Bewley of Scott's instructions and asked her to get Officer Hargrave from the car while she went and talked to her boss.

Thirty minutes later Kelli and her two protectors were just leaving when Kelli's desk phone rang again. She hesitated before answering but then decided it was more likely to be work-related than to be her scary caller.

"Why are you still there? Hurry. It's getting dark out. And take those cops with you, too. I would hate for anything to happen to you."

Kelli once again slammed the phone and looked helplessly at the patrol. "It was him again. And I think maybe he's here, in the building. He knows you're here with me." She looked out her office window but did not see anyone unusual, just the staff and regular patrons; she recognized everybody. She turned back to Officer Bewley, "Please call Detective Rae and let him know we're heading home. But don't tell him about the call. I'll tell him myself. Just ask him to meet me at the house as soon as he can."

Bewley keyed her shoulder mic and had Dispatch put her through to the detective. She delivered the message and the three walked out into the rain and around the corner to the patrol unit. Kelli had decided to leave her car in the lot behind the Society building and ride with them; she'd retrieve it later or tomorrow, didn't matter. This decision worked perfectly because Detective Rae had told Bewley not to let Kelli out of her reach.

49

Tuesday night

Scott and Dean arrived almost simultaneously; Dean was carrying a brown grocery bag and two bottles of wine. The bag contained take-out Chinese that he proceeded to unload onto the kitchen table. Scott thanked Bewley and Hargrave and sent them back on patrol outside.

Kim arrived just as they sat down. Introductions were made as Kim went to the cupboard and grabbed plates, just like she'd lived in the house her whole life, then four forks, and wine glasses from the rack.

"We've got chopsticks," Dean offered. "No thanks," Kim replied. "Have you ever seen a fat Chinese?" She gave her own answer, "No. It's because chopsticks take so much time and effort. A person could starve if they had to use those things every meal. I've always thought that the perfect diet plan would be just to use chopsticks. Forget about South Beach, Atkins, Nutrisystem, all those other plans. Nobody would eat too much with a pair of sticks instead of a fork. And fruits and veggies are easier to grab with those sticks. Moderation by chop sticks. Perfect." Kim picked up her fork and reached for the container of sesame chicken.

The other three stared at her, open-mouthed. All three laughed uproariously and the serious mood was broken. Dinner progressed in a light-hearted manner, each trying to distract the others from the serious discussion they all knew was to come.

About seven, the meal and dishes done, they adjourned to the front parlor and out of earshot of the stalker. Scott turned on the fire and got down to business at last.

"Kelli, Dean and I have reviewed all the material we've gotten and the revised list of six names you gave us. We were able to get it down to just four names: Robert Cobb, Jeremy Deets, Bill Loudon, and Bert Grouse. We eliminated some of the other names as unlikely because they're too old, or, as in the case of Mr. Sanchez, not physical enough to have come up all the stairs, or not familiar enough to Corky. What can you tell me about these four men?"

Kelli was dumbfounded. She'd known three of these men her whole life, at least the Charleston part of it. Surely her intruder was a stranger? *Not somebody I know.* She said as much to the others.

"How did you decide it was someone I know?"

"The perp said as much in his notes. Obviously he's known you at least a year or two, or he wouldn't brag about killing Todd. You told me about your secret admirer in high school. His note said he's wanted you for a long time. I'm betting your high school guy and this guy are one and the same. These three are the ones on the list who have known you the longest and who Corky knows well. We're still doing full background checks on them; right now we're just working through a process of elimination."

"And what if you're wrong?"

Scott exhaled deeply. "Then we're back to square one and we start over with four fewer names to worry about." He gave her a weak smile. "What can you tell me about these three?"

Kelli collected her thoughts. "RJ – you've got him as Robert on your list – is really Sean's friend more than mine. His family lived right around the corner on S. Battery. RJ and Sean are still good friends. I see RJ at the bank now and then; he always gives Corky a cookie so she knows him. She stopped. "I don't know what else you want to know."

"That's fine. We know he's married with three kids."

"Yes. Cathy. I've met her a few times. They seem to be a happy couple."

"Looks can be deceiving," Scott muttered almost under his breath. Kelli and Kim looked at each other; Kim crooked an eyebrow.

Scott continued, "What about Bert Grouse?"

"We went to high school together. He's slightly ...challenged, got teased a lot. Since I was an outsider, too, we sort of consoled each other at lunch, walking home, that sort of thing. He lived a couple blocks over."

"So he might have developed a crush on you?"

Kelli shrugged. "I guess. Maybe. Not that I know of, though. I helped get him the job at the cleaners. He's sweet. Loves Corky; he comes out to the car to see her, keeps a box of Milk Bones in the shop for all his dog friends. Mr. Sanchez thinks the world of him, says he's saved him lots of money on machinery repairs because Bert can fix anything. He's great with anything mechanical."

"Did you date in high school?"

"No. He never asked me out."

"Have you stayed in touch since high school?"

"Not really. We run into each other every now and then, and, of course, I see him at the cleaners. Charleston really is a small town; once you've lived her awhile you start to realize that you see the same people at the same places and you get to know each other. I kept running into Bert at Toast and one day we decided to have lunch and get caught up. That was right after Mr. Sanchez had told me about his leg. Anyway, Bert said he was job hunting and I told him about Mr. Sanchez. He called and the two hit it off. Bert's been there almost two years now." She stopped and looked pleadingly at Scott and then Dean. "It couldn't be Bert, he's a sweetheart."

"And what about the Jeremy?"

Kim spoke up. "I met him, at the kennel. He and Kelli seem to be close, at least they hugged each other."

"Oh, for heaven's sake. I hug everybody, it's the South, it's what we do." Kelli sounded irritated.

Dean grinned. "It's true. Kelli's a hugger, whether you want it or not. She probably hugs the meter reader."

Kelli scowled at him. "That's not true. Besides being the vet tech at the kennel, I've known Jeremy as long as I've known the other two. He was a year ahead in school and I didn't know him all that well but he came to our annual neighborhood Christmas party with his brother, so we got to know each other."

It was Scott's turn to scowl. "His brother?"

"Yes. RJ. Well, half-brother, same mother different fathers. He and RJ always came to the parties, but their parents never did. I used to pass him in the halls at school, said 'hi', that sort of thing, but we never hung out. I hadn't seen him in years, then one day there he was at the kennel. Corky adores him. It was nice for me, too, to see a familiar face, to know the person who would be keeping Corky. He even kept her at the house a couple times, back before Todd died."

"And the last name, Bill Loudon?"

"I already told you everything I know about him. He was the janitor at our high school. He's been at the kennel at least three years, at least as long as we've been taking Corky there. I can't say that I 'know' him, he was just there, the janitor. Pretty grumpy I remember."

"And did you hug him, too?" Scott asked sarcastically.

Kelli sneered at him and replied, "Not that I recall, but if he did something especially nice for me I probably did." She felt like sticking out her tongue at him but decided that would be too juvenile...but he deserved it.

"Oh. I ran into Bill at lunch today. Well, I didn't really run into him; he was eating alone across the dining room from us. I didn't see him until we were leaving."

Scott shared a look with Dean then turned back to Kelli. "Anything else you can think of about these four?"

Kelli hesitated. "Not really. I just can't believe it's any of them. They're friends, well except for Mr. Loudon...and so nice."

"Okay, just one more thing." He reached into his pocket and pulled out a folded piece of copy paper.

"You're beginning to look like a magician, the way you keep pulling things out of your coat," Kelli said jokingly. Scott just ignored her.

"Look at this picture and tell me if he looks familiar." It was the sketch the real estate lady had compiled with the police artist. Kim leaned over Kelli's shoulder since she'd seen two of the suspects, too.

Both women furrowed their brows. It was a picture of a man with dark hair, a moustache, a racing cap, and glasses. He had long dark sideburns, too. "There's something about him that seems familiar," Kelli said, "But I'm not sure what it is. I know I don't know anybody with sideburns like that."

Kim spoke up, "I agree with Kelli, but I only saw Jeremy and Bert for a very brief time. I'd go with her feelings over mine."

Scott retrieved the copy from Kelli's hand and rose. Dean followed. "Okay, then. I guess that's it. We'll follow up and let you know what we find out. We won't contact any of them directly until we have something to talk to them about; if it's one of them we don't want to spook him. He might destroy evidence and I want to be sure we can put him away. It's very difficult to convict a stalker; he can just say he was walking down the sidewalk, or happened to be at the same place as you. Hard to prove without concrete evidence." *Or physical injury*, Scott added to himself.

Kelli hugged both men and said "thank you" as they left. Kim watched the exchanges with a maternal eye.

50

Scott and Dean walked down the street and stopped at the corner. "Let's look at Bill first, then Bert and Jeremy; the RJ guy sounds the least likely, although not impossible," Dean suggested.

"My thoughts exactly. I'll take Jeremy. Meet about four tomorrow and compare notes?" Scott asked.

"Better make it six-ish. I'm covering for someone and won't get back until close to five. I can get the background checks on Bert and Bill underway when I get in in the morning, then pick up the results when I get back in the afternoon."

"How about Montreux in Summerville? No chance of running into Kelli there."

"Not any more. It was a favorite of Kelli and Todd when they lived out there. I'm sure she hasn't been back since he died."

They shook hands and moved off to their respective cars, both determined to find the stalker before he turned into something worse.

Kelli looked at Kim. "I don't know about you, but I'm pooped. I think it's the tension. I certainly haven't been doing anything physical. I'll just let Corky out and be right up."

"Okay, I'll check in with the patrol and make sure all the doors and windows are locked, then I'll head up. I even brought a toothbrush this time." Kim grinned her impish grin and headed for the front door. Kelli and Corky headed for the kitchen door. Kelli smiled at her new friend as they separated, "And I want to hear about your big date today," she called as the two separated. Kelli was gratified by the blush climbing the older woman's cheeks. Kim shook her head in dismay and opened the front door. "We'll see."

Kelli spoke to her dog, "I know it's a bit early tonight, girl, but I'm really tired. I'll give you an extra treat when you come back in." Kelli opened the door and let her dog out.

Kelli busied herself with preparing coffee for the next morning and setting the table for breakfast. She heard Kim come back in and shout that all was locked up and she was heading up to shower. Kelli got two dog treats from the pantry and went to the door to let Corky in, but Corky wasn't waiting at the door as she usually was.

"Yuk! I hope you didn't find something dead out there again. Your breath still hasn't cleared up since yesterday. Nothing like the smell of dead squirrel or bird in bed at night," she muttered to her absent dog. Kelli stepped off the back step and was ready to call her dog when Corky came bounding from around the side of the house.

The two went back inside and up the stairs and to bed. All three got a good night's sleep, with no phone call interruptions.

51

Wednesday

Both women overslept. It felt wonderful! They even took their time showering and heading down to breakfast.

Kelli was the first to voice what they both were thinking, "Wow! No calls last night. Do you think he's moved on to someone else? Maybe it **was** just some high school pranks."

Kim didn't bother to remind Kelli of all the cameras and bugs that had been installed. Or the man who had impersonated a buyer at the open house. She knew Kelli would remember them eventually. Let her relax while she could. "Hmmm. Maybe so," Kim replied abstractedly. "I'm just going to call Scott and give him the good news." She picked up her phone and headed into the foyer while Kelli got out the coffee cups. "And tell him he can call off my minders, too," Kelli called after her.

After just a couple minutes Kim came back. "Scott said he got a good night's sleep, too, for a change. He hopes you're right but he's going to keep the minders for a few more days."

Kelli shrugged and smiled. "Whatever. Here's your coffee. Don't think you can get away without telling me about your big date," Kelli grinned at the other woman.

"There's not much to tell, at least not much that I'm going to tell," Kim grinned back. "Aren't those pancakes ready yet?"

The women sat down at the breakfast table and continued to banter until the patrol arrived to take Kelli to work. The women smiled and hugged and waved goodbye with "see you this evening" brightening their days.

The same patrolmen from the previous day drove Kelli and then escorted her into the Charleston Library Society. The others in the library continued to wonder what was going on but Kelli offered no explanations other than she was helping the Department with some research. That answer didn't make sense to any of them, but the only one brave enough to ask her a question was Gladys.

Kelli suggested to the two officers that they trade shifts, rather than one staying in the office and the other staying outside. They smiled politely and thanked her and Officer Bewley explained, "It would be awkward for Hargrave to accompany you into the restroom."

Kelli blushed and then grinned. "Hadn't thought of that."

As soon as Hargrave had exited and Bewley had resumed her seat near the door, Gladys marched in. "Alright, Kelli, what's going on?" She stood like a drill sergeant opposite Kelli's desk, arms on hips, chin jutting out, and a ferocious glare in her eyes.

Kelli slowly removed her coat, hung it on the hook, smiled and shook her head at Bewley to tell her she didn't need the gun that she had automatically reached for. Then she moved behind her desk and sat down.

"Good morning to you, too, Gladys. What exactly are you referring to?"

Gladys turned to face Kelli, flustered at Kelli's calm and sarcasm. "I'm referring to her," she pointed at Bewley, "and the other one. None of us believes you're doing research."

Kelli breathed out. "Okay. You're right. Someone broke into my house, my grandparents' house, and stole some items. Fortunately nothing very valuable but ones of great sentimental value; even priceless to the family."

Gladys looked as sympathetic as was possible for her, "Oh, I am sorry. But burglaries don't usually include police escorts, do they?" *Why does Gladys have to be so quick?*

Bewley raised an eyebrow at Kelli wondering how she was going to cover this one.

Kelli smiled sweetly at Gladys and explained, "Right again, Gladys, they don't. It seems this burglary was part of a big ring, with some very bad people, gangsters even. So the Department decided it would be a good idea to give me some protection in case one of the gang came after me. After all, I am their only one pressing charges so I'm kinda important to them. Isn't that nice? And it's very hush hush, so don't tell anyone please."

"Oh, for heavens' sake. Our tax dollars at work. Two policemen, uh people, to protect one witness. Seems strange to me but I guess I'm glad you'll be safe. I'd hate to lose the money you bring in for the children's programs." Realizing her faux pas, Gladys cleared her throat and added, "And of course we'd all hate for anything to happen to you." With that she turned and marched out of the office, impatient to share what she had learned with the rest of the staff.

Kelli got up and closed the door after Gladys, then turned to Bewley and they both laughed as quietly as they could, shoulders shaking and big smiles on their faces.

Bewley spoke up, "Even I don't know what we're doing here, but I can tell a fairy tale when I hear one. That was great, and very imaginative. And so quickly! You're amazing."

Kelli sat at her desk and calmed down a bit, "It wasn't all that spontaneous. I knew one of the staff would get the courage to come ask me, so I've been thinking about what I could tell them that would be believable. I think this passed muster, don't you?"

"Oh, yeah; no doubt about that. And by now I bet the whole library knows what's going on."

Kelli smiled at Bewley again and said, "I'm counting on it." She turned on her computer and muttered to herself, "Better get to work."

Across town, in Scott's office, he and Dean starting reviewing the background files on the four most likely suspects.

"Okay," Scott started determinedly, "let's get down to it. It has to be either Bert, Jeremy, Bill, or RJ. I say we forget RJ for now and concentrate on the other three. What do we know about them?"

Dean spoke up. "I think Bill is outside the age parameter. I know he knew Kelli back in school, but he's pushing forty now. His record is clean, no run-ins with the law at any time. It's more likely the perp back then and now is closer in age to Kelli." He looked at the other two. After exchanged glances they both nodded.

Scott summed up, "Okay, Bert and Jeremy it is, at least for now. Let's get to it."

Meanwhile Kelli's day was quiet. No texts from the stalker. No phone calls either. She and her minders grabbed lunch at Toast back on Meeting Street. They both opined that this protection gig was the best they'd ever had; better even than donuts! All three laughed and Kelli grinned at them and then turned serious. "I have to thank you both, you've made me feel very safe. All I can tell you is that I had a stalker who was threatening me. I think you two have scared him away. I've heard nothing from him in two days. So I'm betting this may be your last lunch out. It's back to fast food for your shift tomorrow. I just want you two to know I really do appreciate you." Both officers blushed and didn't know what to say; it was so rare for them to get compliments or thanks from the public. They were literally speechless.

Kelli paid the check and the three of them walked back to the Library in bright sunshine, once again enjoying the warmth and comfortable in each other's company.

That evening he four gathered around Kelli's breakfast room table again. This time Scott brought pizza and beer. The women still opted for white wine. Cork waited patiently under the table for "pizza bones"; she was not disappointed. Conversation centered around their days, mostly dominated by Scott and Dean explaining what they had found and not found in the files.

Once the pizzas had disappeared and all the news was digested, Kelli announced, "I can do without Bewley and Hargrave tomorrow. I think my new "friend" has moved on to another compulsion. At least I think he's given up on me." Bewley and Hargrave were a success." She smiled with only a bit of her elation contained. Scott and Dean were not smiling.

"No, Kelli, not yet. You may be in danger still. Remember we haven't had a chance to talk to either Bert or Jeremy yet; we haven't even found a residence for Jeremy. His LKA, last known address, was at his parents' in Goose Creek, but they say he moved out a few years ago and they haven't seen or spoken to him since."

"Really? I'm surprised. How about RJ? Doesn't he know where Jeremy is? At least we know where Jeremy works, why can't you talk to him there?"

"All very good questions. We plan on talking to RJ tomorrow. We tried to talk to Jeremy at work but he's been on vacation the last few days. Kim is working on finding where Jeremy is living so maybe we can get him there. Until we find out who is behind all this, things are going to stay the same: Kim will continue to spend the nights here, the patrol will continue outside. The only difference is that your minders will be state troopers starting tomorrow; they were feeling left out of the efforts to catch Todd's killer."

Kelli shrugged her shoulders in defeat. "Oh, okay. Whatever."

With that win, the men stood up to go. Scott and Kim had a private conversation outside the swinging door while Kelli walked Dean to the front doors. Then there were hugs and "good nights" all around and the men left.

Kelli and Kim returned to the kitchen and started cleaning up the plates, wine glasses, beer bottles, and pizza boxes. "Well, that was short work," Kim said with a grin. "We make a pretty good team. How about we make it an early night? I don't know about you, but I'm still bushed. I'll go lock up the front if you lock up the kitchen and give Corky her last time out?" The two had gotten into this routine.

Kelli responded, "Sounds like a plan. I'll meet you upstairs in just a minute. After all those pizza bones I'm sure Corky is ready for bed, too. First one upstairs gets the shower first."

Kelli opened the kitchen door and Corky ambled into the back yard. "And no exploring dead things," she said as she closed the door behind her dog.

She turned back to the kitchen and readied the coffee maker for in the morning. She heard Kim shout from the staircase, "Ha! I win. Heading to the shower. See you in a few."

Kelli smiled and checked that all the kitchen windows were locked. Just then the phone rang. Even though she thought she had convinced herself that the stalker was gone, she still hesitated as she walked across the kitchen to the phone on her desk.

"Kelli, hi! It's Hank. Miracles of miracles, they've dropped the case. Sean will be home in a few days."

Kelli plopped down in the desk chair, speechless. All that came out of her mouth was gibberish, "What? How? When? Oh, my God. Hank! That's wonderful." Tears were streaming down her face. "Why, Hank? Not that I'm not thrilled, but you were so sure they would never do this."

"I haven't gotten all the details yet. I'll call you tomorrow after I find out more. I just wanted to let you know the good news as soon as I could. Of course I've already called Nora. She's over the moon and as speechless as you. Sorry to call so late, I'll let you get some sleep. As I said, I'll call tomorrow with more information. Get a good sleep."

Before Kelli had a chance to respond, Hank had hung up. "Oh, my God! Sean's coming home. I can't believe. I have to tell Kim! Where's Corky? If she's playing with a dead bird, no treats for her," Kelli said to the empty kitchen.

Kelli stepped through the door and onto the corner of the piazza. "Corky," she called in a harsh whisper. "You come here right now." There was no response. "Corky," she called a bit louder, no longer worrying if she disturbed the neighbors. She stepped off the piazza and onto the damp grass. It was dark and foggy, the only illumination coming from the street lamp at the other end of the alley and the muted light from the kitchen.

Suddenly a black hood was dropped over her head and her arms were pinned to her sides by two large, rough hands. A deep voice said, "If you want to see your precious dog again, don't fight me. Just walk quietly. I only want to talk, my darling."

Inside the hood Kelli gasped, then stiffened in fear. The man let go of her left arm, in case anyone was looking out their windows. His right arm snaked around her waist and grasped her upper arm. Kelli tried to pry his hand from her arm. He half dragged, half carried Kelli to the back gate. Kelli heard a trunk latch and kicked out, she caught his shin a glancing blow, but not hard enough to keep him from lifting her into the trunk and clamping his hand over her mouth. "Quiet!" he hissed, even though they both knew no sound could be heard from within the thick flannel hood. Kelli started to hyperventilate from fear and lack of oxygen.

"I have Corky. I will remove the hood if you promise to remain quiet and not fight me."

Kelli didn't hesitate. She needed air. She nodded and became motionless. She felt a slight prick in her upper arm and everything began to go black.

Part 4

Austen Butler

'Til Death Do Us Part

52

Wednesday night into Thursday morning

"I swear, Scott, it was just a few minutes," Kim gritted through clenched teeth. She was trying to maintain her professionalism while worried to death about what might be happening to the woman she had come to think of as a younger sister. "We worked out this routine the first night I stayed over. I'd check all the windows and doors in the front of the house, she'd let Corky out and lock up the kitchen. Then we'd meet upstairs, get our showers, talk for a bit, and hit the sack. It's worked perfectly," she hesitated, "until tonight. We figured since she had Corky with her she'd be okay."

"You think?" Scott glowered. "What was different about tonight, then?"

"I got upstairs first and got into the shower. By the time I got out and realized Kelli hadn't come up, she was gone. Corky, too, apparently. I ran downstairs and checked the kitchen. As soon as I saw the back door standing open I called you."

Scott and Dean looked at the almost-tearful cop, wet hair pulled back in a clip, grey CPD sweats, bare feet. Her fear for Kelli was palpable.

The two men looked at each other. Scott took a deep breath and calmly stated, "CSU will be here momentarily. You didn't actually go into the back yard did you?"

"No, I stopped at the kitchen door. I had my flashlight and my gun. I showed the light around and could see the gate standing open. I kinda hoped Corky had gotten out and Kelli was chasing her. I called for both of them, but no response. Maybe someone opened the gate and enticed Corky out? Then grabbed Kelli when she followed?"

Scott was glad to see Kim starting to function like a cop again. There would be time for recriminations later. The important

281

thing now was to find Kelli. Scott had called Dean on his way to Kelli's house; they had arrived within minutes of each other.

Dean spoke up, "How long was it between when you last spoke to Kelli and when you found her missing?"

Kim frowned in concentration. "Maybe twenty minutes? We'd been talking after dinner then decided to go to bed. I headed up front and she opened the door for Corky. Everything was still locked up so it didn't take me very long. I hollered that I was going on up, she didn't reply, but I heard her moving around in the kitchen. I hopped into the shower and was out in under ten minutes." The two men looked in disbelief at each other.

Kim replied to their implied "Yeah, right" with, "Yes. Ten minutes. I live in a house of males with only two bathrooms. I rarely have the opportunity or desire to luxuriate in a bath or shower. My guys get really stinky and I'd rather they bathe than I do."

The men relented. "Got it. What happened next?" Scott asked.

"I started to dry my hair. Then something told me it was too quiet, you know that feeling?" Both men nodded. "I just knew something was wrong. Usually when I come out Corky up on Kelli's bed. I called for Kelli and Corky, got no answer. So I grabbed my mag light and gun. I checked Kelli's room and the guest room where she's been sleeping. I could tell she hadn't been upstairs yet. I ran downstairs, hoping she was just still out with Corky. When I found the kitchen door open I called for them again. Getting no response, I called you, Scott." Kim stopped, her bottom lip beginning to tremble. She bit it hard and continued.

"After I let you know, I called them again from the kitchen threshold and shone my light around as far as it would go. That's when I saw the back gate standing open. I ran back upstairs for my radio and called the patrol, told them to be on the lookout for Corky and Kelli. I guess I was still hoping they were out there together somewhere. I know Kelli's too smart to have left the yard, not even to look for Corky. She would have told me before venturing out; we could have gone together."

Scott exhaled audibly. "Yeah, she's smart. Let's just hope she's smart enough."

The doorbell rang. Dean scuttled from the kitchen to the front door. He brought the CS team up to speed. Two went around the house to start processing what they could in the back yard, one headed directly to the kitchen. Unfortunately they were all-too-familiar with the house's floor plan.

Scott and Kim had vacated the kitchen in favor of the parlor. As the inside tech passed Scott in the hall, Scott told him, "Pull out all the bugging devices, no sense letting him know what we're up to now."

Dean, Scott, and Kim took their accustomed seats in the parlor, each stealing a look at the seat usually occupied by Kelli.

The search for Kelli and her abductor was on.

53

Early Thursday morning

He was practically humming as he drove away. *It worked! I hadn't planned to get Kelli tonight, it just worked out that way. Corky was all alone. I was already parked in the alley behind the house. I was just hoping to get a glimpse of Kelli. But then she let Corky out and she didn't call for her for a lot longer than usual. Corky came as soon as I called her and she jumped right into the backseat, not a peep out of her. Sure, the chew bone had a lot to do with that.*

I was watching on my phone and I saw the men leave. Knew from last night that the woman cop went upstairs once she'd checked in with the patrol, Kelli went up as soon as Corky got back in.

But if Corky didn't come, then Kelli would come look for her. And she did! It worked like a charm.

Kelli first called Corky from the doorstep, then two steps onto the piazza, "Corky! Come here right now!" Then one more step and I came out from behind the camellia by the back door. Christ! You could hide an elephant behind that thing! Came up behind her and now she's all mine. No more grandparents, no more brother, no more Todd. All mine.

He stared at himself in the bathroom mirror, removed his hood, and grinned from ear to ear. *You did it! You did it! She's just across the hall, sleeping like an angel. My angel.*

He went downstairs to the kitchen and grabbed a beer. He rubbed its chilliness across his forehead and skinny, sweaty chest. *That's good.* He snickered to himself as he thought about rubbing his cold fingers over Kelli's sleeping body. *That would be even better.* He giggled again.

The Ketamine had worked just as it should, within five minutes of the injection the banging in the trunk had stopped, but not Corky's whining. *Damn dog!*

The only hard part had been getting Kelli to the car. *She dragged her feet as I walked her to the car, but at least she hadn't struggled. She knew she couldn't escape my vice-like grip, and besides, I had her dog. All my work with weights finally paid off.* He flexed his muscles and giggled again. He felt other muscles getting hard from reliving the evening.

He hadn't liked having to force her into the trunk, but she wouldn't cooperate. His jaw tightened and his eyes grew as pitiless as granite. *Good thing I had the dog to threaten her with. She calmed right down after that, "Please don't hurt Corky." Sounded like that stupid girl in the Wizard of Oz, "Please don't hurt Toto." Guess that makes me the wicked witch. But Kelli will see how perfect we are for each other, as soon as I teach her. She'll love learning about me, too.*

It was easy enough getting Kelli into the house. Just drove into the garage, closed the outside door, and poof! Invisible. Not that many people were up at midnight on a Wednesday. Especially not here in the boonies.

Must have needed more weight workouts, though, because she was just dead weight when we got here – he grinned at his pun and took a sip of his second beer. *God! That stupid dog would not stop barking. Should have given her a shot, too.*

I hated having to drag Kelli up the stairs, but she was so heavy by the time we came through the house and got to the staircase. At least she was out cold and had no idea what was going on. I just dumped her on the bed and went back for the dog. Shame I have to keep Corky around for leverage for a while.

Once I let Corky into the house she stopped barking. She ran right upstairs and jumped up on the bed next to Kelli. And then the whining started. At least whining is quieter than barking. I had to lock Corky out of the bedroom while I put the restraints on Kelli, but all she did was scratch at the door and sit out there and whine. I'm going to have to do something about her before she drives me crazy! Maybe a muzzle will work. The guest room downstairs will be her home for now; I won't be able to hear her down there and neither will anyone else.

I didn't want to tie up Kelli, what's the fun in that? But I know her; she's a fighter, probably a biter, too. I'll just keep her tied up until she realizes how lucky she is to be here with me. I'm sure it won't take more than a couple days. I can always threaten to kill Corky like I did Todd. Nothing and no one will come between us.

I practiced stringing several zip-ties together, got a big bag of assorted sizes and colors at Wal Mart, but that didn't work too well. So I just used them for her hands and ankles, clothesline for the rest. With her hands tied to her ankles and them tied to her neck, she's not going anywhere. She'll have to listen to me. Any movement of her feet or hands will tighten the cord around her neck. A little duct tape over her eyes and mouth, some shooter's foam ear plugs, and gloves on her hands, and she can't figure out where she is. The book about those kidnappings out west called it 'sensory deprivation'. I don't want Kelli hurt, just reconciled and compliant. Willing. The anticipation is so exquisite. He stroked his hardness as his eyes rolled up into his head.

He finished another beer and looked at the clock over the microwave. 3:05. *Better see if she's waking up. I can convince her she's been asleep a whole day, that'll add to her confusion.*

He walked into the hall and up the stairs, whispering to the dark walls and still air, "Come on, Kelli, it's play time."

54

Early Thursday morning

Kelli awoke very slowly. Her head hurt inside and out. *So groggy.* She tried to touch her head but her hands wouldn't move. She tried to open her eyes but couldn't. *Maybe I'm still asleep?*

Gradually full consciousness returned. *Where am I? What happened? Why can't I move?* She tried her feet, but stretching them the least bit caused pain in her neck. *That's weird.* Panic started to envelope her. The more she squirmed, the more her breath was cut off. *Deep breaths. Breathe.*

Okay, Kell, remain calm. Think! Does anything work? Mouth? No. Ears? Why can't I hear anything? Fingers? They feel fuzzy. She tried to spread her fingers. *Mittens? This is getting stranger by the minute.*

Calm down. Keep calm. What do you remember? Memory started to come back. *Back yard. Calling Corky. A man. Hard hands gripping her. A sack of some kind over her head. Car trunk. Then nothing.* She inventoried herself for other pains. *Feels like some bruises on my shins and forearms. Did I fight him? Corky? He said he had her.* Panic for her beloved dog started her to hyperventilate.

No! Breathe through your nose, like in yoga. Deep breaths. You can do this. You know this is someone you know, or probably is, according to Scott. He hasn't killed you so he must want you for some other reason. His notes said he loves you. You can do this. Just figure it out, like a research project. No panic, though, that won't help.

Where am I? Not still in the trunk. Too soft. A bed? That's not good. Any other pains? She'd read that women are more in-tune with their bodies than men, but she'd never paid much attention to hers, never had to, she was healthy. Now she did. No internal changes that she could detect. No pain between her legs. *Maybe rape wasn't in his game plan? Yet.*

Suddenly she felt movement on the bed next to her. The surface she was lying on certainly gave like a bed. She felt a long heavy body next to hers. *Don't panic* she insisted. She started to squirm away from the other body. The other body shifted, she felt it moving closer. Then her bed-companion started licking her cheek. She felt a cold nose. *Corky! Thank God she's okay.*

Kelli tried to reach for her dog, the cord tightened around her neck. Corky started pushing Kelli's shoulder with her nose and whimpering, but there was nothing Kelli could do. Frustration and fear fought for supremacy in her mind. Tears welled in her eyes but found no escape behind her taped lids. Kelli made soft mewling sounds in her throat to try to comfort her dog.

Suddenly Corky jumped off the bed and Kelli could feel her galumphing across the room. Someone had come in, someone Corky knew and liked, otherwise she would have growled. Out of nowhere she heard Scott's voice in her head, "Play along with him. Don't make him angry."

A hand touched her head and Kelli jerked back. Another hand held her head in place. Something was pulled from her right ear, then her left.

"I thought I heard the bed creaking. It's about time you woke up, sleepy head. You've nearly slept the clock around." The hands caressed her cheeks, first the rough fingertips, then the backs of the hands.

Kelli tried to move away from him, but each stretch of her hands or feet tightened the noose again. She stayed still. She could always strangle herself if she got desperate.

"Since you've missed breakfast and lunch, I've brought dinner. Your favorite: tomato soup made with milk, not water, and grilled cheese with cheddar and mozzarella. No mayo. And water, you must be thirsty after sleeping so long." *Subtle. Make everything seem normal, not like you're trying to convince her of anything. This way, when I leave for work, she'll think I work at night, not days.*

How does he know all this? The kitchen camera. But how long has he been watching? A cold fear climbed Kelli's spine, from her tail bone to her scalp. *How long? Maybe longer than we thought.* Nausea made the situation worse. She fought it down. *This is the man who killed Todd. He will not kill me without a fight.*

"I can tell you're thinking, Kelli. That's good. I love your intelligence. But if you're thinking Dean or Scott will rescue you, forget it. They'll never find us. We have all the time in the world to get better acquainted."

The voice. Sounds familiar. But why? Where have I heard it before? Think!

"Now. I'm going to release your hands and feet so you can sit up and feed yourself; it's so hard to feed soup to another person, ends up all over them. But if you consider trying anything at all, remember I have Corky – and a gun. Understood?" Kelli felt cold steel rub down her cheek and across her neck. She nodded minimally to avoid the cord tightening again.

Kelli felt the flexi-cuffs being cut from her wrists and ankles. Then strong hands swung her legs over the side of the bed. She moved her hands to the front of her body and shook them to return the circulation. She rubbed her shoulders to ease their stiffness. She lifted one thigh, then the other, and flexed her feet. The rush of blood to all these areas was worse than the immobility.

She felt his fingers fumbling at the right edge of the duct tape covering her mouth. *Maybe left-handed? Or just nervous?* Quickly the tape was ripped away, taking with it a few hairs that had been trapped under it. Kelli squeaked in pain and put her hand to her dry lips. She forced a small, painful smile to her lips and said, "Thank you. That's much better."

His fingers stroked her lips, outlined her mouth. "I know that hurt, but it'll go away." He pushed the top of a water bottle, *I hope it's a water bottle*, to her lips. "Have a sip. It'll help you feel better. The drugs I had to give you make a person terribly dehydrated and that can cause headaches. Sorry, but I had to drug you. I couldn't have you making noise; it was a long drive here. It was almost dawn before we got here."

"Where's Corky?" Kelli croaked. "She was here a minute ago."

"Not to worry," his voice was hard, like it was being forced through gritted teeth. "I had to lock her outside the room so she wouldn't spill your dinner." He paused, then continued in a more harsh tone, with a pinch to Kelli's upper arm, "Just remember I have her." Kelli nodded silently; she didn't trust herself to talk, she might upset him.

He placed a tray on her lap. He proceeded to indicate the food's location as you would for a blind person: soup's at three o'clock, the water bottle's above the soup bowl, sandwich at nine o'clock. She heard a rustle to the left of the tray. Something cold and metallic touched her hand; her hand recoiled.

"It's okay. It's just the spoon." He opened her fingers and put the spoon against the palm of her right hand. "And here's a napkin, just in case. I know it will be tricky to eat with your eyes covered, but it's a precaution I must take." He laid a cloth napkin on the bed next to Kelli's left hand.

"Now eat. You have to keep your strength up." He sniggered. "While you eat I'll tell you all about Todd's last minutes. It was just a minute, you know. I waited for him to go into the store so I wandered in and waited for him up by the cash registers. You know how they have all those racks of cheap stuff up there? I just pretended to browse them until I saw Todd coming. He got into the express lane 'cause he only had one item, a box of raspberries. There were a couple people ahead of him so it was easy for me to get close up behind him and point the silenced muzzle of my gun right into his back, as close as I could get it without him feeling it. And I pulled the trigger." Kelli heard him chuckle. "His body muffled the little bit of sound that there was. I just walked past him to the exit while he slumped to the floor. I heard someone say "Mister, you okay?" just as I hit the sidewalk outside the doors. Come on. Eat up. You haven't touched your soup. Don't want your energy levels to drop."

Kelli silently agreed with him, but not for his reasons. She ate and only tipped the spoon too much a couple times. She was trying to pick up clues about her captor and her surroundings. *Real soup spoon, not a teaspoon or tablespoon. Feels like sterling, too. Embroidered cloth napkin. Did he buy these to impress me or are they his?* She kept thinking and eating. *Everything I learn will help.* She finished the soup and nibbled at the cheese sandwich, stalling for time. She could here Corky whining from outside the door, sounded like the door was off to the right of where she was sitting.

"All finished? I bet you need to go to the bathroom now." He put his hands under her arms and helped her stand. "Right this way, my darling." He led her a few steps across the room and over a threshold to a bathroom. He pushed the back of her legs against the seat of the toilet bowl.

"Here. Let me help with your zipper. Your hands are probably still numb." Kelli heard glee beneath the man's rapid breathing. She gently pushed his hands away and smiled. "My hands are fine, thanks. I can do it." She had to fight the urge to clench her teeth or reach over and slug him. But she didn't know what weapon he was holding, and she didn't think she was strong enough right now to do much damage. *Wait. Wait for the right moment.*

"No," he snarled, "I insist." He slapped her hands aside. He lifted the zipper pull at the front of her jeans. Agonizingly he pulled it down its full length. "Thank you." Kelli tried to smile at him but she could feel her lips trembling. She hoped there would be no more offers of 'help'.

Once again he slapped her hands away. He put one hand on each side of her jeans and began to pull them down. "Help me, Kelli. Wiggle like you do to get the denim over your pretty ass." He used the jeans to pull her hips from side to side. She almost fell over but she managed to right herself without needing to put her hands on his shoulders. She reached to each side and found a pony wall on one side and a shower curtain on the other. The slacks were slowly guided to the floor, his hands grazing her legs on the descent. Then his hands ran up and down her bare legs, front and back, inside and out. He stopped just at her panty line.

"Step out," he instructed. Kelli did, once again using the pony wall to steady herself. His hand ran around the waistband of her panties. She steeled herself not to tremble.

"I'm sure you can do the rest, but I'll be right here, if you need any help." He laughed and took a step back. Kelli waited for him to move to the doorway. He didn't.

Quickly she pulled down her lace panties, bending as far as she could, using her shirt tail to shield herself from his view, then seated herself, embarrassment coloring every bit of her fair skin. Even though she knew he was watching and listening, she forced herself to take advantage of the opportunity; no telling when he'd give her another chance. The alternative, wetting herself, was unthinkable. Finished she quickly reversed her modest procedure. Her feet searched for her jeans.

"Don't bother. I have them. You won't need them anymore." Kelli held herself firm with difficulty. "Okay. That's fine," she said with dullness, trying out a small smile.

He took her arms and guided her back to the bed. He replaced the zip-ties. He gently laid her on her left side; she knew she was facing the bathroom door even if she couldn't see it. He ran the cord that had been dangling from her neck all this time, through the ankle and wrist restraints and pulled them tight. She heard him rip off a piece of duct tape.

"Could I have a blanket, please? I'm cold." He hesitated, he hadn't considered that. "Of course, my dear, as soon as I finish here." He secured the tape over her mouth, making sure her nose was uncovered. He forced a foam earplug into her right ear. "Comfy?" he asked sarcastically. Kelli nodded, thankful he could not see the mental glare she was sending at him. Nor her thoughts.

Kelli heard him rummaging off to the bed's right. He came back and draped what felt like a quilt over her. "You might as well sleep. There's nothing else for you to do...for now. I have to go out for a bit. Don't want you running away." Kelli heard the bedroom door close after him. She had never felt so alone in her life. At least he'd forgotten to put in the other earplug, the ear that was resting against the pillow. Maybe she could hear something that would help. Corky didn't come back. *Why?*

55

Thursday morning

It was barely an hour after they had arrived at the house when the lead tech called Scott from the alley to report in. Scott put him on speaker so Dean and Kim could hear what he had to say.

"It looks like something or someone was dragged from just off the piazza near the back door, through the gate, and into the alley. We assume the object was then transferred to some type of vehicle. We're searching beyond the alley for any sign that maybe the object was dragged farther down the alley. So far, nada."

Scott concentrated on the tech's words, trying to visualize the situation. "But that would have put the perp onto Meeting Street. Even at that hour there was a greater chance of being seen."

"True. The alley is cobblestone and there's nothing obvious to show what type vehicle might have been there. It's not like on TV where they figure out the make and model and year from a puddle of oil or some other fluid. Of course, if this was TV, we'd have the whole thing solved by now, too, inside an hour."

Like most in law enforcement, they both believed TV cop shows and investigative "reality" shows were reasons the public had lost patience and confidence in their local police; don't all cases get solved in forty-seven minutes? And with no commercials to slow things down? DNA results in TV land come back in minutes, not weeks or longer. Same for toxicology reports.

Dean spoke up, "What about one of the houses surrounding the alley? Could he have taken her into one of those?"

Tech Moss responded. "There are a couple garages and gardens that open onto the alley. We're checking them now. We'll be able to get more definitive views once the sun comes up." Scott looked at his watch as Moss said, "That's still a while from now. We're doing what we can now and the patrolmen are taping off this house's garden and the whole alley; that'll piss somebody off, count on it."

Scott looked like he couldn't care less. "Shit. So we end up unpopular with the residents who can't get their cars out for work. Tough." He hesitated. "Okay, Moss, do what you can as fast as you can once you can see. I'll have officers canvas the neighbors, see if they saw anything, let them know what's going on, and probably piss them off even more. Maybe they'll be happy to go back to bed on this chilly morning. You never know. The public, as we all know, is fickle."

Kim was terrified for Kelli. The problem of stalkers, other than their stalking, was that they were so unpredictable, usually because they were unstable. Anybody who turned a fantasy into reality, especially if it was over a long period of time, as it appears this is, has to have at least one screw loose, probably more. That's what scared Kim the most. "Give me a straight sociopath anytime," she muttered to herself.

She saw Scott click off his phone. "Okay. Here's the game plan." He checked his watch. "It's coming up on four. Not a hell of a lot we can do here before sunrise, just due to the lack of manpower and darkness. We'll get the neighborhood canvas started, even if we have to wake up the whole damn neighborhood. Nobody likes to see a cop on the doorstep at four o'clock in the morning. I'm not hopeful of getting anything from the canvas. We know from the earlier canvas that most of the people in those houses are retired, so they probably went to bed early. We'll hope for something, but not get our hopes up. Maybe someone was coming in late from a party or a movie; we could get lucky."

Dean and Kim looked at him skeptically. Dean voiced their shared opinion of the canvas," You're right. Not much hope there. Maybe there was a late hockey game, but otherwise doubtful. Wednesdays just aren't full of a lot of activity."

"The three of us can get started on a full work-up of our two most likely suspects: Grouse and Deets. All the way back to birth. Some of the background stuff is already done: criminal record, financials, that sort of stuff." He held up a couple file folders from the coffee table. "But I want to know where they were for the last thirty years, where did they go to school, where did they live, work history, family situation, everything we can find. Part of this is already done, but I want all of it. And I want it by noon.

"Dean, you check Grouse's alibi for tonight...last night." He paused. "Seeger, you do the same for Deets." He gave her a stern and-don't –screw-this-up look. Kim knew she was being given a second chance. She'd make the most of it.

"When you check work histories, find out where they were last week when Kelli's house was broken into and Friday night when he got in again. If they worked days, find out what time they left work. You know the drill, anything and everything. I'm going to get one of the patrolmen to search missing persons for the last ten years. If this guy has been waiting for Kelli as long as it seems, maybe he found a surrogate in the meantime.

"And document everything. We don't want this falling apart over a technicality. At this point there's not even much we can charge him with. Trespassing, I guess. Once we find Kelli he can be charged with kidnapping. If it goes to trial we want to be sure we can put him away. We have to find Kelli, both for her sake and to get this freak off the streets."

All three were silent. Each knew if it went to trial the perp could be charged with as much as first degree murder, but that would mean Kelli was dead. No one wanted to say that out loud. Nobody wanted to mention Todd's murder either. *This guy is a ticking time-bomb and we don't know how much time we – or Kelli – have*, they each thought in their own way.

"Okay. Get going. I'm going to take the photos we have of Grouse and Deets over to Ms. Jackson, see if she can identify either one from the open house. I'll see her after I report in to the lieutenant and get the canvas started. If you come up with anything definitive, call me immediately. We'll plan to meet back at HQ at noon, unless we need to get there sooner." All three stood, prepared to separate and get started. Neither Dean nor Kim envied Scott having to report Kelli's abduction to his boss.

"Oh, one more thing." Scott smiled weakly at the other two. "Thanks. Things have been moving really fast for the last few days and I appreciate the work you two are doing." He looked pointedly at Kim. "Kelli being taken was the break we were hoping for, although we all would have preferred a different kind of break, and we will get her back, and alive." Dean and Kim nodded. Scott turned and headed for the front doors, the other two bringing up the rear. Scott stopped and turned back again.

"And don't forget to eat. And get some sleep. You're no good to Kelli if we have to stop to take care of one, or both, of you. That's an order." This time he didn't smile.

56

Thursday morning

He watched her sleep. *She is so beautiful. She's always been beautiful.* He stood just inside the bedroom doorway, admiring his prize. *At last.* She was asleep on her left side, tightly bundled in the blanket he had provided. All he could see was her thick hair tousled across the pillow, her shallow breathing lifting the blanket in a quick staccato, uncomfortable in her sleep. He had given her a mild sedative in the water bottle. *I want more than just watching. I want her to fight me.*

Slowly he walked to her bedside. He sat, his body just touching the soles of her socked feet, peeking out from beneath the blanket. His hand crept under the old quilt and grasped her right foot.

He paused, looking for any reaction, any sign that she was waking. He rubbed his palm up her calf, rough against her silken legs. His thumb traveled up her thigh.

Kelli's mind started to wake. Her head hurt. Her scalp hurt. Her eyes felt like she had fallen into a sand trap face first. *Am I awake? I think so, but I feel so...groggy. I can't see anything. What's that? A spider! There's a spider crawling up my leg. A big spider! Calm, stay calm. Spiders are okay, they don't bite. You don't mind spiders. I do if they're crawling up my bare leg! Bare! Where are my pants? My head hurts so bad it's hard to think.* She fell back into her drugged sleep.

He was hard again; she always had that effect on him, touching her just made him come faster. He panted as he stroked her bare stomach, under her sweater and shirt, running his hands from front to back on her bare skin. His thumb snaked under her bra, rubbing the forbidden fruit.

He jerked his hand back. "No," he yelled to the room. "Not enough. I have to see her eyes, I want to see her love glowing in them, for me, just like she used to look at that loser Todd." His yelling snapped Kelli's mind to attention. She bit her cheeks to keep from screaming.

He stood and yanked the blanket off her. Kelli still didn't move. *Must have given her too much of the sedative.* He rolled Kelli onto her back, goose bumps rising on her legs. Still no movement from Kelli. *She looks so peaceful now, not too comfortable, but not like she's having nightmares. I could feel her glaring at me over dinner, even with her eyes taped shut.* He admired her purple, lace-topped bikini pants. Once again his hands found her, both thumbs rubbing beneath the leg bands of her panties. They stopped and moved back under her sweater, tracing the line of the lace on her bra, squeezing her breasts through the fabric. His panting changed to gasps of pleasure, his head thrown back in a moan of orgasmic exhaustion.

Eventually he pulled his hands from under the sweater and stood, once more admiring his prize, his trophy. "You're all mine, Kelli. And I control you." Frustrated he whimpers, "But this is not enough. I want us to share our love. To be joined as husband and wife, 'til death do us part."

He gently patted Kelli's shoulder and eased her back onto her side, relieving the pressure from her legs and shoulders. He walked around to the other side of the bed and climbed up next to Kelli. He moved over next to her and spooned her. Once again both his hands reached under her sweater, squeezing and rubbing her breasts through the lace bra. They moved down and stroked her bare stomach. Kelli gritted her teeth, glad he was still clothed. After what seemed a lifetime he forcefully removed his hands and slammed his body off the bed. She could hear him breathing deeply at the side of the bed. A squeaky voice said, "Sleep, my darling. I'll be back."

He left the room to change his clothes for work. *Before work, though, I have to take care of that dog. And get some groceries. I guess she'll sleep for a while yet. Have to cut back on the dose next time.* He laughed to himself at the irony that he was going to the same grocery store where he had killed Todd. The potential danger made him hard again.

Kelli finally awoke fully just as she heard the door close behind him. *"Where is he going? How long will he be gone? What has he done with Corky?"* She lifted her head a tiny bit off the pillow and gave it a small shake, trying to clear the fog. *Think, Kelli. What do you know so far? What can you do to save yourself?* Her shoulders sagged at just the effort to think. *Okay. He's organized. Technically good, put in all that gear at the house. About my height. Thin but muscled. Said he took Corky downstairs so either I'm upstairs or Corky is in a basement, or both. Fat lot of good that does. Well, yeah, it does. There are not a lot of basements in the Charleston area. Great. We've left the tri-counties. Could be anywhere. Keep going, Kell. What else do you know? He's patient; he hasn't hurt me yet. He's nuts! Maybe he's making me nuts, I'm talking to myself in my head. Keep going. What else do I know?* She scrunched her eyes tightly closed behind the duct tape. *I know Dean will do everything in his power to find me...and Kim and even Scott will help him.* That made her feel better. *I just have to hold on until they get here, and it's already been over 24 hours.*

How can I keep him at bay? Be nice. Flirt. Flatter him. The important thing is to stay alive long enough to get him convicted, no matter what else he does, staying alive is the important thing. Tears welled up behind the tape. *I'll make you proud of me, Todd, I promise.*

Two hours later he opened the door to the bedroom, a tray in his hands again. "Come on, sleepyhead, wake up. We have a full day ahead of us." Kelli didn't move. He took the wet cloth he had prepared and began wiping her cheeks and neck. Kelli pretended to rouse. "Good girl. " The cloth strayed beneath the neck of her sweater and blouse and slowly wiped her chest above her bra. Kelli stiffened and tried to jerk back, away from her captor and the sickening wet cloth. He spoke calmly and pulled the cloth back out. Then he removed the foam ear plug from her ear. "I'll take the gag off and untie you so you can eat. As long as you promise not to try anything stupid. Remember. I have Corky and a gun. Are we clear?"

Kelli nodded tentatively. He ripped off the tape covering her mouth and sawed through the hard plastic of the cuffs. Kelli said through her dry lips, "Please, there's a big spider on the bed. It was crawling on my leg a while ago. Please get it away." She was starting to panic, she could feel it. For real.

"Shhh. It's okay. It was just me. I love touching you. I've wanted to do this for so long. This and much more, so much more. Ready to sit up?" Kelli nodded again. She didn't need to pretend any more. *Think, Kelli, think. There has to be some way out of this. Keep him talking.* She realized he was still talking and she had no idea what he had just said. He put a water bottle to her lips and she drank greedily. He loosened the noose that was still attached to her leg restraints, then swung her legs over the side of the bed and onto the carpeted floor. He lifted her under her arms to a sitting position. Kelli shook her head, pretending to clear it.

"What time is it? Where are we? Why are you doing this to me?" she asked in a raspy voice. *How long has he been watching me? We assumed he put the cameras in the house while I was in St. Croix, but what if they were there longer? Pay attention to him, Kelli. What's he saying?*

"Here, drink some juice." He pressed the glass into her hand. "Your mouth is dry from the sedative I gave you. The juice will help clear your head, too." She couldn't see him, but she felt him beaming at her, like a proud teacher with a star pupil. "And we've got Irish Breakfast tea, cinnamon toast, and apple cinnamon oatmeal. All your favorites."

Kelli forced a smile and enthusiasm. "Wow! You've gone all out. You really do know my favorites. I had no idea I had such a fan." She put down the juice glass, felt around the tray he had placed on her lap for the spoon and the cereal bowl, pleased with herself when the two connected.

His voice was harsh. "You had no idea? How could you not? I've tried to tell you for years. I started way back in high school with those roses and notes at your locker. Then, this last year, since we got rid of Todd, I've tried really hard: emails, calls, voice mail messages. I was afraid you'd find me out before the time was right. But I was too sneaky for you, too sneaky even for the police. They'll never think to look for us here. We have all the time in the world to be together, to make up for lost time." She felt his leer.

Kelli slowly ate the barely warm oatmeal and sipped her tepid tea. *How long was he in here before he woke me? What did he do?* She stalled, trying to think of something to say and not upset him. *Obviously Scott was right, he is somebody I've known a long time.* "The oatmeal is perfect, thank you so much. It's just the way I like it, no milk." She took another small bite. "I wish I could see you."

"No, not yet, but soon." His thumb rubbed down her cheek to her neck. His right hand curled around the back of her neck. "Soon, very soon." Kelli didn't recognize his hoarse voice.

"Did you know I had to practice several times so I could be sure I knew what to do when the time finally arrived that I could steal you away?" He paused and looked up at the ceiling. "I actually started in high school, and then a couple more while you were in college, and Todd of course. But the girls just wouldn't cooperate, so I had to kill them and find another. The other girls weren't nearly as beautiful as you though." He pats her shoulder. "Not nearly. There's only one Kelli." He beamed at the compliment he has paid her. He softly kissed her sore lips.

Kelli fumbled for a slice of the cinnamon toast on the tray. He had cut it in half diagonally, the way she used to do for Todd. Hesitantly, afraid of the answer, she asked, "Where's Corky?" *Could he be Jeremy? Scott said maybe Bert or Jeremy or RJ or Bill. But Jeremy wouldn't hurt Corky. I don't think Bert would either. Bill is too tall. I can't see RJ dressing up in a Ninja outfit, or any kind of costume for that matter. I'll give RJ and Bill a pass for the time being. Don't guess who he is! If you guess wrong he might get mad. Figure out where you are, then maybe you can figure out how to get away.*

He jumped up, overturning the tray from Kelli's lap. "Don't worry about that damn dog," he shouted. "Nobody and nothing will ever come between us again."

Kelli gasped, then held her breath to calm herself. Finally she asked, "Is that why you killed Todd?"

He had calmed also. He sat next to her on the bed, their thighs touching. Kelli tried not to pull away. Again she realized her legs were bare. She shuddered in revulsion. *What did he do to me while I was asleep?*

Reverently he took Kelli's hand in both of his. "Of course. I knew you really didn't love him. How could you? You love me. I figured your grandparents had talked you into getting married. It sure wasn't your parents. So I freed you for us."

Rage was building inside her. *Where did he get that idea?* Again she heard Scott's voice, "Don't make him mad. For sociopaths it's all about the control. Psychopaths want to control and to deliver pain. But you don't know where the tipping edge might be that turns a sociopath into a psychopath." She took deep, slow breaths through her nose again. *Stay calm. Play along.*

Her free hand reached up to pat his cheek, but encountered only wool. Nonetheless she caressed his cheek. "You know me so well, won't you let me see your face? At least your eyes. You have beautiful eyes. You have that mask on, I still won't see all of you, just your eyes. You are so smart to have planned this special meal for me."

"I've watched you for years. Every minute of your life, you've been with me. Isn't technology great?" He laughed a harsh laugh, delighted with his own smarts.

"I had no idea you knew so much about technology. All those cameras and telephone bugs at my grandparents' house. You have been watching me a long time, I've been there over six months."

"Oh, they've only been in place a couple weeks. I was watching you long before that, years before." He chortled at his big secret.

Kelli thought desperately. *Before? I've only ever lived at three places: the G's, the house with Todd, and at college.* "College? Did you watch me at college? I wish I'd.known. We've wasted so much time."

The slap across her left cheek came out of nowhere. Knocked onto her back by the force of the blow, she couldn't see him moistening his lips with the tip of his tongue. Didn't see the hardness in the front of his jeans. But she felt his hand brush her breast as he reached to pull her back up to a sitting position.

"The blindfold stays on. We'll talk about it at lunch. And don't try to play me." He squeezed the hand Kelli was holding on her inflamed cheek until she yelped in pain.

"Need a bathroom break before your next nap?" *He sounds so pleasant, even though he just knocked the wind out of me with that slap.*

Kelli was horrified at the thought. "No, not right now, thanks." She smiles sweetly, or at least hoped it came off that way.

He laid her back on the bed, so gently. Then re-zip-tied her hands and feet.

She tried to ask without whining, "Can we skip the gag? I promise I won't yell or anything. Wouldn't do me any good anyway, I have no idea where we are. It's really hard to breathe with that on."

He stood in front of her, debating. "We'll give it a try. Remember, I'm right next door and I'll hear you if you make a sound. I also have one of my first cameras in here." He put the roll of tape back onto the nightstand. "I can see you even when I'm not with you, just like at your grandparents'."

"I won't do anything, I promise." She hesitated again, afraid to push her luck. "And can we skip the sedative? Look at me, I can't go anywhere, trussed up like this. You've done such a thorough job of restraining me, you must have thought about this a long time." She tried to smile admiringly. "I think the sedatives are making me sick to my stomach. Thank you so much for breakfast, it helped settle my stomach." Once again she smiled her most winning smile, just slightly pitiful, too. *It's hard to gauge his reactions since I can't see him.*

He knew he should give her a shot, but he didn't want to have to clean up vomit, not even hers.

In his most magnanimous voice he replied, "Okay. At least for a little while. It's not long until lunchtime, then we'll renegotiate.

I need some sleep, too, you know. I can't get it if I have to worry about what you're doing." He grinned again at his disinformation. He had slept while she did, at least for a bit. His plan to disorient her was working.

He spread the quilt back over her. "Just rest then, dear, we'll have play time later, just the two of us." He turned and left the room. Kelli heard the door close behind him, at least she hoped it was behind him. *He could be standing by the door watching me.*

Tears of fear and anger formed behind the tape covering her eyes. She waited, straining to hear if he was still in the room. After what seemed an age she decided she was alone once again. "Think, Kelli, think! You have to find something to help. Think! What else do you know about him? Maybe same background as me, fine china, cloth napkin. Could be either Jeremy or Bert." *At least I can hear another voice, even if it is only mine. Thank God it's not his.* Being able to speak her thoughts out loud made them more real.

Frustration made her try to loosen the restraints but she only ended up with rope burns on her neck. Kelli put her head back down on the pillow and reviewed her thinking of earlier. *Even if he is watching, maybe he can't hear me.*

57

"Nothing? What do you mean 'nothing'."

"Sorry, Scott, that's what we found. Nothing." The senior CSU tech confirmed. It was just after sunrise Thursday morning. Scott had returned to Kelli's house with a box of warm Krispy Kreme donuts for the crime scene techs who had been working through the early morning hours.

"We set up the kleig lights after our initial search. The only thing we still have, even with daylight, are the drag marks from the back door to the alley. From the depth of the marks I'd say either she was drugged and he was pulling her dead weight, or she was intentionally trying to leave the marks."

Scott had grimaced at the "dead weight" comment, but then schooled his face to its normal impersonal demeanor. "I think he would have waited to drug her until he got her to the car, in case somebody was looking out the windows. Must have had another weapon to get her to go with him." The tech wasn't sure if Scott was talking to him or himself.

"That's it, Scott. Unless you have anything else for us?"

Scott considered his reply, "No, that's it. Give the guys my thanks and those donuts." He motioned to the green and white box sitting on the counter. "Sorry about the cliché, but it was the only place I found open this early." He grinned as the tech picked up the box.

Moss laughed. "Not to worry. I don't know anyone who turns down Krispy Kreme, even people who aren't cops." He headed for the kitchen door, then stopped next to Scott, still seated at the breakfast bar. "As always, Scott, it's a pleasure working with you. Some of the detectives watch too much TV and expect us to produce miracles. You're realistic and smart. You know it takes time and a little luck to solve most cases. And now and then science helps, too." He grinned his fatherly smile.

"Thanks, Moss, you, too. I just have the feeling we don't have much time."

The older man opened the kitchen door just as Scott's phone rang. Kim.

"Scott, you better get over here, and bring CSU with you. I'm texting you the address right now."

"On our way. They were just about to close up shop here, nothing to find. I'll stop them and send them on." Scott disconnected and bolted for the front door. He shouted as he bounded down the steps, "Moss, hold on a minute."

Fortunately the whole team was standing on the sidewalk next to their CSU van just starting on their donuts when Scott ran out the front door.

"I need you to go to this address." He stopped and texted it to the older man's phone. "I'm heading there right now. Come on up if you don't see me out front, second floor, number 217." Scott didn't wait for agreement; he knew they wouldn't question him. They'd meet him there and then get the details.

Scott walked over to the patrol car still watching the house and keeping the lookers and rubberneckers at bay.

"You two go inside. Lock everything up tight and stay inside. Nobody gets in without my okay. I want one of you inside at all times. That leaves one of you to check the perimeter or make a breakfast run or whatever. Got it?"

The two young patrolmen nodded in unison. Proud to be included on the case, terrified of screwing up. Scott gave the one closest to him a pat on the shoulder, then turned on his heel and headed toward his car, parked farther down the street. He dialed Dean as he mini-jogged the two blocks along the Battery, past the Civil War mortars, cannons, and the bronze statue of General William Moultrie, famous for having defended Sullivan's Island against the British during the Revolutionary War.

Dean spoke before Scott even had a chance to identify himself, "I was just about to call you. Bert is in the clear, solid alibis for both of the known dates. He works a second job nights and he was at work the whole time. Paying his way through college."

"Okay, so we'll focus on Jeremy. Kim just called. She's got something. Meet us at Jeremy's apartment right away." Scott texted the address to Dean.

"On my way. Any idea what she found?"

"No, I didn't have time to ask her, I had to catch the CSU team before they left Kelli's house. I'm on my way now. See you there." Scott disconnected the call, texted the address to Dean, turned the ignition, shifted into Drive, hit the lights and pulled out. It was normally about a twenty minute drive to the area of Jeremy's apartment from downtown, depending on traffic. Scott figured he could make it in fifteen or less at this hour and with the help of his blue lights. He just hoped Kim had not found Kelli's body.

Scott made the trip in thirteen minutes, the last mile without the lights. Since he didn't know what to expect at the apartment he didn't want to warn Jeremy he was coming. Jeremy could be barricaded in the apartment with Kelli as a hostage. A million scenarios ran through his mind during the drive to North Charleston.

Kim was waiting for him in the parking lot. She looked calm, but excited. She was the first to speak. "I got Jeremy's work record and it was clean. Usually he works nights and most everything happened at night."

"Shit!" Scott interrupted her.

"Except," she paused to be sure she had his full attention. "His schedule changed. Jeremy worked days the week Kelli was in St. Croix, and his days ended on Thursday. Then he had Friday off and has worked days since then. At least through Tuesday, he started vacation as of Wednesday."

"So he could have been our elusive home-buyer on last Wednesday morning. And he could have abducted Kelli last night." Scott shook his head, not enough. "Anything else?"

"You could say that." Kim gave a sly grin. "I had the manager let me in once I'd determined that Jeremy wasn't home. Come on. You have to see this to believe it." Kim led the way up the stairs to the second floor apartment. She used the key the manager had left with her, opened the door, and stood back, motioning for Scott to precede her into the room, much like a circus ringmaster introducing the next act.

"Holy shit!" Scott exclaimed. He was staring at the huge computer set-up with its eight monitors, single keyboard, and what appeared to be Jeremy's own private server to run everything and store the videos. On one monitor he could see one of the patrolmen in Kelli's kitchen.

On the long wall behind the monitors were photos of Kelli. Kelli as a girl. As a teenager. Kelli's wedding. Kelli at work. Kelli swimming. At church. Walking. Reading in her little reading room at her grandparents' house. Kelli in bed with Todd. Kelli and Corky. Kelli at Todd's funeral. Floor to ceiling, wall-to-wall, nothing but photos of Kelli. It took Scott minutes just to make a quick run-through of the enormous quantity of Kelli photos. Some were obviously stills taken from videos.

Dean's voice from the doorway said, "Oh my God!" Moss's deeper voice echoed his sentiment.

Kim turned to the tech, "I walked back out as soon as I saw what was here, didn't want to contaminate the scene. Scott and I have only been this far into the room." She indicated where they were standing, in front of the monitors, Scott still staring at the wall. "We haven't touched anything."

Dean spoke up. "Well, I guess we found our stalker." He looked around the space; kitchen to the left, bedroom and bath to the right. "But I take it no sign of him or Kelli." It was a statement, not a question.

"Unfortunately, no," Scott offered. "But that doesn't mean she wasn't here. Not likely, but possible." He turned once again to Moss. "I want everything you can find. Take photos of everything. Get the computer geeks down here to see what's on that mother of all personal servers. We need to find out where he took her. Call me as soon as you find anything."

Scott turned back to Kim and Dean, both shook their heads in dismay. Scott looked at his watch: 8:47. "You two go home and get some rest, shower, check your kids, whatever. Meet back in my office at three. We already have the background checks going on Jeremy and Bert. I'll let them know to concentrate on Jeremy."

Dean and Kim both started to argue with Scott simultaneously. He held up his hand like a traffic cop.

"No. Do it. I'm going to do the same as soon as I'm sure everything is underway. I'm going to make sure we get his banking records, too. Maybe he has some vacation property or rental property or a storage locker, or even an old family home, maybe a farm. We have to cover all the bases. At this point we know he's been stalking Kelli." He motioned over his shoulder to Jeremy's collage of Kelli. "And we are assuming that he's the one who took her. If he's just a stalker, and not the kidnapper, we're in deep shit. But we have to work with what we have. We'll run down everything we can find about him. Then we'll take it from there. Sound like a plan?" Dean and Kim nodded grudgingly.

"Okay. So there's nothing we can do until we get all this info. So get some rest. By three we should have everything in. We'll review it all, start-to-finish and see what we can figure out about this guy." He paused. "We *will* find her." He stared stonily at the tall state trooper and the round CPD officer. Then he smiled. "Now get out of here. I need your best brains at three this afternoon."

Dean and Kim smiled back and turned and left without another word. They knew Scott was right about the need to rest so they could stay sharp, but they doubted sleep would come easily, if at all. They were wrong.

58

Kelli spoke to herself aloud, "Calm down. Remember 'keep calm and carry on'." She smiled a small smile. This had been her mantra ever since she had read it on a coffee mug in a catalog right after Todd's death. It was either 'carry on' or kill herself. The other option, losing her mind completely, she tried to keep at bay, but it was hard. *Does depression count as crazy? Not clinically, but I guess it can lead to it…sometimes you get so down that it's hard to get back up, hard to do things, hard to talk to people. I guess retreating into a permanent shell could be considered crazy. Okay, that option's out, can't do that.*

Killing myself right now isn't an option really, I'm tied up and have no means of doing it. I guess I could strangle myself with the noose tied around my neck, just straighten my hands and feet and the noose will tighten. She applied a bit of pressure to see how far she had to stretch to get the noose really tight. She felt a charley-horse beginning in her left calf. *Okay, got it. Suicide won't be easy or painless. Take that option away, too. I don't really want to die, no matter how many times I've said it over the last few months. I want to survive and show this bastard he can't win. I want to make Todd proud.*

Option three it is: keep calm. He said there's a camera in this room so I know he can see me, if he's watching. It sounded like a car left a little bit ago, though, so get busy.

We're down to Bert or Jeremy. They both know Corky and she loves them; of course, they give her treats. Kelli smiled as tears welled in her eyes again. "Stop that," she hissed aloud. *But Jeremy has been to both my houses, he sat Corky for me the couple times I went out of town when Todd was unavailable, too. I've known him as long as I've known his brother RJ. Of course I've known Bert since eighth grade, too.* Her brain froze. It was so scary not being able to see, or even move. *Take it easy, Kell, you can do this.*

She thought back to the days before she left town. She saw Bert at the cleaners. He was friendly, but nothing special. *Actually, more interested in Corky than me.*

She dropped Corky at the kennel. Jeremy wasn't there because he was on night shift that week. That left his days free to do whatever. *I wonder what the night schedule was, Sunday through Saturday, or maybe Tuesday to Monday? I guess it could be anything they wanted it to be.*

So with his days free, he could have gone to the open house on Wednesday. Was Bert off work that day? Surely Scott is checking their work schedules. Suddenly she had a quick memory of seeing Teri Jackson hang a "discreet" for sale sign on the wrought iron fence at the house as she had left Tuesday afternoon. *The stalker could have seen the sign. That still didn't let him know anything about the open house, and it was for brokers anyway. Neither of them is a broker.* Kelli rubbed her slapped left cheek against the pillow. She could feel a migraine coming on. Stress did that to her.

Call Teri! Duh. All Teri's contact numbers are on that sign. All he had to do was call Teri to set up a showing and then find some way to get away from her while they were in the house. Maybe while Jeremy was talking to Teri she let it slip that there was going to be an open house, no reason not to. Suddenly she realized she was using Jeremy's name in her thoughts; in her mind at least she had decided he was the stalker. Oh my God! It can't be. She felt deflated, crushed. She'd always been friendly with Jeremy, but never gave him any reason to pursue her, at least not intentionally. "I was just being friendly. Besides, he could never hurt Corky; he loves her." *Or could he? Has it all been an act?*

Kelli felt an overwhelming sadness. Jeremy had killed Todd because of her. *No matter how you look at it, I killed Todd. I'm the reason he's dead. Maybe option two isn't such a bad idea after all. But first, I have to get away from Jeremy.* She took a deep breath and let it out slowly, as she'd learned in yoga. *First, where am I?*

Bedroom. Attached bath directly across from my side of the bed. Toilet separated from the sink by a pony wall. Closet left of the door, opposite the bed. Nightstand on my side of the bed. Queen or king size bed. Corky had had to move over to get close to me, so it's not a full size. Good. So I have a basic diagram of the room.

Smell! What is that smell? It's familiar, doesn't come from the food or Jeremy. Think! What usually creates a smell in a bedroom. Cedar from closets or chests. Moth balls. Perfume. It's my perfume! Estee Lauder's Youth Dew, my favorite. Todd bought me some every year on my birthday; he'd liked it too, a lot. She blushed to remember how much he'd liked it.

But how did it get here? Wherever 'here' is. I had some on the vanity back at Granny and Gramps' house. Did he steal it? I guess he could have, he was in the house enough times. But he couldn't have known it was my favorite, I haven't used it since Todd died. And there were several different perfume bottles on the counter in the bathroom. She strained to visualize the vanity in her bathroom, was anything missing? She couldn't remember.

Suddenly it hit her. *Oh no! No one will ever find me here.* She heard the door open.

"Lunchtime!" This time she recognized Jeremy's voice.

313

59

As he opened the door he wondered what he would find. Would Kelli be mad? Sad? Happy? Complacent? *She's smart and she's had four hours to think about her situation.*

"Lunchtime," he chirped again as he set the tray on the nightstand. "All your favorites again. He was so proud of himself. Kelli wanted to strangle him.

He yanked the blanket off her and stood there admiring Kelli's long legs, her lean body. Her legs still had a tan, *maybe from her trip? Where else was she tanned? I'll have to see after lunch.* He had wanted to get back to his apartment and mount the new photos he'd taken while Kelli slept: her long legs and the purple lace bikini pants. *"Mount", what a perfect word.* But he couldn't get away from work.

"Hungry?" he asked in his most concerned voice.

Kelli realized she was, and she hadn't done anything; at least nothing physical. Her legs and arms were cramping because they hadn't moved more than half an inch in any direction since breakfast.

"A little. Sounds good," she replied in the friendliest tone she could muster. *He seems in a good mood. Should I let him know I've figured out who he is? Play it by ear.*

Jeremy untied her hands and helped her to sit up, swinging her bound legs over the side of the bed again. The blindfold remained over her eyes.

"Better eat before the soup gets cold." Jeremy placed the tray on her lap. He handed her the spoon and once again guided her hand to the bowl of soup. "Water bottle is on the nightstand to your left. Sandwich is at the top right of the tray." He sat next to her, right next to her, their thighs touching. He silently watched as Kelli carefully spooned the warm soup into her mouth. Each time her mouth opened he felt his excitement growing. Shortly, the soup and sandwich were gone.

"See, that wasn't so bad. You did very well. You only spilled a couple spoonfuls on your sweater front. Such a shame. Well, there's nothing to do about it except wash it. Give me the sweater, Kelli." She couldn't see the gleam of anticipation in his eyes nor see the sickly leer that curved his thin lips, "turtle lips" she would have called them.

"It's okay. It's not soaking through to my skin." Kelli hesitated and smiled at him. "But thanks anyway. You don't need to bother."

"It's no bother, Kelli. I said to take it off." His voice was more menacing. Again, the unexpected slap knocked her head back. Her hand flew to her cheek. Tears stung her eyes but couldn't escape the duct tape.

"Now, Kelli, or I'll be obliged to keep slapping you." His hissed voice scared her more than shouting did, hurt more than the slap. She could tell he had moved away from the bed, his heavy footfalls shook the dishes on the tray; he was between her and the bathroom.

"No, you don't need to hit me anymore," she whispered. "I need you to take the tray, though, or I might spill it." He lifted the tray, put it on the dresser across the room. His softer footsteps told her he was somewhat mollified by her agreement.

"Now, Kelli, I mean it." Kelli jumped at his closeness as he snarled into her ear. She hadn't felt him come back across the room.

"Okay, but may I have the blanket? It's cold in here." She tried to look as pitiful as she felt.

"Don't worry, you'll be warm soon enough. I'll see to it." He moistened his lips with his lizard-like tongue. The anticipation was almost too much. He was already hard, just thinking about what was to come, but he was becoming even more excited. "Start at the bottom and pull it up slowly, very slowly." His long fingers skittered down the front of her sweater as he moved directly in front of her. He started to hum.

It sounds like Mancini's Mr. Lucky, but I'm not sure. She heard his breathing become jerky. She grasped the side seams with the opposite hands and started to lift. *I wonder how long I can stretch this out. Surely somebody is looking for me?* Her shaky hands pulled the blue argyle sweater to mid-abdomen; she felt the cold air hit her nakedness. Her fingers fumbled. "No stalling," he snapped. "Do you want me to hurt Corky?"

She pulled the sweater higher, to just below her bra. She heard his breathing stop. *Is he holding his breath? Or maybe he had a heart attack? No such luck.*

"Keep going!" he shouted in a raspy voice. "More!"

As Kelli pulled the bottom of the sweater over her head she felt the lace against he skin, purple if she remembered correctly. She hesitated again.

"Finish. Now!" he raged at her, forcing the words through gritted teeth. Kelli felt spittle hit her forehead. *I think I'm going to be sick.*

Kelli pulled the sweater off her arms and clasped it to her chest. *If only I could see!*

"Drop it, Kelli. Now, or I leave and hurt Corky." Once more he was next to her ear, his moist tongue licking her ear, up and down, up and down. Kelli began to shake from fear and cold. *Stop it, Kell. You've got to hang on.*

Kelli pulled the sweater away from her chest and automatically started to fold it on her lap. He slapped her hand away. "Now the blouse…Kelli tried to look seductive as she unbuttoned each button. Once again she held the blouse in her lap.

"No, Kelli, no undue modesty. It's pointless. Remember, I've seen you in your underwear before, and less. I've touched all your lingerie. This purple lace set is one of my favorites. I'm glad you chose it for me." His ragged breath bounced out the words.

Maybe he'll be repulsed if I'm more aggressive instead of pitiful. Would that be good or bad? I couldn't be worse off. What could be worse? I guess I'll have to try.

Kelli licked her dry lips and gave Jeremy what she hoped was a seductive smile. She arched her back to push her breasts forward.

"I did, Jeremy, just for you. I hoped you'd like purple. You said we'd be together soon so I wanted to be ready." She slowly ran her tongue across her bottom lip, showing just a bit of her teeth. "What do you say, Jeremy, do you approve?"

Suddenly she heard him gasping in front of her. She knew this time it wasn't a heart attack. He slumped to the floor a few feet in front of the bed. Kelli could hear him panting. She wished she had something to hit him with, but with her legs still tied she was afraid she'd fall and he'd recover. Silence. Nothing. She heard no movement. No more panting. No breathing. *Maybe he'd had a heart attack after all.*

"Jeremy?" she whispered. "Jeremy? Are you okay?" She hoped to God he had passed out at the very least. She reached for the blindfold.

"Stop," he croaked from the floor in front of her. "How did you know it was me?" She felt him rising to his knees.

Kelli had prepared for this question once she figured out it was Jeremy. She smiled at him. "Well," she drew out the word seductively. At least she hoped it was seductive to him; this femme fatale stuff had never been her forte. But she had read a lot, including *Fifty Shades of Grey*.

"Way back in high school, when you left me the notes and the flowers, I hoped it was you. But I guess we were both too shy to do anything about it." She smiled at him again.

She hoped he'd keep his distance, but suddenly she felt his breath on her cheek. His fingers traced a line across the skin at the top of her bra. "More, Kelli, tell me more," he whispered into her ear, his teeth just nipped at her lobe. His fingers kept moving across her skin, then down the V between her breasts. Kelli began to shake. She hoped he assumed he was exciting her. She sensed his smile, even blindfolded she could tell he was pleased.

"But then there was nothing while I was in Columbia at college. Finally, after Todd died, you came back."

"If you wanted me, why did you marry him?" His anger was back.

"I was confused. I hadn't heard from you in years. I hadn't even seen you when I came home. I thought you had found someone else."

Jeremy sneered, "No, it's always been you. Oh, I dated, practicing sort of. I was just getting ready for your permanent return to Charleston. I took classes at Trident Tech so I could install cameras so I could watch you all the time. I was ready to declare myself, then you married that trooper." Kelli felt his anger increasing.

"I'm sorry, Jeremy. I was lonely. I thought you had left me. RJ said you had moved away." She silently said a prayer to Todd, *please forgive me*. She knew he would.

She could hear him grinning at her, his anger diffused for the moment. "Well, I'm back now and your husband is out of the picture. I even got that job at the kennel once I saw you with your dog. I knew you'd use the same one your grandparents used before Tuffy died." Tuffy was their Springer Spaniel who had died the same year Todd gave Corky to Kelli.

"I'm so sorry, Jeremy." She choked at the thought of him killing Todd so she'd be free, but she had to keep him distracted. "I'm free now, Jeremy," again she tried her seductive voice.

"Yes, you are. At last." His fingers began to trace circles around her breasts through the purple bra. Kelli was finding it agonizing to keep herself from cringing at his touch.

"Tell me, Kelli," he shouted as he slapped her again, "Why did you call the police if you knew it was me?"

At least his hands are off me. Kelli grabbed her cheek again and sat up straight. She straightened her shoulders and growled at him, "I didn't figure it out it was you until this morning while I was lying here, trussed up like a Thanksgiving turkey." Her right hand groped around the bed and finally found the blanket. She pulled it around her shoulders and held it closed across her chest. "What was I supposed to do, Jeremy? I didn't know for sure it was you." She pitched her voice to a pitiful whine. "Why didn't you tell me? Why were the notes anonymous? I thought it was some weirdo, a stranger." *At least that part's true.*

His hand wrapped around hers where she held the blanket tightly clasped. "Would you have been happy if you had known?"

Kelli smiled brightly. "Of course. I'm sorry about the police. I can call them if you'd like, tell them it was all a big misunderstanding." She hoped he'd fall for it, but knew he wouldn't; Jeremy was too smart.

Jeremy smiled, too, as he replied, "That might be a good idea, Kelli. I'll think about it." He yanked the blanket off her and pulled her arms tightly behind her. A new set of flexi-cuffs was attached to her wrists and the noose reconnected. Kelli gasped as he pulled everything tight.

"Oh, Jeremy, you don't have to keep me tied up. I won't go anywhere. Can't you at least remove the blindfold; I'm getting claustrophobic. After all, I know it's you."

He pushed her roughly back onto the bed; the noose tightened because her feet were still on the floor. His finger traced her jaw line from her swollen left cheek to her right ear. Kelli's scalp prickled, goose bumps covered her arms and legs, and not the good kind either. His tongue traced the skin above her bra, dipping into the cleft. His fingers groped inside her panties. His breathing became shallow. His right hand reached around back and found the clasp to her bra. Kelli stiffened but remained silent. *Death is worse* she kept telling herself, glad he could not see the hatred in her eyes, the determination to punish him someday. She started to choke from the noose.

"Later, Kelli." His breathing returned to normal. "I'm not quite ready to take you to the next level yet. But when I come back the next time, I'll undo all the bindings and we'll have a *really* good time together. Does that sound good?"

Breathlessly Kelli replied, "Oh yes, Jeremy." He lifted her legs and repositioned her on the bed, covering her with the blanket. Kelli took in deep breaths through her nose.

"Get some rest, my darling. You're going to need it." She could tell he was smiling again. "Corky and I are going for a ride."

"Don't hurt her!" Kelli screamed as the door closed.

60

Thursday afternoon

It was just past three o'clock and the three had been at work again for hours, all three dressed comfortably in jeans and polo shirts.

The murder board, or in this case the kidnapping board, had been set up in the conference room. Two white boards arranged side-by-side told the story of Kelli's stalker, starting Friday night when she called 911, and right through the cache of photos at Jeremy's apartment. Kelli's face stared at them from the left side of the board; Jeremy's face from the right.

Scott stood next to the board; Kim and Dean were seated at the nicked up government-issue wooden conference table. "Okay, most of the reports are back." Scott pointed to the stack of pages he'd printed from the multiple online reports he'd received; he still preferred to work from hard copy. "Everything points to Jeremy being our stalker." He paused and grinned.

"Not the least of which is Kim's find of the wall of photos in his apartment." Dean gave Kim a high-five and Kim beamed her cherubic smile.

Scott waved at the array of photos that had been taped to the wall behind them, copies of the photos from Jeremy's, arranged just the way he had them. "So the photos show that Jeremy has been stalking her; that doesn't positively mean he's abducted her. But for the time being we'll assume he has, because we've got nobody else.

"Now for the bad news." Once again he paused; this time to wait for the groans to subside. "The neighborhood canvas, the background search, bank search, property clerk's records...nada. Big fat zero. He was questioned once as a person of interest in the disappearance of another young woman, a teenager actually, but nothing came of it. And she was never found, alive or dead. Maybe a runaway."

"But he has to have Kelli somewhere," Dean piped up.

"By now they could be out of state, in which case everything gets turned over to the Feds."

Kim is thoughtful. "But Viv said he starts a week of vacation tomorrow. I can't imagine he'll show up at work tonight, but what if he does? You know, trying to throw us off."

"The big problem right now is all we have on him is stalking, maybe invasion of privacy. But, with that, every paparazzo in the country would be locked up." The other two nodded in agreement and Dean muttered, "We should be so lucky."

"B&E would be nice, but there's no evidence of "breaking", just "entering", and no evidence it was Jeremy. Nothing."

Kim turned solemn. "What if he's already killed her? And disposed of...the body? Unless we find evidence with him and the body, it's unlikely we'll get a conviction. And if she's dead, there's no point in even trying to get him on stalking. He'll be free to go after somebody else."

Scott tried to boost the others' spirits even though they all knew Kim had spoken their own fears. "We have to assume Jeremy has taken Kelli because he is obsessed with her, maybe even loves her in his own twisted way. So we can hope he's keeping her alive, at least until he figures out his love isn't returned. Kelli's smart, she'll figure out a way to stay alive."

"Even if she is alive, there's no telling what the sick bastard is doing to her," Dean added to the general depression.

"There are things worse than death, especially for a woman," Kim murmured.

The two men nodded knowingly. Scott led off, "Exactly. But dwelling on the unknowns won't help us find Kelli. We have to go with what we do know. Let's get to it." The other two straightened in their chairs and glared at the murder board.

"I'll put an unmarked car at the kennel in case he shows up. He can be brought in for questioning if he shows. In the meantime, I suggest we start back at square one," Scott pointed to the left-most board, "And see if we can figure out where he has her. Unless we can catch him with her everything is circumstantial at this point. I doubt he'll let Kelli see his face or hear his real voice. He's too smart for that. If she lets him know that she knows who he is, her chances of getting out of this alive are slim and none." Scott hesitated. "Unless he's planning to keep her captive for the rest of her life. There have been cases like that, even recently." He hesitated again. "I don't think he's that crazy. At least I hope not."

Kim spoke up, "I know 'murder board' is what you call this process, but how about we just call it 'the board' since we don't know for sure she's dead?"

The two men nodded and shrugged in agreement. Scott remained standing at the boards but Dean and Kim pulled their chairs closer, as if being closer will help them detect better.

"Let's start with last night's abduction." Scott pointed to Jeremy's photo. "Where was Jeremy at five last night?" He drew a straight line at the bottom of the board and wrote the number five at the far left of it. At the far right he wrote the number ten and "abduction" under it.

Kim piped up. "At work. Records show he clocked out at 5:30. Vivian remembers seeing him a little after five. She always makes the rounds before she leaves to let everyone know she's leaving."

Scott wrote "kennel" under the five. "Where was he after work?"

Kim and Dean looked at each other, waiting for the other one to answer. "Don't know. We didn't have a tail on him. Our focus hadn't shifted to him yet."

Scott maintained his calm demeanor although inside he was furious at himself. *I should have worked harder or faster or something.*

"Okay. Moving on." He pointed to the ten and then to Kim. "You last saw her before ten, right, Kim?"

"Yes. I went upstairs to shower a little after 9:30, came back down as soon as I realized Kelli wasn't upstairs, a few minutes after ten." Kim looked wholly remorseful. She grabbed her stomach as another bout of nausea hit her. She'd been experiencing these cramps ever since her friend's disappearance. *How could you be so stupid?* she chastised herself.

Scott seemed to sense her thoughts. "No time for finger-pointing now, we'll save that for the after-case review. We need our total focus on finding Kelli."

He wrote 10:30 on the board. "CSU found nothing at the scene. We are going with the thought that he had some sort of vehicle parked in the alley, since the gate to the alley was standing open. At that hour, though, the neighbors were out, asleep, or in another part of their houses. Nobody saw anything."

Dean spoke up. "The BOLO on Jeremy's car has been useless so far, but it's only been out since we found his apartment stash. We've got every law enforcement force in the state looking for it, but like everything else, no luck. Either he has stashed the car,and Kelli, or he used a different vehicle. We checked the car rentals but nobody recognized his photo." He grimaced. "But there's no telling how long he's been planning this. He could have rented a car last month, or bought a used one a year ago under a fake name."

Scott scowled. "Unfortunately, Dean, you're right. All we can do is work with what we have and hope for a break. Speaking of which, if we can get a DNA sample for Jeremy we can try to match it to the semen samples that were in Kelli's bed. The DNA checked all the data bases for a match, but no luck." He slammed his fist against the board. "There has to be something we're missing."

Kim and Dean looked at each other and silently asked each other, "Is this normal Detective Rae frustration or is he taking this case more personally than usual?"

Scott took a deep breath. He moved farther right, beyond the "abduction" space and wrote Thursday, 10 a.m. "Kim, you got to his apartment about ten this morning."

She nodded. "Yep. Nobody home, so I asked the manager to let me in. Took a while to find him, he was out talking to a resident about a toilet that wasn't working right. After he unlocked the apartment I asked him to wait outside. I made sure he was in hearing distance, though, so I had an impartial witness to me announcing myself as a police officer." She paused for a sip of her lukewarm coffee, definitely not Starbucks, not even grocery grade, but it was free and did the trick.

Kim resumed, "I wasn't more than six steps inside when I saw all the monitors and the wall of photos. I backed out of the apartment and called you. You two got there about eleven and the rest you know." She glanced between Scott and Dean.

"Good job," Scott offered as he writes 11 and "Found monitors and photos @ Jeremy's" on the board. Dean gave Kim his best GQ-model smile, sexy and friendly at the same time. "If only you weren't gay," she poked his shoulder and grinned. "Yeah, I get that a lot. Like you'd ever leave the father of your children." He grinned back at her; another "sister" for his pack.

Scott drew their attention back to the board with a marker tap on the 11. "So where was Jeremy all this time? He'd had Kelli almost thirteen hours at this point. What does it tell us?"

Kim and Dean continued to stare at the board, from left to right and back again. Scott moved to Jeremy's driver's license photo on the board. Under it he wrote as he talked, "Smart. Methodical." Kim offered, "Organized." Scott wrote it on the board.

"Probably has her someplace isolated and big enough to hide his vehicle." Scott added Dean's comments to the board with a big question mark over them. He labeled the comments "locale" and "vehicle".

"I'm guessing he's still in the area, probably within fifty miles," Scott opined. The other two looked skeptical.

"Sounds like wishful thinking to me," Dean said.

"Maybe. But look." Scott tapped the 10 p.m. on the board. "I'm betting he had someplace to lay low within an hour of the snatch. He'd want to get off the streets as soon as he could. Remember, he doesn't know what we know. He doesn't know if we know it's him." He looked from one to the other, seeing tentative agreement in their eyes. "He watched Kelli. He had to know Kim was staying with her. He couldn't have known Kim was upstairs in the shower even if he did see her go upstairs. He had to assume he had only a few minutes to snatch Kelli and get away. At that hour he could have gotten from the Battery to I-26 in ten minutes easy, straight up Meeting Street."

He opened a Charleston-area map on the top of the table and drew a circle about four inches from the coast, using the Battery as the center of the search area. "There's nothing but water to the east, so I'm betting he's somewhere in this area." He pointed to the circle. "Not more than fifty miles out, maybe as close as thirty." Scott's phone rang.

Dean and Kim discussed Scott's theory. "Jeremy's apartment and his brother's house both fall within that circle." Kim put an X to approximate each location. "And the kennel, too," Dean added. Kim put another X.

Scott tapped END on his phone and looked at the other two. "Funny you should mention the kennel. Guess who just showed up for work?" He saw amazement on their faces.

"They're bringing him in now." Scott wrote 5 p.m. as the next time on the line and added "Jeremy @ work; brought in for questioning". "Hope this means my theory works, he *is* still within driving distance." All three looked back at the map.

"That's a lot of land to cover," Kim said. "I hope the interview gives us something more."

61

Kelli felt she had been alone in this bedroom for months. She had no idea what time it was, didn't even know if it was day or night; it was all dark behind the blindfold. Her muscles were cramped and screaming from having to stay in one position for so long. Her tongue was stuck to the back of her teeth she was so thirsty. The silence was unnerving; no car, no sirens, no dogs barking. *Where is Corky? I really have to pee.*

Surely someone has called Nora, told her what is going on? What is Nora thinking? She knew I wasn't coming up the weekend after my trip. She'll tell Sean. Poor Sean. What a homecoming. And worry is so bad for his PTSD. "Worry", "hyper-vigilance", "control", whatever they call it. I think it's hyper-anxiety about everything; PTSDers want to save the world and there are so many things they can't even help; so many things out of their control. Since his return from Afghanistan I tried to tease him about his constant worrying; I told him to prioritize his worrying, no sense worrying about things that haven't even happened yet or things over which you have no control. Nothing helped; he simply can't stop worrying. His hyper-vigilance serves him well as an FBI agent, but it's sure hard on those who love him. His psychologist said he needed a break, going straight from Afghanistan to the FBI was probably too stressful; he needed some recovery time; that old frying pan into the fire thing. Maybe his arrest and incarceration was a blessing in disguise; forced him to take a break. If only poor little Molly didn't have to die for him to get his break.

But Sean loved his job. He said it gave him a chance to continue serving without being in a uniform. Sean was so sure he could handle his PTSD, even though his psychologist said it would probably get worse. Sean told me all this a couple years ago, but told me not to tell Nora; she's a worrier too, but in a more maternal way. Poor Nora!

"Maybe it's better if nobody called her about me," Kelli said aloud. Her own voice in the constant stillness surprised her. "Doesn't even sound like me," she complained. She decided sound was better than the overwhelming silence.

Kelli stopped herself from crying by biting her lip, soggy duct tape was not the way to go. *Or is it? Maybe I can rub it off if it's soggy.* She tried, but it hadn't gotten wet enough.

I have to get away from Jeremy, out of here. For my sake and Sean's.

The door swung open with a loud swoosh. "Oh, poor Sean. Tough. He never had time for me while we were in high school. Him and RJ. Off at that preppy school, but not me. No way. Too good for me. I wasn't smart enough for the parents to spend that kind of money on me. I hope Sean rots in there, I just wish his buddy RJ was in there with him."

"You were listening to me!" Kelli shrieked at him, forgetting to remain calm and friendly.

Jeremy took four long strides and sat next to her. He pulled the blanket back. His palm rubbed slowly from her ankle to her thigh. Kelli knew better than to try to pull away from his touch, it just tightened the noose and angered him.

"Poor Sean. No hugs. No human touch. Human touch? You want some human touch? Exactly what I have in mind." He chuckled and his rubbing increased; his calloused hand climbed up her thigh. Two fingers slid under the legs of her purple bikini pants; one forefinger in each leg opening. His fingers rubbed back and forth, back and forth. Around to the side and back to the front. Then he stopped but his fingers remained inside her panties.

"Don't you think anticipation is a large part of the excitement? Some call it foreplay, but I think it's more like that old song "Anticipation". A much more romantic word." His fingers slid back and forth, now three fingers on each side, roving up to the waistband. "Did you think about us while I was away?"

Kelli swallowed back the bile in her throat. She bit her tongue, literally, to keep from screaming in frustration and fury. She had to distract him.

In her most pitiful voice she smiled weakly, "Of course I thought about you, Jeremy, how could I not? *At least that part's not a lie.* "Jeremy, I'm so thirsty. Could I have some water?"

His hand stilled. Then pulled out of her pants. He gritted his teeth, clearly annoyed at the interruption, but managed to reply, "Of course, my sweet. Can't have you dying of thirst before we get to fuck."

His hands grabbed her shoulders and lifted her upright. He loosened the noose and swung her legs over the side of the bed. Jeremy held a plastic bottle of warm water to her lips. *Must have been sitting on the nightstand all this time; at least it's wet.*

"Enough? Need to pee?"

"No, I'm good. Thank you so much, Jeremy, you are so good to me." Kelli smiled a friendly smile, she hoped. "You are such a good friend."

This time it was a solid upper cut to her jaw that came out of nowhere and knocked Kelli onto her back. "Friend!" he shrieked. "I am much more than a 'friend', Kelli. And you'll see how much more than a close friend when I get back. We'll be very close, I promise." He lifted her back to a sitting position. Kelli could tell her jaw was swelling; she talked around the pain, wheezing for breath.

"Back? Where are you going?" Kelli tried not to sound hopeful. Even though there wasn't much hope anyone would find her here.

"I have a couple errands to run, then I'm going to work." He chuckled. "Can't have your police friends focusing on me while you're missing. They are so dumb; I've outwitted them at every turn." This time his chuckle sounded more maniacal.

"But you'll be gone so long, Jeremy. Please, at least remove the blindfold. I know who you are and I know where we are, what's the point of keeping my eyes covered?"

"We'll see." He chortled, "Did you like that pun?" When he spoke next, Kelli heard the glee in his voice. "Speaking of your police friends. You know that lady cop who's been hanging around you?"

Kelli nodded slowly in the direction of his voice, fearing what might come next.

"She lives in a nice cul de sac in Mount P. with her whoop-dee-doo professor husband." Kelli sensed he was licking his lips. "They have two kids." Kelli gasped. "The youngest boy is a real cutie. I bet she'll miss him." He laughed heartily.

"Jeremy! No! You can't hurt them." She tried desperately to think of something that would stop him. "That's not you, Jeremy, you love animals...and children. Please don't do anything to Kim's family." Tears once again welled behind the duct tape.

"It's up to you, Kelli." He paused for a longer time. His hands once again encircled her breasts, his thumbs rubbed the naked skin above the lace. "Will you play nice with me when I get back? Be more than my 'friend?'"

Kelli caught the sarcasm. She nodded. "Anything you want," she whispered. And she knew she meant it. Anything to keep Kim's children safe.

"That's my girl." Jeremy patted her back and eased her into position on the bed. He started to replace the noose when Kelli spoke up.

"Please, Jeremy, not the noose. My muscles get so cramped from being in one position. And you'll be gone so long this time. You'll want me...flexible when you get back, won't you? So we can play?" She sensed his hesitation. "My hands and feet are still tied. I can't go anywhere," she wheedled. "And you can watch me to see that I'm still here."

His hands dropped. She heard the noose fall to the floor. "True. Okay. I can be nice, too. Real nice." She heard his leering smile.

Kelli pushed her luck. "May Corky stay with me while you're gone? It's so lonely without you." She tried a sexy pout.

She felt him tense beside her. "Sorry, I have other plans for Corky." Kelli felt a sharp prick in her upper arm. *Damn him! Another shot!*

She heard his footsteps cross the carpet and the door close behind him. As her eyes closed she heard a gunshot from the backyard. "Corky!" she yelled as she slipped once more into unconsciousness.

Time, I want more time. But I have to go to work or those stupid cops will find it suspicious. He grinned satanically. *Hell, I have to take these clothes off anyway to change for work.* He went into the room next to Kelli's and checked the monitor. "She's out like a light already." He glanced at his watch and smiled. *Enough time.* Quickly he kicked off his shoes and socks, then stripped off his jeans, flannel shirt and Jockey briefs. He strolled determinedly into the room next door. He stood at Kelli's side of the bed, once again admiring her tanned skin and the purple lace, her sweet face in deep sleep. He was erect immediately.

He hastened around to the other side of the bed and spooned Kelli, his hardness stabbing into her lacey silk buttocks. Her bound hands made an uncomfortable barrier to his desired closeness. He unfastened her bra and slid the straps down to her elbows. He leaned forward as far as he could and reached around her to grab her naked breasts with his sweaty hands, his hardness exploded. "It's too much, too soon, too fast!" Panting in fury he slammed his fists into the pillow above his head. He rolled onto his back and stared at the ceiling, the faux-wood fan went around and around.

With agonizing slowness he pulled Kelli's bra back up and refastened the three hooks. Furious at himself he stood and said to the unconscious woman, "Next time I'll be in better control. No matter what anybody says, I can control myself. I won't disappoint you. I promise."

He roughly returned the quilt over Kelli and then scurried to his room and dressed for work. In fifteen minutes he was on his way to the kennel, visions of his return from work calming and exciting him at the same time.

62

Thursday night

Scott stared through the one-way glass. Arms crossed, a superior grin on his face, Jeremy sat in the interrogation room on the other side. "He looks comfortable," Scott said to Dean and Kim standing next to him.

"The patrolman who brought him in said he didn't say a word the whole drive, from the kennel to here, just kept grinning at him in the rearview mirror," Dean replied with a worried frown.

"Must be all those police procedure manuals we found in his apartment. He knows not to say anything. Once a suspect starts talking it's hard for him to stop," Kim murmured just loud enough for the others to hear. "He's been in custody over an hour," she added. "Hasn't asked for anything. Not a drink. Not a bathroom break. Not even his phone call or his lawyer. Nothing."

"Probably watches a lot of cop shows, too," Dean said with a smirk.

The three stared at Jeremy in silence, wondering what he was thinking, where he had put Kelli.

Jeremy stared back, even though he couldn't see them, he knew the three cops from Kelli's house were watching him. He was still wearing his royal blue vet tech smock. His head was tilted back slightly, giving a better sight-line to the eyes he could feel watching from the next room. He admired himself in the reflected image on his side of the glass. A small smile twisted his lips above his faux Brad Pitt-style beard. He flexed his biceps and admired the macho look he portrayed in the glass.

"Okay, let's see what he's got." Scott lowered his arms, calmed the fists that were bunched at his sides, and headed for the door. Dean and Kim watched him exit. Then they watched him enter the room next door.

Scott pulls out the metal chair opposite Jeremy, his back to the glass. There is nothing else in the room, just the metal table,

331

two metal chairs, and two men. A video camera is secreted in the air conditioning vent over the table. As Scott places a manila folder on the table he feels more like a physician preparing for a patient consultation than a detective. He knows he has to perform careful diagnostics to get what he wants: Kelli's location.

"So, Jeremy, how's it going?"

Jeremy just grinned at him, a very superior grin.

"Okay, you don't want to talk. Fine. I'll talk for a bit." Scott opened the folder.

"So far we have you on invasion of privacy and kidnapping. We're working on confirming that you killed Todd Cavanaugh; cop killing is a death penalty offense; you hanged yourself with those notes to Kelli. Of course, if Kelli dies while in your custody, it's murder one for her death, too, and probably the death penalty. Too bad we can't stick you twice." Scott smiled ruefully. "Of course, that part is up to a jury of your peers. If it was up to me I'd just shoot you now and save everybody a lot of time and money." He paused. Jeremy continued his superior smirk. Scott turned the first page in the folder.

"Seems you had some problems in your youth," Scott said sarcastically. "Window peeping. Aggravated assault. I guess you outgrew those childish things. Moved on to bigger and better crimes." Jeremy's expression did not change.

"What happened to that girl you were dating after high school? Brittany? The one who looked sort of like Kelli? It looks like you two broke up about the same time Brittany disappeared. She hasn't been seen since. I don't suppose you might know where she is?" Scott had a sudden thought. He stood and strode to the door without a word.

Kim and Dean met him in the hall. "Did we search the kennel? Does it have a crawl space, maybe an unused storage area? It would make sense for him to keep Kelli close so he could check on her while he's at work." Kim and Dean looked at each other and shook their heads in unison. "I'll get a team to go check it out," Dean said as he hurried down the hall. "Take an EMT, too," Kim shouted after him.

Scott continued, "One more thing, be sure the techs are checking his cell phone records for any hidden camera views. He must be watching Kelli while he's away from her."

Scott went back to Jeremy. He hadn't changed position since Scott exited so quickly.

"So, how did you meet Brittany? Was she in one of your classes at Trident Tech? Did you kill her because she wasn't Kelli or just because you could? Did your mommy hate you?" Scott saw a brief lifting of the eyebrows, a slight shadow passing over Jeremy's eyes; he pretended not to notice and continued in the same calm-but-curious tone.

"You really did a good job with all the surveillance equipment, Jeremy. Very professional. Of course we left it all in place because we knew you couldn't resist watching and listening. We knew you were there so we only gave you what we wanted you to hear. I think the spy services call that disinformation. Didn't you wonder why we conveniently went to the parlor so often? Or, I guess from your point of view, it was inconvenient. You had to know our crime techs had found the bugs. Are you stupid or just too arrogant to care?"

Jeremy's shoulders dipped; his hands balled into fists on top of the table. His black eyes bore into Scott's chocolate brown ones. He grinned a gruesome smile. "You don't know anything about me," he gritted out between clenched teeth.

"I know enough. We searched your apartment. Found your monitors, all eight of them. Found the Kelli shrine. Found lady's underwear in a box in your closet. Maybe they're yours? Although I have to admit, they were a bit small, and the purple and pink ones are not your color at all." Scott smiled a triumphant smile back at Jeremy.

"I assume you had a warrant? I'd hate to have to sue the department."

"Not a problem for you, Mr. Deets. The manager let us in, with the permission of the apartment owners, of course."

Jeremy just continued to gloat. Relaxation and superiority had returned to his whole demeanor. "You've got nothing. You can't prove a thing. So you found underwear. So what? You can't prove whose they are. I'm out of here." Jeremy stood up and walked firmly to the door. He opened it and stepped into the hall. "And you'll never find Kelli. And if you keep me here, she'll die. Or maybe she's already dead and you'll never find her body," he said in a guttural whisper. "The longer you keep me here, the less time she has, or the less time you have to find her body, while the grave is still fresh. Your call, Detective."

Jeremy turned and headed down the hall, making an exit like a Lauren Bacall movie scene. He had seen the color drain from Scott's face. He knew there was nothing the police could do to him. All they had was circumstantial evidence, nothing to tie anything together. And even his last words were inadmissible because he had been too smart for them. He was in the hall when he said them and he guessed the recording device in the interrogation room couldn't reach that far; Jeremy doubted there were any devices in the hall.

Scott followed Jeremy into the hall and handed him his leather coat that he'd left on the chair in his rush to exit.

Jeremy walked out the front door and through the Municipal Building's entrance, down the steps to the public parking lot and looked for his car. Then he remembered he had arrived in a squad car. He walked back all the way to the front desk and ordered the desk sergeant to "get me a ride. I was brought here under false pretenses and I have to get back to work."

The aging sergeant looked up wearily. "Who brought you in?"

"Detective Rae and his sidekicks."

Without a word, the sergeant picked up his phone and dialed a four digit extension. He slowly explained what was going on and he hung up. "He'll be right here." The sergeant ignored Jeremy and went back to his paperwork.

Jeremy's anger grew each second, but he knew he had to control it. The detective came into view. "Rae, get me a ride to work. This has gone on long enough," he shouted. The sergeant raised his head and listened to their exchange. *A damned witness?* Scott grasped Jeremy's shoulder and pulled him out the door and back to the near-empty parking lot. He stopped them at the top of the cement stairs.

"It will go a lot easier if you tell us where she is, Jeremy. We will find her, and when we do your sorry ass will end up in a place you won't want it to be. I promise you." Scott waited for a response. Jeremy managed to contain his anger and returned his superior smile, nothing more. He looked at his watch. "10:30, Kelli has been missing twenty-four hours." He looked Scott straight in the eye. "I need a ride to work, Detective. Now." He loved being able to order around the brawny cop.

Just then a squad car pulled up to the steps where the two men were standing. "Your ride, Mr. Deets." Jeremy turned on his heel, went down the seven steps and got into the back seat. The car moved off.

Scott returned to Kim and Dean in the observation room, a big smile on his face. "You just let him go. Why does that warrant a smile?" Kim asked, confused.

"Because he's feeling very smug and superior right now, he's beaten the cops. Now he'll lead us straight to his lair and Kelli."

Kim shook her head. "He's too smart – or at least cunning – he'll know we have a tail on him. And he's right, if he doesn't go back to Kelli she'll probably die. What if he has her outdoors somewhere? Animals might find her."

Scott looked from one to the other, returning his gaze to Kim. "Calm down, Kim. We'll find her – and alive. You just have to trust me." She looked deeply into his eyes and saw the confidence there. She looked at Dean standing next to her. Kim and Dean both nodded back at Scott. "Besides, it's only been one day. Few people die of starvation or thirst in just 24 hours. We just need to hurry.

"And we aren't going to wait for him. There has to be something we missed. Jeremy may decide it's safer for him to let her die; so he might never go back to her." He led the two silently back to the conference room and the murder board. "Find it. Start over. Recheck everything. It has to be here."

63

Jeremy ruminated on what the cops might do next. *Follow me when I leave the kennel? Bug my phone?* Finally he had it. *GPS. There must be a bug planted on the car at the kennel.* He laughed out loud, proud to have out-thought the police again. "No problem, Detective Rae, no problem."

The squad car pulled up to the back door of the kennel. As Jeremy got out of the car he saw the nose of the earlier squad car peeking from the side of the building. His Uber squad car pulled off, leaving him standing in the dark. Jeremy made a big show of walking over to his own car and searching it for the bug he was sure was there. After a few frustrating minutes he found it and walked it to the patrolman parked at the side of the building.

"Tell Detective Rae I found his bug. He'll have to try harder than that." With a self-satisfied laugh he turned on his heel and walked to the building's back door. He unlocked it and went in.

Inside he saw a sour Bill sitting at the desk. "Took your own sweet time, Jer. What'd they want you for anyway?"

Jeremy glared back. "None of your damn business, Bill, and apparently none of theirs either. You can go now, I'm here. Sorry you had to stay." He needed Bill on his side, better be nice.

Bill Loudon stood to his full six-five height, grabbed his fleece jacket off the back of the door and headed out the same door Jeremy had just used to enter, without another word. Jeremy watched the door close with a thud. He took out his phone and opened the view of Kelli on the bed; she appeared to be sound asleep, the quilt having slipped down to reveal one purple-covered breast. He rubbed the front of his jeans for a moment, then turned off the picture. "Better check that all the critters are asleep before I do anything else," he said to the small office he and the other techs shared. He stood and walked to their own one-way glass to look into the room of cages where the overnight patients and longer term kennel guests were housed. "Just like at the police office."

He had suggested they install the glass because every time someone walked into the kennel all the dogs started to yap and bark, whether anything was wrong or not. This way any of the techs could check on the animals and not get them all stirred up. He also had installed several video cameras they could use for close-ups of any animals they wanted to check more closely. Most nights it was pretty quiet around the kennel, just the way he liked it.

Slowly he once again opened his phone to the view of the bedroom where Kelli was sleeping. "As soon as I get home, Kelli, we'll be together, I promise" he said once more to the empty room and the sleeping animals. "At last." He could tell that Kelli was becoming more compliant, now that the shock of how he had taken her had worn off. *She seems happy it's me. I want her to enjoy herself, too; but she couldn't have while she was still upset from her abduction. Now, though, now she's ready. And I'm more than ready.* He slammed his fist against the counter top beneath the viewing window. "Tonight, whether she's ready or not," he said through gritted teeth. The noise caused several dogs to start barking.

64

Scott's phone rang. He listened then muttered something into the phone. He hung up and turned to Kim. "Jeremy has gone back to work. I told the officer to stay there and follow him when he leaves. It may be morning until he does, though. He seems to be feeling confident."

"And what if he goes back to his apartment? We know he doesn't have Kelli there." Dean grumbled.

"Well, we've got about three hours to figure out where he does have her. After that he'll leave work and probably lead us on a merry chase through South Carolina."

A computer tech entered the room and handed Scott a piece of paper. Scott scanned it and let out a whoop. "She's alive and indoors somewhere," he said to the other two. "The geeks found eight hidden camera views on Jeremy's phone, they coincide with the eight monitors in his apartment. In one shot they saw Kelli on a bed, apparently asleep." He smiled for the first time in a long time. The other two joined in the mini-celebration as they high-fived each other.

They continued their study of the kidnapping board with new enthusiasm. After a bit, Scott turned his attention to the duplicates of Jeremy's photo wall that were arrayed in the same order on the long wall of the conference room. As he scanned the pictures, he suddenly moved in for a closer look at one of the photos. He turned to Kim and Dean excitedly. "How did Todd die?" he practically yelled across the room.

"He was shot at the grocery store."

"Was he in uniform?"

Dean replied, "No, I don't think so. He usually changed into civvies before he went home."

"Okay. So Jeremy knew Todd, knew what he looked like. But how did he know where Todd was going to be?"

"Right," Kim says, drawing the word out as she grasped where Scott was going.

She picked up his train of thought. "Jeremy had to know Todd was going to be at that grocery at that time."

Dean chimed in, "That seems a bit iffy to me. He would have had to tail Todd for days. Surely there would have been an easier place to kill him."

Scott continued to grin excitedly as he tapped one of the photos. "What if he was killed there because Jeremy knew he would be there at that time? Maybe the grocery wasn't a spur of the moment decision on Jeremy's part." Kim and Dean moved over to the photo wall and stared at the photo Scott was pointing out.

Kim questioned, "But how could Jeremy have known that? It's not like Todd stopped at the grocery every night on his way home from work. Kelli had asked him to stop. She was fixing a special dinner and needed something. She had just found out she was pregnant and was going to tell him that night. There's no way Jeremy could have known that unless…." Kim's eyes lit up.

"Unless?" Scott encouraged her.

"Unless he was a fly on the wall – or had a bug in Kelli and Todd's house!" Kim grinned triumphantly. "Kelli said she and Todd had used Jeremy as a pet sitter a couple times. He could have installed a camera then!" she continued.

"The photo! It's a picture of Kelli and Todd in bed. Kelli has been living at her grandparents' house since Todd's death and the cameras weren't put in *there* until last week. Not to mention the fact that Todd was dead when she moved into the Battery house. So the picture has to be from Kim and Todd's house, not the house on the Battery." She turned to Dean. "Look at the bed posts, does that look like Kelli and Todd's bed?"

Dean looked back at Kim, stunned at her question. "Just because I'm gay doesn't mean I know anything about decorating. Besides, I don't think I was ever in their bedroom and they got new furniture after they moved in."

Kim just gave him a peeved look as Scott said, "Where's the tech's report on those monitors in Jeremy's apartment? There were eight monitors, but only six were views of the house on the Battery. What were the other two looking at?"

The three roughly sorted through the stacks of file folders on the table. "Got it!" Scott yelled as he held a folder aloft. He quickly scanned the sixteen pages for reference to the monitors. "Says the other two show a kitchen and a bedroom. There are screen shots of the two rooms." He handed the photos to Dean. "How about the kitchen? Do you recognize it?" Dean took one quick glance and nodded his head and replied excitedly, "Yep, that's their Cane Bay house. No doubt."

Scott started pacing, thinking out loud. "Okay, so if the house was bugged, that's how Jeremy knew Todd was going to the grocery. All he had to do was lie in wait for him to show up, walk into the store, and shoot Todd when it was pretty clear to do so. Then run out and get in his car and he was gone. Probably had the car out on the street somewhere, where there are no surveillance cameras. Everybody in the store in shock, took them a while to call 9-1-1, at least ten seconds, they would have been trying to help Todd first."

Bringing him down a bit, Kim asked, "But if Jeremy has Kelli at her house, wouldn't she have shown on the monitor when the techs were looking?"

"Good point," Scott agreed. "But not if he was keeping her in another room, or even the living room, as long as it wasn't the kitchen or master bedroom. Then he could have moved her when he had to go to work. Or maybe the techs just didn't notice." A grim look covered Scott's face as he turned to Dean, "Does the house have a basement?"

Dean shook his head.

Scott ordered Dean, "Dean, start drawing a floor plan of the house. Kim, get the techs to open those two monitors and see if anything has changed. I know, I know," he replied at her doubtful look. "Wake them up if you have to. They took the CPU back to the lab so they'll have to be the ones to get the camera views; get them on it as fast as you can. Have them check the CPU's memory, too, I'm sure Jeremy has saved all his camera recordings. I'd like to know the likelihood of Kelli being there right now before we start breaking down doors." Kim scurried out of the conference room and to the nearest phone and departmental phone listing.

Scott looked at Dean, perched on the edge of the conference table. "What's going through your mind, Dean? We've almost got her back. Why aren't you more excited?"

Dean shrugged. "We still have to catch him with her. Otherwise it's her word against his. He's smart enough to have kept her blindfolded all this time, so then her ID will have to be by voice. And you know juries aren't real big on voice recognition identifications, especially if the perp is disguising his voice." He shrugged again. "I'm just playing devil's advocate here."

Scott scowled as Dean continued, "And what if he doesn't go back to the house? We can free Kelli, but not pin it on him. At this point everything we have is circumstantial, no hard evidence either for Kelli or Todd."

"The monitors and the photo wall are hard evidence." Scott pointed out.

"Yeah, evidence of stalking, not kidnapping or murder."

Scott stood still a few seconds and stared at the photo wall, all the photos. Slowly, a devilish grin spread across his face. "I've got an idea, Dean." He pulled his phone from his pocket and started to punch in numbers.

Dean watched Scott and muttered, "Just remember Jeremy is no fool. Crazy maybe, but no fool. He's been ahead of us all along, so we have to assume he has a plan in case we find him. Maybe some kind of booby-trap, or an IED. He won't go without Kelli."

65

Friday morning

Just as Scott hung up on his call, his phone rang back. He listened then turned to Dean. "Jeremy just left work." Scott looked at his watch, 5:30. "A bit early. His shift isn't over until six. The patrol is following him."

"He must know he's being followed. Wherever he goes, it won't be where he has Kelli stashed," Dean replied.

"Right. That was that call," Scott grinned maliciously. "I had two tracking devices put on his car while he was down here, one in the wheel well, one under the front passenger seat. Jeremy found the one in the wheel well; it was hidden just hard enough so he had to search for it, made him feel really superior, according to the patrolman he handed it to; but the other tracker is still pinging nicely. I'm hoping since he found one and he knows we have a tail on him he won't look for another. Regardless of where he goes, we can track him."

Dean grinned back. "So maybe old Jeremy isn't as smart as he thinks after all."

Kim came back into the room. "One of the techs from the job at Kelli's house was covering nights, so he was able to bring up the two monitors at Kelli and Todd's house." Kim paused and passed around a photo printout. "Kelli's there, tied up still, but she looks alive. Looks like a master bedroom, it's got its own bathroom. No movement, though, so I'm guessing she's drugged. Jason will keep watching the monitors and let us know if anything changes." She walked to the wall and compared the bed in the printout to the bed in the photo on the wall. She turned, smiling from ear to ear. "Same bed."

Scott smacked his open hand onto the table. "Yes! We've got him. Dean, you know where the house is, so you'll take point. Now, show me on the floor plan you drew where the master bedroom is."

The three moved down the table to the crudely drawn floor plan. "It's not to scale because I don't know the room dimensions anyway, but you get the idea. Master bedroom is on the second floor, just right of the staircase. Two smaller bedrooms are left of the staircase." His hand moved to the kitchen. "Back door into the kitchen," he pointed. His finger moved again. "Other than windows and the front door, the kitchen door is the only other entrance to the house from the outside." He answered Scott's unasked question and pointed to another door in the kitchen, "This is the inside entrance to the garage."

Kim asked, "There's just three of us. Don't you think we might need some more help?"

Scott ran his hands through his hair then rubbed them across his face. "Good idea. But who do we call? The house where she was snatched is Charleston City domain and Jeremy's apartment is in Dorchester County."

"And Cane Bay is in Berkeley County," Dean added. "Don't forget us lowly troopers, either. We have a vested interest in this case, too."

Scott's phone rang. The other two heard his side of the conversation and it didn't sound good. "Shit! Keep after him; find him and keep me posted." He hung up and turned back to Dean and Kim, a look of fury on his face. "Patrol lost him. Jeremy switched cars at Northwoods Mall. Great big, wide open space in-the-middle-of –the-night mall parking lot, and he lost him. How is that even possible?" He slumped into a chair.

So what if the dogs make a racket? I'm never going back there, they can send me my final check…or not. Kelli and I are getting out of this tourist town. Maybe California. Maybe Hawaii. She's got plenty of money. Gotta love online banking, you can clean out your accounts and nobody even notices. Jeremy grinned his malicious grin as he drove south, away from the kennel and Kelli. He checked his rearview and side mirrors. *Still there. Don't want to lose you yet.*

At 6 a.m. he pulled into the mall parking lot, right next to the Explorer he had rented under his brother's name, using a fake license. The credit card was real, but it too was in his brother's name. *Won't RJ be surprised when the strange charges start showing up?* He chortled. *I never much liked you, big brother. The perfect son. So I'm not 'perfect', not you; no reason to treat me like a misfit.* He slammed his fist against the steering wheel as he got out of his Camry.

He snaked his way around the front of his car and down the Explorer to its door. Parked on the far side of the behemoth vehicle, his smaller car was blocked from the view at the entrance to the parking lot. Jeremy waited patiently for the squad car to appear. Within seconds it did. And stopped just inside the entrance; the patrolman scanned the lot for the missing car. Jeremy saw the driver on his phone, *probably calling that detective.* After a brief conversation the squad car moved slowly toward the south side of the mall and out of sight of the cars parked overnight at the north end of the mall. Jeremy hopped into the Explorer's driver's side, backed the car out and exited the mall the same way he came in. *By the time the patrolman circles the mall and finally sees the other car, I'll be long gone.*

This time Jeremy headed north and west, toward Kelli. He knew the police would continue their search, but they had no idea where he was. *Still. I'll get Kelli and get out of here as fast as I can. As long as I have her, I'm set for life.* As he drove, he contemplated Kelli in a bikini on the beach in Hawaii. His smile spread from ear to ear and down to his jeans. The pulsing in his pants was almost beyond control. *Maybe there'll be time for a little recreation before we leave tonight.* He glanced down at the bulge in his jeans. *Won't take long for this first time.* He cackled like a rabid chicken and pressed his foot harder on the accelerator. *Five more minutes and I'll be there.*

66

"Now what?" Kim asked. "We still know where Kelli is; we can go get her even if we can't pin it on Jeremy. Isn't it best to go get her? Maybe he'll show up while we're there." Kim grinned at the thought of taking down Jeremy herself. Her phone rang.

Scott answered her, "No, he's too smart, he won't go back there, not now that he knows we know it's him. He won't take the chance. You're right, Kim, let's go get her. But we don't need to be the laughing stock of every law enforcement agency in the area; we won't call anybody else in." The three rose and headed for Scott's car. "Dean can give directions to the house from the back seat," Scott announced as they left the conference room.

"Suzi is on her way up. That was the call I just took," Scott informed the other two. "She's been following the tracking devices." The three snagged Suzi as she exited the elevator. Scott pointed to the tablet she was carrying. "Can that thing track Jeremy's GPS from anywhere?"

"Sure. I've got it programmed into…" Scott cut her off and grabbed her elbow.

"Good. You're coming with us."

The four scurried down the stairs and out into the cold and Scott's car, men in front, women in back. Three minutes into their drive Suzi spoke up, "The signal has stopped. He's not moving."

Scott smiled grimly, "Where did you last have it?"

"Looks like Rivers Avenue, around Northwoods Mall."

"That's the second one from the car. Can you track the little one I slipped into his inside jacket pocket?"

"Sure, but it'll take me a few minutes to bring it up. I already have its parameters in here, I just have to get it online."

"Do it. If he's going back to Kelli she could be in trouble." The car sped along Interstate 26, trying to get there in less than thirty minutes.

Kelli slowly awoke. Forgetting about the noose, she stretched her legs to ease the cramps in her hips. The noose tightened and her situation was quickly brought back to memory. "Ouch! Damn you, Jeremy. Come take these damn flexi-cuffs off me!" she shouted to her empty bedroom. But it was reassuring to once again hear a voice other than his. Kelli held her breath and stayed silent for a few moments, trying to detect any other presence in the room with her. Slowly she exhaled. "Just me. Thank God. How long was I out this time?" She tried to open her eyes but they were still covered with the sticky tape.

"Why is he doing this to me? Oh I get that he thinks he's in love with me, but why me? Of all the women in Charleston, why me?" Kelli felt despair creeping up her spine. Her hands and feet were cold, and her nose, a sure sign that the rest of her was getting cold, too. "What do you expect? You have next to nothing on. This quilt isn't especially warm, either, not like some of them Great-Great Granny made." Her mind wandered off to the various colors and patterns in the many quilts she had inherited from her mother's grandmother; nobody else wanted them, but Kelli loved all of them. "At least if this is the one I think it is. Why won't that bastard take the blindfold off? I already know it's him." Kelli hesitated. "On TV, they don't care if the victim sees them because they're going to kill them anyway." She paused again. "So maybe the blindfold is a good thing. But how can it be when I know who he is even blindfolded? None of this makes any sense." Her shoulders sagged in defeat. She heard the door open.

"Hi, honey, I'm home," Jeremy said in his most cheerful voice. "Time to hit the road." He reached for Kelli and started to cut through the plastic cuffs on her ankles. "We may not have much time, so I need you to get up and get dressed as quickly as you can, my darling. We have a hotel reservation in Cincinnati tonight." *We don't, but Kelli doesn't need to know that.*

He cut off the wrist cuffs and the noose, then helped Kelli sit up. He handed her the clothes he had removed the night before.

"How long have I been asleep?" Kelli asked.

"You are a good sleeper, Kelli. Twenty hours this time. It's Saturday night."

Saturday. And nobody's found me yet. I knew they wouldn't think to look here. Jeremy is secretly pleased at Kelli's crestfallen look. He whispered into her ear and made her jump, "Nobody's coming for you, Kelli. You're all mine." With that he ripped the duct tape from her eyes, pulling out a chunk of hair and eyebrows with it.

Kelli's hand reached for her head as tears finally fell. "Why, Jeremy, why? If you want money, I'll get it for you. None of this makes any sense to me."

Jeremy grabbed both sides of her head between his calloused hands. He pulled her to a standing position, just inches from his face. "I love you, Kelli, and you love me. That's why." He snarled at her, "You've got ten seconds to put those clothes on or you're going the way you are."

Kelli reached for her sweater and quickly put it on. She pulled up her jeans and stepped into the shoes that were at the side of the bed. Jeremy grabbed her elbow and dragged her to the door just as she was fastening her jeans.

Hurriedly he pulled her down the stairs and out the kitchen door to the garage. Kelli pulled against his ruthless grip and tried to scratch his eyes with her free hand, but he was too strong for her. Jeremy slugged her hard in her ribs and snarled, "If you fight me I'll just have to give you a shot." Kelli calmed down, but still hung back as much as she could to slow him down, anything to feel like she was in control of something.

He pushed her into the Explorer's passenger seat and attached her seat belt. Before she knew what he was doing, he had fastened flexi-cuffs to her ankles again. "That'll keep you from getting out of the car unless I let you." He hustled to the driver's side, inserted the key, hit the garage door remote that he'd found in a kitchen drawer when he was preparing for Kelli's arrival. *Probably Todd's. He won't be needing it.* He laughed aloud again.

He's lost it completely, Kelli thought in fear. *There's no reasoning with him now.*

347

Jeremy grinned maliciously at Kelli. "Better open the garage door before I start the car. Don't want us to die of carbon monoxide poisoning." He shifted to Reverse and slammed on the accelerator, backing the car out of the garage and into the street.

67

"Next house on the left," Dean said. They had turned off the lights and siren as they turned onto Cane Bay Boulevard, about three miles from the entrance to the Oaks subdivision. Scott stopped the car and surveyed the house and its surroundings. *Nice upscale beginner homes or designed for young families. Toys in yards. Decorations on front doors. Newspapers in the driveways. Kelli's house has a covered front porch, garage to the left of the porch.*

Finally Scott spoke, "No lights. Garage is closed. Looks quiet." Scott shifted back into Drive and slowly pulled the car to the end of the cul de sac. From here they could see the upstairs windows on the side of the house. "The master is the top floor, back window," Dean instructed them. "Still nothing. Maybe he's been and gone."

Quietly the three exited the car and pushed the doors closed without a resounding click. The sun was just starting to come up; at this time of year it was almost eight o'clock before it was fully up. "At least we can see well enough that we don't need our flashlights," Kim whispered. The three pulled their guns from their holsters and approached the house, just two away now, in a low crouch, guns down by their sides.

"What's going on?" a neighbor shouted from his driveway behind them, newspaper in hand, bathrobe open revealing boxers and a t-shirt.

Kim turned and motioned him to be quiet. "I don't have to be quiet. Who are you people? I want to know what you're doing running around the neighborhood with guns. I'm going to call the cops," he continued to shout.

Kim went back and approached him. "We are the cops, Sir. Please just go back inside and call 9-1-1. Ask the Dorchester County sheriffs to come ASAP, tell them there are officers in trouble."

The man still looked distrustful, even though Kim knew he saw the CCPD logo on her shirt. Suspiciously he nodded his head as

he turned and said, "We're Berkeley County here. I'll call them."
He pulled his robe tighter around his bulging middle and went
back into his house. Kim hurried to catch up to the other two.
"We may have more of that," she whispered. "People are getting
ready for work, school, whatever. Probably be a school bus by
here any minute."

"Is he going to call 9-1-1?" Scott asked.

"Said he would. I think he will," Kim replied.

Scott shook his head and cautioned the other two, "Okay,
Kim's got a point. In a few minutes there are going to be too
many civilians around here. If Jeremy is in there with Kelli, he's
probably armed. He'll use her as a hostage if he has to. Let's just
keep everything contained until we get some help here. Then we
can evacuate the neighborhood and call in the hostage rescue
team." He looked at the other two; they nodded in agreement.

Just then Kim's phone vibrated in her pocket. "It's Jason, the
tech who's monitoring the house videos," she whispered. She
listened a minute and hung up. "Jason says there's a man in the
bedroom with Kelli. He's giving her some clothes and she's
getting dressed."

The two men looked at each other and at Kim. Almost in
unison they said, "He must be planning to get out of town. Why
else would he get her dressed?" Again, all three nodded in
agreement.

Scott spoke decisively, "Dean, you take the kitchen door. You
said that's the only other exit, right?" Dean nodded again. "I'll
take the front and the garage. Kim, you get the car and go back
to the top of the street and stop the others when they get here.
Explain what's going on and have them start evacuating the
houses and set up roadblocks." Scott stopped speaking and
listened. "Sirens. If Jeremy hears them come close he may panic.
Kim, stop them as far from this neighborhood as you can."

Kim turned and sprinted back to the car. She quickly pulled
into the closest driveway, turned the car around and headed back
up the street the way they had come in. The sirens were much
closer now. Scott's car with Kim at the wheel crept quietly past

Kelli's Cane Bay house and then sped up as she left the immediate area. No lights. No siren.

Scott nodded at Dean and Dean headed around the right side of the house to the kitchen door. Scott stealthily approached the front door. He wanted to get a look inside the front windows, just to see if he could see anything. He had to get Kelli away from Jeremy.

Suddenly the garage door started to open. Scott slipped back to the wall on the right side of the garage and pointed his gun toward the middle of the two-car garage; he didn't know which side the car was on, but he was damn sure it wasn't going anywhere. Just then Scott saw Dean take up position on the other side of the garage. Dean had a better view into the garage and motioned to Scott that the car was on his side.

The garage door reached its maximum height and a dark blue Explorer rocketed out. Dean and Scott changed their target and shot out the rear tires. As Jeremy fought to control the car, the two law enforcement officers surrounded the car, Dean on the driver's side, Scott on the passenger side, guns aimed at the two heads they could see inside.

Jeremy raised his bleeding head and grinned at Dean. "We almost got away, didn't we? I have no idea how you found us. I had it all planned out." His right hand went to the blood dripping from a gash on his forehead from where his head had hit the steering wheel. He looked at the blood quizzically. "This wasn't part of my plan." He turned to look at Kelli as Scott lifted her from the passenger seat. "Wait for me, Kelli. Please wait," he implored. Kelli just looked at him sadly. "No, I don't think so, Jeremy. I don't think so." She snuggled closer to Scott's warmth and closed her eyes.

Dean opened the driver's door and roughly pulled Jeremy out. Jeremy started to resist. "Please, Jeremy, just give me an excuse," he growled at the smaller man. "You killed my best friend and there's nothing better that I'd like to do than return the favor." Jeremy smiled serenely at Dean, "Yes, I did, didn't I? And y'all never thought of me. At least that plan worked." Jeremy submitted to Dean's rough handling as he was slammed against the hood of the car and flexi-cuffs were pulled tightly around his wrists. Scott and Dean smiled at each other grimly over the hood of the car. Kelli remained cradled in Scott's arms, her tears falling and soaking his shirt front, her feet still bound.

Multiple vehicles came careening down the street, Kim leading in Scott's car, Suzi still in the back seat, holding on for dear life.

Kim slammed the car into Park and jumped out, Suzi not far behind. "Suzi said the tracker was moving again. I didn't know how to contact you without taking a chance of warning Jeremy or distracting you, so we decided to come back. The other guys," She motioned to the six squad cars and the EMT vehicle, "Arrived just as we were heading back. I jumped out and told them to ride quiet and then we all headed here." Kim and Suzi were both grinning. Scott and Dean were, too.

"Is she okay?" Kim asked, worried at Kelli's lack of movement.

"I think so," Scott replied. "Let's get her to the EMTs." He turned toward the boxy vehicle just as Kelli raised a hand from his chest and gave all her heroes a thumbs up.

Epilogue

It's been almost two years since Todd was murdered by Jeremy and a year and a half since he kidnapped me. After I was checked out by the EMTs, Scott drove me straight to the hospital for a full check-up. Physically, I was just a bit dehydrated. Mentally was a bigger problem, but I think I'm getting better. How can you trust yourself or anyone else after such a dismal failure with "friends" as I had? After the hospital, Scott took me home and stayed with me all afternoon.

I thought that year after Todd died was miserable, and it was, so very miserable, but the last fifteen months have been full of absurdities. Once Scott, Dean, and Kim got me out of my house and got Jeremy into custody, all the strangeness began.

I am so glad the Gs decided not to sell their house on the Battery. They came home right after "the ordeal", as I prefer to think of it, to make sure I was okay. They even took the house off the market right away, but planned to put it back as soon as I was up to dealing with it. They stayed with me until they were sure I was back to normal, and then went back to Arizona for the summer. Once they actually experienced an Arizona summer they agreed Charleston is the best of all worlds, and its climate is near perfect, too. They bought a condo out there to use when they need a change of scenery.

Even the Ps – Mom and Dad – sent me a postcard from Indonesia, their latest archeological outpost, to let me know they were "thinking of me"...that was a first. Not the post card, the thinking.

Needless to say, but I will anyway, I sold the house in Cane Bay. No way was I going back into that place. Even though it held three years of happiness with Todd, the three days with Jeremy had invaded every corner. Teri Jackson was glad to get the listing and sold it in record time; that area of Summerville is growing exponentially.

The Gs finally put in a security system and that has helped a lot with my sense of safety. Funny, even though Jeremy had gotten into the Battery House, that didn't bother me as much. But being held captive in my own house really freaked me out.

Of course Corky has been by my side ever since we were reunited. Dean and Kim arrived at the house in late afternoon after I got home from the hospital, bringing Corky and pizza. They'd found her locked up and muzzled in the downstairs guest room. She was dehydrated, too, but we were really happy to see each other. That night Corky slept with her head on my foot, so she'd know if I moved. And Kim stayed the night again, "just in case", as she put it. Just in case I had nightmares or panic attacks.

And best of all, the next morning Sean, Nora and the twins came to see me! It was the best reunion ever. We were all so happy to be back together. And Sean has been visiting me every couple weeks while he settles back in to his job with the FBI.

Back to Jeremy.

He was arrested and charged with several counts of Breaking and Entering, felony kidnapping, and one count of homicide: Todd. After I told them what Jeremy had said about killing other girls, Scott discovered a cold case where a farmer had found the body of a girl Jeremy had dated while I was in college; they were able to pull DNA and match it to Jeremy. Must have happened while he was perfecting his technique.

The first hearing came the day after we left Cane Bay, the next one didn't come until late summer. Between Sean and Jeremy, I have come to believe there is no such a thing as a speedy trial in this country. Back and forth, back and forth that's how the attorneys and the court go. Of course a lot of it is behind the scenes so maybe it just seems as though nothing's going on except arguing about court dates.

At the August hearing Jeremy's attorneys made it obvious they were going for temporary insanity, at the least. I wasn't sure how I felt about that. Part of me wanted him locked up forever so he couldn't fixate on someone else or kill someone else. Part of me felt sorry for him…he must be crazy if he thought I loved him, even after I married Todd.

In November Kim had another baby boy – Aidan. Seems the day of getting reacquainted worked for her and Woody.

Until Aidan's birth Kim and I got together a couple times a week, either here at the house or over at her house. With her permission I got the kids a Golden Retriever for the Christmas after my abduction; Dean and Scott helped me pick her out. The kids named her Millie. Kim got her promotion to detective, too; I am so proud of her.

Last January was Jeremy's trial for the murder of Todd. A slam dunk for the prosecution, according to Scott and Dean. They had his confession to me and the note he wrote. "The guys" as I have started thinking of Scott and Dean, told me I was the star of the trial; that it was my testimony that nailed him. I don't remember anything about the trial. I'm just glad to finally know who did it, even though it still means I was the cause of Todd's death. My psychologist says this is a normal stage of grief: the guilt stage. I don't think I'll get off this stage any time soon. Jeremy was sentenced to life in prison without parole.

Since Jeremy's trial for Todd's murder, my life has been an emotional roller coaster, up one day, down the next.

Joyfully, we had an early Easter this year and everything was in bloom, including the parishoners at St. Philip's. It was time for seersucker and bow ties to come out of the closets; linen, spring colors, and "bonnets" for the women. Spring is my favorite time of year, it's such a cheerful time. Come summer, the men started showing off their straw boaters. Gotta love 'em.

During the weeks, when the Gs were away, and other times, Dean and Scott took turns checking on me…phone calls, out for a quick bite, sometimes a movie, whatever they could come up with.   Fortunately for them, around October this year, I started to feel more secure and I called a halt to the constant attention. It just reminded me too frequently of everything that had happened. That is until Dean met Allen; then it became two, three or four of us. The two being just me and Scott.

When the weather permitted, I've been having all my new friends – and Dean, my old friend, and Allen, Dean's new friend - over for cookouts on the weekends. The kids and the dogs run and play while the grown-ups sit and talk…and enjoy adult beverages.

Earlier this month, more than a year after my capture and rescue, Jeremy came to trial for my kidnapping, no plea bargain for him. Of course I was the prosecution's star witness again. Seemed ironic to me. After a year of berating the prosecution for Sean's situation, here I was supporting them. It was a lengthy trial, at least it seemed so to me. Two weeks. Lots of witnesses, pro and con. Viv and Barbara and Bill from the kennel testified to what a good worker he was, how responsible, always on time, loved the animals. Nobody had much "con" to say about him, except me. Since Jeremy had already been convicted of Todd's murder, I don't see why they even bothered with this trial; why waste the time and money? Just another mystery of the judicial system I guess.

It took two days for my testimony. The Solicitor made me go through everything that had happened, from the anonymous phone calls, to my kidnapping and storage. I was queasy through most of it. I really couldn't believe Jeremy had been in his right mind, but I had been warned not to say that.

It wasn't until the second day that things got really difficult. The defense tried to show that I had enticed Jeremy; that I'd flirted with him, that I was a tease. They tried to get me to say that my hugs were more than just friendly hugs. I had to fight back tears at the injustice of it all…that they could insinuate anything they wanted and get away with it. I felt like I had been raped, by the defense if not Jeremy.

At the end of the second week the case went to the jury. They came back the same day, maybe they wanted to get ready for summer vacation. They found Jeremy guilty of kidnapping, with no finding of insanity. He'll be in prison until his trial for the murder of that other woman; yet another mystery. Scott and Dean are convinced Jeremy practiced on more women and they have opened a task force so they can look for women who look like me who have gone missing in the last twenty years. Who knows how early he may have started?

I'm glad he's locked up, it helps me get over my jumpiness every time a door slams or someone says something from behind me.

Soon after Jeremy's kidnapping trial, and a year and a half since "the ordeal", we had a big party to celebrate all the good things that had happened: Sean's freedom, my freedom, Jeremy's arrest, and all our new friends: Scott, Kim and Woody and their kids Tony, Brandon and Aidan. And of course Dean and his new friend Allen. Dean and Scott barbecued outside and we even rolled the rugs back and danced in the house!

Scott has given me some indications he's tired of playing "big brother" and I think I'm ready to try dating. The hardest part will be learning to trust again. I can start slowly, with Scott; I'm sure I trust him.

I know that dating or even remarrying doesn't mean I love Todd any less. If there's one thing I've learned over my thirty years, it's that love is boundless, and there are all kinds. I know Todd would not want me to become a hermit. Todd loved me and would want me to be happy. If happy means dating or even falling in love again, that's okay with both of us.

I don't know what the future may hold for me, but for now I am willing to find out. I've stopped thinking of Scott as a big brother; he's become a good friend, and a bit more. I'll just take things slowly and see what happens. As Granny always says, "It all works out for the best." We'll see.

Austen Butler

Thank you for reading my first novel. If you enjoyed this, watch for my next publication *In Sickness and in Health* coming to Amazon soon.

To reach me, go to Facebook (AustenButler) or my web site: Austen Butler.com. Feel free to blog me too.

You may email me at austen@austenbutler.com

Made in the USA
Las Vegas, NV
23 January 2021